A California Christmas

Also by Brenda Novak

ONE PERFECT SUMMER

CHRISTMAS IN SILVER SPRINGS

UNFORGETTABLE YOU

BEFORE WE WERE STRANGERS

RIGHT WHERE WE BELONG

UNTIL YOU LOVED ME

NO ONE BUT YOU

FINDING OUR FOREVER

THE SECRETS SHE KEPT

A WINTER WEDDING

THE SECRET SISTER

THIS HEART OF MINE

THE HEART OF CHRISTMAS

COME HOME TO ME

TAKE ME HOME FOR CHRISTMAS

HOME TO WHISKEY CREEK

WHEN SUMMER COMES

WHEN SNOW FALLS

WHEN LIGHTNING STRIKES

IN CLOSE

IN SECONDS

INSIDE

KILLER HEAT

BODY HEAT

WHITE HEAT

THE PERFECT MURDER

THE PERFECT LIAR

THE PERFECT COUPLE

WATCH ME

STOP ME

TRUST ME

DEAD RIGHT

DEAD GIVEAWAY

DEAD SILENCE

COLD FEET

TAKING THE HEAT

EVERY WAKING MOMENT

Look for Brenda Novak's next novel

THE BOOKSTORE ON THE BEACH

available soon from MIRA.

For a full list of Brenda's books
visit www.brendanovak.com.

brenda novak

A California Christmas

mira

ISBN-13: 978-0-7783-1012-9

A California Christmas

To Luci Malone, a member of my online book group on Facebook and a true bibliophile who has come to many of my events, including when I visit the Authors Booth at the California State Fair each summer. I've never seen anyone have to fight so hard just to survive. She's beaten pancreatic cancer not once but twice, and now she's battling it for a third time, yet she forges ahead with such grace, determination and courage. She's an inspiration to me and lifts everyone around her to a higher plane.
Here's to beating it once again!

A California Christmas

CHAPTER ONE

Monday, December 7

Dallas Turner figured he shouldn't be surprised when he walked into his mother's house to find someone who wasn't part of the family in her kitchen. Aiyana had taken *him* in, hadn't she? She'd taken in and raised seven other boys, too. Only a couple of years ago, she'd expanded the campus of New Horizons—the school she'd started twenty-four years ago for troubled boys—to include a girls' side.

But she hadn't adopted any girls yet.

This wasn't a girl, anyway. Although he was seeing her from behind, he could tell it was a full-grown woman who was reaching into the cupboard. A full-grown woman who wasn't entirely dressed.

"Hello?" he said.

Startled, she whipped around, and he nearly dropped the groceries he'd carried in. This was no stranger to him, as he'd first assumed. It was Emery Bliss, someone he'd known when he was living here in the artsy community of Silver Springs, ninety minutes northwest of Los Angeles. He hadn't seen her since he moved away after graduating high school ten years ago, but he recognized her instantly.

She was equally surprised to see him—or to see a man suddenly standing behind her. He didn't know which.

With a yelp, she yanked her T-shirt down far enough to cover her underwear. "Excuse me, I—I didn't expect anyone to be home until this afternoon. Aiyana said—" She blinked several times and her blush deepened. He was no longer the skinny boy with the bad acne whose gaze had so often trailed after her when she returned her horse to the equestrian center of her private school, where he'd worked mucking out stalls, but he could tell she now recognized him. "I was just…getting a bowl of cereal and…"

Her words trailed off as she edged along the counter, leaving her breakfast behind while she stretched her T-shirt down as far as possible, holding it in a death grip with both hands.

"No problem," he said, relieving her of the burden of trying to finish that sentence. She didn't seem to know where she was going with it, anyway.

"I'm *really* sorry," she mumbled as though she'd caused him some terrible injury and escaped the kitchen as soon as she could.

He could hear her footfalls racing up the stairs as Aiyana and his two youngest brothers filed into the house with the rest of the groceries—Aiyana telling them they had only a half hour, at most, before they had to leave again. They were looking forward to playing a particular video game, so this was met with the type of groans one might expect from much younger boys.

"Give us an hour, at least," Bentley, the youngest, a senior in high school, pleaded.

"Just one hour," Liam chimed in. Two years older than Bentley, Liam was working and taking online classes instead of going to college because he'd injured his knee playing basketball and was getting an operation next month.

"No," she said firmly. "We can't miss this appointment."

After setting down the bags in his hands, Dallas pulled their mother aside and lowered his voice so that it wouldn't carry to the second level. "What was *that* all about?"

Aiyana didn't respond right away. She was still preoccupied with his brothers. "You can't start anything interactive where other players are depending on you. We don't have time."

"We'll turn it off the second you say so," Bentley promised, and they dumped the groceries they were carrying on the first horizontal surface they could find and rushed into the living room to turn on the Xbox.

"Mom?" Dallas prodded.

"What?" She gave his hand an affectionate squeeze before disengaging so that she could set her purse aside and put away the food.

Dallas could hear his brothers negotiating which video game to play, since they didn't have time for the one they'd initially planned. Aiyana, Bentley and Liam had met him for breakfast as he came into town from Las Vegas, where he lived in the months he wasn't rock climbing. They'd expected to go directly from there to Santa Barbara, so that he and his brothers could be fitted for tuxedos. Aiyana's wedding was on the nineteenth, and every one of her eight adopted sons would be in the line. But the tuxedo place had called while they were eating and asked to reschedule for later in the day, so they'd done the weekly grocery shopping before they left town instead of waiting until they were on their way home. "What's the deal?"

Confusion showed on Aiyana's face, so he clarified. "Emery Bliss was in the kitchen when I came in." He didn't mention that she'd been wearing nothing except a faded Van Halen T-shirt and a pair of bikini briefs. It was obvious she hadn't planned for anyone to walk in.

"Oh! You saw her?"

"Yes, I saw her." Emery's long blond hair had been mussed, as though she'd only recently climbed out of bed, and she hadn't been wearing makeup, so it wasn't only her state of undress that led him to believe she was staying at the house. "It looked to me as though she's *living* here."

"She is," Aiyana said simply, and went back to unloading the groceries.

His mother didn't volunteer the reason; she made him ask. *"Why?"*

"Why not?" she countered.

"Your wedding is less than two weeks away, for one."

She waved off his words. "It'll be fine. You'll all be here, but Elijah and Gavin have their own houses these days. It won't get crowded until the twins and Seth come home on the eighteenth. Even then, we should have plenty of room."

"I wasn't claiming there wouldn't be enough room—just that…that we'll be busy. We have a lot going on," he added to shore up his argument.

A playful gleam entered her eyes. "What's the matter? Does having her here make you *uncomfortable?*"

As innocent as his encounter with Emery had been, he wouldn't soon forget seeing her ass in those panties, he knew that much. He tilted his head and narrowed his eyes. "Don't start with that."

"With what?"

"You know what. I don't need you playing matchmaker."

He'd wanted to take Emery to Senior Ball back in the day, and Aiyana knew that because she'd tried to help him come up with a clever way of inviting her. But even with his mother's encouragement and the ideas they'd tossed around, he'd never gathered the nerve. He couldn't imagine a wealthy girl from Topatopa Academy, a private school known for providing an elite education, would care to be seen with one of the "bad" boys from New Horizons. He couldn't imagine her parents would be pleased to have her go out with him, either. And during the time he was dithering back and forth, she accepted an invitation to attend the public school's prom with the best player on the Mc-Gregor football team—the running back, who was now in the pros. The McGregor prom was the night before New Horizons' Senior Ball, so while the events didn't *directly* conflict, he'd decided to spare her the trouble of trying to decide whether to attend two formal dances on the same weekend. There was no way he could follow a local hero. She'd be taking a huge step down.

Considering everything, he figured he'd saved himself some rejection by not asking her out ten years ago.

"I'm not playing matchmaker," she said. "I admit that I like Emery. She's a lovely person. And I wouldn't mind if you were to finally fall in love—"

"Finally?" he broke in. "I'm only twenty-nine!"

She closed the refrigerator after putting away the bacon. "Someone has to get hold of you, get you to change your focus and settle down before you kill yourself. The idea of you rock climbing without any safety gear, any ropes..." She shook her head. "It keeps me up at night. But having Emery here has nothing to do with you. That poor girl. I'm just providing a safe haven for her until after the holidays."

"Why would she need a safe haven?" Emery's father, a plastic surgeon, was rumored to have patients who were famous. He made a lot of money. On top of that, Emery had been smart, popular and pretty. What could possibly have gone wrong when she was starting out with everything in her favor?

His mother pulled a tub of mayonnaise from one of the bags and opened the fridge again. "You don't watch much TV, do you?"

"Not in the months I'm climbing." He put some potato chips in the pantry. "You don't understand what it's like. I live out of my van for a week or more at a time." And this year, his climbing season had lasted longer than in previous years. He'd finally found a sponsor, a sponsor who was paying handsomely just to have him endorse their brand of climbing apparel. He'd never had so much money.

"Well, if you don't already know what happened, I probably shouldn't tell you." She reached into another sack. "The more word of it spreads, the worse things will get for her."

"What are you talking about?" He folded the sacks they'd emptied. "And how could telling me make it any worse?"

With a sigh, she dragged him farther from the room where Bentley and Liam were playing, and the stairs where Emery had gone. "After college, she became a news anchor on a popular morning show in Los Angeles. She loved her job, was doing very well at it and had high hopes of eventually moving to New York and taking over a show like *Good Morning America.*"

"But then…" He scowled at her. "Why are you making me drag this out of you?"

She hesitated.

"Mom? This is *me* you're talking to."

"I realize that, but…" She seemed torn. "Okay. She broke up with her coanchor, and he retaliated by posting a video of the two of them online that humiliated her and caused her to lose her job."

He raised his eyebrows. "What kind of video?"

She cast him an exasperated look. "What kind do you think?"

"No…" he said, stepping back.

"Yes! They were having *s-e-x,*" she whispered.

He might've laughed that she'd felt the need to spell it when his brothers were plenty old enough to understand, but he was too shocked. "You've got to be kidding me."

"I wish I were," she said with a frown. "She refuses to show her face in Los Angeles. That video went viral. Everyone's seen it. It even made the national news."

Dallas could only imagine how mortified Emery must've been. As attractive as she was, every male viewer had probably raced onto the internet to have a look. "What about her family? They were always supportive. Why wouldn't she go to them?"

"They don't live in the area anymore. They moved to Boston

two years ago, and her parents are in the middle of a nasty divorce, something she doesn't need to be involved in when she's going through so much herself. Her father is already living with another woman. And her mother is trying to care for Emery's grandmother, who has dementia. That's the reason they moved to Boston in the first place."

"What about siblings?"

"She's an only child."

"Wow." He sank into one of the kitchen chairs. "I didn't realize you knew Emery well enough to take her in."

"I didn't until her mother began volunteering here at the school. A year or so after you graduated, Connie started teaching the boys how to ride. She even donated a couple of the horses. We still have one of them. Anyway, we became close, and that's how I got to know Emery. Whenever Emery came home from college, even after she earned her degree, her mother would bring her over, and she'd help, too. So when the scandal broke, and I saw it on the news, I called to see how she was doing. The poor child wouldn't even pick up the phone. I had to leave several messages before I could get her to call me back. Her mother said she was hiding out in her apartment."

"And when you *did* get hold of her, you insisted she come here?"

"I had to. I couldn't leave her in that situation."

No wonder Emery had apologized when he'd caught her in her underwear this morning. Someone who'd just been through what she'd been through would be extra sensitive to that sort of encounter, even though it was completely accidental. "Wait. So she got fired for sleeping with a coworker? Can that even happen these days?"

"Yes. She signed an agreement when she started at the station saying she wouldn't get romantically involved with anyone in the workplace. But she's considering a wrongful firing suit. This was revenge on his part, pure and simple. He was out to get her when he posted their personal video all over the internet, and their producer—a Heidi Coventry—piled on. Emery thinks it's because Heidi has had her eye on Ethan Grimes herself and was angry when he chose Emery over her."

Dallas didn't know Emery that well. He didn't know Ethan Grimes at all. And yet he felt no small degree of outrage. "Sexism has been such a hot topic, all over the news, and yet this Heidi person, who works for a news station, no less, is only making it worse?"

"I know. I thought in California we'd come further than that."

"The station had better have fired him, too."

"They did, but Emery told me yesterday that she's pretty sure they've hired him back."

"She needs to proceed with that wrongful firing suit."

Aiyana made a skeptical sound. "Even if she does, I'm not sure she'll win."

"How much will it cost to get an attorney?"

"That isn't the problem. She can get an attorney who's willing to do the work for a portion of the settlement. It's the upset and the negativity she'll have to contend with, for months, that she's not convinced she can endure. Not with how hurt and vulnerable she is right now. What's happened to her is beyond embarrassing, and the more attention she draws to it, the more people there will be who hunt down that video."

"It hasn't been removed?"

"From some sites, yes. But this is the internet we're talking about. Once something's out there, there's no taking it back."

That was true. "What's her other choice?"

"To let it all go and try to rebuild her life."

He nearly knocked over the chair he'd been using as he shot out of it but caught it just in time. "Maybe I'd better go have a talk with the asshole who posted it. What's his name again—Ethan Grimes? Who has a name like that, anyway?"

His mother grabbed his arm. "No! Stay out of it. It's none of your business, which is why I hesitated to tell you."

"But if she ever goes back to work at that station, or even in the same industry, she'll never live down that video. She can't be expected to start over at ground zero."

"I agree. And she's always wanted to be a news anchor, has no idea what she'll be if she doesn't continue to pursue her life's dream."

"Why in the world would she allow him to take a video in the first place?" he asked. "I get that she probably loved him, trusted him, all that. But this type of thing has become more and more common. You don't take the chance, especially when you have so much to lose."

"She had no idea he was filming."

Dallas rubbed his forehead. "That makes it even worse."

"I know. It's *so* unfair."

He pictured Emery's big blue eyes and couldn't help feeling protective of her. "What's she going to do?"

"That's what she's trying to decide. If she moves forward with the suit, she'll need to remain somewhere close to LA so she's available to meet with her attorney, take the deposition, go into arbitration or whatever might be necessary. If she decides *not* to move forward with it, she may pack up and move to Boston— where her mother is—and try to get into another line of work. But I've told her she's more than welcome to stay here through the holidays. She deserves some time to get over what's happened and to make the best possible decision."

He shook his head. "What a terrible thing to have to deal with, especially at Christmas."

She checked the doorway to make sure Liam and Bentley were still too preoccupied to be listening in. "Now you understand why I invited her here. I want to help her, if I can."

He walked over to give his mother a hug. "You want to help everyone," he said. He'd always been proud of her. Always been grateful to her, too. He couldn't imagine how he would've turned out—where he'd be—without her.

CHAPTER TWO

Fully dressed, even though she was now back in her bedroom behind a closed door, Emery Bliss paced the short distance at the foot of the bed. She could hear the commotion below, knew Aiyana, Bentley and Liam had returned instead of going to Santa Barbara. She should've pulled on a pair of shorts and a bra before venturing below, but she'd had her mind on the call she'd received from an attorney in LA. She'd never dreamed it wouldn't be safe to run down for a bowl of cereal—not after Aiyana had specifically told her that she'd have the entire house to herself until five or so.

"Damn it." She rolled her eyes at the memory of the shock on Dallas Turner's face when he walked into the kitchen to find her half-naked and helping herself to his mother's food. She hadn't gone down there with the intention of causing a problem, but after everything she'd been through recently, she was so sensitive she didn't feel capable of withstanding *any* kind of blow. When she'd decided to come here, she'd pictured herself with Aiyana and Aiyana's two youngest boys, who rarely interacted with her. They were too caught up in their studies, their girlfriends, their sports and their video games to pay her any mind. Aiyana did so much for so many, they took a new guest in stride.

Emery hadn't anticipated running into the Turner boy she remembered from high school—unless it was closer to the wedding—and she hadn't looked that far ahead. She'd simply jumped at the chance to escape LA and go somewhere no one would think to look for her, so she could create a buffer between her and the harsh judgment and salacious interest she'd received once Ethan Grimes posted that video online.

Had coming here been a mistake?

She eyed the suitcase she'd stashed at the end of the dresser. She'd emptied her clothes into the closet and a chest of drawers so she wouldn't have to dig through all of the belongings she'd brought with her every time she needed to change. But she could pack and fly to Boston, get out of California entirely. She would've done that to begin with if her parents weren't facing their own problems. They each blamed the other for the breakdown of their marriage, so whenever she talked to them, she felt as though she was being torn in two—literally ripped apart.

That was more than she could take right now. She also knew her savings would dwindle fast if she wasn't careful, so she'd been hesitant to spend money on flights she could avoid.

Emery winced at the sound of a knock on the door, then made a face at herself in the mirror. She looked terrible. Her eyes were puffy and her skin blotchy from all the tears she'd cried, her hair was a tangled mop she had yet to comb and what she'd thrown on immediately upon returning to her room covered her but didn't match.

Those small things were the least of her concerns, however. She had to figure out some way to recover from the devastation of losing her boyfriend, her job and, worst of all, her reputation. She had to forget what'd happened at KQLA and focus on the future so she could decide what to do next. But she was so distraught by what other people were seeing when they logged on to the internet and searched for "Emery Bliss sex video" she could hardly cope. This was easily the most embarrassing thing that could ever happen to her.

After clearing her throat so that she'd be able to talk in spite of the large lump that threatened to choke her, she peeked into the hall.

Aiyana stood there holding a bowl of Mini-Wheats and wearing the brightly colored clothes and turquoise jewelry she preferred, her black hair falling down her back in a thick braid. "I'm sorry if Dallas surprised you, dear. I should've called. I honestly didn't think of it, or I would have."

"No, of course you didn't need to call," she said. "This is your house."

"We had a last-minute change of plans, but we will be leaving again shortly and *then* we'll be gone for the rest of the day." She handed Emery the bowl. "Here, you left your breakfast on the counter, so I added some milk and brought it up."

"Thank you." Emery managed a smile for Aiyana's kindness—but then her lip began to tremble.

Aiyana took the bowl back and set it aside before drawing Emery into her arms. "It's going to be okay."

The scent of her flowery perfume filled Emery's nostrils as she rested her head on the smaller woman's shoulder. Aiyana was only about five feet tall but she had the biggest heart of anyone Emery had ever met, and the solidness of her embrace felt so convincing and nurturing that Emery was loath to let her go.

"You don't have to worry about Dallas staying here the next few weeks," Aiyana said when she pulled back. "He won't bother you."

"I don't want to get in anyone's way..."

"You're not in anyone's way. There are eight bedrooms in this house. And Dallas doesn't mind that you're here. As a matter of fact, if I know my son, he'll end up being your best friend and your fiercest protector."

She sniffed, still trying to hold back tears—now caused by the sympathy she was receiving instead of her former mortification.

She thanked Aiyana, and Aiyana said goodbye before heading down the stairs.

When Emery closed the door, she took her cereal and crawled into bed. She'd known as soon as she'd felt Aiyana's arms go around her that she wouldn't pack up and leave. Maybe this wasn't her home, but she felt welcome here. If she stayed, she wouldn't have to face the outside world, wouldn't have to pick sides in her parents' divorce and wouldn't have to witness the decline of her ailing grandmother—not until she felt stronger.

And right now, having the chance to get back on her feet in what felt like a safe environment mattered more than anything else.

It was late when Dallas returned from hanging out with his two older brothers at the Blue Suede Shoe, a popular bar they often visited to play pool or darts whenever he was in town. Elijah and Gavin were both married with children, but Eli, the oldest, helped run New Horizons and lived on campus not far from Aiyana. Dallas rode with him, returning to Eli's house to watch a recorded Lakers game after they left the bar. By the time that was over, it was almost two, so Dallas walked home rather than having Eli drive him.

All the lights were off, so after he let himself in the back door, he was surprised to hear the soft drone of the television. Aiyana rarely stayed up late; she got up too early. And his younger brothers wouldn't be watching TV in the middle of the night. Bentley had school in the morning; Liam had work.

As he neared the family room, the floor creaked under his weight, causing the small figure on the couch to sit up and take notice.

He could tell he'd surprised Emery Bliss just as he had when he first came upon her in the kitchen this morning. Only now if she didn't have any pants on, he couldn't tell; she was covered by a blanket.

"Hello." She lifted the remote as though she felt she should turn off the TV and scurry back to her bedroom.

"Go ahead and finish watching your show," he said before she could hit the Power button. "This is a big house. The TV's not going to bother anybody."

"Are you sure?" she asked.

"Positive."

Standing about ten feet away from her, he shoved his hands in the pockets of his jeans. She was watching an episode of *Dateline*.

"What's this one about?" he asked.

"A young mother has been kidnapped."

"From where?"

"Her house in Iowa. Right in the middle of the day."

Dallas was far more interested in learning if Emery had been able to determine whether Ethan Grimes had been rehired by the television station from which they'd both been fired than getting involved in the crime drama unfolding on TV. He'd thought about her and her situation all day. But he guessed Emery wouldn't be excited to discuss it with him. For one, she barely knew him. For another, it had to be more awkward for her to talk to a man, especially one she barely knew, about the sex video her ex-boyfriend had posted than it would be a woman.

Still, he came around the couch and sat at the opposite end. He'd been so infatuated with Emery ten years ago that he couldn't help wondering what she was like now.

She didn't speak, though, and he didn't interrupt, in case she was as invested in the show as it seemed.

When *Dateline* ended and she navigated to Hulu to put on another episode, he got up and told her good-night. His mother was right—what Emery was going through was none of his business. He needed to leave her alone and give her the space to work out her own problems.

"Aiyana tells me you're a rock climber."

Surprised that she would initiate a conversation when he'd just given up on the idea, he turned to face her. "I like to climb, yes."

"She said you often free solo."

Most people didn't agree with climbing without ropes. They considered it too reckless, too foolhardy. He couldn't tell whether she was one of those who would judge him, label him an adrenaline junkie or whatever, but he couldn't help feeling slightly defensive. "Occasionally. But only when I know the climb well, have done it many times with ropes and feel certain I can make it."

"What happens if you encounter something unexpected, some water or slime on a narrow ledge that makes it too slippery to grip—or a rattlesnake that slithers out of a crack in the rock?"

"Surprises like that generally don't end well," he admitted. "Encountering a rattlesnake while hiking could end as badly, though."

She studied him. "Do you know the guy who climbed El Capitan free solo?"

"Alex Honnold? I've met him. Why? Do *you* know him?"

"I interviewed him on my show in 2018, right after the documentary came out. Since you probably climb in Yosemite, too, I figured you might've run into him."

"I've encountered him in the valley a time or two."

She adjusted the blanket she'd been using. She had on the same faded Van Halen T-shirt he'd seen earlier, but he could tell that she was now wearing a bra. And when she shifted, causing the blanket to fall back, he noticed she was also wearing a pair of pink yoga pants. "How'd you get involved in rock climbing?"

"Unlike Alex, I didn't have the opportunity to start as a kid. I didn't get into it until I was in high school. I began bouldering at Enlightenment Ridge, which isn't too far from here." Climbing had provided an outlet. It was the only thing that quieted his mind and barred unwelcome thoughts from intruding.

"Do you have a sponsor?"

He leaned up against the wall. "I didn't until recently. I got one just a few months ago, as a matter of fact."

"Some climbers don't like the idea of getting paid for climbing," she said.

"Those are the ones who can't get a sponsor," he responded drily, but she didn't give up that easily.

"They claim the money incentivizes guys to climb too fast and take bigger and bigger risks—to be the first to scale a particular rock face in a certain amount of time or whatever, which can be dangerous. They also say that the social media and other attention that goes along with climbing professionally is a problem, because it's so distracting."

"It's a dangerous sport. I'm not going to stand here and argue that it isn't. But I'd rather be making money doing what I love to do. That's the only way I can do more of it."

She raked her long hair back with her fingers and twisted it on top of her head. She still wasn't wearing makeup, but she didn't need any. She was as pretty as ever—just as pretty as she'd been at eighteen. She'd make the perfect news anchor or television host. She had a wide mouth with straight teeth that gleamed when she smiled.

He remembered being absolutely captivated by that smile, too nervous to even talk right when she deigned to speak to him.

"How old were you when you came to New Horizons?" she asked.

"Fourteen."

She let her hair drop. "Were you born in California?"

He nearly laughed. He'd been afraid to ask her anything that might make her uncomfortable, and yet she was veering awfully close to the one subject he didn't like to discuss—his past. "I was," he said simply.

"What part?"

"Bakersfield."

"Do you mind if I ask what happened to your birth parents?"

He hesitated.

"Sorry," she said. "It's the interviewer in me, I guess. I start in right away, but...is that a no?"

"Why don't we trade?" He flashed her a grin. "I ask you something I'd like to know about you, and then you can ask me something you'd like to know about me. Maybe it won't be comfortable for either one of us, but at least it'll be fair."

She eyed him dubiously. "That's okay. The last thing I want to do is discuss what I'm going through."

"Understood. But I'll let the offer stand. Let me know if you change your mind."

He breathed a sigh of relief as he headed downstairs to the bedroom that had been his when he lived with Aiyana. He was fine with leaving things as they were between him and Emery. Satisfying his curiosity where she was concerned wasn't worth digging through the wreckage of his childhood, especially because they'd go their separate ways soon enough. What was the point?

There was no point, no reason to even think about his childhood tonight.

But after he brushed his teeth and stripped off his clothes, he pulled out the letter he'd received and stared down at his name, written in pencil.

Somehow, his father had tracked him down. He'd found this letter in his post office box when he went by to clear it out before coming to Silver Springs. He hadn't opened it, though.

He wasn't sure he ever would.

CHAPTER THREE

Tuesday, December 8

When Emery's alarm went off early the next morning, she fumbled around on the nightstand until she could find her phone and silence it. Ever since she'd arrived in Silver Springs, all she'd done was sleep. It was going on a week now, and yet she *still* didn't have any energy. After pushing so hard for so long—to get her degree in Communications and Media Studies at Cal State LA; to graduate at the top of her class; to launch her career in television; to eat healthy so that she felt good and looked good, something that was important for an anchor; and to make it to yoga every afternoon, all while trying to maintain a relationship with Ethan on the sly—she'd nearly run herself into the ground.

Of course, some of what she preferred to categorize as exhaustion had to be depression. So many things had gone wrong at once, and not only little things. Her parents were breaking up. While divorce was pretty commonplace, it was still extremely painful, and this one had come as such a surprise. When she was living at home, they'd seemed perfectly happy together. What had changed? Her mother couldn't explain the cause of the split—she said she didn't know what went wrong, that her father hadn't complained until he ended it all—and her father refused to explain what had led to his dissatisfaction, except to say that he wasn't fulfilled.

And what was going on with Grandma Adele?

Emery winced every time she remembered her last visit to Boston. When she'd first walked into the room, her grandmother had said, "And who's this beautiful young woman?"

Add to that the indignity of what Ethan had done and the loss of her job, and it was just too much.

How could he have recorded her? He must've set up a camera in his room, one he didn't tell her about, and now her most private moments were being devoured, judged, ridiculed and shared by total strangers. She couldn't stand the humiliation or the betrayal, not only by Ethan but by Heidi. Although she and her producer had never been the best of friends, she'd believed they respected each other on a professional basis. She'd never dreamed Heidi would allow Ethan to destroy her career—especially after he'd already destroyed her on such a personal level by posting that video.

Leslie Simone, a friend of hers and part of the camera crew at the station, had texted her to say she'd heard upper management talking about the situation. Losing both anchors at once had caused their ratings to drop. They needed to stop the bleeding, said that viewers were "attached" to the people they'd been seeing every day for so long. Leslie had gotten the impression they were going to take a step back from what they'd done.

Except...*she* hadn't received a call. They hadn't changed their minds about *her*.

It would be the ultimate irony if Ethan got to go on with his life as if nothing had happened. Of course it would be the man who was quickly forgiven, even though he was the one who'd pursued her despite the agreement they'd both signed when they were hired. He was also the one who'd insisted it didn't matter what they did as long as it didn't affect their work. And he was the one who'd become unbearably controlling, and jealous of anyone who had any contact with her—even her girlfriends. That was why she'd broken it off with him.

Was he heading over to the station right now?

A burst of anger gave her the power to kick off the covers and climb out of bed. It had been only three hours since she'd stopped watching episode after episode of *Dateline* and gone to bed. But she couldn't miss KQLA's morning show. She was dying to see if the station had hired a permanent replacement for her, or if they were still using that amateur Cindy Plank, who'd been after her job for years, as a temporary substitute.

More than that, she wanted to see if Ethan had been given his job back and was there, sitting next to Cindy.

Her hands curled into fists and her muscles tensed. She wasn't sure what she'd do if she saw him on the screen. She was afraid she'd head to Los Angeles and drive her car into the side of the building that housed the station. The possibility made her *that* furious; she'd never felt such intense emotion.

Taking only enough time to pull on her yoga pants, which she'd peeled off before falling into bed, she hurried down the stairs.

As soon as she turned on the TV, she lowered the volume to where she could barely hear it; she didn't want to wake anyone before they had to get up.

Ethan had better not be there...

They'd *both* broken the rules by dating, and they'd *both* been in the video that had caused such an uproar among their viewers. The more religious viewers had written in to complain about her poor character. The less religious viewers had made joke after joke at her expense.

Both reactions had been equally painful.

Her heart thumped in a crazy cadence, almost making her

light-headed as she waited for the news to start. Was he in the studio, putting on his mic?

Calm down. He's not there. The station would never hire him back. If they were going to change their minds, they'd hire me. I was better at the job than he was.

That was what she told herself until the news came on, anyway.

But then, there he was.

"You mother*fucker!*" she yelled.

"Is everything okay, dear?"

The first blast of the TV, before she'd turned it down, must've awakened Aiyana. Or Emery's alarm going off in her room had been louder than she'd thought. The older woman was standing behind the couch in her nightgown and robe, but Emery hadn't heard her coming. She'd been too highly focused, too engrossed in the questions swimming around in her mind and her own torment at the possible answers to those questions.

"He's back!" She pointed at the screen. "He's sitting right there, reading the news as if nothing ever happened. After what he did to me. He…he can't get away with it. He's destroyed my life. My dignity. My…my sense of worth and decency!"

Before she knew it, she wasn't just telling Aiyana these things, she was screaming them, and yelling about what a bastard Ethan was and she couldn't believe Heidi would let him get away with ruining her life.

A little voice in her head told her she needed to calm down. She never acted this way. It wasn't right to do this to Aiyana, who'd been kind enough to take her in.

But once she let go of the monster inside her, there was no way to cage it again. She got so upset that she was afraid she might start throwing things or punching the wall, so she pivoted abruptly to leave the room—and knocked into a lamp.

It crashed to the floor, pelting her legs with glass, but she could scarcely feel it. Mortified that she'd been so thoughtless and clumsy, she dropped to her knees and grabbed a fistful of glass with the intention of cleaning it up so that no one would get hurt—and ended up cutting her hand.

"Don't!" As Aiyana started toward her, Emery stood to search for the closest trash can. God, look what she'd done! The mess on the floor mirrored the mess of her life. Everything she'd suffered was coming to a head in that moment, tearing her apart, ruining all her hopes and dreams as well as tarnishing everything she'd accomplished in the past. And there was nothing she could do about it, not without inviting even more humiliation by trying to pursue justice.

She didn't hear Dallas come up the stairs behind her, so she didn't have any idea when he joined them—not until she found herself caught in his arms and held so tightly she couldn't move.

Then all she could do was drop the glass she'd been trying to clean up, watch the blood drip off her fingers and sob.

"I'm sorry," Emery cried. "I'll leave now. Let me go. I'll pay for the lamp and then I'll be gone."

Dallas could feel her body trembling against his. He could also see streaks of tears as he turned her around and she gulped for the breath to speak. When he'd been awakened by the screaming and cursing, he'd jumped out of bed and jammed his legs into a pair of jeans, but he hadn't even taken the time to button them, let alone don a shirt before climbing the stairs two at a time to reach the living room.

"It's okay." Aiyana came around the couch to reach them. "Calm down. Everything's going to be okay."

"It's *not* okay." She turned her face into his chest rather than look at Aiyana. "It's not right that I would take what's happening out on you. You've been nothing but kind to me. I'll replace the lamp."

Aiyana stroked her hair. "I'm not worried about the lamp. I don't care about things—I care about people. I care about *you*, and you're in a safe place here with us. You can stay as long as you'd like. Maybe you needed to let out all that emotion. But with time, you'll heal. You have to trust me on that. I've seen plenty of broken people put themselves back together again. Dallas is one of them."

Emery seemed to have regained control, but Dallas still wasn't sure whether it was safe to let her go. When he'd grabbed her, she was trying to pick up shards of glass without a care for getting cut, and he'd seen what he thought might be blood on her pink yoga pants. He didn't want her to hurt herself any worse.

"Bring her over here, to the couch," Aiyana told him.

"Hey, what's going on?"

At the intrusion of another voice, Dallas glanced over to find that his two younger brothers had also reacted to the noise. They were standing on the stairs and were, like him, wearing only jeans. Their hair was sleep tousled, and Liam had the waffle imprint of his comforter on his cheek.

"Nothing. We've got it," Aiyana said. "You can go back to bed. You have another hour or so before you have to get up for school."

"Is Emery okay?" Bentley sounded concerned. At the same time, Liam said, "What happened?"

"That's what we're trying to find out," Aiyana responded. "Let us deal with this, okay?"

They were tired enough that they accepted her response without any resistance and shuffled back up the stairs.

Aiyana got a cloth for Emery's bleeding hand and Dallas guided her to the couch.

"I'm sorry," she mumbled to him when he finally let go of her and helped her to sit down.

"Don't worry about it," he said. "What happened?"

Tears continued to stream down her cheeks as she gestured at the TV. "That's him," she said dully, holding her stinging hand to her T-shirt to staunch the blood. "That's Ethan Grimes. They've given him his job back."

Dallas studied the guy who'd been so vindictive to her. He was thin and certainly not unhandsome, with brown eyes, thick slashes of eyebrows and equally dark hair that he wore slicked back off his forehead. But as far as Dallas was concerned, he was also filled with self-importance and came off sort of...smarmy. Dallas wanted to say, "You fell in love with that asshole?" but bit his tongue.

"Here. Let me see that cut," Aiyana said.

Emery held out her hand.

"Fortunately, it doesn't look too deep." Aiyana peered even closer at it. "I can't imagine it will require stitches. For now, just hold this cloth on it until the bleeding stops and I can see it more clearly. I'm going to make some tea. That should be warm and soothing."

"How can they do that?" she asked Dallas, referring to the station, as Aiyana went into the kitchen. "After the Me Too movement and all that lip service about correcting sexism? He signed the same agreement I did. And *he's* the one who pursued *me*. He also caused the scandal, made it public."

"I don't know." Dallas sat down beside her in case she freaked out again. He was waiting for an opportunity to check the blood on her legs, but it was too soon. He was afraid if he drew her attention to the fact that she was hurt in more than one place, she might only get worked up again. "They must know he was the one who put up that video, right?"

She shook her head. "He lied about it. Said his roommate must've put up a camera and posted that video online."

"Why would his roommate do something like that?"

"Ethan claims he must've got off on watching us. And he said Tommy posted the video online because he was being pressured to move out, and he wasn't happy about it."

Dallas dipped his head to catch her eye. "Could that be true? Could it have been this Tommy person?"

"No," she replied immediately. "Tommy would never do anything like that. He's a nice guy. Heidi and upper management are only pretending there's some confusion about who did what, so they have an excuse to be able to continue their relationship with Ethan."

"Did you tell them that?"

"I tried."

"And what'd they say?"

"That Ethan would never post something that would embarrass him as much as it would me, but it *didn't* embarrass him. He's proud of it. And he was happy he had something with which he could totally destroy me, especially because I didn't see it coming."

Dallas clenched his jaw. It was hard not to confront Ethan—to make him pay for what he'd done so that he'd think twice about using revenge porn to hurt any other woman. But Dallas knew getting into a physical altercation with Ethan would be stupid. Ethan deserved an ass whipping, but giving him one wouldn't solve anything. The video would still be out there, available for those who were looking for it. Dallas would just get himself into trouble, and he'd promised Aiyana—long ago—that he would avoid that sort of thing. "So are you going to proceed with the wrongful firing case?"

She stared at the screen for several seconds, watching Ethan talk about a contest for gingerbread houses and a local Christmas tree event.

"Emery?"

She blinked. "I can't face having this negativity in my life as long as it will take to sue the station. And I don't want any more publicity, nothing that will remind people of that video and make them go look for it."

"I understand," he said. "But you can't let them get away with what they've done."

She dropped her head in her uninjured hand and began to knead her forehead.

After a few minutes, Aiyana came back into the room carrying a cup filled with hot tea. "Here you go. Try this," she said to Emery. "Chamomile will help ease the anxiety."

Emery managed a weak smile for her kindness but because of her hurt hand, Dallas took the cup and saucer and held it while Aiyana sat on the other side of her.

"They're betting you won't sue," Aiyana said. "Or they wouldn't have risked hiring him back."

"They know I can't, not without causing more damage to myself. And if I don't win, it'll all be for nothing."

"All adults have sex," Dallas said. "Or most of them, anyway. It's a perfectly natural, normal part of life. So who cares if there's a video of you on the internet? Other than trusting the wrong person, you didn't do anything different than everyone else."

"I wish I could be that cavalier, but even my family, *relatives* can see that video!"

"Only if they go looking for it. And if your family is watching it, there's something wrong with *them*, not you."

She surprised him by laughing, and he laughed with her.

"Look, maybe from the station's perspective you shouldn't have gotten involved with your coanchor," he went on, "but office romances are so common I can't believe employers still require their employees to sign such an agreement. Your relationship with Ethan wouldn't have affected your work if he'd been cool. So why not flip off this douchebag and sue the station despite all the reasons they think you won't? Remove his power to hurt you by refusing to care? Let them know that they've underestimated you?"

"I'll think about it," she said with a sigh.

"Okay. I'd like to see you do it, so I'll keep my fingers

crossed," he said with a grin. "Now why don't you go change into a pair of shorts so that Aiyana can see if there's any glass in your legs."

She looked surprised when she saw the blood staining her yoga pants.

"We'll get this taken care of," Aiyana said gently, obviously eager not to let it undo all the progress they'd made.

"Okay," she said with a sniff, and went upstairs.

"You're so good with people," Aiyana murmured when she was gone.

He took a sip of the tea he was still holding. "I learned from the best."

Emery could've taken care of the cut on her hand and the ones on her legs. They weren't that bad. But Aiyana insisted on checking them with a magnifying glass and removing the few slivers she found with a pair of tweezers. Once she was satisfied that she'd gotten everything, and that none of the cuts were very deep or threatening, she applied some antiseptic and covered each one with a Band-Aid.

"I'm so sorry about what I did to your lamp," Emery said as she sat on the countertop. "I'm going to replace it. I want you to know that."

"Don't worry about it. Now that we're getting married, Cal will be bringing over some of his stuff. I'm sure he has a lamp."

"No, that's not fair. I'll buy you a new one."

"Please don't. Between the two of us, we have more than enough household items as it is. I promise."

Someone knocked on the door. "Hey, I've got to shower if I'm going to make it to school on time."

The voice had to belong to Bentley. He was the only one who had to leave for school. They were in Liam and Bentley's bathroom, where the Band-Aids and antiseptic had been stored.

Aiyana applied the last Band-Aid, and Emery slid off the vanity.

"We're done in here," Aiyana said as she opened the door.

Bentley did a double take when he saw Emery's legs. "Damn!"

"Language," Aiyana warned.

"Right." He looked back at Emery. "You okay?"

"It looks a lot worse than it is. I'm fine—better than the lamp I broke," she said with some chagrin.

A shy smile lit his face, his smooth dark skin contrasting nicely with his large white teeth. "At least I'm not the one to break something this time."

Aiyana swatted his arm, but Emery could tell she wasn't seriously angry. "What you did wouldn't have happened if you hadn't been playing ball in the house."

He pretended to throw a pass to some imaginary receiver. "Hey, I'm a football player. That's what I do."

"You're a running back, not a quarterback, and you had no business throwing that ball in the house," Aiyana insisted with a begrudging smile. "He's hoping to get a football scholarship," she explained as an aside. "We're pretty darn proud of him. But he's not going to let his studies suffer, right?" She winked at him. "You're going to use your brain, too, so that you'll have a fallback in case the worst happens and you don't make it into the pros—or, heaven forbid—you get injured."

"Aw, man, listen to you," he said. "Don't jinx me like that, Ma!"

They squeezed past him on the way out. "You need to be prepared for anything," Aiyana advised.

As Bentley closed the door, Emery couldn't help glancing down the stairs to see if Dallas was still up, but all seemed quiet.

"So are you okay?" Aiyana asked before they parted in the hallway.

Emery knew Aiyana had to get ready for work. She spent long days at the school. "I'm fine. Again, I'm sorry—"

Aiyana waved her words away. "Please, stop apologizing. It's nothing. Really. But I do hope you'll think about what Dallas had to say. Being nice is wonderful, but allowing someone to push you around isn't. Sometimes when people step over the line, you have to let them know you won't put up with it."

Emery was slightly surprised to hear this coming from the nicest person she'd ever met. "I agree."

Aiyana was walking away from her, but at this, she turned back. "You do?"

Emery drew a deep breath. She felt so fragile. But Dallas's words had imbued her with the desire to stand up for herself, to fight back, regardless of what it might cost. "I'm going to call the attorney I've been talking to and tell him to go ahead and file suit."

Aiyana smiled in apparent satisfaction. "Good. They'll learn that they can't treat people the way they treated you."

Although Emery nodded decisively, she knew winning wasn't automatic. She'd have a battle on her hands, one that came with no guarantees.

She paced in her room, trying to work up the nerve, until eight o'clock, when her attorney would be more likely to arrive at his office.

Then she made the call. She managed to reach him, but after it was over, she felt like throwing up.

CHAPTER FOUR

Dallas woke up after ten. His mother would be at work and Bentley at school. Liam would be gone, too. Not only was Liam taking several online classes for college, he was working for Cal Buchanon, the man Aiyana was about to marry, as a cowhand on his cattle ranch not too far from town.

The only person Dallas expected to be home was Emery. Since her main goal in coming to stay with Aiyana was to escape the public eye, he couldn't imagine she'd go anywhere. Although walking around in Silver Springs wouldn't be as difficult as walking around in LA, Silver Springs wasn't all that far away. There would be people who lived in the city for part of the year—people who'd heard about the scandal and may have even watched the video.

The house was silent. Had she left, regardless? Or had she fallen asleep after getting so upset earlier this morning?

He assumed the cuts she'd got weren't any big deal. If they had been, Aiyana would've taken her to a doctor, and he would've heard about it.

He checked his phone. There were no missed calls or texts.

Trying to shake off the last vestiges of sleep, he scrubbed a hand over his face and shoved into a sitting position so he could send a message to his mother.

What happened with Emery after I went to bed? She okay?

He didn't get an immediate response—Aiyana was always busy—so he got up and showered.

By the time he was dressed, Aiyana had a message waiting for him.

Should be. You haven't seen her?

Not yet. Just woke up.

You're not sick, are you?

He was usually well into his day by now, and she knew it. He'd almost always been an early riser. But maybe that was because he often had a hard time sleeping. The nightmares that plagued him had been much worse when he was younger, but he struggled with them even now.

No. Got in bed late. That and I'm taking advantage of having the month off.

I'm glad. You push yourself too hard, especially when you're climbing. The rest has to be good for you.

He'd come home to help Aiyana get ready for her wedding, not because he needed to rest. She was so used to taking care of everyone else he wanted to be sure she received the attention and support she deserved now that she was finally tying the knot with Cal.

His phone buzzed as he put on his shoes. He thought it might be Aiyana, hoping to discuss Emery's situation or checking to see if he'd be interested in walking over when it was time for lunch. She, Eli and Gavin often ate in the cafeteria. They liked interacting with the students, being accessible. That was his mother's secret, how she managed to turn so many troubled boys around. She genuinely cared, she was patient and kind, and she invested the time, gave them the attention they needed.

But it wasn't Aiyana who was trying to reach him. It was Brian Gerlack, the owner of the parkour gym in Las Vegas where Dallas worked during the winter. Dallas had put off coaching until January this year, which was unusual. He usually started the first of November, as soon as the weather turned, but finding a sponsor meant he didn't have to go back at all—not unless he wanted to. Some of the guys who were representing the same brand were after him to travel to Europe to get ready for the IFSC World Cup together, which meant he might not make it back even in January. And that wasn't something he was eager to tell Brian. Brian was more than just an employer. They'd grown exceptionally close over the years, so close that Brian had been talking about retiring and selling him the gym.

Dallas was grateful—for everything Brian had done for him and was willing to do. But now wasn't the time to lock himself in. Dallas had finally achieved what he'd been after all along. He could climb to his heart's content—*and get paid for it*. He couldn't commit to an entity he'd be responsible for without any reprieve, couldn't strap himself down indefinitely. Just thinking about being stuck in one place—especially in such a big city—made him claustrophobic.

With a frown, he silenced his phone and went upstairs. What Brian offered him was a great opportunity. But he'd recently been given a better one. If he became a real contender in the sport, someone like Alex Honnold, he could always use his name and experience to open a gym later.

But if he got hurt before he had enough recognition and couldn't continue to climb…

What then? Where would he find the capital? It would be much more difficult to get a start if Brian had already sold the gym to someone else.

He put two slices of bread in the toaster and was scrambling eggs at the stove when he heard a sound behind him. He knew before he turned around that it was Emery.

"You okay?" he asked, glancing behind him.

She'd just rolled out of bed, too. Dressed in another pair of yoga pants—these gray—she had her hair pulled back. "I feel terrible about how I behaved earlier. That tantrum was childish and…ungrateful and…and ridiculous." She rolled her eyes. "I'm embarrassed."

"Don't worry about that. It's not the first time my mother's lost a lamp." He cast her a wry grin. "I broke a few when I lived here."

"But if it was when you lived here, you were much younger," she pointed out ruefully.

"I've gotten better at managing my emotions over the years," he said with a shrug. "I've had a lot of practice handling disappointment."

She didn't seem overly pleased by his response. "You're saying I haven't had any practice? That I'm spoiled?"

"I'm saying that the trouble in your life started later than mine. That's all. You get better at navigating setbacks once you handle a few."

She could tell he meant no insult. "True, but that's no excuse. It's so nice of Aiyana to let me stay here, and I—"

"It's fine," he broke in. "She understands what you're going through." He used his spatula to point at the coffeemaker. "Coffee?"

She got a mug from the cupboard and poured herself a cup. "Thanks."

"How about some eggs?"

"Only if you've got enough. Otherwise, I can have granola and yogurt. Or cold cereal."

"There's plenty."

He pulled out a plate, buttered the toast and gave her a piece of it as well as a big scoop of eggs.

"Did Aiyana tell you?" she asked.

"Tell me what?"

"I've decided to go ahead and sue the station," she replied as he set the food in front of her. "I talked to my attorney about it this morning."

He returned to the stove to dish up his own breakfast. "You confident in that decision?"

"I feel it's the right thing to do," she hedged. "But I'm scared. It could get ugly. Ethan could go to the media, cause the story to blow up even bigger, when all I want is for it to go away— the sooner the better."

"You should expect the worst. You need to be prepared or your commitment will waver."

Biting her bottom lip, she stared down at her food. "How do I get prepared?"

"You have to know your own mind, remain determined." That was how he tackled each new climb. It was determination that carried him through every challenge.

"At Christmas," she added glumly. "Who wants to deal with such negative—and embarrassing—stuff at Christmas?"

He thought of her parents' divorce and her grandmother's deteriorating mental state, but she didn't mention those things, and he didn't bring them up, either. He rummaged through the refrigerator for ketchup, grabbed the last piece of toast he'd buttered and the rest of the eggs, and sat down with her at the table. "I can't imagine anyone would. But Ethan whatever-his-last-name-is brought this fight to you."

"Right." She watched as he took his first bite. "There's just one thing."

He swallowed. "What's that?"

She cleared her throat, obviously uncomfortable. "I hate to ask you this, but…" Her eyes skittered away from his only to return a second later, and her shoulders lifted as she drew in a deep breath. "I can't quit imagining it, can't quit feeling as though… Well, it's the elephant in the room, isn't it?"

"If there's an elephant in the room, I don't know about it," he said, mystified.

"You'll understand as soon as…" She twisted her hands in her lap. "Maybe if I just broach the subject, get it out of the way, I'll be able to relax and…and won't have to feel so self-conscious and humiliated every time I see you…"

He swallowed. "Sounds good to me. What are you talking about?"

"You haven't…" She squeezed her eyes closed. "You haven't watched the video, have you?" she blurted out.

He waited for her to open her eyes, which she did with a wince, as though she was afraid of what she might hear. "No."

Her eyes widened in disbelief. *"Really?"*

Skepticism showed in her voice, but there was hope in her face—and it was the hope that made him glad he was telling the truth. "Really," he said with more authority.

She pushed her eggs around her plate. "Most people, especially old acquaintances, would look it up the moment they heard of it. Curiosity alone would tempt someone to watch it. I admit—" her face reddened "—if I wasn't the one going through this and someone told me there was a sex tape on the internet featuring you or anyone else I knew from high school, I'd be tempted to look it up. I was a news anchor, after all. I've been trained to jump on any piece of potential news, even if it's only gossip. I'm sort of ashamed of that now that I'm on the other end."

"It's human nature," he said.

She took another bite. "So why haven't you looked it up?"

It sure as hell wasn't because he wasn't interested. Like she'd said, curiosity alone dictated he have a look. He guessed he felt even more curiosity than others, because of his earlier romantic interest in her.

Before he'd dropped into bed last night, he'd nearly gone online to see what all the fuss was about. How bad was it? How much of her could be seen? Should she be as embarrassed as she was? Was Ethan putting on an act, playing the great lover, knowing he was videoing the whole thing? Did he ever look toward the camera?

The thought that Ethan might have done something like that had made Dallas want to punch him in the face. He'd used his anger as an excuse to grab his laptop. He gave himself several other excuses, too—it was no big deal, everyone else had seen it, it might help him calm Emery's fears and convince her it was no big deal if he knew what *exactly* was involved. It wasn't like it would change his opinion of her. What would it hurt?

She didn't even have to know.

But before he could type her name in the search engine, he'd realized that it *would* hurt something—it would hurt *her*—and decided he wouldn't abuse his mother's trust, that he would be the man she wanted him to be, and he would be the friend Emery needed in this moment. Even if she didn't know he'd done it, he'd be taking something intimate from her that she hadn't offered him, and he didn't want to do that to her or any other woman.

He chewed slowly, trying to decide how honest he should be about the close call. She'd been honest with him. But he wasn't the one struggling with trust. So he decided not to reveal that he'd nearly broken faith with her—even before he knew it was somehow important to him to maintain it. "Because it wasn't meant for me," he said simply.

In the end, that was the reason he'd set his laptop aside and gone to sleep without allowing her coanchor to embarrass her any further, so it was true.

She sagged in relief, as if his words were soothing to her bruised and battered heart—probably her ego, too—and Dallas was glad he'd made the right decision. He was also ashamed of almost making the wrong one.

"I appreciate it," she said. "I feel so violated, and…and wounded, you know? As if Ethan somehow blew away any hint of respectability and dignity I had. So it's especially nice to be able to be with you and not feel as though you're seeing that video playing in a loop in your mind whenever you look at me."

Because he'd nearly succumbed, he felt unworthy of her praise and changed the subject. "Being cooped up in this house all the time, thinking about what happened, can't be making things any easier. I've got to get some Christmas shopping done. I usually wait till the last minute, but this year, with how busy we'll be with the wedding, I figured I'd drive over to Santa Barbara today and see what I could find. I have nieces and nephews who are getting older and understand that Christmas means presents." He chuckled. "So I can't be quite as derelict as I've been in the past. Any interest in going with me?"

She started to decline. She seemed horrified by the possibility of facing strangers who might've seen her in such a compromised position. But he convinced her that the people in Santa Barbara might not recognize her. It was chilly out; she could bundle up without looking odd or out of place. "A day out will be worth the risk. You have to start circulating again at some point," he said. "Facing your detractors might help you put it behind you."

"I'm not ready for that," she insisted.

"Why wait? Why let anyone make a prisoner out of you?"

She rubbed some of the bandages under her yoga pants. "I've got all of these little cuts, for one."

"Are any of them very deep? Do they hurt?"

"Not really, but I'm using whatever excuse I can," she said wryly. "Maybe I'll brave it after Christmas."

"You don't need to do any shopping?"

"I can do it online."

"And miss all the decorations and holiday cheer? The congested traffic? The crowds? The fake tree in the center of the mall?" He nudged her elbow as he finished eating. "The Salvation Army person who rings that little bell?"

She laughed but then narrowed her eyes. "Something tells me you're not all that excited about holiday decorations yourself."

"I like them," he insisted. "And going out might only get harder the longer you put it off. Why not have some fun? Forget everyone else? I'll be with you. How bad can it get?"

She took a few more bites and swallowed before nodding as though she'd come to a decision. "Okay."

Knots formed in Emery's stomach as Dallas parked at La Arcada Courtyard, a quaint shopping and dining area in Santa Barbara with 1920s Spanish Colonial architecture, red awnings, several fountains and ivy crawling up the white stucco walls. She hadn't spent much time in Santa Barbara, not since she was a kid, but it remained familiar to her and felt generally less threatening than the LA metropolis, which was filled with the television viewers she'd been so excited to cultivate once she graduated from college.

"You ready for this?" Dallas asked as he turned off the engine.

They'd been talking most of the drive, so she'd been able to push this moment to the back of her mind—the moment when she'd have to get out and face strangers who might recognize her and be familiar with the scandal surrounding her. Even with Dallas beside her for moral support, even with Santa Barbara seeming quite removed from LA and her relationship with Ethan, she felt the jagged edge of anxiety drag through her, tearing at her confidence. She wished they could return to

New Horizons Boys Ranch immediately, so she could retreat inside Aiyana's home. She was safe there. No one could find her—other than Aiyana and Aiyana's immediate circle, of course.

"I don't know..." She stared out at the people scurrying past the bronze dolphins cavorting in the middle of the walkway between two rows of shops.

The weather was far better than they'd anticipated. Although it had been raining when they left, the sun had come out since. It was turning into a beautiful day. She could wear a coat, but she might look odd pulling up the hood like she wanted to do.

"You don't care what these people think," Dallas said.

She glanced at him. "That's easy for you to say. You've never been embarrassed this deeply."

"How bad could that video be?" he asked. "Maybe I should watch it so that I can understand."

Her gaze had drifted right back to the window. At this, she whipped her head around to look at him again. "No!" she said desperately. "I'll get out."

She heard him chuckle and knew his comment had been a ploy to pry her from the van, but the more she got to know him—and the more she liked him—the more mortified she became at the thought that he might see what so many already had. It was becoming progressively more important to her that he *never* see that video.

Her knees threatened to buckle when she landed on her feet, but she managed to stay upright and move out of the way of the door so she could close it.

"Where should we go first?" he asked, coming around the van.

She studied the shops as though she were about to face a firing squad and grabbed a pair of sunglasses out of her purse. "I don't care," she muttered as she put them on.

He laughed at her morose response but surprised her by taking her hand. "We got this. Come on. No one is going to say anything to you without answering to me."

She expected the next few minutes to be excruciating. But people were more interested in their own shopping than they were her. When no one stopped to stare or point, she began to relax, but she didn't let go of Dallas. The warmth of his hand, calloused in places because of his climbing, felt more reassuring than she wanted it to. She'd always prided herself on being a fierce, independent woman. But Ethan Grimes had dealt her such a leveling blow. She hated that she'd been stupid enough to get involved with him in the first place. She should've been able to ascertain the kind of man he was much sooner.

"See? Everything's fine," Dallas said as they stopped to gaze up at a historic mission bell hanging over another sculpted dolphin, this one spouting water.

She checked the walkway to be sure a crowd wasn't forming to laugh at her. She knew that was ridiculous, but she was so self-conscious. "Thanks for...for helping me through this."

"Of course."

The afternoon flew by. They admired the elaborate Christmas decorations both inside and outside the various stores, grabbed a late lunch at a sidewalk café, picked up a few gifts and tossed a coin in a fountain that had sculptures of turtles climbing onto rocks. On a bench that had a statue of Benjamin Franklin at one end, they sat and enjoyed an ice cream cone.

By late afternoon, Emery was finally to the point where she could remove her sunglasses and talk and laugh freely, even walk without having to cling to Dallas. But just as they were getting ready to head back to Silver Springs, they drifted into a quaint and expensive chocolate shop. She was planning to send a box of chocolates to her mother, thought it might help encourage Connie during this difficult period, when she realized the woman behind the counter was someone she'd known in high school.

"Sidney," she said, the word pulled from her automatically as soon as Sidney looked up.

"Emery! What are you doing here?"

Emery felt the hair on the back of her neck stand up. Sidney had been one of those friends in school who was nice to her face but talked about her behind her back—the kind of friend who was jealous of any success she had and would be relieved, almost eager, to see trouble come her way.

At first, Emery hoped that Sidney hadn't heard about Ethan, the sex video and her subsequent firing from the news station. But with the way social media worked, she knew that wasn't realistic. It took only one person from her old high school to hear the news and share it, and then *everyone* would know. And surely there'd been at least one person who was privy to her downfall. Something *this* juicy spread fast.

"Just shopping for Christmas." Emery conjured her best imitation of a smile, hoping it would mask her nervousness and insecurity. "What are you doing here? Do you live in Santa Barbara these days?"

"I do. My aunt owns this store, and since I was tired of small town life and was talking about moving closer to the coast, she asked me to help out with it until after the holidays."

"What will you do then?" Emery asked, trying to keep the focus off herself for as long as possible.

"I'm an interior designer—have a BFA from the Pratt Institute in New York City."

Emery wasn't familiar with the Pratt Institute, but Sidney was so proud of having gone there it had to be something special.

"I'll be starting my own business after the first of the year," she added.

"That's wonderful," Emery said. "I'm happy to see that things are going well for you." She indicated the chocolates in the glass showcase. "I was just hoping to order a box of candy for my mother."

"Of course. What kind would you like?" Sidney asked, but the moment she finished packing Emery's chocolates and had wrapped the box in Christmas paper and put a pretty bow on top, she said, "So…do you still live in LA, or did you leave because of…you know?"

Sure enough, she knew—and she couldn't resist putting Emery on the spot.

"I still live in LA, but I'm staying in Silver Springs for a few weeks, what with the holidays and all." Emery didn't add that her parents were no longer there, or that she'd have to move away from LA eventually, because she couldn't bear the thought of returning.

Sidney lowered her voice. "It must be hard."

"Why would it be hard?" Dallas had been moving along the display case. He acted as though he was going to order a box, too—and maybe he was—but Emery knew he'd also been monitoring the conversation.

Sidney's eyes lifted to his. "Is this…your new boyfriend?" she guessed.

Emery didn't have a chance to respond before Dallas spoke again.

"No, but I'd like to be," he said. "You saw that video, right? Damn, it was hot! *Any* man would be lucky to have her."

Sidney's jaw dropped. In one fell swoop, Dallas had removed her power. He'd tackled the situation head-on, as if Emery didn't have anything to hide or feel awkward or embarrassed about, and that left Sidney with nowhere to go. "I… I guess," she stuttered.

Dallas took his time choosing a box of chocolates for Aiyana. Then he insisted Emery sit with him at one of the little tables in the shop, where they ordered a hot chocolate and sipped it slowly, proving they were as comfortable as could be.

"Enough already. I'm dying to get out of here," Emery whispered once Sidney was busy helping some other patrons who'd wandered in.

Dallas checked his watch. "We'll leave as soon as she's available, so that we can say goodbye."

"I didn't even want to say hello," Emery grumbled.

He laughed loudly as though she'd just made a great joke and they were having a grand time together. Then he lowered his voice. "You can't dictate how most people will react to you. But you have to remain in charge, can't give them the power to hurt you—or they will."

Her attorney had suggested she hire a PR company to handle the debacle. If she hadn't lost her job on top of everything else, she would've taken that recommendation. Now she could see why a PR company might be important. With a little strategy, she could spin what'd happened in a more favorable light and outmaneuver her detractors. They didn't have to know she was dying inside.

The customers Sidney had just helped were walking out the door when Sidney glanced over. Surprisingly, there was no hint of the smugness in her expression that had been there when she mentioned LA. She seemed almost jealous again—jealous that such a handsome man would shrug off what Emery had done instead of making a joke out of it, out of her.

"Incredible," she muttered to Dallas after Sidney picked up their empty cups and disappeared into the back.

"What?" Dallas said as he stood.

"Attitudes are as catchy as the flu."

"Exactly."

"We appreciate your help," Emery said to Sidney when she returned to wipe off their table.

"No problem." Her gaze shifted to Dallas. "Merry Christmas," she said, obviously eager to please him.

"Merry Christmas," he said with a wide smile and once again took Emery's hand.

CHAPTER FIVE

It was after eleven when Aiyana sat on the couch next to Dallas. His younger brothers had gone up to get ready for bed, and Emery was in her room, possibly asleep. "How'd it go today?"

Dallas continued flipping through TV stations. He didn't watch a lot of TV, just a show here or there on his computer. Not only did he sleep in his van in one campground or another throughout the summer, he went to bed early so he could get up at the crack of dawn. And during the winter—until this winter—he spent most of his time at the gym, coaching or working out so that he could maintain his strength and earn enough to carry him through the next climbing season. "How'd what go today? Shopping? Fine."

"You and Emery get along okay?"

"Of course. Why?"

"You were gone all day."

He eyed her dubiously. "What are you implying?"

She arched her eyebrows, unwilling to back down even though the look he was giving her warned her not to make a big deal of the time he'd spent with her houseguest. "It means you were having fun."

After glancing back toward the stairs to be sure Emery wasn't coming down, he lowered his voice. "I was just trying to help her."

The way Aiyana smiled made him suspect she didn't believe him, so he leaned forward. "You know better than to play matchmaker," he said. "Even if she were interested, which I'm sure she's not—she's going through too much right now to even consider getting into another relationship—it would only set her up for heartbreak. I wouldn't make a good husband."

She rolled her eyes. "Says who?"

"Says *me*. Climbing has come between me and plenty of other women. This relationship would be no different." He knew that wasn't strictly true. It wasn't climbing that made him leery; it was a lack of trust. The only psychologist he'd ever found helpful had told him he had abandonment issues. But anyone who'd been through what he'd been through, especially at such a young age, would be angry and walled off.

"Eventually, you'll be looking for something more...fulfilling than climbing," she predicted.

He settled on SportsCenter since he knew his mother wouldn't stick around long enough to watch anything even if he chose a program she'd like better. She had school in the morning, was already up past her bedtime. "I don't find anything more fulfilling than climbing," he said. "I'm happy the way I am," he added the moment he saw the concern enter her eyes. Aiyana had saved him in so many ways; he refused to cause her to worry. "I'm good."

She sighed as she glanced away, then looked at him again, this time catching and holding his gaze. "I got a letter a couple of months ago."

He tensed. He could tell by her somber tone that this wasn't just any letter—and since he'd recently received a letter himself, he could guess what she was about to say. "From my father?"

"He's been in contact with you, then? You didn't say anything, so I assumed he didn't follow through."

Dallas pictured the crinkled envelope he'd taken out of his duffel bag last night. He didn't pick up his mail often, handled almost everything online, so his father's letter had been waiting in his post office box for over a month. "He wrote me, if that's what you mean by 'followed through.'"

"What'd he have to say?"

"I don't know."

"You didn't open it? What'd you do with it? Throw it away?"

"Not yet. But I might. What'd your letter say?"

"That he was eager to reach you, that he had something to tell you he felt you should hear."

The bitterness that welled up surprised Dallas. He'd thought he'd come to terms with his childhood—even though it had warped him in a way he couldn't seem to fix, like a constant wind permanently bends even a strong tree. "As far as I'm concerned, he's dead. I don't want to hear anything he has to say."

She rested her hand on his forearm. Her touch had always soothed him. He'd watched Eli handle the horses they had on the property in a similar manner, knew it was because of the trust he'd developed with them that they responded as they did. Dallas supposed the same mechanism was at work here, too. So maybe he could trust. He trusted Aiyana, didn't he? It just didn't come easy.

"He claims he's sorry for what he did to your mother and sister, Dallas," she said. "That he's spent the past twenty-three years regretting his actions."

He didn't believe that for a second. No amount of regret could change the past, anyway. Dallas was six when he'd watched his father, in a drunken rage, shoot and kill his mother and sister. He turned the gun on himself afterward, but managed only a superficial wound before being hauled off to prison. Dallas went to live with his mother's mother—until she died of chronic disruptive pulmonary disease a year later. Then he was put into the foster care system, where he acted out so badly he was passed around from home to home until he turned fourteen and the state, in a last-ditch effort to correct his behavior, sent him to New Horizons.

Fortunately, that brought him into contact with Aiyana. Because of her—and the stability she offered—not only did he graduate, he was accepted to UC Santa Cruz. He only attended one year before dropping out, but at least he finished high school. If not for Aiyana, he wouldn't have done that much. If not for Aiyana, he'd probably be in prison, like his dad. The group of friends he'd fallen in with in Bakersfield, where he'd spent his life up until that point, was getting heavily involved in using and selling drugs.

"Why does he want to talk to me?" Dallas asked. Then he voiced what he suspected, what he'd told himself that letter probably contained, which was the main reason he hadn't opened it. "Don't tell me he's up for parole. Does he expect me to come speak at his hearing, and try to help him get out? Because that's not gonna happen."

"That's not what he said," Aiyana replied. "He told me he was just hoping to get a message to you."

"So that's how he got my address? You gave it to him?" He scowled. "Why? You know how I feel about him."

"Actually, I don't," she said calmly. "You'll never speak of him."

"Because of how I feel," he responded in exasperation.

"I'm sorry if I made the wrong decision. I should've asked you before I gave him your address. Even though you've never opened up about him, I know you have issues with him, and rightly so. But I figured it was safe to give him a PO Box. It's not as if he could ever show up at your door, even if he *did* get out. And I thought—" her hand rubbed his arm in a loving gesture "—if he's truly sorry, it might do you some good to receive an apology. Sometimes when people take responsibility for the things they've done—no matter how terrible—it can heal old wounds."

Dallas didn't think the man he remembered was capable of

true remorse. He was too narcissistic for that. "I'm fine. There's nothing he could do to help me even if I wasn't. Whatever he says, they're just words."

She let go of him and sat in silence for a few minutes before changing the subject. "We're having a rewards assembly tomorrow morning at school, for those who have attained at least a B average so far this semester. I was hoping you'd come and teach the boys how to scale the climbing wall. Gavin and Eli don't know much about climbing, so I bet they'd be grateful. And it would allow them to concentrate on helping the boys with the sports they *are* good at."

"What time?"

"Eight."

"Of course," he said. There was nothing Aiyana could ask of him that would be too much—not that this would be even a minor sacrifice.

"Thank you." She stood and kissed him on the head. "Good night."

As he listened to her climb the stairs, he thought about what she'd told him: *Sometimes when people take responsibility for the things they've done—no matter how terrible—it can heal old wounds.*

Was that true? Could he fix what *he'd* done that easily?

Sadly, no. Jenny wasn't around to apologize to.

Wednesday, December 9

The buzz of her phone woke Emery. She blinked at the light streaming through the cracks in the blinds, realized it was morning and started fumbling through the blankets. Last night, after she'd returned from Santa Barbara and climbed into bed, she'd been shocked to receive a text from Ethan. That he'd have the nerve to contact her after what he'd done, that he'd feel safe enough to do so, boggled her mind.

But the temptation to rub her nose in the collapse of her career was probably too great for him. Also, he didn't know that she was going to sue him as well as the station. Her attorney hadn't even drawn up the paperwork yet, let alone filed it and had it served.

She threw off the covers, finally locating her phone when it hit the carpet with a dull thud. The ringing had stopped by the time she climbed out of bed to get it, but she could see who'd been trying to reach her. It was her mother.

After a yawn and a stretch to help gather her faculties, she climbed back into bed, burrowed deep into the covers and braced herself for this conversation.

"There you are!" her mother exclaimed as soon as she answered. "But...what's wrong?"

"Nothing. Why?"

"It sounds as though you're losing your voice."

Emery cleared her throat. "I just woke up." She checked the clock on the nightstand. It was almost nine, which was late, but not *that* late, considering how hard it had been to fall asleep last night. Although she'd been exhausted, she couldn't quit obsessing about the lawsuit—how long it might take to complete and what it might trigger. Neither could she quit thinking about the day she'd spent in Santa Barbara, the way Sidney had behaved in the chocolate shop, the implications of that encounter and the man she'd gone there with.

And then Ethan's audacious text.

She hadn't responded to her former coanchor. It was so hard not to tell him to get lost. But she figured she should try to lure him into revealing something that might help her case. She'd have only a short window before he became aware, a gap during which he might be confident enough to brazenly say something that would prove her allegations to be true.

"This late?" her mother said. "It's almost noon!"

Emery tried to focus on the conversation. In her family, sleeping in was a mark of laziness. She couldn't help but chafe at her mother's overblown reaction. "You're on Eastern time. How's Grandma?"

Her mother sounded weary when she answered. "She's not improving."

Which meant she was getting worse. Emery could hear it as surely as though her mother was shouting it into the phone. "Does she still recognize you?"

"On a good day."

Emery closed her eyes. "I'm sorry."

Her mother's voice hardened. "Have you heard from your father?"

She hadn't. She rarely heard from Marvin since her parents' marriage fell apart. He was too caught up in his new life, and his new woman. She felt forgotten, left behind. He knew what Ethan had done to her, but he'd scarcely reacted to it, even though he used to be protective of her, of all of them—the defender of the family. Emery was so bewildered; she couldn't figure out what'd gone wrong, but her father seemed to be walking away from her. "No."

"He's cut off my access to our bank accounts. I have no way of buying anything."

A thread of panic ran through those words, causing Emery's stomach to churn. Connie obviously hadn't expected Marvin to act as he was, either.

Emery had no idea how long her own small savings would have to last. She wasn't even sure she could get another job, not a decent one, what with all the slut-shaming that was going on as a result of that video. But how could she not help? "How much do you need?"

"A few hundred bucks, if you can spare it. I hate to ask, but Grandma doesn't have anything besides her social security. It barely covers the utilities and her car insurance, and I've got to get groceries."

"Of course. It's no problem," Emery lied. Connie hadn't been able to pay her back the last loan. Her mother had no income, had always been a stay-at-home mom. But she couldn't let her mother and grandmother go hungry. Fortunately, her grandmother, Adele, didn't have a mortgage, so they didn't have a house payment in addition to all the other bills. But she couldn't continue to support them. Her father had to be fair with Connie and split the assets they'd accumulated in their marriage.

"Thank you, honey. I'm sorry to bother you with this. If I wasn't at such loose ends, maybe I'd be able to figure out something else. But it's all I can do to hold myself together and be there for your grandmother."

"I know," she said. "It's okay." But it meant she'd have to call her father, have to remind him of his duty to his first family, and she wasn't convinced that would go well. "I'll Venmo it to you."

"You're a lifesaver."

Although Connie had sounded relieved when they hung up, Emery was more worried than ever—about her mother, about her grandmother, about her future job opportunities. Christmas was a terrible time to look for work. Even if she could face doing it, she didn't think it would be wise to set herself up for failure.

But things couldn't continue like this.

It wasn't until several minutes later that it occurred to Emery that her mother hadn't even asked how *she* was doing.

She had to be almost as humiliated as Emery was. She could no longer brag about her daughter, who was on TV. She probably had extended family and friends who were watching that video, too. Not talking about it was her way of not acknowledging it, of shelving it completely.

With a sigh, Emery dragged herself out of bed. All she wanted to do was go back to sleep, but maybe Dallas would be home. Maybe he'd make her breakfast again. It felt surreal that she'd been reduced to relying on people who were barely more than acquaintances.

But she was infinitely grateful they cared enough to help.

The assembly ended at lunchtime, but the boys were so excited about the climbing wall, and having someone there who could show them how to scale it, they weren't in any hurry to go to the cafeteria.

"You'd better get something to eat," Dallas warned the last of the stragglers. "You'll spend the afternoon hungry if you don't."

"Can't we stay here and climb?" one boy asked. "Please?" Thick red hair, which stood up in back, and a face full of freckles made him look as young and untainted by the world as a boy his age should be. But the scars on his arms told a different story. Most of the students who came to New Horizons had difficult backgrounds, which was why Dallas didn't ask what'd happened to this one. His own arms had scars that looked so similar he was fairly certain he could guess what'd happened to this poor kid.

"I'll tell you what," he said. "Ms. Turner rented the equipment for the entire day. If you'll go to lunch and to the rest of your classes, you can come back after school's out. I'll be here until four-thirty."

"Cool!" the boy cried, and his friends made similar exclamations as they hurried out of the gymnasium.

"Let's walk over and have some lunch ourselves," Gavin said.

Dallas turned. He'd seen Aiyana and Eli go with the boys to the cafeteria and hadn't realized his other brother was still around. "Sounds good to me."

While Eli helped Aiyana administrate, Gavin handled much of the grounds and maintenance. What his mother had created was thriving, and Dallas was once again grateful to her—grateful to know that she was still providing a safe and stable place for lost boys, like the kind of boy he'd been, to finish growing up.

Briefly, he considered coming home to work. There was certainly a need he could fill here—and he wanted to do it.

He just didn't know if he could take the daily reminder of his own childhood. He'd been running from the past for so long, he wasn't sure he could ever stop.

CHAPTER SIX

Dallas wasn't home. Emery had checked the main floor and called downstairs a few times to say good morning—all with no response. It soon became obvious she was alone in the house.

With a sigh, she sat at the kitchen table and reread the message she'd received from Ethan. I miss you. He'd sent just those three words, but she nearly went ballistic every time she saw them. How did he expect her to respond? He acted as though he hadn't destroyed her career, *her life*.

Maybe he didn't care.

Her jaw tightened and her fingers itched to type a vicious retaliation. She'd never in her life been so incredibly angry. But she had to tamp down that anger and *think*. Only then might she improve the situation.

He'd opened communication between them. Maybe his arrogance would work in her favor and cause him to miss the trap she was setting for him.

So… What could she say that would cause him to admit he was the one who'd put that video on the internet? To tell her how things had transpired when KQLA hired him back? Was there a chance he'd let it slip that Heidi knew he was guilty of sabotaging his coanchor's career? That upper management had turned a blind eye to his toxic behavior? Allowed him to submarine a fellow employee without any reaction—except to give him his job back even though he was as guilty of breaking the "no romance" rule as she was? ·

It was a long shot. Ethan wasn't stupid. He was just feeling comfortably in command at the moment. But she had to try.

She pictured his big white teeth and wide smile, the care he took styling his hair and choosing the right clothes, as she mulled over various responses. Would riling him up or placating him work better?

She hadn't quite decided when she received a message from Aiyana.

We're having lunch in the cafeteria. The food isn't bad. Come over and eat with us, if you feel like getting out.

Thanks to Ethan, she doubted she'd ever feel like going out again. The question was whether she could *drag* herself from the house for any type of public interaction, let those around her whisper and murmur and shoot her curious, if not damning, glances.

Would she have the resilience to weather that?

She still felt so raw. But Aiyana had said "we." Since Dallas wasn't home, that "we" likely included him. He'd protected her yesterday, made it possible for her to not only leave the house but to relax and have fun, even after she bumped into Sidney.

She bit her lip as she texted Aiyana back. She had to put herself out there and at least *try* to heal. Dallas had said it was all in her attitude, that she could determine how others reacted to her by shrugging off what'd happened as though it wasn't any big deal. They would take their lead from her.

She'd seen proof of that yesterday. But it required more strength and determination than she'd ever had to muster to tell Aiyana she'd come when she didn't have him or anyone else to walk over with.

Once she got there, maybe Dallas could help her decide how to respond to Ethan. Because he wasn't emotionally embroiled in this nightmare, he could be more objective…

After pulling her hair into a messy bun, she changed into some jeans and a blouse, dabbed on some blush, lipstick and mascara, and rushed out of the house without giving herself time to reconsider. She could do this. What were the chances that any of the students had heard about her or seen that video?

The possibility couldn't be *too* great. They were young and busy with school and sports. Who would point out a news clip like that to them—especially here, at a correctional school? While going to New Horizons, where most of them boarded, they were somewhat isolated.

That meant she likely only had to worry about the teachers.

Once she stepped inside the cafeteria, however, and all eyes turned her way, Emery felt she was being skewered by a thousand tiny daggers. There weren't any girls on the boys' side of campus, and only about half the staff were female. Of that half, most were quite a bit older. She told herself *that* was the reason she was drawing so much attention, that it had nothing to do with the intimate video making the rounds online.

Dallas stood and waved her over, and instead of turning and rushing back to the house, as she was dying to do, she let her eyes latch onto his tanned face, with his blue eyes and sandy-blond hair, and smiled confidently, as though she were her old self.

"Hi," she said, still smiling as she drew close enough to speak. But she could feel her lips tremble. She hoped no one would notice.

He studied her as though he wanted to say something encouraging. But he didn't. Maybe he thought it would be too patronizing or would embarrass her in front of the others. Instead he said, "Have a seat. I'll grab you a tray."

As he walked over to where the food was, she sank down next to his brother Eli and Eli's wife, Cora, a teacher at the school, both of whom she'd seen at the house several times. Gavin sat across from her, by Aiyana. She'd met him, too, but only once since he lived off campus and didn't come to the house as often. Fortunately, Eli and Gavin were tall enough to shield her from some of those who were still staring at her. The students were probably only curious if she was a new teacher or something, but she couldn't bring herself to look beyond those at the table to determine if the interest she felt was really that casual.

"Heard you went shopping yesterday," Gavin said.

She could tell he was trying to put her at ease and was grateful. "Yes. I…er…we got some Christmas shopping done," she said, even though she'd been too worried about spending money to buy more than that box of chocolates for her mother and a pretty picture frame for her grandmother. Dallas had picked up a few more things for his family. "It was fun."

"Good. Maybe Dallas can manage to get his gifts wrapped this year," Eli said. "Usually, he just hands us each a sack."

Gavin laughed. "I'd make fun of him, but until Savanna came along, I wasn't much better."

"Neither were you, not until you married," Aiyana told Eli. "It's Cora who does all the shopping and wrapping, isn't it?"

When Cora shot him a look that made him concede the point, they all laughed.

"That just means Dallas needs a woman in his life," Eli said, and the awkward silence that fell immediately after made Emery squirm. Dallas was one of the most vital men she'd ever met. Although he was a little rough around the edges—certainly didn't bother with anything but the most practical haircut and clothes—there wasn't an ounce of fat on him, his mind was quick, his smile impossible to resist and his eyes spoke volumes with a single look. If she had her guess, most women would find him attractive.

But after what she'd been through, she wasn't looking for another relationship. And when she *did* start looking, she hoped to find someone who was already established, who had more direction in his life. She had no problem with Dallas climbing half the year, but she wouldn't want to be involved with someone who needed so much time alone.

"I'm sure he'll find the right woman," she mumbled.

Dallas returned and slid a tray of spaghetti and meatballs, with a piece of garlic bread and a box of chocolate milk in separate sections, in front of her.

"Thanks," she said, relieved when he sat down, because he made just as good a shield as Gavin.

She stared at her food, far too nervous to eat. "This looks… delicious," she said lamely, and picked up her fork.

"I'm glad you made yourself come out," he said softly, for her ears alone. "It'll get easier."

She nodded as though she believed him and pretended to eat while the others talked and laughed. She didn't have much to contribute to the conversation. The ambient noise kept her on edge; she was waiting for the moment when a teacher approached the table and recognized her. She thought something like that was happening when a boy walked up just as the bell rang.

"Do you remember me?" he asked.

Her breath lodged in her throat, and her face burned with shame. She didn't remember him, couldn't remember ever seeing him before. But if he knew her, she felt certain he had to have heard about the sex scandal.

Before she could respond, however, he said, "Probably not. I was only about six when I saw you."

She'd been so prepared for the humiliation of being called out in front of everyone at the table, that it took her a moment to process that he was talking about years ago. "Where—where did we meet?" she managed to say.

"I was staying at my cousin's house. You know Avery Till-erman, right?"

She recognized the name. Although they'd lost touch, she'd gone to high school with Avery. They'd both been part of the equestrian club. "I do."

"That's my cousin."

"Oh. What's Avery up to?" She was reluctant to continue this conversation, was afraid of where it might lead. What if he called Avery to say that he'd run into her, and Avery informed him of her recent disgrace? But she couldn't risk cutting him off too soon, either. Then he'd have even more reason to mention her to Avery. *I saw your friend, and she was so rude to me.*

"She's a veterinarian. Just opened her own practice here in town last year."

Shit. Avery lived in Silver Springs? That meant he probably *would* say something to her. "I'll have to look her up, say hello."

When he pulled out his phone, she caught her breath. "I can give you her number..."

"Right." She let her breath seep out slowly. "Um, that would be great." Her hands felt unwieldy as she clumsily created a new contact.

After she managed to type in Avery's name and number, she set her phone aside—with absolutely no intention of contact-ing her. "Thank you."

"No problem."

"You'd better hurry or you'll be late for class," Aiyana broke in, her words acting like a cattle prod that made him lope away.

Emery watched him and the rest of the students filter through the double doors like sand passing through the bottleneck of an hourglass.

"You finished eating?" Dallas asked, bringing her mind back to the people around her.

She nodded, and even though she'd taken only a few bites, he didn't press her. He grabbed her tray along with his own, emptied both into the garbage and stacked them one on top of the other.

Emery sat still, waiting for the room to empty completely. She wanted to be certain everyone was in class before she attempted the walk across campus to Aiyana's house. She'd heard Eli recruit Dallas to help with some PE classes—a teacher wasn't feeling well—so she figured he'd be staying at the school. She'd have to decide what to say to Ethan on her own or wait until later, when Dallas was available to offer his opinion.

But he surprised her by telling Eli he'd be a few minutes late and insisted on walking her back to the house.

"You did it," he said, once they were on their way. "You braved being in public on your own. Way to go."

Emery had her head bowed, her eyes focused on the ground in front of her, but she couldn't help looking around every few seconds to make sure she wasn't going to run into someone who might stop her and sound the alarm. "It was a mistake."

"Why?" he asked in surprise.

"Because I'm afraid that boy who approached me will tell his cousin I'm in town, and Avery will mention the video. If that happens, if just one student hears the news, it'll spread through the school in no time."

"Some people will invariably find out, Emery," he allowed. "You have to expect that."

And weather it. That was the part he didn't say. "But *kids*?" she responded. "Young *boys*? You know how salacious that will be to them. I came here to escape what was happening, to feel safe—not to expose an entire boys' school to that video. If New Horizons starts buzzing with the news, I won't be able to stay. At that point, it'd be better to hole up inside my apartment in LA and order DoorDash until I run out of money."

He smiled as though he was tempted to laugh at the pathetic picture she painted, but he didn't. "Hopefully, Avery will surprise you and not share that information with her young cousin."

She cast him a sideways glance. "You really think it might go that way—with *my* luck?"

"Why not give her the benefit of the doubt until she proves me wrong?"

"Because I don't know her all that well—I never did. She wasn't part of my close circle of friends. She was just someone I knew from the equestrian club and a couple of projects we did together in history class. That was the only reason I was at her house when that boy saw me. Avery and I were working on a group project."

"I haven't heard anything about your sex video that leads me to believe it was anything other than two consenting adults who were in a monogamous relationship. It's not as if you were moonlighting as an expensive escort, or swinging with another couple, or you were discovered having sex in public. From what my mother has told me, you didn't even know you were being filmed."

"I didn't! That Ethan would do something like that is…it's disgusting."

"You just happened to be a well-known news anchor," he said. "And a beautiful one, at that, which caused the video to go viral. What you were doing on that video—it's nobody's business but your own, and there's got to be other people who see it the way I do."

She would've been pleased by the compliment he'd embedded in that response. Dallas wasn't the type to say things he didn't mean. And *beautiful* seemed a strong adjective for him, so it was a flattering one. But she was too buried in her own misery to take any pleasure in what he'd said. "Most of the world isn't that broad-minded," she grumbled. "You should read the scathing messages I got on social media until I closed all my accounts."

"People can be cruel, especially when they're hiding behind a computer. Forget those bastards."

Shrugging it off sounded good in theory. But she couldn't do it. She was too sensitive to the criticism, too embarrassed to be caught in such an indelicate situation and too hurt that Heidi and the rest of the management team at KQLA chose to keep Ethan and not her, even though she felt she was the better anchor.

Maybe it was that they could pay the woman they hired to replace her a little less than they'd been paying her, since her replacement would be starting at the bottom of the pay scale.

Emery's blood boiled when she thought that the station itself would benefit from what Ethan had done to her. "He wrote me."

"Who?"

"Ethan."

"What?"

"He did," she said as they were coming up to the house. "He texted me last night."

Dallas stopped walking. "What'd he say?"

She got her phone out to show him. "Can you believe it?"

He shook his head as he read Ethan's text. "No, I don't believe it. What a prick! What're you going to say to him?"

"I'm dying to let him have it, but maybe there's a smarter way to handle this."

"I don't know how you've held back," he admitted as he started walking again.

She hurried to keep up with him. "It hasn't been easy, but if I can set my emotions aside and… I don't know…draw him in somehow, maybe I can turn the tables."

"How?"

"That's what I wanted to ask you. If he'll admit that he posted that video and that he did it because he was angry with me, I can prove it was all about revenge. And if I can prove it was all about revenge, I might not be able to get my job back, but at least the station will have to compensate me for the loss. Then maybe I'll have the means to hang on long enough to put my topsy-turvy world back together again."

"Would he trust you?"

"I think so. Based on this message." She lifted her phone again, which she hadn't yet slipped back into her purse. "I get the impression he regrets going so far and is testing the water to see if maybe it's not too late to get me back."

"After what he's done? That dude's got some nerve."

"He has such a high opinion of himself that he can't imagine being rejected. That's why he flipped out when I broke up with him. Because he's handsome and popular from being on TV, he gets a lot of attention. He acted as though I should feel grateful to be the woman he'd chosen."

A muscle moved in Dallas's cheek. "Like I said, what a prick."

"I can see him for what he is now that it's too late. I wish I'd seen it sooner. But this text suggests I might be able to use his conceit against him—to at least walk away from the train wreck of my professional career with some kind of settlement."

Dallas sighed as they reached the house. "It's so hard not to drive to LA and kick his ass."

"I admit, part of me would love to see you do that. But I'd rather outsmart him. Then *you* won't get in trouble."

He held the door while she walked in but didn't follow. "Then tell him you miss him, too."

She turned to face him and took over holding the door. "That's it? I was thinking about telling him that my life hasn't been the same without him and seeing if maybe we could meet up."

"No. That's too fast. Make him work for it, or he might suspect something's up. Besides, I *hate* the idea of you meeting him in person."

"He's never been *physically* abusive—"

"I don't trust anyone who's done what he's done and neither should you."

She tucked some loose strands of hair behind her ears. "True. I was just thinking I might be able to video *him,* for a change.

Be able to show the judge, or whoever decides my case, what a jerk he really is."

"You can record the conversation when he calls—while maintaining a safe distance."

She blinked in surprise. "How do you know he'll call?"

He winked at her. "Because he's thrown out a hook, and you're going to make him think you're biting on it. Of course he'll try to reel you in."

CHAPTER SEVEN

Every once in a while Dallas thought he saw Jenny. He knew it couldn't be her. His sister, older by seven years, was gone. As much as he wished otherwise, there could be no doubt of that. He was the one who'd crawled to her after their father, dripping blood from when he'd attempted to shoot himself, dropped the gun and ran from the house. Dallas had known she was dead well before the police and paramedics arrived. He'd never forget her pretty eyes staring sightlessly at the ceiling.

That image haunted him.

And yet, in a cruel trick of his imagination, there were moments when Dallas could swear he caught glimpses of her. Other times, he thought he could hear her whispering in his ear, usually when he was just waking up.

Run, Dallas! Hide! And don't come out until I call you!

It was as if his mind reverted to when she was alive, and he had to accept the fact, again and again, that her life had been brutally and needlessly cut short by their own father. If he had to name the most heartbreaking thing he'd ever had to endure, it would be that. He missed his mother, Dora, but what he felt for her was complicated. Love and longing, certainly, but plenty of anger, resentment and a sense of betrayal, too—for not getting away, for not protecting them as a mother should.

That wasn't the case with Jenny, however. She'd been strong where their mother was weak, had always been there for him when he was frightened or hurt. And in the end, she'd paid the ultimate price.

He'd give anything to be able to go back and make that day unfold differently.

"Hello? Dallas? Are you listening? I'm talking here."

Dallas jerked his gaze away from the blonde girl with the long hair and the pink ski coat, the sight of which was what had taken him back twenty-three years, and once again focused on Eli as they crossed the campus. He'd just spent the afternoon substituting for PE on the boys' side of campus and now his brother was hitting him up to take over after-school practice for the girls' basketball team. "What?"

"I said you've never played much basketball. Do you feel comfortable coaching?"

It wasn't easy to shake off the nostalgia triggered by the sight of that girl, who, from the back, looked so much like Jenny, and who would've been about the same age as Dallas remembered her. "No."

Eli's eyes widened. "What?"

The girl went into a classroom and disappeared from view, making it easier for him to focus. "I'm going to invite them over to climb the wall. The boys who are there right now would love that."

With a startled laugh, Eli caught his elbow and pulled him to a stop. "When were you going to tell *me* about your plans?"

"I don't know. It just occurred to me that I should stick to what I do best," he admitted. "And I promised some of the kids who were having fun with the wall at lunch that I'd be around to help them after school."

"I'll tape up a notice that you'll be there from four to five, because you need to work with these girls on basketball for that long. They have a game tomorrow," Eli pointed out.

That changed things. Eli was right; Dallas couldn't let them go into a game unprepared. "Oh. Hmm. Okay." He wiped a bead of sweat running down the side of his face. It was cool and overcast and smelled of rain, but whenever he remembered his sister, he grew hot and clammy. "I guess I can attempt to teach them *something* about basketball." He grimaced as he tried to decide what that might be. "There's a YouTube video for everything, right?"

"The girls are only thirteen. Help them focus on improving their defense by boxing out. That could easily take up the whole practice."

Dallas glanced toward Aiyana's house, a two-story, sprawling farmhouse, sitting way off at the edge of campus. With all the buildings and trees in between, he could see only the chimney and part of the roof. But he wanted to return there, to learn if Emery had messaged Ethan, and if Ethan had indeed tried to call her, as he'd predicted. "Why can't *you* handle this practice?" he asked as they started walking again.

"Because I have a staff meeting in ten minutes."

"Right. You told me that. But you didn't say why you couldn't reschedule it."

"I need to make sure we have enough donations to be able to provide Christmas for those who would otherwise be overlooked or forgotten, and I'm running out of time."

That was a good reason to have Dallas do the coaching, all right—one he couldn't complain about. "Then you'd better go. You don't need to walk over with me. I haven't been on this side of campus very often, but I can find the gym."

"It's okay. I'll at least introduce you before I abandon you."

Dallas remembered *his* first Christmas at New Horizons, before Aiyana had adopted him. He would've been one of those boys who didn't get a gift if she hadn't orchestrated it. "I'll donate a couple hundred bucks to the cause," he said.

"Are you sure?" Eli asked.

He shrugged. "Why not?"

Eli shot him a quizzical look. "Because this thing called *money* that you don't seem to care about? It can keep you fed and put a roof over your head."

"Who needs a roof when you can sleep under the stars?" he joked. Since it was just him, he didn't have high expenses. And now that he had a sponsor, he had more money than ever before, anyway.

Eli rolled his eyes. "Not everyone can live as simply as you do."

Before he could respond, Dallas noticed a woman marching purposefully toward them. He assumed she was a teacher. Dressed in a no-nonsense skirt and jacket with low heels, she clutched a stack of books to her chest.

"Oh jeez," Eli murmured.

"What is it?" Dallas asked.

"Mrs. Seamus. She can be a pain in the ass."

Dallas was eager to hear why Eli thought so—he seemed to like most of the other teachers on campus—but this one was drawing too close for them to continue talking without being overheard.

"Mr. Turner?" she said as soon as she reached them.

They both could've answered to that name, but Dallas knew she wasn't talking to him.

"Is something wrong, Mrs. Seamus?" Eli asked.

"I hear we had that female anchor from LA on campus today," she replied.

"Emery Bliss?" Eli filled in.

"Yes."

"Not in any official capacity," he assured her.

She looked taken aback by his response. "She was in the cafeteria, wasn't she?"

"She was."

"My question is *why*? I don't think she has any business being here, do you?"

Dallas felt his spine stiffen. "Why do you say that?"

Although he was the one who'd spoken, she continued to direct her complaint to Elijah. "An hour ago, I caught two girls in my class trying to look up—" Her voice turned squeaky, and she cleared her throat. "*Well*, they were trying to find a video that was recently posted of Ms. Bliss online." One eyebrow arched above her thick-framed glasses. "I assume you're aware of the one I mean."

Eli sighed before responding. "Yes, but...how'd they find out about that?"

"It's been on the news, Mr. Turner."

"I can't imagine many of our students watch the news, Mrs. Seamus," he said, coming right back at her.

"They may not *watch* it, but some have smartphones and a few others have laptops. Those who don't can access the internet at the computer lab. And even if that weren't true, most have parents, brothers, sisters, cousins and friends who talk. In other words, they get the same information as the rest of us. When I walked over to see what all the fuss was about, Chanel Rogers clicked to what she was supposed to be doing, but I pulled her aside after class and she told me Jimmy Graham, also one of our students, was excited to have seen Ms. Bliss in the cafeteria today. So he texted a friend who lives in LA to say that she was on campus. And his friend told him—"

Eli lifted a hand to stop her. "I can guess what his friend must've told him."

"Right, and then he told Chanel and who knows how many of our other students. Word will have traveled through the whole school by tomorrow. Can you imagine the memes that are probably already circulating? This will distract even our best students," she predicted disapprovingly.

"I know that isn't optimal, but—"

"Optimal!" she broke in. "May I remind you that Chanel is only thirteen—and Jimmy is fourteen?"

"I know the ages of our students," Eli said. "But...what is it you're suggesting we do?"

"I'm suggesting Ms. Bliss return to her own home as soon as possible, of course."

"What if she needs a safe haven?" he asked. "What if she was wronged and is struggling herself?"

"Then I feel sorry for her, but she's not our responsibility. We have to do what is best for our students. Seeing they get what they need—and protecting them from anything that could be harmful—is a job I take very seriously."

"We *all* take our jobs seriously," Eli said, obviously offended, but she didn't allow him to interrupt.

"The young people who come here have been through a lot. Helping them find peace and happiness and gain control over their lives and behavior is no small challenge. Why make it any harder than it has to be?"

Instead of answering what was essentially a rhetorical question, Eli defused the situation by checking his watch. "We have to go or we'll be late," he said. "But I understand your concerns, and I'll take them to my mother."

She didn't like being put off. "I'm not being petty," she insisted. "You know how impressionable our students are."

Dallas wanted to tell Mrs. Seamus to stay out of it; Emery had enough problems right now. And it was nearly Christmas. Why couldn't she get a small reprieve so she could heal and try to enjoy the holidays? But as soon as he opened his mouth, Eli sent him a sharp look that caused him to reconsider. He didn't work for the school; he needed to let his brother do his job.

He heard Eli tell Mrs. Seamus he'd get back to her and allowed himself to be steered away. "Last I checked, Mom had the right to decide what was best for this school," he grumbled when the teacher was out of earshot.

"That woman drives me nuts," Eli confided.

"She comes off pretty militant," Dallas said.

"She is."

"So why did Mom hire her?"

"Because, for all her inflexibility and focus on the letter of the law, Mrs. Seamus cares about her students. She works hard, is completely devoted to them."

"But she's crossing a line here. Mom should be able to open her home to whomever she wants."

He expected Eli to agree, so he was surprised when Eli said nothing.

"You don't think so?" Dallas challenged.

Although they'd reached the girls' gymnasium, and basketball practice was supposed to start any minute, Eli paused before opening the door. "If Mom didn't live on a school campus, especially a school campus like this one, I'd say yes—for sure. But Mrs. Seamus has a point. Taking care of our students is our number one goal."

"Having Emery here isn't hurting anyone!"

"Dallas, I like Emery, too. And I'm eager to help her. But I don't know that I can completely buy into the statement that having her here won't hurt anyone. What's going on with her really *isn't* something we want our students to be aware of or focus on. They're too young for that video."

"Like you told Mrs. Seamus, it's already out there, in the media."

"But like *she* said, seeing her around campus draws their attention to a scandal they probably wouldn't have paid any attention to if not for that."

Dallas scowled. "They're more streetwise than the students who go to almost any other school."

"Which is part of the problem, right? They would be more drawn to stuff that's too old for them than other students of the same age."

"So what are you saying?" Dallas asked.

Eli appeared to be torn. "Probably nothing. Mom's already invited her. It's not as if she'd ever ask her to leave. But it could get uncomfortable for a bit. Mrs. Seamus won't be the only one to criticize this move, and I don't want anyone saying anything about Mom that might upset her before the wedding."

"They'd better not," Dallas said.

"And yet they will, and they will feel as though they have the right. All it will take is for Mrs. Seamus to start complaining to the other teachers, and those who agree with her will rally behind her and make their opinions known."

"After all the good Mom has done?"

"*Everyone* has their detractors, Dallas," he said, and swung the door wide.

The house smelled of garlic, onion and cilantro when Dallas walked in after helping with the climbing wall, as promised, once he finished basketball practice. Someone had been cooking. He hoped whoever it was had made enough for everyone. The spaghetti he'd eaten at lunch was now a distant memory.

"Hello?" he said as he ducked his head into the kitchen.

Emery was at the stove. "Hi."

Judging by her smile, she was in a stronger, more confident mood. She was bouncing back, he thought, and cringed inside as he remembered his conversation with Eli. What her fellow anchor had done wasn't going to fade away fast. "Where is everyone?"

"No one else is home yet," she said. "But I hope they get here soon. I made some chicken enchiladas. They'll be out of the oven in ten minutes."

"Smells amazing."

"There's homemade salsa." She indicated a bowl on the table. "Come taste it."

He helped himself to the chips she'd put out, too. The salsa contained just the right amount of cilantro and hot pepper, and she'd made a bowl of guacamole that was topped with crumbly, salty cotija cheese—a particular favorite of his. "Delicious. But where did you get the groceries? I can't imagine we had ingredients like cotija and cilantro in the fridge."

"No." She lifted her chin proudly. "I braved going to the store."

She obviously considered it an accomplishment, and it was. She was afraid to show her face in public, which was why he'd gone to the trouble of walking her home after they ate in the cafeteria earlier. "And? How'd it go?"

"There were a few people who stared at me, but I ignored them, grabbed what I needed and got out of there."

"Good job. Don't let anyone or anything hold you back." He swallowed the food in his mouth. "It was nice of you to make dinner, by the way. I'm starving."

"I wanted to make myself useful. I don't want to be a burden."

"Don't worry about that. We have no expectations. Everyone hits a rough patch now and then." He scooped up another bite of salsa. "Did you message Ethan?"

"I did."

"And?"

"I said what you told me to."

"How'd he respond?"

She checked her phone, which was sitting on the counter while she cooked. "He hasn't, yet."

"Hmm."

"It's been five hours." She was stirring something in a saucepan on the front burner but turned to face him. "Why do you think he hasn't messaged me back?"

"I have no clue. But don't give in to the temptation to text him again. Not yet. Let's wait and see what he does."

"What if he just lets it go?"

"Then we'll come up with a different strategy to draw him out, but we shouldn't give up on this one too soon. He might've had a busy day."

"He's probably out spending all the money he's making because, unlike me, he still has a job," she grumbled sarcastically. "If he doesn't go to the gym after work, he has his teeth bleached, gets Botox injections or goes to the tanning salon—and that's if he's already had a facial, a manicure and a pedicure."

Dallas chuckled as his mother came into the house.

"Smells like heaven in here," she said. Aiyana looked tired but she had good color in her face. Dallas knew she worked too hard, but there was no getting her to slow down, so he'd stopped trying. He hoped, once she married Cal, that Cal would be able to persuade her to take it a little easier. "Emery made dinner," he told her. "Mexican food. And what I've tasted so far is incredible."

"That's wonderful. I'm hungry."

"Me, too. Where're Liam and Bentley?" he asked. "The food's almost ready."

"Liam's with a friend, so he'll miss dinner. Bentley went over to Eli's to play with the kids. I'm sure he assumed it would take me an hour or so to get a meal together. This will be a pleasant surprise. I'll text him to let him know we don't have to wait tonight—thanks to Emery."

A timer went off, and Emery donned a pair of oven mitts so she could pull out a pan of enchiladas that were bubbling in a cheesy sauce with green chilies.

"Look at that," Dallas said.

"I'm going to run upstairs and change," Aiyana said. "I'll be right back."

Dallas pulled some plates from the cupboard. "I'll set the table."

After starting toward the stairs, Aiyana doubled back. "By the way, thanks for helping out this afternoon. I don't know if Eli told you, but Susan is sick again. Otherwise, I could've had Tobias Richardson step in. He's usually the one who substitutes on the afterschool stuff, if we need him, but today he had to go over to the cookie store."

"Jada couldn't do it? Susan's her mother."

"No. With the baby and her social media business, Jada can no longer take that on, too," she said. "Maya goes over when she can, of course. She loves to help her grandmother. But a fourteen-year-old can't manage the store all by herself. And you know that Maddox is too busy here."

"Why doesn't Susan hire someone?"

"It's hard to hire an employee for such a short time. Business will die down again in just a few weeks."

"True," he allowed, and Aiyana went upstairs.

"Who's Tobias?" Emery asked when she was gone.

"He helps with the grounds and maintenance here at New Horizons—and, apparently, the coaching, if necessary."

"How is he related to Susan?"

"He's not, technically. He's Maddox's brother—Maddox is the principal of the girls' side of New Horizons—so there is that connection, I guess. She owns Sugar Mama, a cookie shop in town."

"I'm familiar with it."

"Sounds like, with Christmas coming up, she's extra busy. So it's a bad time for her to be sick."

Emery poured the refried bean mixture she'd been making into a bowl and carried it to the table. "I hate to ask, but...she doesn't have cancer or anything serious, does she?"

"Not cancer, no. Lupus. And she lost her husband a couple of years ago, if I remember right, so she's on her own with the store. She has a son who helps out when he can, too, but Atticus has his own job and his own life, and I'm sure he can't be there whenever she needs him. He's in a wheelchair besides, so it's hard for him to reach into the cooler to dish up the ice cream for the cookie sandwiches and other stuff she sells."

Aiyana's voice came down to them from upstairs. "Emery, would you mind if I asked Cal over to dinner?"

"Of course not! I would love to see him."

"Great."

As Emery dished up the Spanish rice she had waiting on a back burner, she lowered her voice. "I expected Aiyana and Cal to get married years ago. Why do you think they've waited so long?"

"That's a mystery to me, too." Dallas was so loyal to Aiyana that he almost left it at that, but he thought it might be encouraging for Emery to know the truth. "She's hinted that, like me and the other boys she's tried to help, she has a past and that past informs the present," he added.

"Are you saying something happened in her childhood to make her reluctant to marry?"

"That's my guess. But she won't open up about it, so I don't really know."

"Sorry. I didn't mean to be too nosy. My curiosity got the best of me, I guess."

"No worries. I'm curious about it, too. She seems to have everything figured out, so it's hard to imagine that she ever lost her way. But as she often says, anyone can make a tragic mistake."

"That's true." Emery seemed thoughtful as she brought the rice and beans to the table. "How often do you think Susan needs help?"

"I couldn't tell you." He looked closer at her. "Why? You're not considering offering to step in, are you?"

She lifted her hands palms up. "I'm available, right? I doubt I can get another job so close to Christmas, and I wouldn't want

to get one here, anyway, since I don't plan on staying long-term.
But I could help this Susan get through the Christmas rush."

"That's really nice of you," he said. "But…it would mean facing the public on a daily basis."

She suddenly seemed less certain. "I realize that. But someone told me I can't let anyone or anything hold me back." She offered him a half smile. "I have to get back out there at some point. And I would hate hiding here while someone is too sick to run their business, especially so close to the holidays."

Lying low for a little longer would probably be more advisable. After running into the likes of Mrs. Seamus, Dallas understood that. But it was nice of Emery to care. "Maybe she'll get back on her feet."

"If she doesn't, and she's open to having me step in, at least I'll be working in my hometown—a small community and one that's slightly removed from LA. That wouldn't be a bad place to start."

"True…"

"And if she can afford to pay me, even if it's only minimum wage, a paycheck would help shore up my dwindling savings. My mother's going through a hard time, so it would be a boon to her, too."

For all of his encouragement, Dallas wasn't overly anxious to see Emery put herself out there when he wouldn't be there to act as a buffer. "Well, take some time to think about it. Make sure it's something you really want to do."

"Okay," she said, but he knew she was going to do it. She wanted to help Susan—and he could tell she needed the money.

CHAPTER EIGHT

Ethan's answer came that night. Emery couldn't help but wonder if he'd purposely waited until it was late in hopes of getting her to come over and, possibly, stay the night. But if that was his intention, if he imagined she'd ever sleep with him again, he was even more delusional than she'd thought.

As soon as the text pinged her phone, she hurried downstairs to tell Dallas. They'd finished a movie only a few minutes ago, which they'd watched together after everyone else went to bed. But she was fairly certain he was still awake and would want to hear the news. After all, he'd asked her a couple of different times if she'd heard anything.

"Dallas?" She knocked softly on his door.

When he opened it, he wasn't wearing a shirt. It was no big deal. He was in his own bedroom, getting ready for bed. But the fact that he was only half-dressed gave her enough of a shock that she almost wished she hadn't come down. He was so firmly in the friend category that the last thing she wanted was to find him sexually desirable, especially after all she'd been through. She didn't think she'd be capable of trusting a man for years to come. She also didn't want things to get awkward between

them, and knew it would be easier not to think about sex if
Dallas wasn't so attractive.

She told herself not to let her mind drift in that direction,
but it was difficult to stop it. Climbing had made his shoulders,
arms and torso into a work of art. At a minimum, she had to
appreciate the sheer beauty of his body.

"What's up?" he asked.

She blinked several times before remembering why she'd
come down. "Um, Ethan."

He stepped aside to let her in. "You've heard from him?"

"Yeah." As she slipped past him, she could smell the scent she
already associated with him. Although it was subtle to begin
with, something she could detect only when she got close
enough to him, it was slightly stronger in his room, with both
him and his belongings in such a confined space. It wasn't cologne she noticed; nothing that contrived. She couldn't name it,
but it was earthy and appealing—definitely all male.

The room suddenly felt too small for the both of them, and the
fact that a bed took up most of the space made her self-conscious.

He shut the door—probably to give them some privacy, so
they wouldn't wake the others or just out of habit—but it made
the room shrink even smaller. "Did he call you?"

"No. He's still testing the waters. He sent another text."

"What a coward," he said in disgust. "What'd the message
say?"

There was a chair at the desk in the corner, but there were
clothes draped over the back of it. She didn't feel comfortable
sitting there or on the bed, so she stood in the middle of the
room, gripping her phone tighter than was necessary. "He said
that he regrets what happened between us and hopes I'll be able
to forgive him one day."

"That's sort of an admission of guilt," he said, as though
weighing it in his mind. "Isn't that what you wanted?"

"It's not specific enough. If I took it to Heidi, she'd just say he could be referring to the breakup."

He rubbed the beard growth on his chin. "Is there any chance he could be sincerely sorry?"

This question caught her off guard. She'd been so busy hating Ethan she hadn't even considered the possibility that he could be experiencing genuine regret. "I guess there's a chance," she allowed, but she didn't find it very likely. Anyone who could do what he did couldn't have a diligent conscience to begin with.

"If you decided he was, could you ever forgive him?" Dallas asked.

"No. What he did was too personal. It cut me so deeply I don't know if I'll ever get over it."

When he sat on the bed, she noticed his bare feet. He was completely relaxed, totally casual. They were friends, so he had no reason not to be.

She needed to calm down, but her heart was pounding for no reason.

"He's a dumbass if he thinks a woman ever could get over that," he said. "To abuse your trust in that way..." He shook his head. "Every woman he dates from now on will have to wonder if there's a hidden camera somewhere."

"I hope his future girlfriends protect themselves better than I did." She sat on the corner of the bed so she wouldn't look as uncomfortable as she felt. They'd both been on the couch earlier, hadn't they? Why was this any different? "What do you think I should say back?"

"Tell him you appreciate the apology."

"That's it?"

"Less is more," he explained. "You want *him* to be the one who's talking."

"True." Once she typed the words and sent the message, she could tell Ethan was writing back. "He's on right now," she told Dallas.

The smooth, tanned skin of Dallas's arm touched hers as he scooted over to see for himself.

She read:

Is there any chance we can get together and talk? I feel like things got so out of control there in the end.

She knew Dallas had read it, too, when he said, "It's working."

Emery wrote:

I saw you on TV. You got your job back, huh?

Dallas nodded. "Yeah, lead him there. That should be good."

I went in and pled my case to Heidi. You could do the same. I'll put in a good word for you.

"After getting me fired he's trying to play the hero?" she muttered. *"Unbelievable."*

"Bastard," Dallas concurred.

I doubt it will help. There has to be a scapegoat, right? Some casualty to appease viewers who were angered by that video. So if the station has already rehired you, they can't rehire me.

Her phone started to buzz while they were waiting for Ethan's response. "He's calling!" she announced, and came to her feet.

Dallas jumped off the bed, too. "Wait. Don't answer it yet."

"I don't know if I dare answer it at all," she said. "What if I can't fake being nice?"

"You have to. He'll find out about the suit soon. This could be your only chance." Dallas grabbed his phone from where it was charging on the nightstand. "Remember, just let him do most of the talking. I'll record the whole thing."

"No, I got it. I downloaded an app that will allow me to record an incoming call—but I have to answer it first." After taking a deep breath, she hit Talk. "Hello?"

"It's me."

"I know," she said, and put him on speaker while searching for the IntCall app she'd installed, hoping for this opportunity.

"Are you okay?" Ethan asked when she didn't speak right away.

His tone was conciliatory, beseeching. She decided he was a much better actor than she was, because he couldn't really care about her. "Barely," she admitted. She figured there was no reason to pretend when it came to that. He had to know what a devastating blow he'd dealt her.

"I can't believe everything that's happened," he said as though *he'd* somehow been a victim, too.

She had the recording going. Giving Dallas a little nod to let him know, she breathed a sigh of relief. "It's been crazy," she said into the phone, fighting to get those three words—such a gross understatement—through a throat that was already threatening to close off with anger and frustration.

She hoped she wasn't about to burst into tears; it suddenly felt like it.

"We should never have let it come to this," he said.

Let it come to this? *We?* He'd caused it! Or was he saying— *you should never have left me. Let this be a lesson to you.* "I never saw it coming," she admitted.

"That Tommy would load that video... It's unconscionable. I still can't believe it."

Her mouth dropped open and her gaze jerked to Dallas. There was no way Tommy had filmed them and put that video on the internet. She liked Tommy and knew Tommy liked her. It was Ethan who'd done it. But he was determined to pass the blame. "Why would *Tommy* do it?" she asked.

"I tried to tell you before. He was pissed at me. You know I asked him to move out, right?"

Only because he was anxious for her to move in. But once they'd broken up, he didn't need Tommy to move out. At that point, the problem had been solved. So even if Tommy were the type to do something vengeful, he wouldn't do it once he knew he could stay, would he?

Before she could respond, Ethan said, "I think he has a thing for me, if you want the truth."

"A *thing* for you?" She'd thought Ethan couldn't surprise her any more than he had, but this proved her wrong. She'd never seen any sign of interest from Tommy and she'd never heard Ethan make such an assertion before.

"He's gay, you know. I think he was jealous of you the whole time, and this was his way of getting you out of the picture."

But Tommy had a boyfriend. They seemed content with each other. And she'd already stepped out of the picture by the time that video was loaded.

Ethan's story wasn't making sense, but he was doing his best to sell it.

Mentally harnessing her emotions, she fought to keep her voice steady. "Have you talked to him?"

"I have. I told him I could never trust him again and that he had to get the hell out of my apartment. I kept worrying that the little bastard was filming me in the shower or getting dressed or whatever. It's creepy."

Poor Tommy. Beyond a cursory hello or goodbye, she didn't know him that well, had only spoken to him a handful of times. But her impression of him was so different from the picture Ethan was painting. She wished she had Tommy's phone number. He might be able to tell her something that would disprove Ethan's version of events. "And he said…"

"He claims he didn't do it—swears on his life. But who else could it be?"

You! It was you! Emery wanted to scream into the phone, but she felt Dallas touch her arm—a reminder not to lose her composure.

"Do you have his number?" she said. "I'd really like to give him a piece of my mind."

"No, I deleted his contact information from my phone as soon as he moved out. I don't ever want to talk to him again."

That was convenient. The expression on Dallas's face suggested he was thinking the same thing. "That anyone could do that... Well, you're right," she said. "It's unconscionable, and I hope whoever recorded and posted that video burns in hell."

"So where are you?" he asked.

"What do you mean?"

"I've been by your place a hundred times. Your car is never there."

She heard Dallas swear under his breath and pulled the phone away so that Ethan wouldn't realize she was with someone. "I'm visiting a friend," she said. "I couldn't stay in LA, not with everyone watching that video."

"Then where are you?"

"Silver Springs."

"Even though your parents are in Boston these days?"

"I have friends here."

"Who?"

"No one you'd know."

"Are you looking for another job?"

"Right before Christmas? No."

"When will you be coming back to LA?"

"At this point, I can't say."

"I hope it's soon. I'd really like to see you. I'll even come there, if you'll give me an address."

She shifted her hold on the phone. "Maybe if you admitted that you were the one who recorded us and then put that video up on the internet, we could make up, Ethan, put this all behind us. But the fact that you're trying to blame it on Tommy, when Tommy would have no motivation to do it, makes me realize that you're a liar on top of everything else."

"I'm not lying!" he cried.

"Tell me the truth, and maybe I'll be able to forgive you." Dallas had suggested she let Ethan do the talking, but Ethan wasn't saying anything that would help her. He was using this call to try to rewrite history. And soon it would be too late to press him; he'd know she wasn't going to forgive him—she was going to sue him. "You did it, didn't you? You wanted to hurt me, so you posted that video."

She was hoping he'd say something like, "You hurt me first!" But he didn't. He fell silent.

"Ethan?"

"What?" His voice was now morose.

"Why did you make that video? Had you recorded us before?"

"You're such a bitch," he snapped, instantly vicious, and hung up.

Emery threw her phone on the bed and covered her face. "Damn it!"

Dallas tugged her hands away. "Don't let him mess you up again. You did the best you could," he said, and pulled her into his arms.

Contrary to what it probably seemed to Dallas, she wasn't all that emotional. Not normally. But her helplessness in this situation created so much frustration it surfaced in the way of tears. "I hate him," she whispered, trying to choke them back.

"He's obsessed with you. You heard him, right? He's driven past your house a hundred times. Consider yourself lucky to be rid of him, and that it only took a leaked sex video."

"Only?" She could feel the solidness of Dallas's body, the strength in his shoulders, and as much as she didn't want to admit it, she felt better now that she was in his arms.

"He could've done a lot worse." He smoothed the hair back

from her face, like one might do with a child. "He's so removed from reality that I wouldn't put it past him to turn into some kind of stalker. Maybe you got out when the getting was good."

She'd never thought of it that way. "You think he might be dangerous?"

"I'd hate to accuse him of that, because I don't really know. But he's definitely missing a sensitivity gene."

"He only cares about himself." She tilted her head back to be able to see Dallas's face. "Wading through my drama can't be any fun for you. I'm sorry that I'm in your mother's house and that my situation is such a downer right now. I'm not normally like this."

"I don't mind."

The moment she started to notice how long his eyelashes were, she told herself to move away from him. He smelled and felt too good for her to be able to think clearly.

But she didn't withdraw. Her feet seemed to be stuck to the floor, and her heart was pounding again—only this time it wasn't in anger. She was beginning to feel something much more pleasant, and the unexpected reprieve made her reluctant to change anything.

Suddenly curious to know what it would be like to kiss a man like Dallas, she studied his lips. They were nice lips; well-shaped and soft-looking. He was so different from Ethan or anyone else she'd dated—much more rugged but also… What? She couldn't decide. It felt strange to dub him as guarded when he'd been so nice. But he was holding back, reserving a part of himself that he didn't allow others to see or know.

What was he like when he wasn't holding back?

The change she felt in his body let her know he'd felt the change in hers, and that broke the spell. They both stepped back at the same time, and she quickly wiped the tears that were left over from that call with Ethan. "I'd…uh…better go to bed. I'll try to figure out a way to reach Tommy in the morning. He might be able to tell me something that will help."

"Is he on social media?" he asked.

"I don't know. I've never looked for him. Until I decided to move forward with the suit, I didn't have any reason to contact him. I knew Ethan was full of shit coming up with that bogus story. But now... I may have to prove it."

"Instagram or Facebook might be an easy way to reach him."

"I'll check. Thank you for...for coaching me through this," she said. "I appreciate your friendship."

His mouth quirked as though he knew she was labeling their relationship as a way to get them back on stable ground. "I appreciate your friendship, too," he said. "And don't worry, I know I'm not the kind of guy you need," he added with a wink.

Emery was breathless by the time she reached her room. She'd only scaled two flights of stairs, but she felt as though she'd run a mile.

What had just happened? There'd been that business with Ethan, which was upsetting. Then Dallas had tried to comfort her, and it had worked far better than either of them had expected. Not only had the anger and frustration, her constant companions of late, drifted away, she'd felt a flicker of *desire*.

She almost couldn't believe it. Here she was in the depths of despair and yet she'd wanted to kiss *Dallas*? Right on the heels of having Ethan shout profanities at her and hang up?

Humans really were resilient, she thought as she dropped onto the bed. She'd figured her sex drive was gone for good, or at least for a while. That video was enough to make her want to remain celibate for the rest of her life. But Dallas had just proved that celibacy probably wouldn't become her reality—and that meant she had to be careful or she could get herself into trouble again. She knew Dallas would never do anything like what Ethan had done, but her heart was too fragile right now. She had to protect it.

Besides, Dallas's friendship was what was pulling her through this mess. She couldn't risk losing it.

Trying to forget what was, she told herself, a minor blip and would amount to nothing if only she could forget about it, she opened her laptop and set up a new account on Instagram. She wanted to see if she could find Tommy.

He wasn't listed by name, but sometimes people on Insta used only their handle. She tried various possibilities with no luck and decided to check Facebook. She couldn't imagine Tommy used Facebook very often. Not many of her friends did. But it was possible he'd set up an old account—or she might be able to find someone associated with him who could get him a message.

Her phone dinged with a text. She cringed for fear it would be from Ethan—another attack. She hadn't blocked him, even though she probably should, just in case he texted something she could use against him.

But it wasn't Ethan; it was Dallas. Any luck?

Apparently, he wasn't asleep yet, either. She thought about that brief moment in his room but quickly shoved it into the back of her mind. He was obviously letting it go, so she didn't need to worry about it, either.

Not on Insta. Trying Facebook now.

If he's not there, do you remember his boyfriend's name? Maybe you could find him.

It was a good suggestion. She *did* remember Tommy's boyfriend's name, because it was the only time she'd ever met a Thiago.

Sure enough, she found someone she thought might be him and followed the account so that she could send him a message:

If you know Tommy, please tell him that Emery Bliss, Ethan Grimes's ex-girlfriend, needs to talk to him. Ethan is trying to claim Tommy's responsible for something I know he's not, and I could really use his help. Tell him I'm sorry to have to ask.

She braved leaving her number, even though she wasn't one hundred percent certain she had the right guy. At least she had a chance.

Closing her laptop, she set it aside. She didn't expect to hear back from Thiago tonight. It was too late. She told Dallas:

I found someone who might be Tommy's boyfriend and left him a message. Thanks for suggesting I look for him.

That's what friends are for.

He added a wink emoji that let her know his response meant more than the cliché alone. He was referring to that encounter in his bedroom, was letting her know he understood the boundaries.

She sent a laughing emoji back to him, brushed her teeth and changed into the T-shirt she'd be wearing to bed. What happened with Dallas was nothing, she told herself; she didn't need to worry.

But as she fell asleep she wasn't thinking about the catastrophic events that had brought her to Silver Springs.

For a change, she was thinking about a pair of pretty blue eyes with long golden eyelashes.

CHAPTER NINE

Thursday, December 10

Before she left for work, Aiyana had come down to Dallas's room to ask him to put up the artificial Christmas tree. She said they'd decorate it tonight if he could just bring it in from the garage. It was later than she usually put it up, but with her wedding coming up so soon, she was running behind.

He expected it to be an easy request but frowned when he found the box. It was huge! He didn't know how she thought just one man could carry it in alone. "I know you think I'm strong, but this is ridiculous," he muttered as he pulled out his phone to call Eli or Gavin to ask if they could stop by the house and give him a hand.

Before he dialed, however, he thought of Emery. He didn't need a lot of help. If he had his guess, the box was more awkward than it was heavy. The two of them could probably manage it—if she was around.

He went back into the house and yelled up the stairs. "Emery?"

When he received no answer, he walked up to find her door closed and some music playing.

He knocked loudly so she'd be able to hear him above the alternative rock band she was listening to, and she opened the door wearing a white blouse with a wraparound tie and a slim-fitting black skirt. She'd also put on makeup. "Wow. You look great," he said. "You going somewhere?"

"Last night I told your mom I'd be willing to help Susan with the cookie store until after New Year's, when I need to get on with my life, and she set up an interview."

He wondered if Susan had heard about the disgraced news anchor from LA and if it was going to be difficult for Emery to face her. Right now, Emery seemed intent on getting ready, so it was tough to tell if she was nervous. "What time do you have to be there?"

She checked her phone. "In an hour. Why? What are you doing?"

"I was going to offer to make you breakfast in trade for a few minutes of your time."

"I'll take that deal. What do you need?"

"A little help bringing in my mother's Christmas tree." As he let his gaze slide all the way down to her high heels, he tried not to acknowledge, even though he definitely noticed, that she had a nice figure. "But you might not want to do it dressed like that. The box is dusty."

"I can kick off my shoes and throw on a robe," she suggested.

"Are you sure? I could ask one of my brothers to stop by instead..."

"No need. I'm here. And I'm stronger than I look." She flexed as she grinned at him. "At least I'm not crying today," she added as if she knew he'd be relieved about that.

He chuckled because he *was* relieved and jerked his head toward the stairs. "It's in the garage."

"Great. I'll be right there."

He went down ahead of her, and she put on a robe and came to join him.

He held the door going into the garage for her to come through. Then he pointed at the giant box that contained his mother's fourteen-foot artificial Christmas tree, which already had the lights on it. "It's that beast right there."

Her eyes went wide. "Wow. That's bigger than I expected."

"That's what I thought when I first saw it." He rested his hands on his hips. "You still game to give it a try?"

"Of course. Why not?"

She got on one end, he on the other, and they managed to lift it. From there, he did his best to bear most of the weight as she helped carry it inside. "You okay?" he asked as they struggled to squeeze it through the door.

"Fine. You?"

"I'm happy I'm not trying to do this on my own," he admitted.

They both blew out a sigh and dusted off their hands once they'd maneuvered the tree into the living room and put it by the window where it could be set up. "Thanks," he said. "Now... what would you like to eat?"

"How extensive are your cooking skills?" she teased.

"I live in my van half the year, so keep that in mind."

"Not a wide repertoire, huh?"

"I typically eat greens and beans. As long as I get enough protein and vitamins, I don't care too much about the taste. I'm definitely no chef."

"An omelet?" she queried.

"That I can do."

She went up to remove her robe while he returned to the kitchen.

"Any word from Tommy?" he asked when she was back and pouring a cup of coffee from the pot he'd put on as soon as he got up.

"Nothing yet," she said. "I checked as soon as I rolled out of bed. I'd really like to hear what he has to say. Maybe he was aware of Ethan's hidden camera. It's possible I'm not the first woman Ethan ever recorded. If Ethan made a joke about filming his sexual exploits, or Tommy saw him purchase the equipment or found the packing material in the trash, it could make a big difference in my case."

"It'd be awesome if he ran across the camera months ago."

"Wouldn't it?" She added a dash of cream to her coffee. "My attorney would be so excited. He called me this morning. He plans to file the paperwork tomorrow."

"So only one more day before Ethan and the station learn that you're coming after them?"

"Yup." She took a careful sip. "And I'm a little scared. I haven't blocked Ethan's number. Since I didn't get anything useful out of him last night, I'm hoping being served with a lawsuit will set him off, make him say something he wouldn't have said otherwise."

The ding of the microwave signaled that the bacon was done. As Dallas got it out, he could easily imagine how angry Ethan might get. "Are you sure you should even answer if he does call?"

"I have to. He won't say anything on voice mail. He knows I could play that for someone else, but he doesn't know I'm recording our conversations. I'll have a much better chance of having him go ballistic and screw up if I answer."

"True. Last night, I got the impression he's really torn. He wants you back, so he's tempted to play nice, but he's angry that you don't want him, which makes him act badly instead. I just... I hate to think of what he might say to you."

"That's exactly how it is. When we first broke up, he alternated between bringing me gifts, telling me he loved me and sending flowers to making me think he might explode. And as things progressed, and he realized I really wasn't coming back, he got nastier and nastier."

Finished cooking her omelet, Dallas brought it to the table. "How nasty did he get?"

"Called me every name in the book, said I'd never amount to anything without him, that I'd come crawling back on my knees, that I wasn't good in bed anyway—you name it." She carried her cup to the table and sat down. "He hurled every hurtful thing he could at me. Then, as if that wasn't bad enough, I came out from work one day to find a dog pile in the driver's seat of my car."

Dallas had already started to make his own omelet. "You've got to be kidding me."

"No."

"And you think it was him?"

"Had to be. I almost always lock my car, but I was running late that morning, the parking lot was fenced and we had a security guard at the door of the building, so I didn't bother digging out my key fob."

He hesitated while chopping more onion. "But the security guard didn't see anything?"

"No. That's another reason I think it had to be Ethan. The security guard would recognize Ethan's car, so I doubt he'd bother to watch him from the moment he parked to the moment he walked into the building. It would be easy for Ethan to leave that 'smelly bomb' for me as he passed my car."

Dallas dabbed the last of the bacon with a paper towel. "Does Ethan have a dog?"

"No. Which is why he claimed it couldn't be him. But when the dog pile thing happened, he was pretty angry. The day before, I refused to let him come over, and I saw this weird look in his eye. It was like he suddenly *hated* me. He was embarrassed that I would break up with him, didn't want anyone to think he couldn't have me or any other woman he wanted, but I'd had enough. By then I'd realized he's not a nice person." She finally took a bite of her omelet and chewed slowly before saying with complete conviction, "I know in my gut that it was him."

Dallas used a spatula to turn his own omelet. "How long after that dog shit incident did the video show up online?"

"It was the very next day. What he'd done hadn't hurt me enough. He was looking for something else."

"How did you find out that he'd posted the video?"

She swallowed what was in her mouth. "Oh God, it was horrible. I was in the middle of getting a pedicure, just hoping to relax for thirty minutes and forget about the messy breakup, how awkward it was going to be to see Ethan every morning and deliver the news without every viewer we had reading in our body language that we suddenly couldn't stand each other. I was also worried about how we were going to keep our little problem from coming to the attention of Heidi and others at the studio. And on top of that, my mother was falling apart because she'd just learned my father had moved in with another woman. So there I was, closing my eyes and thinking I had a much-needed chance to recoup, when the woman next to me started whispering loudly to her neighbor on the other side. They'd say something to each other, crane their necks to get a better look at me, then nod and whisper some more. Finally, I said, 'Excuse me. Is there something wrong?'"

He lifted his omelet out of the pan and onto a plate. "Did they tell you?"

She frowned as she stared at the bite she held on her fork, her mind obviously back in that nail salon. "The woman closest to me said, 'Aren't you Emery Bliss?'"

"You must've thought they recognized you from seeing you on TV," he said as he brought his plate to the table.

"I did. I was sort of flattered," she said, looking slightly embarrassed. "But then the other woman said, 'Is that really you in that steamy video online?' I told them that I wasn't in any steamy video, that I was a news anchor and they must've confused me with someone else. Then she and her friend started laughing. They left it at that, but kept shooting each other these side-eye looks as though the joke was on me. And it was. Right about then my phone started to blow up. I was getting calls and texts from almost everyone I knew—'Oh my God! What's going on? Have you seen it?'"

"That must've made you sick to your stomach."

"It did. I'll never forget what it felt like to click on that first link and see myself naked." She closed her eyes and shook her head. "I felt like throwing up. And so many people on Facebook and Instagram were calling me a slut or making fun of me. It felt as though everyone I knew—even those I didn't— were gathering around me to taunt and jeer and throw rocks."

Again, Dallas had to fight the urge to contact Ethan and take this fight into his own hands. "Did you call Ethan and ask what was going on?"

"I did. I called him immediately. My heart was pounding so hard I thought I'd pass out, and my mind was reeling as I tried to figure out who'd recorded us, and who would hate me so much that they would post that video online." She laughed without mirth. "It wasn't until I talked to him that I realized."

He shoveled a forkful of omelet into his mouth. "That it was him?"

She nodded. "He wasn't upset at all. He was smug, almost gleeful. So then I began to catch on. I realized *he* was the one who'd recorded it and put it out there—to punish me for breaking up with him."

"Did you accuse him?"

"I did. And he laughed. He's lied about laughing since, when I tried to tell Heidi about that call," she explained. "But that was exactly what he did."

"Too bad you didn't get it recorded."

"Now you know why I'm hoping he'll do something like that again."

"The guy deserves to have his ass kicked," Dallas ground out, once again feeling the desire to do just that.

"What he deserves and what he's getting seem to be two very different things. I can only hope this lawsuit will make the situation a bit more fair."

"When will you need to meet with your attorney?"

"I don't know. So far we've been taking care of everything via Skype."

He got up to pour himself some more coffee. "If you ever have to drive to LA, I'll go with you, if you want."

"I would love that. Thank you." She checked the time. "I'd better get a move on. I don't want to be late for this interview. It might be the only job I'm able to get," she added with a rueful laugh.

"Good luck with it."

She rinsed off her plate and put it in the dishwasher. "You don't have to go to town in the next ten minutes, do you?"

Although she kept her eyes on what she was doing instead of looking at him, he knew where she was going with this. "No. But I'll take you."

She smiled at him, obviously relieved. "Thank you. I have my car, but... I don't know. It's easier to be with someone who's supportive—helps me feel like less of a pariah."

"I get it. And I don't mind."

She started to leave the kitchen but stopped at the last second. "By the way, don't think I haven't noticed that you're not fulfilling your end of the bargain."

He was just getting up to rinse his own plate. "What bargain?"

"You said I could ask about you as long as you could ask about me. Well, I've told you just about everything there is to know about the nightmare I'm going through—I've even told you the embarrassing stuff—but you haven't said a word about yourself."

"I'm not that interesting," he joked, hoping to pass it off that easily.

She arched one eyebrow. "Does that mean our friendship only goes so deep? I share and you encourage?"

He thought of the night before, when he'd held her against him in an effort to comfort her, and nearly kissed her. It'd taken him an hour or more to dampen the desire created in that moment. Long after she was gone, his mind kept circling back to it, imagining what it might have been like had he gone through with it. He didn't want to fight that battle again, so as far as he was concerned, maintaining some emotional distance was a good idea. It might help him maintain some physical distance, too.

He didn't want to screw up with her while he was home. He wanted to help her.

"There's just no need to go into it," he said.

Emery smoothed down her shirt, checked the tie on it to be sure it was still in a perfect knot and brushed a piece of lint off her skirt. "Wish me luck," she said as she sat in the passenger side of Dallas's van looking at the cheerful Sugar Mama sign just down the string of shops on the main drag.

Dallas rested one arm over the steering wheel. "Don't be nervous," he said. "She needs your help, which means she should be very friendly."

He'd been coaching her the entire drive, trying to help her calm down. She'd never thought she'd be so afraid to apply for a minimum wage job, but she felt anyone who hired her, especially in such a small town, could come under fire. So she was frightened she might get turned down, even for this.

"Right." With a deep breath, she got out, cast a parting glance at Dallas—and received a nod of confidence. After a quick smile to signify that she was okay, or at least determined to see this through, she straightened her spine and focused on Sugar Mama while forcing her feet to carry her to the door. It was a darling shop, decorated in pink and brown—with both stripes and polka dots—and it was fully decked out for the holidays.

Open the door. Close it. Smile. She couldn't chicken out the way she wanted to.

"You must be Emery Bliss," Susan said as soon as the bell went off, announcing her presence.

Emery assumed it was the way she was dressed that indicated she wasn't simply a customer and swallowed to ease the dryness of her throat. Would Susan mention the recent scandal? Would Emery have to explain what'd happened? Make excuses? Apologize for what she'd done, even though it should've been a private matter between her and her boyfriend?

Susan's gaze ran over her, making her think that maybe she would. She didn't seem overly welcoming.

But then she smiled. "You're a beautiful young woman. You remind me of my daughter."

"Thank you."

"And you seem familiar. Where do I know you from?"

Aiyana obviously hadn't mentioned her situation. Susan didn't seem to be aware that she'd even been a news anchor. Emery didn't know whether to be disappointed that the matter wasn't already out in the open or grateful that she had a chance to circumvent it—although not mentioning it would be taking a chance. Susan could so easily find out and get angry that she wasn't notified. But Emery didn't feel as though she had to sacrifice her self-respect for a mere four weeks of work. "I grew up here."

"Oh! I've been here forever, so I've probably seen you around. Aiyana just said you were an old friend visiting for the holidays. I didn't realize you were one of our own. Who are your folks?"

Emery gave Susan her parents' names, and as soon as she mentioned that her dad was a plastic surgeon, Susan nodded. "I've heard of him. I don't know that we've ever met, but—"

"They live in Boston now. My mom and Aiyana are close, and since I live in LA, Silver Springs was much less expensive to come for the holidays, so…"

"I see. How long will you be staying?"

"I don't know yet. But I hear you only need help with the

store for a little while, and I would love to be able to lend a hand."

The dark circles under Susan's eyes and her sunken cheeks suggested she was struggling. She was tall and thin—too thin—and she looked tired even though it was early yet.

"Some days are better than others," she responded with a brittle smile. "But for some reason, this month has been particularly rough. I've had to rely on my son-in-law's brother far too much. Fortunately, he makes sure I have what I need."

"Did you say your son-in-law's brother?"

"I did. My son-in-law is the principal at the girls' side of New Horizons, so he can't help much. And my daughter is really busy with the kids and her social media business. So Tobias, his brother, helps me out a lot."

"That's really nice. He must be a good man."

"He is. I didn't think so for many years, but I was wrong about him. I feel bad about that."

Emery didn't know how to respond to such a comment, so she went back to Susan's health. "Maybe the long hours are what's giving you trouble. The Christmas season is wonderful, but it's busy."

"True. I'm grateful for the extra business, but it's hard for me to put in so many hours without ever getting a break, especially because the damp weather causes my lupus to flare up." She rested her hands in the pockets of a cute apron that matched the decor of the shop. "So. When would you be available to start?"

"Whenever you need me," Emery replied, a little startled that Susan was going to hire her that easily. "You could even call me at the last minute, if you begin to feel poorly, and I could run over."

"You realize that business drops off steeply after Christmas, so if you do stay in town..."

"Don't worry. I won't be staying into January. I'm fine with helping only as long as you need me, even if that's just a week or two."

"That'll work." She sagged slightly as though she'd been concerned she didn't have much of an opportunity to offer. "I can't afford anyone in the off-season. Do you have experience working in a place like this or something similar, like an ice cream or cupcake shop?"

"I'm afraid not."

"Not even during college?"

Her parents had paid for college. Because of them, she'd been able to focus exclusively on her studies, hadn't had to work, which was why she could hardly begrudge the money she sent to her mother now. "No."

"Well, it's easy enough—which is why it doesn't pay a whole lot."

"I understand."

"I'll go a dollar per hour over minimum wage, since you're being so flexible with me. Is that acceptable?"

Emery felt a wave of gratitude. Maybe she wouldn't make a great deal of money, but any amount would help mitigate the drain on her savings. "It will. Thank you. I appreciate it. When would you like me to come in for training?"

A group of people walked into the store, so Emery stepped off to one side, praying no one would recognize her while she waited for Susan to serve them. Fortunately, they were intent on the menu, which took up the whole of one wall, didn't even glance over at her as they chose various cookies, ice cream sandwiches and a whipped mocha drink.

Once Susan had rung them up and they'd sauntered out, Emery breathed easier.

"Can you be here when I open on Saturday?" Susan asked. "At ten?"

"I can," Emery told her.

"Great. I'll see you day after tomorrow, then."

As she left, Emery felt a little guilty that Susan didn't know she was hiring a woman with such a damaged reputation. But she was so eager to leave the recent debacle behind her she wasn't about to spread the word herself.

"What'd she say?" Dallas asked as soon as she climbed back into his van.

"I got the job," she announced. "Saturday will be my first day."

"Congratulations." He started the engine and put the transmission in Reverse. "What should we do to celebrate?" he asked as he twisted around to look behind them.

"How about dinner later—on me?"

He quit looking for a break in traffic. "Are you sure you want to spend the money?"

"I'm a working girl again. I can afford it," she joked.

"I have an idea," he said.

"What is it?"

"Have you heard from Tommy or his boyfriend?"

She opened Facebook on her phone to check. "No. Still nothing."

"Then let's go to LA."

"Where I'm bound to run into people who'll recognize me?" she said, horrified. "No thanks. That's why I'm here—to avoid anyone who might've seen that video."

"But I've been thinking. Ethan claims he kicked Tommy out and removed all of Tommy's contact information from his phone, right?"

"Yes."

"Do you believe that?"

"Not necessarily."

"How long has it been since you two broke up?"

"It was the week before Thanksgiving." She'd begun to grow disenchanted with Ethan a couple of months before that, but it wasn't until then that she made it official.

"So not that long ago."

"Not really. What is that? Three weeks?" Providing the time-line reminded her of how quickly her world had been laid to waste.

"And how long after you broke up was it when he loaded that video onto the internet?"

She grimaced at the memory. "It was the last day of November. I remember because that was the day I had the pedicure appointment."

"It's only the tenth of December now," he pointed out.

She studied him in confusion. "I don't get what you're saying."

"What are the chances Tommy was able to find another place to live in one week? Ethan blamed him for posting that video, so it stands to reason he wouldn't have thrown him out until after it went up. If it went up on the thirtieth—that isn't very long ago."

"I still don't get what you're saying."

"I'm saying Tommy might still be living with Ethan. He might be *trying* to move, but there's a good chance he hasn't been able to find another place and pack and remove all of his belongings, not in that short time."

She seemed skeptical. "Unless he just moved in with Thiago."

"If he and Thiago wanted to move in together, why did Ethan have to kick him out?"

"Ethan could be lying about that. We know he's lying about plenty of other stuff."

"It's possible. But practically speaking, that's a quick move. Why don't we drive to LA and stake out Ethan's house, see if we can't catch Tommy? Even if he's moved, he might not have gotten all of his stuff, so we might be able to catch him."

Emery pictured Tommy returning for a final load. It would be so great to get his side of the story, and the longer she waited, the less chance she'd have of Tommy being anywhere near Ethan's house. "It's worth a shot," she agreed. "But you've already done so much for me…"

"My mother doesn't need me at the school today. I have the time. And I think Ethan should be held accountable. If we can find Tommy and you can get a leg up on this thing, I stand to gain some personal satisfaction."

If she hadn't already put on her seat belt, she would've hugged him. Her life had steadily improved since he came into it. "You've been really good to me. Thank you—for not judging me and for…for believing me and supporting me."

"Oh, I'm still judging you," he said with a completely straight face, and they both started laughing as he pulled out and turned toward LA.

CHAPTER TEN

"That's it right there?" As they rolled slowly down a densely populated street filled with small, single-story houses, Dallas pointed through the windshield at the address Emery had given him. White stucco and with a red tile roof, it reminded him of a Mexican villa, especially because it had palm trees lining one side of the property. There was also a large sycamore tree turning most of the front lawn to dirt and exposed roots, and a plethora of cars parked up and down the street.

Emery slid down in her seat as they passed by. "That's it."

Ethan went to such great pains to take care of his physical appearance that Dallas had expected him to live in a nicer place, but it was expensive to rent a house in LA. Dallas had also taken the time to Google the starting salary of a news anchor and knew that Ethan's job didn't pay as much as some might expect—maybe fifty to seventy thousand dollars a year. "That his car?"

She shook her head as he indicated a black SUV parked in front. "No, must be a guest of one of the neighbors', because it doesn't belong to Tommy or Tommy's boyfriend. There's rarely any on-street parking around here—at night, anyway—so people park wherever they can, and if they don't get up and go to work, their car can sit around all day."

"Does Ethan use the garage?" Dallas checked his watch. "It's nearly three. He should be off work. Do you think he's home?"

"He's got to be off by now, but he doesn't park in the garage. It's filled with his mother's storage. If he was home, his car would be in the drive."

"Why does he have his mother's storage in his garage?" Dallas asked.

"She downsized when she moved to San Diego, doesn't have a big place. She's planning to come back for it eventually, but who knows when that will be. He's a Mama's boy. In her eyes, he can do no wrong, and he adores her for it."

"We're lucky his garage is full," he mused. "Now we'll know when he's home and when he isn't. What does he drive?"

"A brand-new white Audi A4."

Dallas brought his van to a sudden stop. "Are you serious? He's living in *this* house with a roommate while driving a car that's almost forty grand?"

She rolled her eyes. "I know. I was with him when he bought it. He spent way more than he should have. He always spends his money before he gets it. But his mother gave him the down payment, so that helped. It's important to Ethan to keep up appearances, and more people see his car than his house."

"What a pretentious fool." Giving the van some gas, he went around the corner and weaved back through the neighborhood. He wanted to get a feel for the layout of the streets in case he had to drive off without warning. He didn't trust Ethan. If Ethan figured out what they were doing and got angry, Dallas would have to protect Emery, not only himself. He figured he'd better be prepared. He didn't know if Ethan owned a gun or some other weapon, and after what he'd been through with his father, no one was going to be harmed on his watch.

Once he felt comfortable, he cruised down Ethan's street

again and was lucky enough to find a spot to park where they could see the house but didn't feel they were too conspicuous.

"So now we wait?" she asked when he turned off the engine.

He adjusted his seat so that it wasn't as close to the steering wheel. "Now we wait. Hopefully, Tommy will show up instead of Ethan, and we will have the chance to approach him."

"That would be awesome." She looked at her phone again. "I still haven't received a response on Facebook, and even though I left my number for Thiago to give him, Tommy hasn't called."

"I haven't given up hope that he will. In the meantime, we'll do what we can."

Her face looked pinched, nervous, as she studied the house.

"How long were you and Ethan together?" Dallas asked.

"We started dating about ten months ago. He tried asking me out before that, but I didn't want to get involved with anyone at work. I'd signed that agreement and meant to honor it."

"Were you ever in love with him?"

She took a few seconds to consider the question. "I *thought* I was. I was in love with his potential—but the man he is on the inside doesn't match the handsome package. I finally had to admit the truth and quit making excuses for him. Whenever he'd be a jerk and we'd argue, he'd blame me for setting him off. It took me a while to realize he was manipulating me, making me feel responsible for his own bad behavior."

Dallas shifted to get more comfortable. "I looked up revenge porn on the internet while you were in your interview at the coffee shop."

"And? What'd you learn?"

"That posting a digital image in an attempt to harass someone is a crime."

She leaned back and put her feet up on the dash. "Revenge porn is called cyber-exploitation. It's a form of nonconsensual pornography, and it's illegal in California, but the penalties aren't very big. And proving what Ethan did was a willful act meant to cause me injury isn't that easy."

"How could anyone argue that it wasn't a willful act meant to cause you injury? You lost your job because of it."

"But if push comes to shove, he could claim consent—that I knew about the recording and gave my permission for him to do whatever he wanted with it."

"What woman would give permission for something like that?"

"Someone who wanted the attention. Someone who thought that being in the spotlight might bring future opportunity. Someone like a news anchor who was just a little too eager to 'make it.'"

Dallas felt his eyebrows jerk together. "Can he change his story after the fact? He's claiming he didn't put it up in the first place, not that you gave consent."

"Because he doesn't know the defenses that are open to him yet. It's possible, if he gets the right attorney, they might go that way."

"I'm pretty sure if the police confiscated his computer, they could prove it came from his IP address."

"If only they would expend the time and resources."

"If he was smart, he'd get rid of it right away, just in case. Maybe he already has. That would be a small price to pay to maintain his innocence."

"It's possible he didn't use his computer. If he knew it was a crime, he might've been careful enough to use Tommy's. Regardless, the police are so busy working on bigger cases—rapes and murders and bank robberies—that they aren't going to search his house, confiscate every computer connected to him and bring in a forensics team to take a look at the hard drive. That would cost taxpayers a fortune, and, from their perspective, it would come with very little reward, even if they nailed him. The crime is called 'harassment by means of an electronic device,' and it's only a misdemeanor. So nothing will likely happen from a criminal standpoint. My attorney said the worst Ethan would get on the criminal side would be six months in jail, a fine of up to a thousand dollars or both."

Dallas rummaged around in his console until he found a pack of gum and, after offering Emery a stick, which she accepted, he put a piece in his own mouth. "Six months in jail would be serious for a pretty boy like Ethan. I can't imagine he'd fare well with the type of men he'd meet in there. It would also publicly embarrass him the way he embarrassed you, and he'd lose his job for real this time."

"We'd still have to prove intent—that he didn't accidentally post that video when he meant to post something else, that it was him and not Tommy using his computer or whatever. Mr. Costa—"

"Mr. Costa's your attorney?"

"Yes. He said if Ethan hired anyone who was any good to defend him—and I know he would get the best because his mother would step up to pay for it even if she had to sell everything she owns—he'd be unlikely to serve time. That means it would come down to a fine, which, even at a thousand bucks, would be nothing for what Ethan did to me, especially since he retained his job and I didn't. That's why we're suing him in civil court. We can get a lot more than a thousand dollars if we win. And if my lawyer and I can create a strong enough case, the police might go after him, too."

"They're not now?"

"They claim they're looking into it, but from what I understand, if we do their work for them, make it easy, we'll have a better shot."

"I remember hearing about the civil case that Nicole Simpson's family filed against O.J."

"It provided their only justice," she said sadly. "Taking the civil path might prove to be my best recourse, too."

Dallas spotted a car coming down the street. "That's a white Audi, isn't it?"

Emery sat up, then ducked down. "Damn. It is. That's Ethan."

They watched as he parked, gathered his shopping bags and went into the house. He didn't seem to notice them. "Are you okay if we stay here to see if Tommy comes?"

"Yeah," she said, but after two hours of waiting they began to despair that he would ever show up. They were also getting hungry; it was dinnertime.

"I'm going to the door," Dallas announced.

Once again, Emery sat up straighter. *"What?"*

"Why not? It'd be smarter than hanging out around here indefinitely. He doesn't know me. He doesn't know we know each other, either, so he has no reason to suspect we might be in contact. I could ask for Tommy, see what he says. Maybe if Tommy's not there, he'll tell me where I can find him. At a minimum, he might clarify whether Tommy has really moved—and if he has, we can safely assume we're wasting our time sitting here."

She puffed out her cheeks as she mulled it over, but agreed in the end. "That makes sense."

"Okay. Be sure to stay down."

"Will do."

As Dallas got out, he was hoping Ethan would do something to give him an excuse to throw just one good punch. As far as he was concerned, a broken jaw might not be everything he deserved, but it would be the quickest form of justice.

Emery curved her nails into her palms as she watched Dallas cross the street, walk down a couple of houses and cut across the lawn under the sycamore tree. It wasn't until he was almost to the door that she got the idea to text Ethan. If she distracted him, if she made him believe the fight was elsewhere—somewhere far removed from his front door—he might be less suspicious of his visitor.

He would certainly never guess she was behind what was going on.

I thought you wanted to talk. But then you curse at me and hang up?

The symbol indicating he was looking at her text appeared on her screen the moment Dallas reached the stoop.

When Dallas knocked, the ellipsis disappeared.

She waited to see what Ethan would do first—answer her or answer the door.

After a minute, he came out.

His encounter with Dallas lasted much longer than she'd expected. Ethan flashed his best smile, shoved his hands in his pockets and leaned against the doorjamb as they talked—like some kind of GQ model.

Dallas stood back a few feet, and although she couldn't see his face, he seemed every bit as affable. Eventually, they both pulled out their phones and Dallas typed something into his while looking at Ethan's—a great sign as far as Emery was concerned. Then they talked and laughed a while longer.

Finally, Ethan watched Dallas walk away.

She ducked down as Dallas approached, didn't dare put her head above the dashboard, especially because Dallas murmured, "He's still there," as he climbed in.

"Did you get anything?" she asked.

He didn't answer; he didn't even look at her. He started the engine, drove past Ethan's house and waved. For Ethan to still be outside, he either really liked Dallas, or he was suspicious of him.

It wasn't until after they'd turned the corner that Dallas pulled over and she was able to get back into her seat and put on her seat belt. "What happened?"

His teeth flashed as he grinned. "Tommy *has* moved in with Thiago, but Ethan gave me his phone number."

"No way!"

"It's true." He handed her his phone with the contact information on the screen.

She smiled when she saw it, then settled back as he pulled from the curb and merged into traffic. "You two looked like old friends. What'd you say to him?"

"I made a big deal about recognizing him on TV, told him how attractive he was and said if he ever wondered what it was like to be with a man, I'd be interested in helping him explore."

"You've got to be kidding me!" she said with a surprised laugh. "You hit on him? And he believed you were sincerely interested?"

"All it took was a little flattery."

"Knowing how vain Ethan is, I shouldn't be surprised. But... how'd you bring up Tommy?"

"I asked if he was home."

"And Ethan gave you his number?"

"Not quite *that* easily. First I made up some bullshit about having met Tommy at a bar—and hinted that he took me home."

Her jaw dropped. *"You didn't..."*

"I had to have *some* reason for knowing where he lived."

"Since they live together, that was a risk." She couldn't help admiring his nerve.

"I was assuming they have completely different circles and rarely even saw each other."

"Fortunately, that would be true."

"It helped that I knew Thiago's name. And that he and Tommy went through a rough patch a few weeks ago. Ethan assumed that was when I met Tommy, and I played along."

"Wow. I had no idea you were so devious," she joked, unable to quit smiling.

He arched a remonstrative eyebrow at her. "I prefer to think of it as clever," he said. "Anyway, it worked out. You now have the ability to contact Tommy and, hopefully, counter all the lies

Ethan has been spreading." He slung his arm over the steering wheel, looking casually in charge as he glanced over at her. "I'd call that a good day's work," he said proudly. "So I'm ready to take you up on that dinner invitation."

"Sounds good to me. Now that the stress is off, I'm starving."

"You used to live in this city. Where should we go?"

"Beer & Salsa in Burbank. There's always a wait, but you'll never eat better shrimp fajitas."

"Done," he said, and followed her directions to the restaurant. They'd been together so much the past few days and were so happy in this moment it felt perfectly natural to be holding hands as they walked in.

"What are you doing up?" Eli asked.

Aiyana clicked away from her word processing program, where she'd been proofing some grant requests, and switched her phone to her other ear as she yawned. "You don't live here anymore. How do you know I'm up?"

"I'm still on the same campus and can see that the light's on in your bedroom."

"Only if you're looking for it."

"I always check on you," he admitted.

She smiled at his protectiveness. She was a lucky woman to have the happiness—and the people in her life—she had now. She'd never dreamed so many of her children would be able to overcome the tremendous odds that had been stacked against them, or that she'd end up with someone like Cal. Rarely did she feel worthy, which was why she'd waited so long to marry him. She was expecting life to get difficult again; it seemed it always did. But she'd been with Cal long enough that she was beginning to trust him and the bond they shared, which was why, she supposed, she'd finally given in on the matter of marriage. "I don't know," she admitted. "Can't sleep. What are *you* doing up?"

"Little Xander's teething."

At the mention of her newest grandson, only six months old, Aiyana felt some of the tension that had been troubling her tonight ease. She'd loved being a mother, but she'd taken on an incredibly difficult family—adopting eight boys who were victims of severe emotional, and sometimes even physical, trauma. Trying to help them heal and make sense of the world had required constant effort and a great deal of perseverance.

But being a grandmother wasn't like that at all. Thanks to the men her sons had become—at least the older ones who were in that stage of life—and the women they'd married, they were providing a solid foundation for the next generation. She was excited to think she wouldn't have to worry about her grandchildren the way she'd had to worry about her children.

"Is it the stress of the wedding that's bothering you?" Eli asked.

"No. I'm fine with the wedding."

"You're not having second thoughts…"

"No."

"Good, because if you were to back out now, it would break poor Cal's heart."

That was true. He loved her fiercely, and he let her know it. "I would never do anything to hurt him."

"So if it's not the wedding, what is it? A particular boy or girl at the school who isn't doing well?"

"There's always someone to worry about at the school." Sadly, more than one. But that was the nature of her business, what she'd chosen to do.

"Is this a little closer to home, then? Is it Dallas?"

When she didn't answer, she knew Eli would understand he'd guessed correctly.

"What's going on with Dallas?" he asked. "He seems to be doing okay to me. The same, anyway."

"I just keep thinking…" She got up and began pacing around

her bedroom. "What would make someone want to scale dizzyingly high, steep rocks—*mountains*—with no safety gear? When one mistake would mean certain death?"

In the daytime, when they were both busy, Eli would probably have said something like, "He's not the only one who does it. It's a sport, and all sports can be dangerous. He'll be okay." Although she didn't buy that, she understood he said those kinds of things to relieve his own worry—to refuse to face the reality of the situation.

But late at night like this, when the immediate pressures of work and family felt so far away, he was prone to be more open and honest. They had their best discussions in moments like these. "Maybe he puts himself in such dangerous situations to make him fear death and *want* to live."

"Meaning he doesn't feel that way naturally?"

"I'm just throwing out ideas."

"The chances he takes make me feel as though my heart is caught in a blender, and any moment it could switch on. I keep waiting for the phone to ring with news that would devastate me, and I never realize that more than when he's home and I'm *not* scared for him. That's the only time I get a reprieve, the only time the fear retreats and I can breathe freely."

"I'm sorry, Mom. That's the last thing he'd ever want to make you feel."

"I agree. The fact that he does it anyway suggests he *has* to do it. But *why*? How many times can one person cheat death?"

"You know he feels responsible for his sister's murder, feels as though Jenny might've been able to get out of the house if she hadn't tried to draw their father's attention away from him so he could hide."

"I do. But he was *so* young—"

"Doesn't matter. He has to cope with a great deal of survivor's guilt."

She opened the top drawer of her desk and pulled out the

letter she'd received from Dallas's father. "And I gave the man who killed her Dallas's address," she said with a sigh.

"*What?* You've heard from his father?"

She took the letter from its envelope and stared at the tiny, cramped printing—all of it in pencil. "He wrote me from prison, pleading for a way to contact Dallas. And I…"

"Felt sorry for him?" Eli asked incredulously.

"No, not that. I was hoping he'd say something to Dallas that would heal old wounds, something that might make it possible for Dallas to forgive himself for living instead of dying that day. I thought maybe then Dallas would quit rambling around, taking such foolish chances and denying himself the community and support of his friends and family."

"I'm guessing it didn't work out that way."

"Dallas isn't happy that I gave Robert his address. He's received a letter from him, but he hasn't opened it. Says he's not sure he ever will."

"Maybe that's for the best," Eli said. "Maybe what his father has to say will only make matters worse."

"In the letter he sent me, Robert sounds sincerely sorry. But you could be right. I might've made a mistake."

"You never know," Eli said. "It's possible that it's a *good* thing this is coming up again."

"In what way?"

"If Dallas has to face it and rethink it all as a man, he might come to better conclusions than he did as a child, might finally be able to get beyond it."

"I hope so. It's not as if he's been willing to go to therapy—not since I took him to that one psychologist, Dr. Smith, who retired after a couple of years with him. Remember?"

"He told me a psychologist couldn't change the facts."

"He told me that, too," she said, "but he seemed to do a lot better when he was working with Dr. Smith. The nightmares eased a bit. I know that much."

"Maybe he'll try therapy again one day. We can't force him. Where is he now?"

"He took Emery to LA."

"You don't think there's any chance of them getting together, do you?"

"I don't know. At first I was hopeful, but if he won't settle down, it will only drag her into the same morass of worry I'm in."

"Maybe she'll be able to fulfill him. Having Cora come into my life made a huge difference for me."

"Yes," she said, as though that made her more optimistic. But while Eli had been severely abused as a child, he hadn't watched his father murder his mother and sister.

That made everything permanent.

CHAPTER ELEVEN

It was probably completely natural for Emery to touch him so often. They were friends, they'd had a couple of drinks, and they were out forgetting about Ethan and having a good time. Dallas just wasn't used to having a woman take his hand, grab his arm or spontaneously hug him—not unless she was also open to a sexual relationship. And, as a result, his mind kept shooting off in a completely different direction, one that was decidedly *not* platonic.

But he didn't have a lot of female friends. He spent half the year climbing, surrounded almost entirely by men. Even during the winter, when he worked at the gym, he dealt with more men than he did women. His students had mothers, of course, but they were usually married or too old for him. And Emery was particularly attractive…

After a delicious Mexican dinner, where they'd talked and laughed for nearly two hours, they'd decided to leave his van at Beer & Salsa and take an Uber to Rodeo Drive. They'd both had one too many margaritas, so they weren't ready to drive back to Silver Springs, and Emery wanted to see the Christmas decorations in this ritzy area. He suspected she also wanted to show him her city. It was obvious by the way she talked about living in LA that she loved it.

As they strode along, she slipped her arm through his, and he once again told himself it was no big deal. She didn't mean anything by it. It had been much warmer before the sun went down, so warm they'd left their jackets behind, and now it was growing chilly—that was all. But the awareness he was beginning to feel, despite trying to ignore it, was getting so distracting he was having trouble focusing on what she said.

"What do you think?" she asked.

He didn't have an answer. He'd missed every word except the last question. He'd been too busy imagining what it might be like to kiss the girl he'd been too afraid to ask out back in high school—even as he chastised himself for considering it.

"I…" He looked down into her expectant face and smiled apologetically. "I'm sorry. I zoned out there for a second. What'd you say?"

She pulled her arm away. "It's okay. Are you getting tired?" she asked as though she was suddenly worried she might be boring him. "We can go home, if you're ready."

"No. I'm not able to drive quite yet. I just…had something else on my mind. What was it you said?"

"I suggested we go to the beach. Have you ever been to the beach at night?"

"Not this late," he replied.

"It'll be dark, but the moonlight reflects off the water, and you can hear the surf crashing onto the shore. It's quite an experience."

Considering what he was feeling, the beach might be too isolated. But just knowing she wasn't receptive to the kind of intimacy he was beginning to crave would keep him in line. He was still a little buzzed, so they needed to do *something* until he sobered up. "You won't be too cold?"

"Not if we build a bonfire," she said eagerly.

"I didn't realize you could still do that." He loved California as much as anyone, but it had to be the most overlegislated state in the union.

"Only on some beaches. But I happen to know which ones." She grinned mischievously up at him. "Should we Uber there?"

She was obviously enjoying herself. She'd been so miserable lately that Dallas was glad to see her forget about the recent past for a while. Since he didn't want to do anything to ruin her reprieve, he figured he might as well let her finish out the evening in whichever way she liked. "Okay. Why not?"

She pulled out her phone to request the rideshare. "I'm too full to eat anything else, but what do you say we stop by the liquor store on the way and buy a bottle of wine? We have to get firewood, anyway."

Dallas felt his pulse pick up. This trip to the beach was beginning to sound very romantic. That made him uncomfortable, given that he was already struggling with a growing desire to touch her in a way that was decidedly beyond friendship. But she didn't seem to be aware of that or think anything of putting them both in such an intimate situation.

It would be okay, he decided. She'd made it clear that she wasn't in the market for another relationship, and that was a boundary he would never cross, especially with a woman who'd so recently been through what Emery had been through. "I won't sober up if we continue to drink," he pointed out, trying to nix the wine, at least.

More control was better than less, he thought. But she had her mind made up. "Then we'll sleep on the beach," she said as if it didn't really matter one way or the other.

It was too hot to sit close to the fire, and it was too cold to sit far away from it. But if they stayed on the cheap blanket they'd purchased, right at the edge of the circle of light leaping and dancing on the sand, it was comfortable. Maybe a little *too* comfortable. Emery didn't want to leave this place. She found it surprisingly cathartic. As a news anchor, she'd covered almost everything there was to do in the sprawling metropolis, was always looking for something new to report or a fresh angle she could use to highlight a place or activity people may have seen or done before. But she looked at the city, and this beach, with different eyes now that she didn't have to package it for the viewers of KQLA's morning show. She didn't have to worry about creating an enticing hook, how best to present the information in the shortest amount of time or how to follow up with a highly engaging social media post so that she could extend her reach and continue building her career.

The pressure was off; she could simply sit and enjoy.

She had to admit, for the here and now—*this* moment in isolation from all others—it was nice not to have an agenda. Relaxing with Dallas while sipping merlot from a cheap plastic champagne flute and listening to the crack and spit of the fire above the powerful crash of waves not far away made her grateful just to be alive.

After the past month, it was wonderful to feel as though that was enough.

"This was worth the effort," Dallas decreed, tipping his head back to gaze up at the sky.

He was wearing a contemplative expression as he studied the stars.

"You must see the sky without the intrusion of city lights all the time," she said, "what with camping out so often."

"I do."

He didn't elaborate, didn't describe his life, but she was curious about it. What would it be like to face such formidable physical challenges on almost a daily basis? To look down and to know that a fall would be certain death? And what about the other aspects? To be totally indifferent to what most other people—people like Ethan—prized so highly? To not care about getting a more lucrative job, a bigger house, a nicer car or any other material object? Dallas seemed content to have only what he needed to get through each day. And it was clear he didn't give a damn about impressing anyone, which was partly why he *did* impress her. He was free in a way few people were.

"You told me you mostly live on beans and greens. But you're not a vegetarian, like Alex Honnold. I've seen you eat meat."

"Occasionally. But from what I saw in that documentary about him, we have a similar approach to food."

"In what way?" She remembered one scene that showed Alex whipping up a big pan of beans or something else on a camp-style stove and eating it right out of the pan. "As long as it's healthy, you're happy?" she guessed. "You're not too picky?"

"Basically. During my climbing months, food is simply fuel."

She poured him another glass of wine before wedging the bottle back into the sand. "Doesn't it ever get lonely spending so much time by yourself?"

It took him a moment to answer. Then he said, "Sometimes. But climbing is worth it to me. The challenge keeps me engaged. Besides, I think everyone gets lonely once in a while."

"I didn't while I was working," she mused. "Or I was too busy to notice. But I've certainly felt alone since Ethan did what he did. Worse than alone. For the first time in my life, I've felt hated and reviled. That's been hard. Everyone wants to be liked, and I'm betting that's especially true for someone like me—the type of personality who would aspire to become a TV anchor."

"Probably," he agreed.

Emery was doing most of the talking, but she couldn't seem to stop. She was happy for the first time in a long while. But the alcohol seemed to be having the opposite effect on Dallas. He seemed happy enough, or possibly he was merely content, but he was growing more and more reserved. "Anyway, enough about Ethan," she said, assuming he had to be tired of that topic. "I don't know why I brought him up again." She

lifted her wine. "This is delicious, by the way. You said coming here was worth it, but you have to admit that bringing the
wine was a great idea, too."

He held up his glass to clink it against hers. "I readily admit
it."

Closing her eyes, she focused on the caress of the wind against
her cheeks. "Right now I feel pretty damn invincible," she said.
"Don't you?"

"I'm not sure *invincible* is the word I'd use," he said wryly.

Opening her eyes, she pulled the hair whipping around her
face out of the way. "Why not?"

A small smile tugged at his lips before he twisted around to
stare down the beach. "Never mind."

"What are you looking for?" she asked, distracted as she followed his gaze into the darkness. The only things she could see
were the whitecaps of the foamy waves, and the far-off light of
a ship at sea.

"It's hard to believe that with four million people in LA, we
can be *this* alone," he said.

They hadn't encountered anyone after they were dropped
off, while they were building their bonfire or spreading out
the blanket—no voices, no lights, no movement, other than the
constant thunder of the waves and a few sand crabs that scurried
to get out of their way. "It is," she said. "It seems like we're the
only two people on Earth. And here we are, sitting at the edge
of the greatest ocean, breathing in the salty sea air. It's gotten
chilly, but it's worth the cold. I love the ocean."

"I wish I had a jacket to offer you." He pulled part of the
blanket they weren't sitting on up around her. "There's this, but
maybe it's not enough. Would you rather go?"

She snuggled close to him, reveling in the warmth of his solid,
muscular body. "Are you kidding? We have a lot of fire left."

Although he seemed stiff at first—stiff enough that she almost
pulled away, assuming such close contact wasn't welcome—he

soon shifted to make her more comfortable and his arms went around her. "Are we staying until it dies down?"

"I'd stay a lot longer than that, if I could," she said, watching the flames.

"I don't have to be home until the wedding," he joked. "You're the one who has to work on Saturday."

She laughed. "Maybe I'd get my fill if we really could hang out until tomorrow night." She poured herself some more wine. They'd almost finished the bottle. "How do you like living in Vegas?"

"I like it."

"It doesn't get too hot for you in the summer?"

"I'm never there in the summer."

She was feeling a nice buzz, knew she should stop drinking, but she took another sip. "Where do you climb most often? Other than Yosemite?"

"I like Utah. Big and Little Cottonwood Canyons and Zion National Park. Have you ever been to either of those places?"

"No. But I've heard a lot about Zion."

"You really have to see it in person. Moab is also special. There's nothing quite like Canyonlands and Arches National Park."

She heard the reverence in his voice and understood how passionate he felt about nature. "I've seen pictures of both."

"Pictures don't do them justice."

She removed her shoes and dug her toes into the damp sand at the edge of the blanket, eager for more sensory input, more celebration, a way to continue to block out the recent past and the difficult challenges that loomed ahead. "What do you do in the months when you're not climbing?"

He drained his glass. "I coach at a parkour gym."

"Do you like that?"

"I don't mind it. The owner is great. Better than great. He's sort of like a second father to me. And the kids are awesome. Anyway, it gets me through the winter."

"Do you ever worry that your lifestyle might be... I don't know...a little hard on your relationships?"

"Not really."

"You never intend to marry and settle down?"

When she glanced up at him, she saw that his lips were slanted into a self-deprecating smile. "I doubt there's a woman out there who could put up with me."

"It wouldn't be easy to tolerate your wanderlust," she admitted. "But you never know. Alex Honnold is with someone. Or he was when I interviewed him. I can't say if they're still together."

"Maybe I'll meet the right person someday," he said, but he spoke noncommittally.

Emery spread the blanket out so that she could lie on it. "I'm getting tired. What about you?"

"I'm not too bad, but thanks to all the wine we've drunk, I'm not ready to drive."

She patted the blanket. "Let's take a nap, sleep it off. This night has been so fun. I don't want it to end quite yet, do you?"

He eyed the spot next to her with obvious reluctance. "No, but... I don't know if lying down together would be wise."

The scent of the fire filled her nostrils as she stared up at the black velvet sky. She'd had too much to drink, all right; the world was beginning to spin faster and faster and faster. "In what way?" she asked, covering a yawn. She thought she could guess. She wanted to touch him, too. It was the alcohol, she told herself.

But he didn't explain. "Never mind," he replied and curled up with her.

Dallas wasn't sure who started it. He only knew that by the time he came fully awake, he and Emery were kissing. Her hand was up his shirt, touching his chest, and he had a raging hard-on.

He tried to come to his senses, to gain control of the situation, but they must not have been sleeping long because his thoughts were still fuzzy. "Emery?" he said, trying to pull away.

"What?" she murmured, her mouth moving down until he could feel her tongue on his neck.

He struggled to catch his breath—and to resist the urge to slip his hand up *her* shirt. "Did I start this—or did you?" he managed to ask.

"I don't know," she replied. "But you feel—" she bit his neck "—and taste—" she kissed his jawline "—and smell—" she nuzzled her nose up under his ear "—better than anything."

He felt every muscle tense with the desire to respond in kind. Instead, he swallowed hard and resisted the impulse. "I appreciate that, but you've been through a lot. We don't want to make it any worse."

She jerked her head up and looked around. "How? There's not another soul out here. Even if we *weren't* alone, it's so dark someone would have to literally stumble over us to realize we're here."

"That isn't it," he said. "We're still drunk. At least I think we must be." With the sudden injection of so much testosterone, as well as the jolt of the surprise, his thoughts were growing decidedly clearer. Was she sobering up, too?

"That could be true. But it's been a really horrible month, and I need to feel something good. A second ago, you seemed to want the same thing."

She hadn't misread what his body was telling her. He was trying not to be selfish. "I do. It's just…this is sort of sudden and could possibly ruin our friendship. You might want to reconsider—"

She sat up so abruptly he swallowed the rest of that sentence. He assumed he'd talked some sense into her and what had started so quickly had ended just as fast. Although he'd done the right thing, losing the satisfaction he craved created a sharp pang of disappointment.

But she didn't stand up to go; she pulled off her shirt.

"Holy shit," he whispered when she guided his hands to her full, soft breasts. "You're not making this easy. Will you…will you stop and think for a second? Can we make sure this is going to be all right?"

"I *won't* think," she said. "I refuse."

"But you might regret this later."

She was already working on the buttons of his shirt. "Do you have birth control?"

"In my wallet."

"Then I won't regret it."

He caught her wrists. "What about afterward? What about tomorrow?"

"Tomorrow I can go back to trying to rebuild my life, and we can pretend this never happened. This is just a…a time-out. A onetime thing. Neither one of us is looking for a relationship, so what can it hurt? We're both consenting adults, and we don't have any emotional expectations."

He had to admit she made a great case.

"Are you in?" she asked.

When he hesitated, she faltered. "Dallas? Are you saying no?"

"I'm definitely *not* saying no. I'm simply trying to…clarify. Are you sure you won't be upset with yourself, or me, in the morning? You won't be embarrassed to see me? You won't give up your new job, leave Silver Springs and head back to your apartment to spend Christmas alone? *Nothing* will change?"

"I'm positive."

She sounded so definite he knew he was going to move forward despite the fact that he probably shouldn't.

"Then what do we have to lose?" he said, and pulled her back down on top of him before rolling her onto her back. "But I say we start over. If this is only going to happen once, there's no way I want to race for the finish line."

Emery had never been one for casual sex. She knew it could create all kinds of problems. Before she started seeing Ethan, she'd been so caught up in her work she hadn't even gone out very often. She'd put up a profile on a dating site and left it there, but after meeting several of the men who contacted her, she'd grown discouraged and quit logging in or following up. She supposed that was how she fell into a relationship with Ethan—there was no one else in her life, and she got worn down from interacting with him every day.

Considering that abstinence was her typical MO, at least when she wasn't dating someone, she couldn't believe she was doing what she was doing with Dallas, and that she'd been the one to encourage it. This was the most sexually aggressive she'd ever been. But she guessed that she was, in part, making a statement. This was her way of flipping Ethan off for wrecking her life, her way of refusing to allow what he did, or the judgments of those who saw the video he'd posted, to stop her from enjoying her sexuality.

It didn't hurt that Dallas was built as well as he was, that he could kiss better than anyone she'd ever kissed before or that she genuinely liked and trusted him.

They made out for so long she was beginning to wonder if he was still hesitant to go further. But once he turned his attention to the rest of her body, she understood why he'd waited. By then she was so excited, she was especially sensitive to his touch and couldn't help gasping when his mouth moved to her breast and his fingers slid even lower.

"God, that's good," she whispered and let go, allowed him full access without holding back. So when he finally pushed inside her, she thought she might climax immediately. He must've been close to climax, too, because he lowered himself to his elbows and kissed her again. Although she enjoyed the kiss, like all the others before it, she also understood he was taking a slight break from focusing on what was going on below the waist, so that he could maintain control.

"I've never made love on the beach," she said as she waited.

He lifted his head. "Me, either. Now I'll be ruined for doing it anywhere else."

"You'll have to bring every woman you want back here." It was completely the wrong time to make such a statement. But she needed to remind herself not to get *too* caught up in what they were doing. This didn't mean anything. That was the point of casual sex.

"I'd rather not talk about other women right now," he said.

"Smart man," she teased.

He didn't keep the banter going. She was trying to put some emotional distance between them—their lovemaking was growing pretty feverish and intense and all-consuming—but he wasn't playing along. From what she could tell, he welcomed the intensity, didn't seem concerned with emotional distance, because he turned the focus back on her, which enhanced the overall experience but did little to help her maintain the proper perspective.

"Are you cold?" he asked when she suddenly quit responding, for the first time worried that they might be making a big mistake. "We can stop."

She nearly brought it all to a halt. Because he was so considerate, he'd given her the opportunity.

Except she couldn't do that; it wouldn't be fair. He'd given her plenty of chances to stop before it went this far. It wasn't as though she really wanted to quit, anyway. She'd just gotten spooked by how well it was going.

"No. I don't feel the cold," she admitted, and so that reality couldn't intrude again, she closed her eyes and concentrated on the occasional pop coming from the glowing embers of the fire, the cool wind on her naked, sweat-dampened skin and, most of all, the sensation of Dallas filling her with each thrust. "You feel incredible inside me," she admitted as soon as that flash of reluctance was cast aside. "Just the way I knew you'd feel."

That was too personal. But this whole thing was getting away from her, and she couldn't seem to stop it.

"I'm glad to hear that, because with you beneath me, I feel like the master of all I survey," he said, and they both laughed.

"Maybe the wine has something to do with that."

"Nope, it's all you," he whispered, and rolled onto his back, pulling her with him. "Let's try it this way, so that you can be in charge. Maybe you'll be able to work off some of the anger and hurt you've been feeling lately."

She was eager to try. Resting her hands on his firm chest, she began to move slowly and deliberately. The intensity on his face made her feel powerful. She liked being on top. Here, alone with him on the beach, she felt as free as he probably did when he was climbing.

Once she began to move faster, his hands gripped her thighs to help her, and she cast away the rest of her reserve, threw back her head and rode him in earnest. When she felt his body go rigid, she was afraid he might come too soon. That one moment when she'd freaked out had cost her; she wasn't quite there yet. But he didn't.

Her release was both powerful and oddly cleansing. It was almost as if her body had gathered up all of her frustration and unhappiness and annihilated it in one grand explosion that rippled through her, bringing the most exquisite pleasure.

When she gasped, she heard Dallas make a similar sound and felt slightly exultant. Besides everything else, she'd brought him to climax with her.

"That was close," he admitted, sounding relieved as she slumped over him and tried to catch her breath. "I was hanging on for all I was worth."

"I could tell. But you made it. And it was so damn good."

"You know what they say about rock climbers."

"No, I don't," she said, suddenly languid and relaxed and tired again.

"Neither do I," he said, and they laughed as he wrapped the blanket around them before drifting off to sleep.

CHAPTER TWELVE

Saturday, December 12

"Will you be okay if I leave for a few hours?" Susan asked.

Startled by the intrusion of her employer's voice, Emery blinked. She'd been staring off into space, lost in her own thoughts. "I'll be fine," she insisted with a polite smile, but she wasn't as confident as she was pretending to be. She'd spent the past two hours training at her new job. What she had to do wasn't hard. But as long as Susan was around, and she only had to do what she was told, her mind tended to wander.

After Dallas brought her home early yesterday morning, they'd both slipped quietly into their respective bedrooms, hoping Aiyana and his younger brothers wouldn't realize they'd been out all night. He'd been gone when she woke up; he spent Friday working for his mother, helping to get ready for the wedding, which was going to be at the groom's ranch. Aiyana had asked him to set up several tents and fill them with tables and chairs. Emery had heard something about a gazebo, too, and going to Santa Barbara to pick up the wine. He'd gotten back after Emery was in bed. Then she'd left before he was up this morning, so she hadn't seen him since their night on the beach.

That didn't stop her from thinking about him, however.

"I need to lie down for a couple of hours," Susan said. "But the weather's turned again, so it shouldn't be too busy. I never get as many customers when it's wet."

"Right." Susan looked pale and moved as though she was struggling to keep going. "I got the store. Don't worry about anything. I hope you feel better soon."

Susan thanked her, and Emery maintained her smile until Susan made her way gingerly out the back door to her car, which was parked in the alley. Then, as if fate was determined to make a liar out of Susan, the store got busy in spite of the bad weather. Emery had to focus on what she was doing to keep up, especially because she'd never worked a cash register.

Three hours passed and Susan didn't return. So when Emery heard the bell ring over the door at three-thirty, she didn't think anything of it. It had been ringing all day, and it was the front door, not the back. Whoever had just walked in wouldn't be her employer.

She was so intent on continuing to manage the store alone— and get a large, boisterous family their ice cream cones and sandwiches—that she didn't even look up until she heard a deep voice she immediately recognized.

Dallas. He was there with his two younger brothers. Dressed in faded jeans and a gray, long-sleeved T-shirt that had a picture of a stick figure rock climbing that said Roam Free, he'd just had his hair cut. Emery could tell Liam and Bentley had been to the barber, too. No doubt they were getting ready for the wedding.

She felt a strange sensation in her stomach the minute she looked up, knew her odd reaction to seeing Dallas was a result of Thursday night and cursed herself for being foolish enough to get so intimate with her new friend. Now she wouldn't be able to stop herself from undressing him with her eyes.

He smiled, and she smiled, too—shooting for a perfunctory expression to cover her sudden self-consciousness—before finishing with her current customers.

"Hey," she said once the large party left.

His eyes searched her face. She wasn't sure what he was looking for, but she could guess. He had to be wondering if she was going to be true to her word and treat him the same as she'd treated him before they made love. "We were in the neighborhood and thought we'd drop by and see how you're doing on your first day," he said as Bentley and Liam hunched over the ice cream case, trying to decide on what they wanted.

"I'm doing okay." She checked the clock. "Except that I've been on my own for the past several hours. I keep thinking Susan will be back, but…"

"Do you know where she went? Because it's sort of strange she'd leave you alone so long already."

"I didn't think anything of it in the beginning. She wasn't feeling well, and I was glad I could spell her so she could go lie down. But now I'm starving and wondering whether she's ever going to take over so I can buy some food. I would've packed a sandwich if I'd known I wouldn't be able to get away."

"I'll grab you something from down the street," he said. "What would you like?"

"No, that's okay. I'll survive. I'm just beginning to worry that something might've happened to her. She gave me her cell phone in case I had a question or couldn't figure something out. Maybe I should call her."

"I'll have an ice cream sandwich with confetti ice cream and sugar cookies," Liam piped up, so intent on the treats offered in the store he seemed oblivious to their conversation.

Bentley chose Oreo cookie ice cream between white chocolate chunk macadamia nut cookies.

"And what would you like?" she asked Dallas.

He ordered a coffee, said he wasn't much for sweets when she asked if he was sure he wouldn't rather have ice cream, and paid for the three of them.

"Thanks for coming in," she said, and breathed a sigh of relief when he was gone. She'd promised him it wouldn't be awkward between them, and she was trying to keep that promise by acting as though it wasn't. But their night on the beach had definitely altered *something*.

Fortunately, she had a break in the amount of traffic in the store after that, and she used the time to clean up. She still hadn't decided whether to bother Susan. Maybe her new employer had been so exhausted she'd dropped into a deep sleep and Emery shouldn't disturb her.

She decided to give Susan one more hour before calling and went into the back, where no customers would be able to see her eat a cookie to stave off the hunger pangs. But before she could take her first bite, the bell sounded over the door.

"Shit," she muttered, and put the cookie down before walking back out front. She was expecting another customer or set of customers, but it was Dallas with a white bag in one hand. His brothers were probably waiting in the van or looking at something else because they hadn't come back with him.

"Turkey and Swiss," he announced, handing the sack to her over the main ice cream freezer. "We can't have you getting hangry on your first day of work."

His grin was the sexiest she'd ever seen. Or maybe she only thought it was sexy because she'd so recently been naked with him.

She cleared her throat. "Thank you." She was trying not to concentrate on how great that night had been, or how much more handsome he seemed to her—and she'd already found him handsome before. "I really appreciate this. Here, let me pay you for it." She started to get her purse, but he spoke up to stop her.

"No, don't worry about it. It's only a sandwich. Besides, you paid for the Mexican food we had in LA, remember?"

How could she forget? Every detail of that night seemed to

be indelibly imprinted on her brain. "Because you helped me with the Tommy situation. I owed you dinner."

"You didn't owe me anything. What's happening with Tommy, by the way?" he asked. "Have you heard from him?"

"No. I called yesterday and left a message, but so far...no response."

"Hopefully he'll get back to you soon."

"That would be nice. According to an email from my attorney, Ethan wasn't served yesterday so he will likely be served on Monday. I hope to hear from Tommy before Ethan finds out I'm suing him and starts raising hell. But I'm afraid Tommy doesn't want to get involved, or I would've heard from him by now. To be honest, I wouldn't blame him. This isn't his problem. He had nothing to do with it."

"If Ethan's slinging lies about him, he might care enough to try to clear it up."

"We'll see."

He started to leave but turned back at the last second. "I just want to make sure..." He gave her that sexy grin again while scratching his shoulder. "You're okay with...you know, what happened Thursday night on the beach, aren't you?"

She was surprised he would bring it up. She'd been planning to pretend it never happened, thought that might be the easiest approach for both of them. "Of course."

"Good. I'm glad. I'd hate for that to turn out to be a problem."

"Thanks for caring," she said, and meant it. She doubted many guys would bother to follow up. She and Dallas weren't likely to have much contact once the month was over and they both went back to their regular lives. It wasn't as if he had to worry about how she felt.

He winked before walking out.

She stared after him for several seconds once the door closed, but hunger eventually drove her to take the sandwich he'd bought her into the back. At last, she could eat.

She'd just finished when someone else came in. Quickly wiping her mouth and throwing the napkin and the sandwich wrappings in the trash, she hurried out front. A tall man with bottle green eyes and tattoos covering both arms stood there.

"Susan around?" he asked.

"Not right now."

"I'm Tobias." He held out his hand. "Susan's daughter is married to my brother, Maddox."

"Nice to meet you," she said. "I recognize your name. When she hired me, Susan mentioned she wouldn't have been able to get by without your help."

"You might have noticed her health isn't the best, so I try to pitch in now and then—when I can."

"She appreciates it. She told me you're a good man."

His eyes widened. "Are you sure she was talking about *me*?"

"Is there another Tobias in this small town?"

"Not that I know of," he said, a slight smile curving his lips. "She told me she'd hired someone, but I wasn't sure when you were starting, so I thought I'd stop by and make sure she was okay for today. Saturdays are usually busy, and what with the holidays…"

"It was crazy in here earlier, even with the rain. But she went home to rest. As a matter of fact, since you know her so well, you might drive over and check on—" She fell silent when she heard the back door. "Never mind. That's probably her now."

Sure enough, Susan rushed around the corner without even putting down her purse. "Emery, I'm so sorry! I meant to be back long before now. Normally, I struggle to sleep for any length of time, so I don't know how I conked out for so long. I should've set an alarm."

"It's fine," Emery assured her. "You must've needed the sleep."

"But it's your first day, and you've been on since ten without a break. You must be hungry. I brought you some leftover spaghetti you can heat up in the microwave in back."

"Actually, some of Aiyana's sons stopped by not too long ago and brought me something to eat." She was reluctant to mention that it was Dallas specifically who'd done this. She preferred to act as though she was a friend to the whole family.

Because she was, she reminded herself.

"Oh good." When Susan looked at Tobias, her face brightened immediately. "Tobias!"

"Hello," he said. "I just swung by to see if you were doing okay today. Looks like Emery's helping a great deal."

Susan glanced around the store and seemed satisfied with what she saw. "Yes, she is." She turned to her. "Everything go okay while I was gone?"

"It was busy, but when you own a store, busy is good."

"That's true," she agreed, seemingly relieved that the world hadn't gone to hell simply because she'd overslept.

"Is there anything you need me to do while I'm here?" Tobias asked. "Carry in supplies or change out ice cream tubs or whatever?"

Susan took him in the back and had him refill the flour bins, since he was there, anyway, but he walked out fifteen minutes later. "It seems you two have a strong friendship," Emery said, wondering why Tobias, who wasn't related to Susan, was so diligent about seeing to her needs.

Susan watched through the window as he climbed into his truck and drove away. "Life can be strange," she said simply.

Thinking about Thursday night and how it had changed her the past two days—so much that she couldn't seem to get back to the person she'd been before sleeping with Dallas—Emery absolutely understood.

"Yes, it can be."

"How was your first day?" Aiyana asked as soon as Emery walked through the front door.

Emery stopped short when she saw Aiyana sitting in the living room with Cal, Liam, Bentley and Dallas, all of whom were spread out on the floor, making wedding favors. Emery bit back a smile at the sight of Cal's big, calloused fingers struggling to tie a dainty red-striped ribbon with a thank you card attached to it around a clear glass mug filled with hot chocolate mix, crushed candy cane and mini marshmallows. Emery thought it was a particularly cute favor, given the season, but she had to laugh at Aiyana's "work crew."

"Great. I earned some money, which was all I was hoping for."

Aiyana finished a bow and set the lidded mug aside. "How's Susan? Dallas told me she stranded you at the store for hours, and I know she wouldn't do that if she was well."

"She wasn't feeling too great at first but seemed better after she had a chance to rest."

She pulled a new mug into her lap and wound the ribbon around the neck of it. "Good. Have you eaten dinner? I cooked a roast with some vegetables, if you're hungry."

Emery stole a glance at Dallas, who was sitting with the mugs he'd completed lined up on one side of him and the sea of mugs he had yet to do on the other. "I ate a late lunch," she told Aiyana. Unsure whether she should thank Dallas again for being considerate enough to grab her that sandwich, she decided not to draw attention to his kindness, in case Aiyana read too much into it. That was another consequence of Thursday night, she realized. Now they had something to hide. "I brought home cookies in case everyone would like dessert," she announced.

That was all it took to get Liam and Bentley to abandon their posts. They jumped up, probably as eager to get out of tying bows as they were to get hold of the sack she carried.

"Do you need help with the favors?" Emery offered.

"If you don't have any other plans tonight," Aiyana replied. "As you can see, I have a few recruits, but Liam and Bentley are dying to go AWOL, and we've invited a lot of people to the wedding, so it's no small task."

Knowing how popular and well-known Aiyana was in this area—Cal, too—Emery had no doubt the entire town would turn out. Even more than the locals. A great number of her former students and teachers would come, too.

"It's Saturday night, Ma!" Liam complained. "And Jake is throwing a Christmas party. We don't want to miss it."

"That's important," Cal said. "You should go. After all, this is only our wedding, something that will happen just once in a lifetime."

Emery smiled when he shot her a grin.

"I'm excited about the wedding," Liam said, taking his words at face value instead of the sarcastic way they were intended—probably to reassure Cal, just in case he *was* feeling a bit of disappointment. "But the people who come don't need to take home mugs of hot chocolate mix. They probably have a big can of it from Costco in their pantry like we do."

"We still have to make them," Aiyana insisted.

"Why?" Bentley pressed.

"To thank everyone for coming." She rolled her eyes. "Guys don't get it," she said to Emery. "To them, this is wasted effort."

"Hey, hey," Dallas complained. "Watch yourself. I'm cooperating. I've done more of these things than you have. I must be close to a hundred by now."

It was obvious he'd done far less than that, but Aiyana didn't call him out.

"And I've done at least—" Cal frowned at what he'd accomplished "—ten in the same amount of time."

They all laughed as Emery stepped over some discarded boxes to reach the stairs. "I can help. Just let me go put my purse away and change."

"Now that Emery's available, can *we* can take off?" Liam asked his mother.

"Why not?" Emery heard Aiyana reply in exasperation. "I'm going to have to retie all of yours, anyway."

"What's wrong with mine?" Liam demanded, a scowl in his voice.

"You can't see how sad those bows are?"

Emery chuckled as she scaled the stairs, closed her door and stripped off the sweater and pants she'd worn to work.

Once she had on her sweats, she returned to the living room but only Aiyana, Cal and Dallas were there. "Liam and Bentley left already?"

Aiyana rolled her eyes. "They had one foot out the door when we started."

"At least you still got us," Cal said, trying to be helpful, but his response made Emery laugh again because she couldn't tell whether he'd finished even three more while she was changing.

"I'm picking up speed," Dallas announced.

Emery took Liam's place instead of Bentley's when she sat cross-legged on the floor simply because it was farther from Dallas. "Let me show you how it's done," she joked.

For the next few hours, they tied and loaded mugs into boxes, then moved the boxes into Cal's truck, Dallas's van and Aiyana's trunk.

"Okay. That will have to be enough for one night," Dallas said. "Eli just texted me. My sisters-in-law are making and freezing the potatoes for the wedding, so I promised Eli and Gavin I'd meet them at the Blue Suede Shoe once they got the kids to bed."

"We have almost three hundred," Aiyana said, finishing up her count. "That should be enough."

"Good. I'll see you in the morning." Dallas bent to drop a kiss on his mother's cheek before turning to Emery. "Would you like to come along?"

"I don't think so," she said. "I'll probably just...go to bed."

"Why not get out for a while?" Aiyana asked. "Relax and have some fun with people your own age? It might be a nice break from spending every night in your bedroom."

She'd just been to LA with Dallas, and they'd made love on the beach, so she hadn't been spending *every* night in her room. But she wasn't about to point that out. Aiyana was mostly right—since she'd come to Silver Springs she'd scarcely left the house. "I'm still reluctant to be seen in public," she admitted. She'd managed to get through the day at Sugar Mama without anyone drawing the connection between her and the sex video, but maybe that was because no one had looked at her too closely. They were too busy celebrating the holidays and being dazzled by the cute shop and delicious offerings.

And no one would expect someone involved in such a big scandal to be working in a small-town cookie store.

"Everything went smoothly when we went to Santa Barbara and LA," Dallas pointed out. "And you were in town all day today. Did anyone say anything that upset you?"

"No."

"Then come. You have to start living again at some point."

"You'll be with your brothers," she said. "I don't want to intrude."

"You won't be intruding. We could use another person for darts and pool. If you come, we won't have to recruit anyone else."

She had to hand it to him. He wasn't letting Thursday night stop him from remaining her friend. She wished it wasn't such a big deal in *her* mind. "Okay," she said. "Let me go change again."

CHAPTER THIRTEEN

Dallas could tell Emery was self-conscious about being recognized. Although she was friendly to Gavin and Eli, she was quiet, and he caught her surreptitiously glancing around at the crowd every few minutes.

"You okay?" he murmured to her as he relinquished his cue stick to someone in the party waiting to use the table after they were done.

They'd just finished their third game of pool. Emery was terrible at darts and not much better at billiards. She admitted she hadn't played either game very often, so Dallas hadn't been surprised. She was a career girl. He couldn't see her spending much time hanging out in bars or billiard halls. But she was his partner, which meant Gavin and Eli slaughtered them the first two games. The third game, Dallas managed to play better than he'd ever played in his life—and his brothers probably weren't competing very hard—so he managed to pull out a win. They were going to try beer pong next. But he could tell Emery was slightly reluctant to go over to that corner of the bar, where there were a lot more people.

He was tempted to take her hand, to offer some support and

reassurance. But after Thursday, things were different between them. He was careful not to touch her, and he could tell she was being careful not to touch him. They had to get back to where they'd been before they let their relationship turn physical. Otherwise, he was afraid it would destroy Emery's recovery. He was beginning to understand that it could mess him up, too, although he wasn't entirely sure how or why.

"I'll buy the drinks," Eli announced, and Dallas didn't argue. Eli and Gavin had lost; they were supposed to buy. Dallas had picked up the first round and Emery the second.

"I'll be right back," he told Emery and Gavin and took a bathroom break while Eli went to the bar.

He expected all three of them to be waiting when he returned, but only Eli and Gavin were there, lounging against the wall, talking and drinking a beer. "Where's Emery?" he asked.

Eli angled his head toward the dance floor, and Dallas followed his line of sight to find her in the arms of some big, bulky dude he'd never met before. "Who's *that*?"

"Beats me," Eli replied. "Came up and asked her to dance."

Dallas told himself he didn't mind seeing her with another guy. Why would he? He was *glad* she felt safe enough to get out there. They were only dancing, anyway. It wasn't as though that would make him jealous even if they were a couple.

But when he found his gaze migrating back to the two of them again and again, that tingle of awareness—that sense that she might mean trouble for him in some way—ran through him again. Could it be that Thursday night had meant more to him than it should have?

"How long *is* this song?" he suddenly blurted out.

Gavin and Eli blinked at him. Only then did he realize he'd interrupted a conversation he'd been pretending to listen to.

"Why are you in such a hurry for it to be over?" Gavin asked.

Dallas scowled to cover the gaffe. "I just… I thought we were going over to play beer pong."

His response sounded weak, even to his own ears.

"There's still plenty of time for that," Eli said. "What's the rush?"

"There isn't one," he mumbled. After that he didn't dare show any impatience for fear his brothers might misconstrue his concern.

The song finally ended, but another one started and Emery remained on the dance floor. It was really starting to bug Dallas because the guy she was dancing with kept pulling her up against him, and she'd have to readjust their relative positions, over and over, to get more space. Then he saw her break away as if she'd been patient long enough, and the dude grabbed her arm and whipped her back around to face him as though he wouldn't let her leave.

A murmur rippled through those who'd noticed, and other people began to stare as it became apparent they were having a problem.

Dallas stalked over. "Something wrong?"

The guy's head swung toward him like a bull spotting a red cape. "Nothing that's any of your business," he said with a sneer.

Dallas sized him up in an effort to determine, if this situation escalated, whether he'd be a real threat. Young, maybe twenty-two, he was about six foot four, two hundred and twenty pounds, and he had broad shoulders, massive biceps and beefy hands. He obviously spent lots of time pumping iron, which was probably why he thought he could be an asshole and get away with it.

He was also drunk.

"How do you know whether it's my business or not?" Dallas asked.

"Because I wasn't talking to you—I was talking to *her.*" He still had a hand clamped around Emery's wrist. "And like I was trying to tell her, I didn't mean to make her mad. I thought she was hot in that video. Hot's a compliment, right?"

"That isn't what you said." Emery's face was flushed, her jaw clenched. "At least not all of it."

"You mean the part about your tits?" he said, starting to laugh. "Aw, man, come on! That was a compliment, too."

"Let her go," Dallas said.

"*You* stay out of it!" the guy snapped. "I'm trying to apologize to my famous partner here so we can finish our dance."

Dallas lowered his voice to make it clear he wasn't messing around. *"I said let her go."*

"Dallas, it's okay." Emery glanced worriedly between them. "I don't want to drag you into this. I'll just… I'll finish the dance. He apologized."

"See?" The way the guy jutted out his chin acted as an exclamation point. "There's no reason for you to get involved."

They were making a scene, and Dallas knew she wouldn't want that. But he'd brought her here, and he wasn't about to let anything go wrong after she dared take the risk of coming with him. "You don't have to dance with this drunken prick if you don't want to," he told her, and took her arm to lead her off the floor.

Eli and Gavin were both hurrying over as a large hand gripped Dallas's shoulder. He felt himself being turned, but when the blow came, it mostly missed. He'd been prepared for it, had jerked his head to one side just in time. It was the other guy who was surprised when Dallas used the momentum of his turn to add power to his own punch.

His opponent looked dumbfounded at the immediate and decisive retaliation. Maybe he'd expected Dallas to start by cursing, yelling or lobbing more threats. But Dallas wasn't about that. He was more than happy to enforce what he felt was only right.

The dude didn't crumple to the floor as Dallas halfway expected. He shook his head as though he had to clear the cobwebs out of it. Then he touched his mouth, spotted blood on his fingertips—blood that'd come from his nose, which looked broken—and his eyes narrowed as he came after Dallas again.

"Get her home," Dallas said, shoving a stunned Emery into the safety of Eli's chest.

The guy managed to get both arms around Dallas and pull him down while Dallas was trying to make sure Eli got Emery clear of the action. Then, as Eli guided Emery out of the bar and Gavin held back the guy's friend, who seemed all too eager to jump in, the fight turned into more of a wrestling match than a boxing match. But Dallas was a better wrestler than he was a boxer, anyway. Anyone who had any street fighting experience knew how important it was to be good on the ground, since almost every fight ended up there.

After narrowly escaping being pinned underneath his opponent, Dallas used all his strength and flexibility to break away and tried to jam the guy's arm up behind his back.

The dude managed to get free before Dallas could fully achieve the hold he was striving for, but Dallas maintained his balance and used the leverage of being higher off the ground to get on top, where he pressed his sudden advantage and really let loose.

At one point, the guy succeeded in bucking him off, and they rolled around on the floor. Dallas took a few blows, but there was no pain. The only thing he felt was determination and fury. As they crashed into other people and chairs and tables, someone yelled to call the cops. After that, all sensory input dissolved into a blur. Dallas couldn't see anything except his opponent, and he couldn't hear anything except the blood rushing through his ears—until Gavin and several others pulled him off the stranger.

"Dallas, that's enough," his brother said.

The words came to him as though through a long tunnel. It didn't *feel* like enough. It felt as though Dallas had barely gotten started. Although his opponent's head had struck him in the jaw when they fell, and he could taste blood from a cut lip, he didn't want to stop fighting. It'd been so long since he'd allowed him-self this kind of outlet. Because of Aiyana and her love—and, he hoped, the maturity he'd gained as he grew older—he'd learned to channel his negative emotions into the physical exertion of climbing. But he'd grown up using his fists. Fighting was the most effective release of the anger he carried around inside him, and now he knew that remained true to this day.

It wasn't until the moans he heard registered in his brain that he realized the other guy was still on the floor, curled in on himself, holding his face. Dallas had gotten the best of him. The dude couldn't even get up. But Dallas wasn't overly surprised. It didn't matter that the guy was taller and had at least forty pounds on him. Emery's dance partner had no idea he was dealing with someone who had a lot more experience.

Dallas preferred winning to losing, but he felt no sense of pride or achievement. He was determined this asshole wasn't going to use his size and strength to intimidate Emery, or give her a hard time in any way, but he didn't care about him spe-cifically.

The person he was really fighting was his father.

And that was a fight he could never win.

Emery sat in the living room with what was left of the sup-plies they'd used to make the wedding favors stacked to one side. She was alone, but she wasn't watching TV. She was reluctant to turn it on for fear the noise would awaken Aiyana or the boys. She didn't want them to know about the fight at the bar quite yet; she felt responsible for it and wanted to be sure that Dallas was okay before she had to face his mother.

She was staring at the Christmas tree and its reflection in the window, watching the tiny lights twinkle as they appeared to race around, when she finally heard the door.

Dallas came in the back way, as he had when he'd returned after being out with his brothers the last time.

She stood, listening to his footsteps as they progressed down the hall.

"What are you doing up?" he asked the moment he saw her. "It's really late."

"What do you think?" she asked, slightly put out that he'd let her stew for so long. "I've been worried about you. Why didn't you text me? Let me know you were okay?"

He scratched his head. "Sorry. I've been over at Eli's, getting cleaned up in case my mother was awake. I didn't want the sight of blood to freak her out, especially with her wedding next week. She's been through enough of that sort of thing with me."

He had a Band-Aid on his cheek, but there was no way to hide the fact that his eye was swollen or that there was a cut on his lip. "Meaning you get into fights often?"

"I used to," he said.

She was surprised he could state it so unapologetically. She couldn't imagine someone resorting to violence *habitually*. She'd never known anyone who was prone to getting into fights, which was just another reminder that they came from different worlds.

She was grateful for his help tonight, though. And for everything else he'd done, so she was oddly torn. "You're okay?"

"I'm fine."

She folded her arms across the sweatshirt she'd donned when she got home. "I'm sorry you had to do that. I hate that you got hurt because you were trying to protect me."

"Doesn't make it your fault," he said. "That dude was asking for an ass kicking."

"He was a jerk," she agreed. "I didn't want to dance with him in the first place, but I could tell he recognized me, and I just... I didn't want him to make a big deal out of my being there. I thought if I danced with him, maybe he'd be cool and keep it to himself."

"Considering how it turned out, that's pretty ironic," he said with a mirthless chuckle.

She noticed that his right hand was bandaged. "You didn't break your hand, did you?" she asked, instantly alarmed.

"No. It's just a sprain."

"You've been to a hospital?" He'd come home late, but not late enough for *that*.

He laughed. "No."

"Then how do you know?"

"I've broken it before," he said simply.

Incredulous, she shook her head. "I used to report on revenge porn and bar fights... I wasn't *involved* in that sort of thing."

"You'll get back to what you're used to eventually."

He was obviously spent, and she could understand why, after such a tremendous surge of adrenaline. She was feeling the effects of it, too, although she couldn't imagine it was to the same degree. "Right," she said so that he wouldn't feel the need to continue to encourage her. "I'll let you get to bed."

"Okay. You get some rest, too. And please don't worry about what happened tonight. You did nothing to cause it."

"I *did* cause it, though—just by being at the bar."

"You had as much right to be there as anyone else. *He* was the one who was out of line."

That was true—and yet the fight wouldn't have broken out if not for her. She kept wondering if she should've tolerated the idiot's groping and suggestive language even though she could tell he was leading up to trying to get her to go home with him. "The police didn't come, did they?" she asked as an afterthought. "You're not in any trouble..."

"The police got there before I could leave. But they didn't threaten to arrest me or anything. I didn't start the fight, and there were plenty of witnesses to back that up."

"So he's the one who's in trouble?"

"He could've been. He's lucky it broke out on the dance floor.

Even though we ran into a few tables and chairs, we didn't break anything. So there were no property damages. And I won't be pressing charges. The medical bills and other stuff he'll have to contend with will be punishment enough."

She felt her eyes widen. "Medical bills! What happened to him?"

"He has a broken nose, at least. I'm fairly certain he has a broken jaw, too. Having that wired shut for several weeks won't be fun."

"I'm glad it's him and not you."

"Me, too." He offered her a weary smile as he started past her, and she told herself to let him go, let the evening end right there. But, for some reason, she couldn't stop herself from reaching out to catch his arm as he went by. He was just close enough to touch and she wanted to touch him badly enough that she'd done it almost involuntarily.

He froze, but instead of meeting his gaze, even though she knew he *had* to be looking at her, she watched her own hand slide down the soft, tanned skin of his forearm.

He allowed her to lace her fingers through his. But then he said, "Emery..." and she knew by the tone of his voice that it was a warning.

She kept her gaze on their entwined fingers. "What?"

"I don't have any reserves tonight. If you're not careful, what happened on the beach will happen again."

Finally, she lifted her eyes. "That's just it," she said. "I want it to."

When he was shuffling in the back door, Dallas had been so tired and sore he could barely walk, but as he took Emery's hand and led her down to his room, he experienced a fresh surge of energy.

At first, he was afraid she'd feel the need to do a lot of talking—to try to explain what she was thinking or feeling or determine what he was thinking or feeling so they could, once again, lay down some ground rules to avoid future trouble. She hadn't done that when they'd started this last time; he had. But she'd nearly freaked out in the middle.

Tonight, he wasn't in the mood to contend with any of that. That they wanted each other so badly didn't make a lot of sense—they came from such different backgrounds and were heading down completely different paths—but in his mind it didn't have to make sense. He was fine with the inexplicable, with random attraction, with living in the moment. But as good as Thursday had been, tonight he craved total silence. He didn't want to hear anything *or* see anything. He wanted to connect with her through touch alone, to feel her bare body against his and savor the exquisite sensation he knew that would create for as long as he could stop himself from taking it further.

Fortunately, she seemed to understand his need for silence, because after all the excuses they'd allowed themselves before, this was exactly the opposite experience. They were going to take what they wanted, but he got the feeling they weren't going to acknowledge that they were once again crossing a line they shouldn't cross.

He didn't switch on the light. He just closed the door behind them and turned to face her in the dark, his hands resting loosely around her waist. It was somehow more erotic that he couldn't see even the outline of her—and that they had no business doing what they were doing.

Maybe it was the allure of the forbidden that was getting the best of them...

She didn't move, didn't touch him or try to kiss him. She just stood there, only an inch from him. It was almost as if they were held in place by magnetism alone. He knew it would require significant energy to pull away.

He could feel her soft breath on his face as he rested his forehead against hers. He could also feel his heart beating against his chest, and wondered if hers was thumping just as hard.

"Your room smells like you," she whispered when he didn't make a move.

"Is that good or bad?" He'd never noticed, never even considered it.

"It's good. I like the way you smell."

"I like the way you *feel*," he said.

Rising up on tiptoe, she kissed him so gently he could tell she was afraid she'd hurt his busted lip.

"I'm fine," he insisted. "You don't have to be careful."

Still, her tongue ran over the cut as though she was making a physical apology before lightly meeting his tongue, at which point every muscle in his body went rigid.

It's just a kiss, he told himself, and yet it had such a powerful effect on him it nearly turned his knees to jelly.

He lifted the bottom of her sweatshirt, and she raised her arms so that he could pull it over her head. He tossed it on the floor as she removed his shirt, drawing out the anticipation as she took her time going from one button to the next. When they'd been in the living room, he hadn't been able to tell whether she was wearing a bra—it hadn't been obvious either way thanks to the thick material of her sweatshirt—but he'd guessed she wasn't and he'd been right.

As he ran his fingers down the smooth skin on either side of her spine, she leaned forward just enough that her nipples grazed his bare chest. "That has to be one of the best things I've ever felt," he said and, reaching up to cup her breast, lowered his head to take her nipple in his mouth.

The moment he heard her sigh, he knew he wouldn't be able to continue the slow pace they'd set for much longer. Slipping his good hand inside her yoga pants, he said, "Take these off."

After she complied, he lifted her onto his bed and spread her knees apart as he climbed on with her. She reached for his zipper, but he gently knocked her hands to the side so that he could kiss his way up her thigh.

She was quivering as he neared his target, but then her legs suddenly snapped together as though she'd deny him access. "I feel too vulnerable for that," she said with a nervous laugh.

"Vulnerable? Or self-conscious? Because there's no reason to be self-conscious with me. But if you really don't want me to—"

"It's not that I don't want you to..."

"Then let me," he whispered. And not only did she allow him to open her legs, her hands fisted in his hair, her back arched and he heard her groan in spite of how quiet they were trying to be when he touched her with his tongue.

CHAPTER FOURTEEN

Sunday, December 13

When Emery woke up, she felt surprisingly good, and she knew why. She hadn't gotten a lot of sleep—it'd been four o'clock before she'd returned to her room—but the night had ended on a much more positive note than it had begun. Just remembering her time in Dallas's bed made her smile.

He was an incredible lover.

"I must be crazy," she whispered to her reflection as she sat up and stared at herself in the mirror over the dresser. What was she doing staying here, working in a cookie store and having sex with Aiyana's son? She'd never imagined she wouldn't be in LA, delivering the news. But, thanks to Ethan, her life had taken a ninety-degree turn.

Part of her thought she should leave Silver Springs right away, put a stop to the madness and quit being a burden on Aiyana and Dallas. But Aiyana had made it clear she was welcome, and Dallas insisted he wanted her to stay, too, at least through the holidays, at which point they'd both have to get back to their regular lives. Sure, she'd been recognized at the Blue Suede

Shoe and in such a sensational way that word of her presence was
bound to spread and spread quickly. But she'd expected the locals to become aware of the fact that she was in town eventually.

So how would that change things?

She'd face some judgment, criticism and curiosity while working at the cookie store. But at least she had a job here, was making some money, and she had a safe place to come home to at
night. What would she do in LA? Sit around and feel sorry for
herself? Obsess over Ethan being able to retain his job despite
what he'd done to her?

A loud clang and some other noises, coming from below,
trickled up to her. Someone was in the kitchen.

It had to be Aiyana. Emery had been staying in the house
long enough to know the younger boys would sleep in as late
as Aiyana allowed them to. And Dallas deserved to sleep, after
getting banged up in that fight.

Determined to help with the wedding before she had to go
to work, Emery kicked off the covers and climbed out of bed.
She had to shower before heading to the store, but she didn't
want to do that now in case Aiyana needed her to do something strenuous.

After she brushed her teeth, she pulled her hair into a pony-
tail, donned some sweats and hurried down to see what might
be on the agenda.

"You're up early," Aiyana commented when Emery joined
her in the kitchen.

"I have to be at work at one but I was hoping there was something I could do this morning to help you get ready for the
wedding. It's the last weekend before the big event. You must
be overwhelmed."

"Oh, I'm not taking the wedding too seriously," she said as
she rinsed the beaters of the electric mixer. "I'd like it to be a
nice event, of course, but I'm too old to obsess about the details. Cal loves me, and I love him. That's what's important. If

I forget something or the food or music doesn't turn out exactly so, hopefully our guests will understand." She gestured at a bowl filled with batter. "You ready for breakfast? I'm making buttermilk pancakes."

After becoming an adult and working hard to take care of herself, it felt wonderful to be able to stay with someone like Aiyana, who was so nurturing. It wasn't as if her own mother could offer her a soft place to land during this difficult time. "Looks delicious. Thanks. Would you like me to set the table or do something else to help with the meal?"

"If you could get them on the griddle for me, that'd be great. I'll go roust out the boys. It's harder to get them up than you might expect."

Emery buttered the griddle Aiyana had already plugged in and chuckled as she listened to the ruckus going on upstairs.

"Right *now*," she heard Aiyana say. Then either Liam or Bentley responded, with a big measure of complaint, "It's Sunday! Why do we have to get up so early?" And she said, "Because we have work to do."

Emery was being so careful to pour the batter such that the pancakes wouldn't fuse together that she didn't hear Dallas enter the room behind her.

"Morning," he said.

She whirled around, holding the spatula she planned to use to turn the pancakes. "Oh! You startled me. Good morning."

Her pulse picked up, but she knew it wasn't from being surprised. Just having him so close did that. As much as her mind insisted on continuing to call him a friend, her body had no hesitancy claiming him as a lover.

He was wearing a pair of jeans that fit so well she couldn't help noticing, and a plain gray sweatshirt. "Sleep good?" he asked as he went over to pour himself some coffee.

The air felt pregnant with all the things they were attempting to ignore. Last night had been... Memorable. That was probably the best way she could describe it. They were good together in that way. There was a palpable energy sparking between them even now, but she wasn't about to address what'd happened. She was going to pick up and move on, exactly as she had after Thursday. "I did. You?"

He didn't answer, but he smiled as he sat down with his cup, and Emery used the few seconds she had before Aiyana returned to take stock of the injuries to his face now that it was easier to see the bruising. "You look better than I thought you would."

He took a sip of his coffee, drinking it black. "That fight last night was nothing."

"Your mother won't think it was nothing when she sees your face." Emery bit her bottom lip as she considered how Aiyana might feel at learning her son had been hurt trying to protect her. She didn't want Aiyana to regret being kind enough to take her in. "What are you going to tell her?"

"That some jackass at the bar picked a fight with me."

She felt a wave of relief. "You won't mention me?"

"I don't see why I'd need to."

Their eyes met and held for several seconds, and she knew that, like her, he was probably remembering their time in his bed, especially when his eyes ran over her before returning to his coffee. "I appreciate that," she said.

"Dallas!" Aiyana yelled as she crossed the living room on her way to the stairs that led to his room.

He cleared his throat and looked toward the door. "Right here."

"Oh. Good. You're up," his mother said, even though she hadn't quite reached the kitchen. "Are you hungry?"

"Do you have to ask?" he replied. "I'm always hungry."

She stopped as soon as she crossed the threshold and saw his face. *"What happened?"*

"I got into a little scuffle last night. That's all."

"That's *all*? You're going to look like you've been mugged in my wedding photos!"

Emery winced and opened her mouth to explain what really happened. After what Dallas had done for her, she couldn't let him bear the brunt of his mother's displeasure. But Dallas shot her a quelling glance. "If you think I look bad, you should see the other guy," he joked.

Frowning, Aiyana lowered her voice. "You know better than this…"

He arched his eyebrows. "This one couldn't be helped," he said, suddenly serious and surprisingly firm.

The edge to his voice indicated he wouldn't be questioned, and Aiyana backed off. "Okay. You're an adult now. I'll stay out of it. Just tell me this—is the other guy okay? He isn't in the hospital, is he?"

"He might be," Dallas allowed.

Emery was shocked by his honesty, but continued to turn pancakes on the griddle as she heard Aiyana say, "Oh, Dallas."

Emery couldn't withstand the disappointment in her voice, couldn't let him take the blame. He didn't really deserve it. "It was my fault," she admitted. "Some guy was bothering me, and when Dallas tried to get him to stop, he started a fight."

Aiyana's expression immediately relaxed. "Oh, that's different," she said, putting a reassuring hand on Emery's arm. "Don't worry. I just panicked for a second. If there's a fight around, somehow my son always finds it."

"That's not true," Dallas argued. "At least not anymore. It's been years since I've been in a fight."

Her face took on a sardonic expression. "I guess I'm still traumatized."

Liam and Bentley came thundering down the stairs at once, shoving each other as they entered the kitchen, each fighting to be first.

"Hey," Dallas barked when they bumped the table, causing his coffee to slosh over the side of his cup.

"Sorry, bro." Liam pushed Bentley off him since Bentley had landed in his lap. Then he leaned forward to get a better look at Dallas's face. "Whoa, what happened to you?"

"Ran into a door," Dallas said flippantly.

"No, you didn't," Bentley said as though he wasn't that gullible and slid into his own seat. "You were in a fight, weren't you?"

Dallas took another sip of his coffee. "Not a big one."

"What happened?" Liam asked.

"Doesn't matter now," Dallas replied.

"Really? That's it?" Bentley was obviously disappointed. "That's all you're going to say?"

"Yes, it is," Aiyana broke in. "Let's leave it there for now."

Bentley shot her a disgruntled glance. "Fine, what do we have to do today?" he asked as he helped himself to the pitcher of orange juice already on the table.

"Cal needs you to help clean things up at the ranch." Aiyana got some plates from the cupboard. "We only have one more week until the wedding."

"What will we be cleaning?" Liam asked.

"The grounds. Mowing, weed-eating, trimming. That sort of thing."

"I sure hope I don't have to muck out the barn again," Bentley grumbled.

"When we finish, can we go bouldering with Dallas?" Liam asked. "He said he'd take us while he's home."

"Not today," Aiyana said. "By the time we finish at the ranch, it'll be dark."

Emery got the impression she wasn't eager for Dallas to encourage his younger brothers' interest in the sport he loved, and she could understand why.

"But next week's the wedding. We can't go then, either," Liam complained.

"We'll have our chance," Dallas told him. "Mom and Cal are heading to the coast for a few days after the ceremony. We'll clean up on Sunday, so she doesn't have to face that when she gets back, and climb on Monday. You'll be off school that week for the holidays, so we'll have plenty of time."

"*Okay*," Liam said, putting a heavy emphasis on the second syllable to show his displeasure with having to wait.

"When I get married I'm going to elope," Bentley announced.

Aiyana set silverware in front of each of them. "Why's that?"

"You've been planning and working on this wedding for months and months—and yet it'll be over in a matter of hours. Seems like a waste of time and money to me."

"Weddings aren't meant to be practical," Dallas reminded him.

Aiyana came up behind Bentley and dropped a kiss on his cheek. "We'll see how fast that changes once you're in love and your bride wants all of her friends and family see her promise you forever."

A grudging smile tugged at his lips as if to say he already knew she was right, and they all laughed.

"Shh, I hear something," Liam said, lifting one hand.

When everyone quit talking, Emery could hear what he did—the jingle of her phone. "Oh, that's me," she said, and handed Aiyana the spatula as she hurried up the stairs.

The call had transferred to voice mail by the time she reached her room, but she recognized the number. She'd called and sent several text messages to it since Dallas had gotten it from Ethan.

"No, no! Don't go anywhere—I'm right here!" she mumbled, afraid she'd missed her one chance to speak to Tommy, and that, for some reason, he wouldn't pick up when she called back.

"Hello?"

The second she heard his voice, she breathed a huge sigh of relief and closed her door. "Tommy, it's Emery."

"I know," he said. "You've been blowing up my phone for two days."

So why had he waited so long to call her back? "Sorry about that, but I'm in a terrible mess."

"I've seen the video," he said simply.

She cringed. She felt so violated. "Ethan is claiming you posted it."

"That's what you said in your messages. But where would I get something like that?"

"The story he gave me—as well as upper management at the studio to save his job—goes something like this. You have a thing for him, so you were jealous of me. You must've been spying on us while we were making love, secretly recorded us and posted that video online so I'd blame him and refuse to get back together."

"That's ridiculous! I'll be honest with you. I *do* have a thing for Ethan. I always have. Besides being straight, he's vain, shallow and selfish. But, God help me, there's something about him. That's why it was hard for me to make this call. I knew it would mean siding with you against him, and I preferred to stay out of it."

"Even to proclaim your innocence?"

"I had nothing to do with that video. I didn't make it, and I certainly didn't load it onto the internet."

"I believe you. There's no doubt in my mind Ethan posted it to get back at me for breaking up with him. He's using you as a scapegoat. But we can't let him get away with what he's done. It's unfair to both of us."

"What do you think *I* can do?"

"Help me."

"How?"

"Did you ever see any recording equipment in the house? Run

across a hidden camera? Remember Ethan talking about filming his sexual exploits? Anything along those lines that might help place the blame where it rightly belongs?"

"I never saw any recording equipment. But that doesn't mean anything. These days all you need is a cell phone. He could've put his phone in a stand on the dresser, had it recording the whole time, and it's entirely possible you didn't notice. Even if you saw it, you'd probably assume he was charging it."

Sadly, that was true. She'd been far too trusting. "You don't remember picking up on anything about him making his own pornography? Never heard him mention recording himself with me or anyone else?"

"No. I once told him about a friend of mine who used a similar recording to blackmail a partner into returning some paintings, which he'd stolen when he moved out, but that's all."

Emery sank onto the bed. She'd been so convinced Tommy would be able to provide some information that would help her case. But saying he had a friend who'd once threatened cyber-exploitation wasn't going to do anything. "You're sure? That's it?"

"That's it."

Letting her head fall into her hand, Emery massaged her temples. "Okay. Thanks," she said in resignation, and was about to hang up when she thought of another question. "Wait! Tommy?"

"Yes?"

"Why'd you move out?"

He hesitated, which seemed odd. Most people could readily name a reason for moving. "Thiago and I decided to live together."

But why now? He'd been with Thiago for six months. And since they'd recently gone through a rough patch, Emery was under the impression their relationship wasn't as solid as it had been before. "Why? What changed?"

After another pause, he said, "Nothing, really. We've wanted to move in together for a long time. That's all."

She'd guessed that might be the case. But his response still begged one question. "Ethan wasn't mad that you didn't give him thirty days' notice so he'd have time to get someone else in there?" She knew how strapped Ethan was financially, what with the new car payment, the amount of credit card debt he carried, and the way he liked to buy clothes, shoes and watches. He wouldn't be happy to pay twice as much rent, especially when he wasn't expecting the added expense.

"Sorry, I just arrived at work and the restaurant's busy," Tommy said. "I'd better go."

She hadn't realized he was driving while talking to her. "No problem. I don't want to hold you up. Thanks for calling me back."

"You bet. Good luck with everything," he said and then he was gone.

With a sigh, she put her phone back on the nightstand and started to go down to finish her breakfast and clean the kitchen. But the more she thought about her conversation with Tommy, the more it troubled her.

He never did answer her about moving out so suddenly and leaving Ethan without a renter. Had he been evading her question?

She told herself no. She could easily imagine him arriving at work and being distracted.

But there was something else.

She came to an abrupt halt before entering the kitchen, where she could still hear everyone else finishing up breakfast, then pivoted and went back up to her phone. Tommy worked as a waiter for an upscale seafood restaurant in Malibu that served an elegant brunch on Sundays. She'd been there; Ethan had taken her several months ago. They'd asked for Tommy so they could sit in his section. But they'd been told Tommy never worked on Sundays—something Ethan, who was oblivious to almost anyone but himself, hadn't been aware of even after living with Tommy.

Today was Sunday. And yet Tommy had said he was at work. Had his schedule changed?

She assumed it had, but she looked up The Lobster House, anyway, found the website and called the number listed. "Has Tommy come in yet?" she asked the woman who answered.

"Tommy doesn't work on Sundays," she was told.

"He must be subbing for someone," she said. "Can you check the restaurant, please?"

"I'm positive he's not here. Everyone has shown up for their shift. But…one sec."

Butterflies rioted in Emery's stomach as she listened to the classical music coming through the phone. Fortunately, she didn't have to wait long. "Nope. Tommy's not here," the girl said when she came back on the line.

"Thank you." Emery hit the End button and stared at the phone in her hand for several seconds afterward, Tommy's words circling around and around in her mind: *I just arrived at work and the restaurant's busy.*

Why did he lie to her?

CHAPTER FIFTEEN

Susan was waiting for her when Emery walked into Sugar Mama—but not in the way Emery had expected. She'd assumed her employer would be looking forward to having her arrive so that she could leave the store and grab some lunch or, possibly, take another nap. But Emery could tell Susan had been waiting for other reasons.

"There you are," she said, even though Emery wasn't so much as a minute late.

"Is something wrong?" she asked.

"No. I just… I heard about what happened at the Blue Suede Shoe last night, and—"

"Word is spreading that fast?" Emery had expected gossip, but it hadn't even been twenty-four hours!

"A friend of mine was at the bar when the fight broke out."

Of course. That was how it worked in a small town. It wasn't that everyone knew everyone else; it was that everyone knew someone who knew someone and so on. "I'm sorry that it happened, but it wasn't my fault. It wasn't Dallas's, either. The guy I was dancing with was drunk, and he was saying some very inappropriate things to me."

"Because of that sex video that was posted online right after Thanksgiving."

Emery's heart sank. The fight had brought the scandal to Susan's attention. Was she about to be fired from another job? "Yes. But that wasn't my fault, either. My ex-boyfriend posted that video to embarrass and humiliate me."

Susan's lip curled in disgust. "What a terrible betrayal of your trust."

Emery blinked in surprise. "What?"

"I spoke with Aiyana about it this morning. I can't believe you were fired from your job—a job you loved—and yet he's still working at the station."

"It's enraging," Emery admitted, but she still wasn't sure she was safe. Susan didn't strike her as a particularly broad-minded person.

"It's too bad he did what he did, especially right before the holidays," she said. "What a way to ruin Christmas. But I'm glad you had the courage to apply here, even though it puts you in contact with the public. That couldn't have been easy."

Emery's mouth fell open before she had the presence of mind to close it. "You don't think I'm a terrible person? You're not afraid there will be people who'll criticize you for hiring me?" She didn't dare add that some of those people might go so far as to quit patronizing the shop.

"No. If I've learned anything after what I've been through in my life, it's that it's not up to me to judge." She smiled. "If anyone gives you any trouble while you're here at work, be sure to let me know and I'll take care of it."

Although she didn't plan on involving Susan, she was grateful for the offer. "Thank you."

"You're welcome. Now I'm going to bake a fresh batch of chocolate chunk cookies—we're running low—while you watch the front, okay?"

"Okay," she said, but before Susan could disappear into the back, Emery called her name.

Her employer turned.

"Thank you. I can't tell you how much…how much your support helps right now."

She nodded. "No problem. Next time you see Tobias, tell him he *has* taught me something," she added with a wry grin.

"I'm not sure what that means," Emery admitted.

"It means everyone makes mistakes."

That didn't explain what had gone on between her and Tobias, but when Susan went to do her baking, Emery knew it was all she planned to say on the matter.

"You're in a good mood."

Aiyana focused on Cal, who was dusting off his hands after rearranging lawn furniture. "I am?"

"You were smiling a second ago, while staring off into space," he said.

"Oh." She laughed as she watched Dallas, Bentley and Liam set up an outdoor bar under the shelter of an open-air barn. "I was thinking about this morning."

Cal, his silver hair combed off a face weathered from the many years he'd worked outside, squinted at her. "Something happen that I'm not aware of?"

Once again, she recalled the many covert glances she'd noticed between Dallas and Emery this morning at breakfast, the way Dallas seemed to mark wherever Emery was at in a room and how quickly he'd come to her defense at the bar last night. He liked her; Aiyana could tell. "It's Dallas."

"What about him? Don't tell me you've finally convinced him to give up climbing without safety gear."

"Sadly, no. He's as stubborn as they come. As stubborn as *you* are," she joked. "But I'm hoping he'll take more care if he finds someone he loves so much he can't bear the thought of not being with her."

"Like I have?"

She cupped his cheek. "Yes."

A twinkle entered his blue eyes. "Who might that be?"

Emery had been there earlier, helping right along with the boys, until she'd had to leave for work. "My houseguest, of course."

"I thought that might be the case. Anytime she started to lift something, if it was heavy, he hurried over to do it for her."

"He's definitely watching out for her," Aiyana agreed.

Cal folded his arms across his button-down work shirt and plaid wool overshirt. "I can see why he might like Emery. She's smart, she's nice and she's beautiful. Not quite as smart or nice or beautiful as you, but...close," he added with a wink.

She took the gnarled hand she'd come to know so well and studied the veins tunneling under the sun-spotted skin, the thick calluses on his palms, the heavy silver and turquoise ring he always wore because she'd given it to him. "You've loved me since the moment you met me," she said, remembering the day twenty-five years ago that he came to her aid in a city council meeting and, as one of the largest landowners in the area, helped advocate for her to be able to start New Horizons. "Haven't you?"

"I have," he confirmed without hesitation. "And I will love you till the day I die. There's never been anyone else for me."

Never in her life had she expected such devotion, never had she dared rely on it. She was embracing his love now, and part of her was far happier for doing it. But there was still another part that was frightened and waiting for it all to go bad. "I'm a lucky woman."

"I hope I make you feel that way."

"I can't believe we've been together for so many years."

"This has been a long time coming," he said, obviously referring to their marriage.

She pursed her lips. "I don't see any need for a ceremony, not at our age. A piece of paper doesn't change anything between us."

"It's important to me."

"Which is why I finally agreed, but I'm yours regardless."

He took off his cowboy hat—used to shade his face, not to make a fashion statement—and wiped his brow. "So you think Emery might lasso Dallas?"

She smiled at his terminology. She was marrying an old cowboy and not only the hat proved it. "I'm hoping she will—or someone else who's deserving. All I want is for him to be happy."

"Eli and Gavin got lucky. He could, too."

"Not everyone has what we have. Look at Seth." Her fourth-oldest son had lost his wife of only a few weeks to an infection from a cat scratch, of all things, and she feared he might never get over it.

"You never know what might happen as the years go by. It took us a while."

She looked around at all they'd done to prepare for the big event. "Yes it did." Her phone went off and she glanced down.

It was Eli. Planning to call him back later, she silenced the ringer. She wanted to finish their work first.

But then she received a text from him that read:

Call me ASAP.

"Mom? Cal? Where should we put this?" Dallas called out, lifting the handle of an old, rusty plow. "I'm guessing you don't want it around the wedding party. Someone could fall and get hurt on it, especially a child."

"You're right," Cal said, and since Bentley and Liam already had their hands full planting poinsettias all along the edge of the barn, he walked over to help Dallas drag the old plow to a safer part of the ranch.

Aiyana, meanwhile, couldn't budge. She felt as though her feet were encased in concrete as she stared down at the words on her screen.

ASAP. Eli wasn't easily excitable, so she couldn't help the terror that rose up inside her.

Before she could call him, however, he called back.

"Hello?" she said, answering immediately this time.

"Where are you?" he asked.

"Still at Cal's with some of your brothers, getting ready for the wedding. Why?"

He didn't offer to come over and help. She'd already told him she preferred he spend the weekend with his wife and kids. He put in long hours at the school—they both did—and she had enough help on hand with his single brothers. She'd told Gavin the same thing when he said he'd come. "Are you sitting down?" he asked.

Her eyes sought the people she loved. The ones who were with her were fine. She could see that. But she couldn't be sure about Ryan and Taylor, the two boys she'd adopted who were the same age. Or Seth, in San Francisco. The three of them wouldn't be home until Friday. "How bad is it?" she asked. "Has anyone been hurt?"

"No, it's not that."

She closed her eyes as she drew in a deep breath. She'd never forget the call she'd received when Seth's wife died. "Then it can't be *that* bad."

"It's not good."

Her chest tightened. "Tell me."

"Someone, an older man, just came by the school, looking for you. I ran into him after taking Cora and the kids to see Santa."

"Who was it?"

"Said his name was Robert Ogilvie."

Aiyana covered her mouth. "That can't be right."

"That's what he said."

She dropped her hand so that she wouldn't have to raise her voice. She didn't want anyone else to hear her. "Robert Ogilvie is in prison."

"Not anymore," he said.

Emery told herself she shouldn't—obviously, Tommy wasn't willing to be helpful—but thirty minutes before closing, she couldn't stop herself from texting him again.

Sure you were at work. Why'd you lie to me? What have I ever done to you?

She doubted he'd respond. She'd had trouble getting him to answer her before. But she wanted him to know that she was aware of his dishonesty.

She waited fifteen minutes, but when he didn't reply, just as she'd suspected he wouldn't, she added:

At least I'm learning who I can trust. Maybe it really was you who filmed and posted that video.

A customer walked in. It wasn't until she'd made the man's ice cream sandwich and he was gone, and she'd said goodbye to Susan, who was staying behind to clean and lock up, that she was able to check her phone again.

Surprisingly, Tommy had answered.

I had nothing to do with it.

So why won't you help me? You're that in love with a total narcissist—a narcissist who will never return your feelings.

His response came as she was getting into her car:

What's done is done. There's nothing I can do to fix it. Why should I ruin my relationship with Ethan? He just loaned me $300 so Thiago could pay his electric bill. Ethan might be an asshole, but he can be a nice asshole—sometimes.

After she started her car, she called Tommy via Bluetooth so she could drive.

"If he's being nice to you, it's for a reason," she said as soon as he picked up. "You realize he *wanted* you to move out, or he'd be furious that you did. He needs help with the rent."

"Why would he *want* me to move out?" he asked skeptically. "We were getting along fine."

"Think about it. What he did to me is a crime. He has to cover for it—and his story is far more believable if you're not still there, living with him."

No response.

"Tommy?" She heard him sigh. "Do you think he gave you that money because he cares whether you keep the lights on?"

"When you put it that way..."

"He only cares about himself, and you know it."

"Maybe so. But like I said, what's done is done. There's nothing we can do about it now. The video is already out there."

"There *is* something we can do."

"What's that?" He sounded suspicious.

"I'm suing him, and you could help me."

"Whoa! You're kidding."

"I'm not. He'll be served tomorrow."

"Are you sure you want to do that?"

"Why wouldn't I?"

"Because he'll win. He never plays fair. He's so used to getting what he wants he cheats if he has to."

"That's the kind of thing I need you to tell my attorney! How he throws a tantrum like a child anytime he gets upset. How he tries to get revenge. That's all important in establishing who he is and why he might've done what he did."

"Shit. I'm going to have to get involved—right after he loaned me money," he said as though realizing he couldn't avoid it.

"Again, he didn't do that for you."

There was a long silence.

"Will you at least talk to my attorney? I'm only asking you to be honest about who Ethan is, what he's like and what you might have heard about me or that video or both."

More silence.

"Tommy?"

"Okay," he said in resignation. "I don't know that I can really help. I hate ruining my relationship with Ethan for nothing. He'll never forgive me, and you know that. But what the hell. I don't live with him anymore. I guess it doesn't really matter."

She breathed a sigh of relief. Tommy had always been a little starstruck. He loved being personally acquainted with a local celebrity. But Ethan wasn't a true friend to either one of them. And it wasn't fair for him to get away with destroying her life. Everyone who could needed to stand up and stop him. Otherwise, he could go on to victimize someone else. "Thank you."

"Are you going to be able to get back on at the station?" he asked.

"If I win the suit, they might *have* to offer me my job back."

"You're suing them, too?"

"I am."

"Damn. You are the wrong person to piss off."

"I'm only demanding what's right."

"But would you want to go back to the station even if they made you an offer?"

"I doubt it. I'll probably try to continue my career somewhere else. I might even move to New York."

"What are you doing now?"

"I work at a cookie store in Silver Springs, where I grew up. But only until after the holidays. Then I'll have no income whatsoever."

"That sucks."

"It's frightening, and it's all Ethan's fault."

"I'll do what I can."

He sounded more committed, but she still worried he'd change his mind. "Okay. I'll have my attorney call you tomorrow."

"Good luck getting through the holidays."

She remembered how upset and depressed she'd been when she first arrived at Aiyana's. She could barely get out of bed, barely leave her room, and here she was working. Apparently, Dallas had made a big difference; nothing else had changed. She enjoyed his friendship and support—among other things.

It was those other things that worried her. She couldn't make another mistake. Not at this juncture. She was already trying to rebuild her life.

CHAPTER SIXTEEN

Aiyana had to tell him, didn't she? She couldn't risk having Dallas be blindsided. A man who could murder his whole family wouldn't be likely to care about how it might affect his one remaining child to be confronted by him. If Robert Ogilvie possessed a sensitivity gene, he wouldn't have been able to do what he did in the first place.

That meant he'd most likely come to Silver Springs for selfish reasons. He'd been in prison for twenty-three years. The entire world had changed since he'd been locked up. Aiyana could see where he might be lost and bewildered and looking for some way to establish a life on the outside, but with so much time gone by, there probably wasn't a soul left who could or would help him. The only thing he had on the outside was a son.

What if he wouldn't be willing to leave until he located Dallas and saw for himself that his son wasn't going to forgive him and allow him back into his life?

She watched Dallas joke around with his brothers, pinning them to the ground when they tried to challenge him, as they put away the mower and other tools. As the older brother, he was obliged to put down the younger upstarts, who loved wrestling with him. He was happier than she'd ever seen him, and yet she knew he still battled the demons that had plagued him since his mother's and sister's murders. She wasn't sure he'd ever find the peace she wished he could have. He felt too responsible for Jenny's death, wouldn't allow it.

How would this latest development affect him?

She wanted to kick herself for ever responding to Robert. Now she saw his attempt to reach out in a completely different light. He'd sent those letters—the one to her and then to Dallas—just before being released, intending to establish contact, so he could examine the possibility of building a relationship with Dallas. Having someone to help him would make everything easier.

But was Robert really clueless enough to think what he'd done could ever be forgotten? That Dallas wouldn't feel more loyalty to Jenny, if not his mother?

"You okay?" Cal came up to her while wiping his face with a handkerchief. He still worked as hard as a much younger man. She loved how strong and driven and eminently good he was. "You were so happy a few minutes ago."

"And now I'm worried," she admitted.

"The wedding will come off without a hitch. We're almost ready. What's left to do?"

"I'm not worried about the wedding." She checked to be sure Dallas, Liam and Bentley couldn't hear her. "Robert Ogilvie is out of prison."

Concern entered his expression. "Dallas's father? Already?"

"*Already?*" she echoed. "It's been nearly a quarter of a century."

"But he was sentenced to forty years. And it's my opinion that he should never get out. He murdered his wife and daughter!"

"True, but he cooperated with the police, confessed and showed remorse—once he was caught. That, along with good behavior, must've shortened his sentence. His age probably factored into it, too. I bet the parole board no longer saw him as much of a threat."

"Hey, he's only in his sixties."

Cal was sixty-one, eight years older than she was, but she was too caught up in this latest development to laugh at his wounded pride. "Statistically speaking, men your age don't commit murder."

"Well, he'd better keep his distance from you and Dallas, or I might prove to be an outlier."

She knew he was only joking, but she also knew he'd do anything to protect her, if necessary. "He's here, in Silver Springs, Cal."

He lowered his voice. "How do you know?"

"Eli called. Robert was over at the school, looking for me and asking about Dallas."

"You don't think he means to harm Dallas in any way…"

"No. But just reentering his life could push Dallas into a very dark place."

"What should we do?"

"We have to prepare him, let him know that his father is no longer behind bars. What other choice do we have?"

Cal rubbed the salt-and-pepper beard growth on his chin. "Dallas is a man now, Aiyana."

"What does that mean?"

"We can no longer protect him. As difficult as it might be, he has to be the one to deal with this. Once he learns Robert is in town, he might head back to Vegas, which would mean he'd miss the wedding, but—"

"That's how you think he'll react?"

"I do. I think that's what all those hours of climbing are about—they're his escape. But, considering the circumstances, you wouldn't hold it against him if he missed the wedding, would you?"

She'd been looking forward to having all of her children

home, was planning to have a family photograph taken. But she would never ask Dallas to stay if he would be happier elsewhere. "Of course not."

"Just be sure to let him know that, so he feels he can leave if he needs to."

"Actually…"

"Uh-oh, I know that look," he said. "What are you thinking now?"

"Before I tell Dallas that Robert's in town, why don't I try talking to Robert? Maybe he's not as bad as his past would indicate. It could be that he's sincere in his remorse. He stated as much in his letter. And if that's the case, I might be able to convince him to leave without contacting Dallas. If I have to, I might even offer him some money to leave us alone. Then we can enjoy the wedding and Christmas as a family before we have to break the bad news."

"If you could work that out, it'd be better than blowing up everything and having to deal with all that emotionality and upset right now, when we have so much going on," he agreed.

"Yeah. Why let Robert ruin Christmas and the first family get-together we've had in recent years? The boys come back whenever they can, but it seems as though we're always missing someone. Because of the wedding, this will be the first time in a long while that they'll be here all at once."

She expected Cal to chime in again, as supportive of this idea as she was beginning to feel, but he didn't do so quite as readily as she would've liked. "What?" she said, looking for reassurance.

He put an arm around her. "It's a bit of a risk, but I suppose you can determine how receptive Robert is once you've talked to him."

She nodded, somewhat relieved just to have worked out a course of action. Even if Robert was every bit as bad as history would indicate, and she had to rely on bribery alone to get him to leave, she was willing to give him a significant sum, if only he wouldn't ruin the next two weeks. "Can you keep the boys busy here while I go talk to him?"

"They won't be happy when I mention more work—they think they're done—but I can come up with something. How will you find Robert?"

"He told Eli where he's staying."

"You're not going to his motel! We're talking about a known murderer, Aiyana. I don't want you over there, not unless I'm with you."

"I'll be fine. You stay here and keep the boys with you. I'll call the motel and have Robert meet me somewhere else."

"Demand that it be a public place."

She didn't want to meet him at his motel, but she didn't want anyone to see her talking to him, either. "He has no reason to kill me."

"I don't care," Cal said. "He's fresh out of prison. I'm not willing to take the chance."

She decided to have Robert meet her under the pavilion at the park. It was a public place, so she wouldn't be ignoring Cal's wishes, and yet there weren't a lot of people who frequented the park during the rainy season.

It would be public but private. "Okay," she said as she rose up on tiptoe to kiss him.

No one was around when Emery got home. In the winter, the store closed early on Sundays, even through the holidays, so it was only six-thirty. She figured Dallas, Aiyana and the others were still at Cal's, getting ready for the wedding.

She considered going over to see if they needed another pair of hands. She hadn't been able to do much before work. But she was becoming infatuated with Dallas and thought it might be wise to take a step back. Now that she was capable of leaving her room and being seen in public, she was going to meet an old friend, Cain Brennan, for dinner, who was in town for the holidays and recognized her when he'd come into the store earlier.

After a shower so that she would no longer smell like fresh-baked cookies, she got ready and hurried out of the house. She didn't have to meet Cain for an hour yet, but she wanted to be gone before Aiyana and her family could return. Otherwise, she was afraid she'd cancel her dinner with Cain. She was far more interested in seeing Dallas, hadn't been able to quit thinking about him all day.

She drove slowly but still arrived far too early to go in. She sat in the parking lot and called her mother, who immediately asked if she'd spoken to her father and started to complain about the mess she was in.

Emery hung up as soon as possible so that she *could* call her father. She'd been putting it off. She felt fragile enough without having what would, no doubt, be an upsetting conversation with the man she'd believed she could always rely on, but who had let her down right when she needed him most.

Even after she sent the call, she checked her watch, hoping for an excuse to hang up and continue to procrastinate this conversation. But she still had thirty minutes before Cain was due to arrive. Considering the brevity of her conversations with her father these days, that would be more than enough time.

You can't cry. That was the only caveat. If she was going to meet an old friend who may have heard of her humiliation, she was at least going to do it with some dignity and not walk into the restaurant with swollen eyes, a red, splotchy face and smudged mascara.

"Hello?"

The second she heard her father's voice she tightened her grip on the phone. He felt like a stranger to her. That was something she could never have imagined growing up. "Dad?"

"Emery, what's going on?"

He asked that question so casually it was hard to believe he'd been paying the slightest attention to the catastrophe that had destroyed everything she'd built.

Or he no longer cared. That was the possibility that really hurt.

"Nothing," she said. Why bother telling him, yet again, that she'd been deeply wronged and had no idea how to cope with the embarrassment and humiliation? That she'd lost her job and wasn't likely to find another one, at least in TV, not with such a scandal on her record.

She was an adult. She had to stop leaning on her father at some point.

She'd just never expected to lose his support so suddenly or so completely. "I'm calling about Mom."

"You mean you're calling *for* her." He sounded bitter, but she forced herself to overlook the tone of his voice.

"She has no money, no way to get by."

"Why can't she work like the rest of us?"

Emery drew a steadying breath, once again warning herself not to get emotional. "She has worked. It hasn't been for a paycheck, but she has done a lot for our family."

"You've been grown for years now."

"But she's never really held an actual job. And she didn't see the divorce coming, had no time to get prepared. It's not easy to jump into the workplace when it's been decades. What is she trained to do? Technology has changed so many things over her lifetime. Let's face it—she's not even that great at working the television remote."

"She can learn, can't she?"

Spoken with true sympathy. Emery gritted her teeth. "She was your wife for thirty-one years. And she's got Grandma to take care of. She can't train for a job and enter the workforce right now."

"Her mother isn't my problem."

He'd never really liked Adele. She could be controlling, difficult. No doubt he was taking some small pleasure in being able to walk away. "What if your roles were reversed?" Emery asked.

"My mother is already gone."

"That's beside the point, and you know it."

"Look, I don't want to argue about this. If Connie needs money, all she has to do is sign the offer my attorney sent over."

By not helping her, he was trying to force her to accept his latest offer. This was a part of her father she'd never thought she'd see; she didn't want to see it even now. "She told me she would, except it's not a fair offer."

"How isn't it fair? I'm the one who's earned all the money. It was my schooling, my hard work that's carried us the past thirty-one years. She should be grateful for what I'm offering her. Instead she's being greedy."

Was this really her father talking? Or the woman he was with? No doubt Deseret was demanding he hang on to as much of his money as possible so that she could spend it.

There were so many arguments Emery could launch. But she had a feeling Connie had already tried them all. So she simply said, "When you refuse to help her, *I* have to step in, and I'm in no position to be sending money to her and Grandma right now."

"Then don't. I just told you, she has other options."

"She can't sign that deal, Dad. It's not fair."

"How do you know? What's not fair is having her involve you and complain about me. It's not fair that she's turned you against me."

"Dad, please," Emery said. "I can't take this right now. I'm not in a good situation myself."

"You should never have gotten involved with Ethan Grimes. You signed that agreement, knew you weren't supposed to."

"So that makes everything that's happened *my fault*?" she cried. "Are you really saying that? You're living with your medical assistant, for crying out loud. Obviously, you've had an in-office romance, too. Only what you did was much worse. At least neither Ethan nor I was married!"

"How dare you!" He was yelling now, too. "Who do you think you are?"

"I used to be your daughter."

"Don't start with that. I don't have to put up with your judgments!"

"*My* judgments? You're the one looking for any excuse not to do the right thing."

"I have other people in my life right now. I can't think only of you and your mother. It's time you both took a little more responsibility for your own lives."

Those words hit her like a punch to the gut. Was he really that desperate to please the young woman he'd taken up with? "Forget it. Mom and I will get by without you," she snapped, and hung up.

She was breathing hard as she checked the time. Sure enough, their conversation hadn't lasted long. It hadn't gone well, either.

She started the car. She needed to get out of there. She didn't feel like going out with someone she hadn't seen in years, didn't have the fortitude to explain why she was in town—if Cain didn't already know—working for minimum wage at a cookie store. What she wanted was to see Dallas, to feel his hands on her body, and what had just happened made her crave that contact even more than she had before.

What was he doing tonight? Should she text him? See where he was?

No. It doesn't matter. The way things were going, it would be far too easy to wind up hurt all over again.

Determined to stay the course, she texted her mother that her father wasn't going to soften, that she'd done all she could where he was concerned and they'd talk about it in the morning. Then she turned off her car and got out.

She'd wait in the restaurant. Maybe if she was inside, and she'd already checked in with the hostess, she'd be more likely not to cancel dinner with Cain and go find Dallas.

Aiyana had no idea what to expect. She'd never met Robert Ogilvie. He'd been in prison for eight years before Dallas ever came to New Horizons. She'd seen pictures of him, of course, when she researched his crime in order to gain some perspective on Dallas, who'd been her student before he became her son. But Robert hadn't even been forty years old in the articles about the shooting where she'd seen his mug shot and another picture of him being led out of the courthouse when he was on trial.

What did he look like after almost a quarter of a century behind bars? From all reports, he'd been handsome and congenial in the beginning—not someone anyone would believe to be dangerous. She'd read that the neighbors had been shocked when they learned what he'd done. But the number of years it'd been since then, and being locked away for so long, had probably taken a toll.

Would she be able to recognize him?

Although it started to drizzle while she waited, she was sheltered by the pavilion. She pulled her coat closed for warmth and shifted nervously, keeping an eye out for movement. He didn't have a vehicle, so it wasn't as if headlights would announce his arrival. He'd said he'd walk, that his motel wasn't far. Being more familiar with the area, she'd known it would take him at least thirty minutes, and he'd be soaked by the time he arrived, but she hadn't offered him a ride. That defeated the purpose of meeting him out in the open.

Finally, a tall, lean figure emerged from the darkness. He was wearing a stiff pair of brand-new Levi's and a cheap button-down shirt, with no coat.

He walked tentatively, swiveling his head around every few seconds as though scouring the trees for some kind of threat. Did he think he was about to be ambushed? That her invitation had more to do with revenge than the discussion she'd suggested they have?

Or was he just jumpy from having spent forty percent of his life in a cage? Child killers typically didn't fare well in prison.

"Over here," she called, and squared her shoulders. She'd soon be face-to-face with a man who'd taken the lives of his wife and daughter and would've killed Dallas, too, if he could've found him. Just because Robert had served his time didn't change the depravity of what he'd done.

But she was a little less scared of him once she could see how timid and uncertain he was—and how careful he was to stand far enough away from her.

She drew a calming breath. "I'm glad you could make it," she said, keeping her voice cordial. He looked enough like the man in the article from twenty-three years ago that she could tell who he was. She could even see a little of him in Dallas. But she wouldn't have recognized him if she hadn't expected to encounter him. He'd lost a lot of his hair, had big bags under his eyes and he was rail thin. Prison had aged him by a lot more than the years he'd spent there.

"Thank you for calling me," he said politely, almost obsequiously. "I don't mean to bother you, especially during the holidays, but I was hoping to speak to Dallas." He lowered his voice. "I know he might not be excited by the idea of…of hearing from me, but I'd appreciate the opportunity to apologize in person—if possible."

"That's why I gave you his post office box. So you could apologize," she said tartly. "You didn't mention that you were getting out, or that you would try to visit him."

"I was afraid you wouldn't respond if I told you that," he admitted. Then, more defensively, "Regardless of everything else, he's still my son."

She felt her spine stiffen. "No, he's not. He'd be dead if it were up to you. He's *my* son. And I'll be damned if you're going to get anywhere near him."

He stepped back as if blown there by the power of her conviction. No doubt he was surprised; she was known for her kindness. Not only that but he'd lived with his crimes—and men who had committed similar terrible acts—for so long he'd probably lost all perspective. But, like any other mother, she could be fierce when one of her children was threatened.

"He..."

"He what?" she challenged when he didn't finish.

He squinted at her before shifting his gaze to his feet. "He should be able to decide for himself."

She couldn't help remembering Cal pointing out the same thing only an hour or so earlier. *Damn it.* She knew they were both right and hated that she couldn't simply step in and force Robert to go away for good. Was she out of line for even wanting to? Could he hold the key to putting Dallas's heart and mind to rest, bring him closure and a worthy explanation at last?

She doubted it, which was why she was struggling with this. "I can't believe he'd ever agree to see you, but you're right, it's not my decision. I am, however, going to ask you for a favor."

"A favor?" he responded, looking up.

"Don't worry. I'll make it worth your while."

He wiped away the water dripping into his eyes from what was left of his hair. "What do I need to do?"

"Leave town. I'm getting married on Saturday, and I don't want you to ruin it. Then there's Christmas. Don't bother us until it's all over."

He hesitated. "I don't plan to ruin anything. I just want to see Dallas."

"You've made that clear. But you've waited this long. Why does it have to be right away?"

"It doesn't. It's just that—" he cleared his throat "—I don't plan to settle here. There's no work for...for someone like me.

And since I don't own a car, it's hard for me to get around if there isn't a bus or some other form of public transit. If I leave, I'm afraid I won't have the means to come back."

She wished he wouldn't. "I'll give you the money. All you have to do is disappear for a few weeks so that Dallas isn't faced with your release right now."

He studied her suspiciously. "I wouldn't want him to think I sold out. That...that the money meant more to me..."

"Oh for God's sake!" she snapped. "You killed his mother and his sister! Do you think taking some money from me is going to be a big deal?"

As soon as she put it that way, he shoved his hands in his pockets and bowed his head. "I guess not."

She attempted to calm down. She dealt with difficult situations all the time, wasn't normally so easily rattled. She told herself it was because this situation was particularly close to her heart. But it was more than that. She wanted to hate Robert as much as she hated what he did, and he was making that hard for her. He looked and acted too contrite to evoke the same level of anger she'd felt before.

Why, oh why, couldn't people be easily categorized? Labeled "good" or "bad" and that was that? Instead, the lines constantly blurred, making life so complicated. It upset her that she could feel *any* empathy for Robert Ogilvie. Was he merely pretending to be humble and sincere? Was he playing her?

Possibly. She had to remember how little compassion *he'd* had when he committed those murders. "Thank you."

He studied her for a moment. Then he said, "How much are we, um, talking?"

She went with the figure she'd decided upon while driving over. "A thousand dollars."

His eyes widened. "That's a lot of money. I don't think I'll need that much. A few hundred should be enough."

Except he was starting with almost nothing. Prisoners only

received a small amount of "gate money" when they were released, and he'd probably spent most of that just buying some street clothes, coming to Silver Springs and renting a motel. And she wanted to rest assured that he'd stay away until January, didn't want to worry that he'd get desperate and come knocking on her door right as she was attempting to enjoy her wedding.

"Times have changed. It takes more to get by these days than it did when you were on the outside." She reached into her purse for her wallet, planning to give him all the cash she had on hand, and the difference in a check, when he stepped away, shaking his head.

"Actually, no. That's okay. I don't want to take any money. I'm hoping to get a job soon. I'll just…try to get by until I might be able to see him."

"But you have to leave town. You understand that, right? You have to go to LA or somewhere else," she reiterated.

"I understand. I was planning to go to LA, anyway—after I saw Dallas. I figure it might be easier to find work there."

She didn't think it would be easy for a sixty-three-year-old ex-con to find work anywhere, especially if a potential boss were to Google his name. He'd not only committed murder, he'd killed his own wife and one of his two children. Besides, what was he trained to do? He'd once worked in finance, but she doubted anyone with a felony record could go back to handling big money transactions. He would probably be better off in prison, and she had a feeling he understood that. "I'd rather have the peace of mind of knowing you'll be able to keep your word," she said. "It'll take at least this much to get to the city and rent a room. Even if you find a job in that amount of time, it'll be a week or more before you get paid."

He nodded. "Okay."

She got the money out but didn't give it to him right away. First, she had to clarify a few things. "Have you told anyone in town who you are? That you're related to Dallas? That you're just out of prison? Anything like that?"

"No. The only person I've spoken to—at least enough to even mention my name—is the fellow over at the school, when I went there looking for you. I didn't even know Dallas was in town until then. The PO Box you gave me is in Vegas."

"You must've given the motel clerk your ID."

"I did, but he didn't seem to look twice at it."

After so long, she couldn't imagine his name would be enough to spark recognition, especially if the clerk he was dealing with was young enough.

"That's good to know." She handed him the money and quickly wrote a check for the difference. She guessed he didn't have a bank account yet, but he could get one in LA.

"Thank you." He seemed ashamed to accept her help, but she hadn't done it for him.

"You're welcome," she said stiffly and, as she watched him walk away, wondered if he was sincere when he said he wasn't interested in money. Even if it was true that he just wanted to apologize, he had to be hoping for Dallas's forgiveness. And she didn't think Dallas could ever give him that, not after enduring the tragic loss of his mother and sister and being cast adrift at such a young age, at the mercy of the state until he was adopted.

She didn't think it was fair of Robert to even ask.

CHAPTER SEVENTEEN

Cain arrived on time. He was wearing designer jeans with a bur-gundy V-neck sweater that couldn't quite hide the thickening of his middle, smelled strongly of cologne and smiled a little too broadly when he saw her—and Emery immediately regretted agreeing to meet him. He'd presented dinner so casually when he bought the cookies. A bite to eat. A chance to catch up as old friends. She hadn't expected it to be a date. She'd driven to the restaurant herself; in her mind, that was a clear indication. But she could tell by the way he was dressed, and the way he put a hand at the small of her back as they approached the hostess, that he had a different take on the evening. Apparently, what he'd said and done before was merely intended to get her to lower her defenses enough to have dinner with him.

She wasn't capable of going out with anyone right now, she thought in a moment of panic. She shouldn't have come.

But then she remembered having sex with Dallas, on two dif-ferent occasions, and told herself if she could do that, she had to be capable of having dinner.

"I was so surprised when I saw you in the cookie store," he said after they'd been seated.

"Same here." It hadn't only been a surprise when he walked in—it had been a bit of a nightmare, since she'd been afraid of running into someone she knew. People who were familiar with her from before would naturally be interested in the salacious scandal she was currently navigating, and she didn't care to resurrect old relationships at the moment. She just wanted to hide out, heal and regroup.

"So how long will you be staying in Silver Springs?"

She'd already answered that question at the cookie store, but he was making small talk, trying to ease into the dinner, so she pretended as though this was the first time she'd heard it. "Just until after Christmas."

"Do you know which day you'll be going back?"

"That's a bit loose right now." The day she had to leave the refuge she'd found wouldn't be easy. She felt safe at Aiyana's and at risk almost anywhere else. But she was hoping to be up to the challenge by then. She couldn't stay with Aiyana forever.

Fortunately, the waitress brought their waters and offered a wine list, which distracted Cain. Emery was afraid the conversation had been drifting toward where she was currently staying—he hadn't asked that yet—which would inevitably lead to why she would be living with Aiyana in the first place. Did he know about the video? If not, she wasn't going to tell him. If he could misrepresent what this evening was meant to be, she could certainly neglect to mention what Ethan had done.

"Would you like a glass of wine?" he asked.

She smiled. Having a drink might help her get through the evening. "Sure."

She selected a white zinfandel, he a glass of rosé. "It's nice of you to help out at the cookie store while you're here," he said as the waitress went to get their drinks. "My mother says the owner is having health problems."

"She is. But how does your mother know? Is she a friend of Susan's?"

"Not really, but they know each other. My mom's still really involved in the Chamber of Commerce," he added by way of explanation.

Emery hadn't known his mother had ever been involved with the Chamber. She hadn't paid much attention to that sort of thing when she was in high school, hadn't known Cain that well. They'd shared a few classes but that was it. She remembered him as a shy, awkward boy, but he seemed to be more outgoing as an adult.

"What are you doing for work these days?" she asked, trying to guide the conversation to topics she deemed safe. She knew from the conversation they'd had at the cookie store that he lived in the Bay Area, but that was all.

"I dive into water tanks," he replied.

The ice clinked in her water glass as she set it down. "What for?"

He chuckled. Apparently, he was used to getting such a reaction. "To vacuum up the sediment on the bottom."

"You're talking about the public water supply..."

"I am."

"You make a great case for using a filter at the tap."

"Don't worry, someone sprays me down with an antimicrobial before I go in."

That hardly made her comfortable with the idea. There was just something off-putting about a guy in a wetsuit vacuuming up sand and other debris from the water people were meant to drink. "You must not be claustrophobic," she commented.

"I'm not. And it's quite safe. The same person who sprays me down before I go in keeps an eye on my air supply when I'm in the water, so I have help if I need it."

"It'd be terrible if that person had a heart attack or fell asleep on the job," she mused.

He slid the candle in the center of the table over to one side so that it wouldn't be directly between them. "It would. But it would be highly unlikely that the equipment would fail at the same time. So I guess I'm playing the odds."

"How'd you get into that?" she asked, feeling as though she might be able to salvage the next few hours, after all. She was genuinely curious about his line of work.

"My ex-girlfriend's father works for the City of Berkeley. He wanted us closer so that he could see his only grandchild—she has a little boy from a previous relationship—and he knew someone who knew someone who was looking for a diver. Since the job paid more than I was making, we moved, and I stayed on even after we broke up."

The waitress returned with their wine and asked for their order, so they took a moment to study the menu. Emery requested the tilapia with couscous, and he ordered a cowboy steak smothered in onions and mushrooms with scalloped potatoes.

"What about you?" he asked after the waitress left.

A knot formed in the pit of Emery's stomach. "What about me?"

"What are you going to do for a living? Will you try to get on at another TV station? I hope so. I've seen you deliver the news. You're fantastic."

She caught her breath. He knew. He must've known all along, or he went home and told his family that he was meeting an old friend and they informed him as soon as they heard her name.

Fortunately, he didn't seem too shocked, and, as embarrassing as the whole thing was, she was slightly relieved that she wouldn't have to dodge the issue for the rest of dinner. "I don't know," she admitted. "I'm suing the station for wrongful firing, and I'm suing Ethan Grimes for posting that video, which I had no idea he'd even made. Until I can get through that, I'll probably try to scrape by working some low-profile job like I'm doing at the cookie store. I don't feel as though I can move forward until this thing is resolved."

"What a jerk," he said.

"I never dreamed that someone I was dating would do something so despicable."

"He comes across as a nice guy on TV, but I know you can't always tell from someone's public persona."

"Trust me, he's his own biggest fan." She took a sip of wine and braved a question she knew she probably shouldn't ask but had to know. "How'd you hear about it?"

"Word swept through town," he said vaguely.

"Let me guess—your mom told you." He'd just indicated that his mother worked for the Chamber of Commerce, so she'd be privy to town gossip, and his mother was the one who'd told him about Susan.

"Yes and no. I've sort of kept tabs on you since high school. My mother knew I'd be interested so, yes, she told me."

"You've kept tabs on me? From the Bay Area?"

"Well, not like a stalker, but if your name ever comes up I pay attention to it. You were so popular in high school—I'm sure I'm not the only one."

She imagined all the people who had to be talking about that video and the wine began to sour in her stomach. "Have you seen it?"

When he flushed, she had her answer.

"Just a glimpse of it," he said, trying to minimize his exposure, but she doubted that he was being strictly honest. Her gut told her he'd watched it all the way through—maybe more than once. And that was enough to make her, once again, regret coming to meet him.

"I appreciate that you didn't watch the whole thing, that you saved me that embarrassment," she said to see how he'd respond and could tell he had indeed been lying. Instead of accepting her gratitude, he barely murmured a response and then acted overly preoccupied with the food the waitress was carrying to their table.

Fortunately, however, he no longer seemed eager to talk about the video.

"I'm sorry about what you've been through," he said when the waitress left. "You deserve to be treated a lot better than you were."

Then why didn't *he* treat her better when he had the choice? He could've chosen not to watch it.

Or was she being too hard on him? Measuring everyone by Dallas's reaction, which she'd found so comforting and supportive?

He said something she'd missed, so she tuned in again. "Excuse me?"

"I said it would be fun to go to a movie after this. Would you like to do that?"

"Not tonight," she said. "I'm pretty tired. And I can't be out too late, since I'm staying with someone. I wouldn't want to wake up the whole household when I got home."

"Aiyana wouldn't mind."

So he didn't only know she'd been the victim of cyber-exploitation, he knew where she was staying? No wonder he hadn't asked. "Maybe she wouldn't mind, but her wedding's Saturday, and I wouldn't want to be the reason she isn't able to get enough rest. Besides, she's not the only one at the house."

His gaze met hers. "Dallas is there, right?"

"Yes. So are Liam and Bentley," she felt the need to point out.

"But they're younger. Dallas is our age."

"That's true. Do you know him?"

"I know of him. My mother says he's a hothead, always looking for trouble. I'd be careful of him, if I were you."

Somehow she managed to swallow her food. "What makes you say Dallas is a hothead?" she asked, and then it dawned on her. "Oh, you've also heard about the fight at the Blue Suede Shoe."

"It's a small town," he said by way of explanation, but he knew so much about her she had to wonder if he'd truly been surprised to see her when he walked into the cookie store—as he'd stated—or if it had been orchestrated in advance. Was the fact that she was working there something else his mother had told him?

"Yes, it is," she said and did what she could to maintain the conversation from there, but midway through the meal, she needed a break and escaped into the bathroom. Cain had set her up. He knew all about her and her situation and was trying to date her. She supposed she should be flattered, but she was more irritated and upset than anything else. He'd lied about being surprised by their meeting at the cookie store, and she felt sure he'd lied about viewing that video of her with Ethan. He'd even lied about tonight being about old friends getting together to catch up. Maybe they were polite lies, innocuous lies, lies any person might tell in his particular situation, but they were still lies. He was using her situation to try to get her into a relationship with him, and that bothered her.

Her phone chimed, so she dug it out of her purse.

She'd received a text from Dallas.

What are you doing?

Wishing I was with you.

She told herself not to send that, but did it anyway. It was true, and she needed truth right now.

He responded:

Want to go out and see the Christmas lights?

She knew the answer should be no. The way she was craving his touch, she'd end up back in his bed before the night was through.

Her thumbs hesitated over her phone before she finally typed her answer.

★ ★ ★

"How'd it go?" Cal murmured.

Aiyana knew he'd been dying to ask ever since she met with Robert, but this had been his first opportunity. She'd played off her early departure from the ranch by acting as though she'd simply gone to start the tacos she'd just served for dinner, and it had worked beautifully. No one had questioned her absence.

Now they'd all eaten, but the boys were still hanging around the kitchen table, talking and laughing while she cleaned up. "I'll tell you later," she mouthed so she wouldn't draw their attention.

"They're caught up in their own conversation," Cal said. "Just tell me if he's leaving."

She nodded.

"That's a relief. How much did it cost you?"

"A thousand dollars."

His scraggy eyebrows shot up to indicate he was shocked by the amount.

"I know it's a lot, but I needed some reassurance that he wouldn't come back until January. This is really important to me. Now he will have no excuse."

"Mom, where's Emery tonight?" Bentley asked, breaking into their conversation.

Cal opened the cupboard closest to the sink and got out a toothpick as though that had been his purpose in going over near Aiyana in the first place.

"Still at work, I guess," she said as she glanced back at her son.

He didn't seem convinced. "It's nearly nine o'clock. I don't think the cookie store stays open that late on a Sunday. Not in the winter."

She added more hot water to the suds in the sink. "Then I don't know."

"Do you know, Dallas?" Bentley asked.

Dallas glanced up from his phone. "Haven't talked to her."

"That's bull," he cried. "Who have you been texting if not Emery?" He tried to grab Dallas's phone out of his hand, but Dallas snatched it away.

"No one," he said with a scowl designed, no doubt, to warn his brother off.

"It has to be a woman," Bentley insisted. "Or you wouldn't have freaked out a minute ago when Liam wanted to use your phone so he could download that game he's been telling you about."

"That has nothing to do with it," Dallas said, but he didn't sound very convincing, even to Aiyana.

She told the two younger boys that it was time to go up and do their homework—she knew they both had plenty of studying to do with finals this week—and waited until they were gone to ask Dallas, "Is Emery okay?"

He grinned. "I never could hide anything from you."

She hoped the reverse wasn't true. Now that she'd done what she'd done, it would be even worse for Dallas to find out about Robert. He might get angry that she'd talked to his father on her own instead of giving him a chance to decide for himself, angry that she'd spend so much to get rid of him for only three weeks or just angry that his father was out of prison despite what Robert had done. "When is she coming home?"

"She's on her way. But she won't be staying. We're going out to look at the lights."

"The Christmas lights?" she asked in surprise.

He looked confused. "We wouldn't be going out to look at the *traffic* lights."

She ignored his sarcasm. "I've just never known you to pay much attention to holiday decorations."

"I like them as much as most other guys," he said, but she knew what he liked was Emery.

"Sure you do," she said, and she and Cal started laughing.

★ ★ ★

As soon as Dallas saw Emery's headlights, he went outside
to meet her. He didn't want her to come in. Then his brothers would hear her and realize she was home—and that she was
going back out with him.

"Where have you been?" he asked when she turned off her
engine and opened her car door. He was curious since she was
so reluctant to go out in public.

"On a date, apparently."

He hadn't expected that response. She'd been out with someone else? There was nothing official between them, but it felt
like someone had punched him in the gut. "With who?"

"Cain Brennan. Do you know him?"

He struggled not to reveal the jealousy that was burning
through his veins, but his jaw suddenly felt too stiff to move
properly. "Never heard of him."

"He went to my high school."

"So his parents are rich?"

"His mother owns a window covering business that's been
around for years and years. I think she's somewhat of a busybody in town—at least that was the impression he gave me. His
father's a dentist and does quite well."

They sounded like an ordinary family—the type of family
he'd always envied, since his had been so screwed up. "How'd
this...*date* come about? Did he hear you were in town and call
you, or—"

"He came into the cookie store earlier. It was just supposed
to be dinner with an old friend, but he sort of pulled a bait and
switch on me."

A spark of hope did battle with the negative emotions that
seemed determined to strangle him. "A bait and switch?"

"He painted it as one thing but showed up with other ideas."

She sounded so annoyed that Dallas suddenly felt better, good
enough to joke it off. "At least you got a free meal."

"No, I insisted on paying my half and left right after we ate, even though he was intent on getting me to go to the movies with him."

"You didn't want to go?"

"No. I didn't want to be with him—I wanted to be with you."

He let his eyes slide down, taking in her long eyelashes, the lips he'd kissed, the breasts he'd touched. "So is *this* a date?"

"I don't know," she said. "I just hope it ends with you inside me."

"How about if we start that way?" He jerked his head toward his vehicle. "Let's go."

CHAPTER EIGHTEEN

They didn't speak as Dallas started the van and drove them out of town. The radio was playing, but Emery could still hear her heart pounding in her ears. Her mouth watered in anticipation of once again tasting him, and she looked forward to running her nose over his smooth, warm skin and smelling that unique and wonderful scent she associated with him.

As soon as he found a private spot in a grove of trees, he pulled off the highway, out of sight, and parked. He left the music playing as they got in back, where there was a bed, and yanked anxiously at each other's clothes, trying to get them off as fast as possible.

It didn't take long, but when Emery felt Dallas's bare chest come against hers, she couldn't wait for him to get even closer.

They were kissing so deeply they were breathless within minutes. "Nobody kisses as good as you do," she told him when he pulled away to run his mouth down her neck. She didn't say so, but nobody felt as good as he did, either. Her hands moved along the muscles that rippled across his back as he lifted her and twisted so that she was beneath him.

"Keep talking like that and this won't last long." He was joking, but the ragged edge to his voice lent truth to those words, and she found his level of arousal as intoxicating as everything else about him. How was it that while her life was in the midst of a complete meltdown, she was having the best sex she'd ever experienced?

"I'm just glad you decided to come home for Christmas," she whispered as she outlined his ear with her tongue.

"So am I," he told her gruffly, eagerly, and brought her knees up as he pushed inside her.

When it was over, Dallas dropped onto the mattress beside Emery. The way they'd made love was far more intense than it had been before, but Emery didn't care to examine the reason.

"That was amazing," he said.

She had to agree. For whatever reason, they were perfect sex partners. She'd never felt such raw desire for anyone else and was a little rattled by it. What was happening to her? She seemed to be a completely different person than she'd been before—a far more reckless and passionate person—and that frightened her. Where would it all end? And would she be able to get back to the woman she'd been before?

"Sorry. I would've waited until after I'd shown you the lights," he said as he nipped at her shoulder. "But I kept thinking of the silkiness of your hair and the softness of your skin and the fullness of your breasts. And then you showed up looking like a wet dream in that dress, and said what you said, and I lost all control," he added with a laugh.

She pressed her lips to his neck, still luxuriating in how much he appealed to every one of her senses. "It's not too late to drive around and enjoy all the holiday cheer, is it?"

"Absolutely not. Maybe we can get some ice cream while we're out, too."

She ran her fingers down his arm, struck by the sheer masculine beauty of it. "Sugar Mama is closed."

"Another ice cream store has opened up not far from the main part of town. It doesn't offer fresh-baked cookies or ice cream sandwiches—it's more of an old-time parlor with giant creations doused in caramel and chocolate sauce—but I'm definitely in the mood for something indulgent, aren't you?"

"We've been pretty indulgent already," she said. "But I could go for some ice cream."

"Then we'd better hurry, before it closes."

She sat up and started putting on her clothes—but became slightly self-conscious when he didn't follow suit. He lay back, locked his fingers behind his head and simply watched her. "You're not getting dressed?"

"Not yet."

"Why not?"

"I like what I'm seeing. You're beautiful, Emery. I've always thought you were beautiful."

She felt herself flush as she flipped her hair out from under her dress and started looking for her panties. "You remember me that well from high school?" Although she remembered him, she couldn't recall much about him, except that he attended "that" school, the one with all the troubled kids.

He plucked her panties out of the bedding and handed them to her. "Yeah," he said with a mysterious smile that led her to believe there was more to his answer than it might seem.

She hesitated before taking her panties from him. "Why are you smiling as though you have a secret?"

"No reason," he replied, but he pulled her back into the bed, rolled her onto her back and, as one hand curved possessively around her bare ass, kissed her so powerfully she told herself she shouldn't like it.

But she did. A lot.

"I had a thing for you in high school," he admitted.

"You did?"

"I almost asked you to the senior dance."

"No way!"

"It's true." He got up and started to dress, and this time she made it a point to watch him. "What are *you* looking at?" he joked.

"You," she said, playing along.

His lips quirked into a sexy grin. "Because..."

"I like what I see," she said, and sat up, grabbed him by the shirtfront and hauled him in for just as possessive and powerful a kiss.

Emery felt inexplicably happy as she and Dallas sat in a corner booth at Blake's Ice Cream Spot. Decorated like a 1950s soda fountain in red, white and chrome, it served hamburgers, hot dogs, homemade chili and French fries, as well as gigantic ice cream creations.

"Wow, this place is packed," she said to Dallas as the waitress wove through the crowd to bring them water. "I wouldn't have expected this on a Sunday night."

"Eli, Gavin and I came here last time I was home," he said. "They serve great garlic fries."

"I thought I smelled garlic."

"Should we get some?"

"Why not?" she said with a shrug.

"There are benefits to making love *before* eating," he joked. "We should do it more often."

She laughed and they ordered a large garlic fry to share, agreeing that ice cream would come later.

The waitress had left, and they were talking about the *Saturday Night Live* skit Dallas had just shown her on his phone, when Emery felt the weight of someone's stare. She'd been so caught up in Dallas—so content just to be with him—she hadn't scoped out the place for people who might recognize her, as she'd made a habit of doing since she came to town.

"Something wrong?" Dallas asked when she straightened.

A prickle ran down her spine as she scanned the faces that surrounded them, searching—until she found what she was looking for. "Oh my God," she whispered, jerking her gaze away
from the person she'd just seen.

"What is it?"

"Don't look now, but that's Cain Brennan over by the juke-
box."

"The guy you had dinner with earlier?"

"Yes. I never dreamed we'd run into him. What could be
the chances?"

"In such a small town? Not too bad—if you're both looking
for a place to hang out on a Sunday night. Very few businesses
are open."

From what Emery could tell, Cain was with a male friend
or relative. It wasn't as though he'd been following her. But she
was embarrassed for him to catch her out and about, especially
with Dallas. She'd told him she was too tired to go to the movies—and he'd warned her against getting involved with Dallas.

Was it apparent that she and Dallas were a little more than
friends?

She tried to imagine what Cain might've seen when they
walked in. How would an onlooker have interpreted their body
language? They'd been having a great time, but they hadn't been
holding hands or anything. They'd agreed not to touch in public. It wouldn't be wise to start tongues wagging. But the sheer
magnetism of their attraction could be more apparent than she
realized.

"He won't quit staring at me," she complained. "Should I go
over and say something? Apologize?"

"Apologize for what?"

"For not wanting to go to the movie with him?"

"No. I don't think an apology would make him feel any better. It might only embarrass him. I'd just let it go. It is what it
is, you know?"

"You're probably right."

Their ice cream came, and Emery tried to enjoy it, but with Cain there, watching her so closely, she was too uncomfortable. She waited for Dallas to eat as much as he wanted. Then she said, "Let's get out of here."

"You got it," he said, but just as he tossed twenty-five dollars on the table to cover the bill, she noticed movement out of the corner of her eye and realized that Cain was walking toward them.

"Here he comes," she muttered.

Dallas squeezed her leg under the table. "It'll be okay. Just smile and act like there's nothing wrong. There *shouldn't* be anything wrong. You have the right to say no if you don't want to go out with a guy."

"But I said I was too tired!"

"Because you were attempting to salvage his feelings. That it didn't work out isn't your fault."

"Hey," Cain said as he reached the table.

She forced a smile. "Hi."

"Looks like you got your second wind." His own smile appeared brittle, and his voice sounded more high-pitched than she remembered it being at dinner.

"Yeah. I'm feeling better," she said lamely.

"Have we met?" Dallas asked.

Emery got the impression he'd inserted himself to draw Cain's attention, so that she could feel more comfortable with the situation and was grateful to him for taking the lead.

"No." He held out his hand. "I'm Cain Brennan."

Dallas shook with him. "Dallas Turner."

"I know."

Emery could feel Dallas's surprise. "I thought you said we haven't met."

"We haven't, but most people in this town are familiar with you and your situation."

Emery could tell he'd surprised Dallas again. "My situation?"

"With your father just getting out of prison, it sort of brings it all up again." He clicked his tongue in apparent disgust. "You'd think a man who killed his wife and one of his children would spend the rest of his life behind bars."

Dallas went rigid beside her. "What are you talking about?"

Cain's eyebrows knitted. "You don't know?"

"How is it that *you* know?" Emery asked, mortified for Dallas. She was shocked to hear this history with his father, but now she could see why he might be reluctant to talk about his past.

"When I saw Dallas walk in, I was curious, so I did a Google search. With just a few keywords, I found this." He flashed his phone at them. "It's only a short article—what your father did is hardly news after so long—but I figured you, of all people, would be keeping track of him," he said to Dallas. "I sure as hell would be. He tried to shoot you, too, right? Tried to kill you when you were just a kid? I'd be afraid he might come back to finish the job."

"Cain, that's enough," Emery said, but it was too late. The news that his father had been released from prison had hit Dallas like a bombshell. Her, too. His father had killed his mother and his sister—and had tried to kill *him*? And she'd thought her own situation was bad. She'd gone on and on about it, soliciting his help. She felt awful now.

"Let's go before I break this fool's jaw," Dallas ground out, his face stony.

"I told you he was a hothead," Cain said as Emery scrambled from the booth.

They headed to the exit without responding.

"Sorry if I ruined your evening," Cain called after them, but Emery could tell by the smile in his voice that he wasn't sorry at all.

Everyone else was asleep by the time they got home, and Dallas was glad. The dark, quiet house meant that it wouldn't seem odd when he said good-night to Emery and went straight to his room, where he could be alone. He wanted to get hold of that letter his father had sent him to see if Robert had mentioned getting out of prison. Maybe it was his own fault that he'd been blindsided tonight. Maybe that was the reason Robert had written in the first place.

He closed the door behind him as soon as he walked into his room and went straight to the drawer where he'd stuffed the envelope.

"Damn you," he muttered to his father, scowling at his own name, written in what had to be Robert's hand. Most people would easily recognize the writing of their own parent. But Dallas hadn't seen enough of Robert's to be able to distinguish it.

This was the first time his father had ever reached out. Part of Dallas couldn't believe it had taken him almost twenty-five years. Another part was angry that he'd tried to contact him even now.

With Cain's words still echoing in his ears, he pulled out his pocketknife so that he could carefully slit open the top. For all he knew, the way his father had sealed the envelope was intended to give him hepatitis, if not something worse. Robert simply wasn't someone who could be trusted. He was a consummate actor, could fool just about anyone—at least when he was sober. Even before the murders, he'd been embezzling from the financial planning company where he worked. He'd just been caught the week he'd opened fire, which is what had pushed him over the edge. Although he denied it afterward, Dallas firmly believed he'd planned to kill his family, take off and start over.

The letter inside was written on lined paper—it, too, in pencil.

Setting aside the envelope, Dallas spread what turned out to be one page on the desk at the side of the bed and ironed out the folds.

Dear Dallas,

I've thought about you so often over the years—every day,
if you want the truth. You might scoff at this, but I feel as
if I know you. I can remember holding you, feeding you,
teaching you to walk and to throw a ball as if it was only
yesterday. For me, time has stood still. But I understand that
everything must've changed for you and you can't possibly
remember me, at least not in any favorable light. You were
too small when I did what I did to be able to hang on to
the man I was before that day.

Filled with disgust and too many other emotions to name,
Dallas squeezed his eyes closed and shook his head. That day?
What about everything he'd done before? But Dallas had already known this letter would be full of lies and, therefore, difficult to read.

With a heavy sigh, he steeled himself, opened his eyes and
continued reading:

My actions must seem unfathomable to you, the actions
of a crazy person. I wish I could claim that I was crazy.
It'd be easier to forgive myself. But I'm not sure depression would qualify, even a depression as dark as the one
that encompassed my mind in that moment. I've attended
group therapy for years here in prison, and if it has taught
me anything, it's to take responsibility for my actions and
try to apologize. But in this case, there's no way an apology could ever be sufficient, and I know that.

Lip service. This was all bullshit. Dallas couldn't help but
clench his jaw. Robert wasn't taking any responsibility for everything that led up to that day, was blaming it all on one act
caused by depression, but only because depression had become
such a buzzword, which made it a ready excuse. He'd never

mentioned being depressed before—certainly at the time and not even in court. It was alcohol that brought out the worst in him, not depression, but anyone who would embezzle, especially when he was making a decent living as it was, had to be an asshole to begin with.

Still, I'm willing to talk to you about how it all came to pass—not as an excuse, only as an explanation—so that you will at least know what made me snap. The murder of your beautiful mother and sister is not something I like to dwell on. Since I can't take any of it back, or fix it in any way, it just reopens a wound that will never heal. But if it might help you come to terms with the past, to understand how a father who really did love his family could do what I did, I'll tell you everything—not that I pretend to truly understand it myself.

Dallas laughed without mirth. He was saying all the right things—exactly what his therapist must've told him.

Please let me know if you'd like to meet. You have never written me, or come to see me. Maybe you're better off left as you are. But I've nearly served my time. I'll be getting out soon and wanted to let you know that. I also wanted to offer to do whatever I can, little though it may be.

Love,
The man you once knew as "Daddy"

Dallas sat there, letting it all sink in, and didn't realize he was weeping until a tear dropped off his chin. Frustrated that his father could still cause him pain—after so long—he swiped at it with impatience and irritation. But he knew it wasn't just sorrow for the loss of his mother and sister that he was feeling;

it was sadness for what might have been if only his father was capable of the sincerity to which he pretended.

Carefully folding the letter back up, he shoved it into its envelope and put it in the drawer. He didn't want to see his father. Robert was right. Depression wasn't an excuse he could accept, because he didn't believe his father had been depressed. It was narcissism, not depression, that drove him that day, just like every day.

He tried not to think about Robert or anything else as he got ready for bed. He was tempted to head back to Vegas and be done with Silver Springs. It was easier to forget his past when he kept moving forward, kept rolling on, constantly looking toward the next day.

But he couldn't leave before the wedding, would never do that to Aiyana.

It was at least an hour later, when he was still staring at the ceiling—sleep miles and miles away—that he heard a knock. It was so soft that at first he wasn't positive there was really someone out there.

"Come in," he said.

Emery slipped inside the room, wearing an overly large T-shirt. He didn't know if she had anything on underneath.

"Sorry to bother you," she said. "I just… I couldn't sleep. The way things ended tonight… I was too worried about you."

"I'm fine." He heard the remoteness in his own voice, the "leave me alone" tone of it, and felt bad, but he didn't know how to bridge the sudden distance between them.

"Are you sure?"

"Positive." He could tell she wanted him to open up to her the way she'd opened up to him about Ethan and that sex tape. She had to be surprised by what she'd learned tonight. He hadn't mentioned what his father had done—even that his father was in prison.

"Okay." She hesitated for another few seconds, giving him a second chance.

He wanted to reach out to her, to pull her into bed with him. But he struggled with the fact that it felt as though he needed her. He couldn't help fighting that dependence; the desire alone suggested he should deny himself, or maybe he'd come to need her, which he couldn't allow.

"I guess I'll see you in the morning," she said at last and turned to go.

Before she could let herself out, he managed to force her name past the lump in his throat. He could help her with Ethan, could reach out because she needed him. It was much harder for him to admit when he needed someone.

"Yes?" she said, looking back at him.

He didn't answer, couldn't answer, but he lifted the covers.

She didn't react right away. He held his breath while she stood there, deliberating. For some reason, he couldn't bear to see her go, and yet he had too much pride to ask her to stay, too much fear of how she made him feel and the vulnerability those emotions created.

His heart jumped into his throat when she closed the door, padded across the floor and crawled into bed with him.

He kissed her immediately, parting her lips with his tongue, and started to remove her shirt. He assumed she wanted another sexual encounter. He certainly wasn't interested in talking. He expressed himself much better physically, and he looked forward to converting all the negative emotion coursing through him into sexual energy—and a release.

But she resisted, letting him know that her shirt would stay on.

"Emery?" he said, slightly confused.

She didn't answer. She just pulled him into her arms, pressed his head to her shoulder, and combed her fingers through his hair in a soothing and hypnotic motion. She was refusing to let him change this into something sexual; she was asking him to accept her comfort on a different level. For him, it was a deeper level.

He wasn't sure he was capable of that. But as the minutes ticked by, he found himself settling more comfortably against her. Then he started to relax. And, at last, he was able to drift off to sleep.

When he woke the next morning, she was gone.

CHAPTER NINETEEN

Monday, December 14

The following morning, while Emery worked at the cookie store, she kept checking her phone. She was worried about Dallas. He'd seemed so tortured last night, and she felt terrible for how consumed she'd been with her own problems while remaining oblivious to his.

She was hoping to hear from him, that they could talk about what she'd learned. She understood that his past wasn't his favorite subject—he preferred to suppress the pain—but she thought having a shoulder to cry on might be therapeutic for him. Whether or not he was willing to open up would also reveal if he really trusted her.

So there was that. And her lawyer had said that Ethan would be served today, that he might even be served at work. Since they were also suing the TV station, it made sense to serve them both at the same time.

How would they react? She was especially worried about Ethan. She'd seen how vicious he could be when angered. Would he post something else on the internet—another video or some

naked pictures of her she didn't know he possessed? She had
no doubt he'd strike back or try to do something to get her to
drop the suit.

She remembered the many times she'd showered at his house
while getting ready for work. Had he secretly filmed her?

The possibility made her queasy. She felt as though she was
just beginning to cope, didn't want to backslide. She'd expressed
her concerns to her lawyer this morning over the phone as soon
as she left Aiyana's, and he'd said they'd be lucky if Ethan *did* post
something else. Then they'd have fresh evidence against him.

But that was easy for her lawyer to say. His primary concern
was winning the case. *She* had to survive the next few months
and couldn't bear the thought of further humiliation. With the
holidays approaching, people were finally turning their attention to other things.

Or maybe it only seemed that way because she was keeping
her head down and staying out of sight. Either way, by the time
she returned to LA, she hoped the scandal would be mostly forgotten—was loath to face a whole new onslaught of embarrassing photos or video.

"I'm going to run down the street and grab a bowl of soup.
Would you like me to bring you something?" Susan asked.
She'd been in the back baking all morning. With Emery there
to serve any customers who came in, and to watch the front,
Susan didn't have to get up quite as early and could bake some
of the less popular cookies after the store opened. It was nice to
see her looking more rested.

"No, thanks. I'm good." Emery had to keep moving and was
too anxious to eat. She counted the bowl of oatmeal she'd eaten
for breakfast as a mistake. It was still sitting heavy in her stomach.

"Okay. You've got the store," she said, and went out the front.

As soon as her boss was gone, Emery checked her phone again.
Nothing from Dallas. Maybe he was waiting until she was home
and they could talk in person. But she hadn't heard from Ethan,

either. Or the station. Had the process server done his job? Was he there now? Or was he so busy he'd put it off another day?

She hated the thought of it not happening right away almost as much as she feared the consequences once it *did*. If she had to sue them, she wanted to get it over with as soon as possible.

The store was so busy over lunch, Emery couldn't obsess about anything. But when things slowed down an hour later, she sat on a stool behind the counter, nervously tapping her foot while performing a Google search on her name to see if anything new popped up.

Nothing.

Thank God. Except she was once again presented with a link to the original video. As soon as she petitioned one place to pull it down, claiming copyright infringement, another put it up. Trying to get rid of them all was like playing a game of Whac-A-Mole.

The bell sounded, and Emery jumped to her feet.

"It's just me," Susan said. "I brought you a bowl of broccoli cheddar soup. I know you told me not to, but it's after one. I can't imagine you won't be hungry before long, and I don't want you to be miserable."

"Thank you." It was a thoughtful gesture and Emery was grateful. If only she wasn't sleeping with her hostess's son, who had a tragic background, and suing her former employer and her former boyfriend, she might be able to relax enough to eat.

"Margie Brennan, who owns the drapery business down the street, was at the café," Susan said. "Normally she doesn't talk to me. I'm not among the business owners here in Silver Springs who can afford to participate in all the promotional things she tries to get the Chamber of Commerce to do. But she made a beeline for me when I was waiting to order the soup."

Emery tensed. Susan had to be referring to Cain's mother, who ran a drapery business, and Emery was slightly concerned with what she might have to say to Susan. "What did she want?"

"She said that you went out with her son last night and asked me what you were like."

This fortified Emery's impression of Cain's mom as a busybody, which didn't ease her mind. "What did you tell her?"

"That you're a wonderful person."

"Despite the video."

"That had to be what she was getting at, yes."

After how Cain had behaved, Emery couldn't believe *she* was the one who could be considered unsuitable, but she knew she'd probably face this with almost any guy she dated in the future. Modern feminism or not, fair or not, her reputation had been ruined.

Cain was so different from Ethan, and yet she saw a commonality—a vindictive streak in them both. After what she'd been through with Ethan, she definitely planned to steer clear of Cain. "Actually, she doesn't have anything to worry about. I have no romantic interest in her son. We grabbed a quick bite to eat—but only as friends. We went to high school together."

Susan rolled her eyes. "If he's anything like his mother, I can see why you wouldn't be overly excited about him. Margie thinks she's better than everyone else. And he's just as special, of course. Like I said, I haven't had a lot of contact with her, but whenever I do, it seems she's singing his praises. Is he really that great?"

Emery's opinion of Cain was decidedly less flattering than his mother's. "He has an interesting job," she said, trying to avoid making a statement either way.

"That bad, huh?" she said with a laugh.

Emery couldn't help laughing with her. "Yeah, that bad."

"What does he do that's so interesting?"

She started to explain how he dived into water tanks to suck up the sediment, but her phone buzzed, and when she glanced down, Caller ID showed KQLA.

They must've been served with the lawsuit. She couldn't think of any other reason they'd contact her right now. No doubt management would be angry and shocked...

She told herself she shouldn't answer it, but she couldn't resist. Her curiosity was too great, and the only way to ascertain how things might go was to hear what they had to say. "Can you excuse me?" she said. "I can't miss this call."

She wasn't sure she even gave Susan the chance to respond. She pressed Talk as she hurried out the back way and into the alley, where she could have some privacy. "Hello?"

"Emery, this is Heidi."

She could hear the tension in her former producer's voice. They must've been served, all right. "What can I do for you?"

"There must be some misunderstanding here."

It was chilly, and Emery hadn't grabbed her coat, but she could scarcely feel the cold. "What kind of misunderstanding?"

"The reason we had to let you go has nothing to do with the video that showed up online."

Showed up online? Emery made a noise of disgust. "Heidi, nothing just *shows up* online. Someone has to put it there. Ethan loaded that video on a popular revenge porn site and then emailed a link from a fake email account to every local and national news station he could think of. This was a cyberattack, and cyberattacks are illegal."

"He claims he *didn't* do it, and there's no way to prove he did, so how are we supposed to know who to believe?" she asked defensively.

"Common sense?"

"That's between the two of you. We let you go because the chemistry between you and Ethan wasn't right anymore, and you know how important it is for the two major anchors of any newscast to have a certain...rapport on camera. That's part of what creates viewer loyalty."

"You think viewer loyalty has been improved with me gone?" Emery asked.

"If we hadn't removed you, we would've received complaints. And we're still working on your replacement, so we're in a building stage. But you have no right to sue us," she insisted. "That's my point. You were no longer the right person for the job, and we should have the right to make that decision."

"I was doing an excellent job," she argued. "There's no way you can say I wasn't. I was never late, I never missed a broadcast and I never received any disciplinary action. I worked hard and did everything I could to be a great anchor—and our ratings were better than ever."

"It just wasn't working between you and Ethan anymore. Besides, it wasn't just *my* decision. There was general agreement around here."

She sounded as though she was trying to convince herself of that. "I don't believe it happened the way you're trying to portray it, Heidi. I believe you've wanted to date Ethan for a long time and got jealous when we started seeing each other. Then he posted that video, and you saw it as your chance to get rid of me for good. But even if Ethan was interested in you, why would you ever want him? You've seen what he did to me. If you think you can trust a man like that, you're mistaken."

"I don't want to date Ethan," she said.

Emery knew better. She could not have mistaken the dirty looks she'd received once she and Ethan got together, nor the adoring looks Heidi had lavished on him. "Even Ethan knows how you feel about him. And he uses that to his advantage and laughs about it behind your back. I hate to be unkind—I know it can't feel good to hear that—but it's true."

Silence.

"Aren't you happy you decided to hire a guy like that back?" Emery asked.

"Just drop the suit," Heidi snapped, and disconnected.

Emery was shaking when she let the hand holding her phone drop from her ear. It was difficult to believe she could win a suit against her former employer. They had so much more money and power and access to good lawyers. From what she could tell, slapping them with a lawsuit had acted like a whack to a beehive. The internal buzzing that it had started was probably quickly escalating into a deafening roar as they closed ranks and gathered all their firepower for the fight ahead.

Before this thing was over, they'd make her doubt her ability as a news anchor; just what Heidi had said on the phone made her face sting as though she'd been slapped. And with so many people pointing a self-righteous finger at her, she was afraid shame would get the better of her, too. Maybe, in the end, the judge would side with the chorus of people who'd called her a slut online and told her she'd gotten exactly what she deserved.

She let her breath go in a long exhale as she checked the time. She hadn't specifically told Susan she was taking her lunch break, and she'd left her soup inside. But she hoped Susan would assume she'd started her thirty minutes off the clock, because she couldn't make herself go back in right away.

She kicked a rock across the alley. Had she made a mistake picking this fight? Would she regret it?

She pulled up Dallas's number and sent him a text.

I just heard from the station.

He hadn't contacted her, as she'd hoped, but she was so drawn to him she couldn't help contacting him. It felt as though she was caught in some kind of tractor beam—one she didn't even want to escape. When she'd held him as he slept last night, she'd stayed awake for quite some time just reveling in the sensation of having him there in her arms. She found it deeply satisfying, which was bizarre. She couldn't remember ever lying awake with Ethan for any reason other than concerns about her parents or planning what she was going to do for a particular story at work.

She tried to tell herself she wasn't falling in love—it couldn't happen that fast. But she'd dated a lot of men and never felt quite as she did now...

What did they say?

She breathed a sigh of relief when she saw his response. She'd been afraid, after last night, that he might try to push her away simply because he struggled with intimacy, and he felt he'd let her get a little too close. She knew what'd happened last night—the time she'd spent in his bed, comforting him—wasn't the type of thing he allowed just anyone.

They're trying to spin it a different way, change their reason for firing me.

Don't let them scare you. That they called you tells you they're worried.

Heidi *had* tried to convince her that she didn't have grounds for the suit...

They wouldn't have bothered if they weren't.

His reasoning made sense. It was probably Heidi who'd initiated her firing, as Emery had always suspected—lobbied all those in upper management who had a say. And now that doing so had turned into a problem, Heidi was scrambling to cover her ass.

Of course she was.

But if the station had been served, Emery was fairly certain Ethan had been served, too. How was he taking the news?

I'm afraid Ethan will do something to get revenge, like he did before when he was mad at me. Tell me again that I was right to pick this fight.

They picked the fight. You're only finishing it. And if he does anything, I'm going to have a little talk with him.

After which Ethan would very likely have a broken jaw. Emery felt terrible for enjoying the image that conjured in her mind, but she couldn't think of anyone who deserved to be punched in the face quite as much as he did.

Maybe it wasn't politically correct, but instead of telling Dallas she didn't condone violence, she used the kiss blowing emoji to respond. She was grateful he was there to hold her hand through this and wanted to support him, too.

You've been so good to me. I want you to know that I'm here for you, too. That if you'd like to talk about your father, what happened to your family or even what happened last night in the ice cream store, I'm more than willing.

Thanks but it's ancient history, so there's nothing to say.

She frowned at his response. It hadn't felt like ancient history last night.

Apparently, he could help her, but he couldn't accept help. He preferred to internalize everything—lock it up and soldier on.

Did that mean he'd never be able to open up enough to fall in love himself?

Dallas had spent the day driving to Santa Barbara for the tuxedos and was glad for the time alone. He'd said nothing about his father's release from prison to his family—and would say nothing, least of all to Aiyana. That would only start her worrying about him, and she didn't need anything else to worry about before her big day.

He wished he could block Robert's release from his own brain but, hard as he tried, he couldn't get his father off his mind. Forty years had seemed as though it would last forever. He'd expected Robert to be in his late seventies when he got out. *If* he got out. Some people didn't live that long. Dallas had been holding out hope that Robert would be one of them and that he'd never have to face the prospect he was suddenly faced with now.

How was it that the bastard had been released *seventeen years* early? After what he'd done?

Dallas's jaw clenched as he pictured his father able to move about at will and interact with innocent people who had no idea what he was capable of. What if he married again? Would he tell his next wife what he'd done to the last one?

His phone rang when he was about half an hour from home. It was nearly dinnertime. He could've returned earlier if only he'd made the effort, but he'd spent a couple of hours doing yoga at the beach. He did yoga as often as possible, especially when he couldn't climb.

He expected the call to be his mother, wondering where he was. But it was the owner of the gym where he worked—again. Dallas had been dodging Brian's calls for over a week, which was unfair, both to Brian as his employer and Brian as the father figure he'd come to be.

This time he made himself pick up. "Hello?"

"There you are. God, what does it take to get you to answer your phone?"

"It's possible I've been out climbing. Have you thought of that?"

"No, because you're in Silver Springs. You told me that your mother is getting married, and I'd bet my life on the fact that you wouldn't miss it. You'll be there until the big day is over."

Brian knew him too well. But he didn't yet know about the

contract Dallas had signed with Xtreme Climbing Apparel. Dallas had been hesitant to tell him. He wanted to wait until he could break the news in person. "That's true. I'm trying to have some family time. So what's the emergency?"

"I want to find out if you're going to buy the gym and take over for me or not. If you don't want it, I need to find someone else. I'm not getting any younger, you know."

"You're not ready to retire quite yet," Dallas said, hoping to God it was true. He was afraid to turn this opportunity away. If he didn't perform as well as his competitors, he could lose his sponsor. Then where would he be?

"I'm getting damn close," Brian said. "Will you be able to make the commitment?"

"You have to know *now*? It's not only my mother's wedding, it's nearly Christmas."

"What's that got to do with anything?"

Nothing, really. Dallas was just trying to buy some time. "Can't we talk about this when I return?" Even if he decided to train in Europe, he planned to go to Vegas first and spend a week or two with Brain.

"*Will* you return? That's the thing. I thought you were coming back in November."

"Some things came up this year."

"An unusually warm fall that allowed you to keep climbing? That's the only thing that came up—until your mother's wedding."

It was much more than that, but Dallas didn't correct him. He was still holding out for a better time to talk to Brian. "I'll be back in January."

"Is that a promise? I don't want to waste my time waiting for you if you're not going to come through. Maybe I should be looking at other options. You're not the only climber in the world, Dallas."

"I'm aware of that."

"But you are one of the best," he relented. "And you're one hell of a coach. I like having you involved. But, damn, you don't make it easy."

"We'll talk about it in January."

"Why put it off? I'd like to go into the holidays with something concrete to tell Janet."

Dallas liked Brian's wife. And the request was a fair one, but… "I can't focus on such a big decision right now," he said. "My father was just released from prison."

Brian was one of the few people he'd told about his background, probably because Brian had had an abusive father, too, and they went out for a beer so often when Dallas was in town that it would've been harder *not* to tell him.

Still, Dallas hadn't intended to mention the latest; it'd just come out.

"You gotta be kidding me," he said.

"No."

"When? *How?*"

"I have no idea. I just found out myself." Before he left Silver Springs, he'd searched for the article Cain had referenced, hoping to glean more information, but it didn't give an exact date. It'd merely indicated that Robert's parole had been granted and he would, indeed, be released.

"So where is he?"

"That's anyone's guess. I can't imagine he has the money to travel very far from San Quentin. Even if he worked the whole time he was incarcerated, what do they pay? Twenty cents an hour?"

"That could add up to a small amount of seed money, given enough time. How far is Silver Springs from San Quentin?"

"About a seven-hour drive. He could take a bus, I guess. But I can't imagine why he would."

"To see you, of course. Who else has he got? Does he know Aiyana?"

"Not personally, but he must've learned about her. He sent her a letter. Sent one to me, too, but it was delivered to my PO Box in Vegas."

"He might try to find you."

"He'd better not."

"What'd he say in the letter?"

"Nothing, really. Just some bullshit to make him look less like the psychopath he must be."

"Did you ever think you'd hear from him?"

"Not after so long."

"How will he get by and make a living?" Brian asked. "Does he have any family who will take care of him?"

"None. He had a younger brother, but he and both parents are dead." Since Robert had purchased the gun shortly after his parents were run off the road by a sleepy semi driver, Dallas had always believed their deaths might've contributed in some way—if only because they wouldn't be around to help him pay back the money he'd stolen. He was used to his parents being around to give him anything he wanted.

"No cousin? No uncle? That sort of thing?"

"No one in our extended family would be happy to see him. They have their own lives, their own problems." None of them had stepped up to take Dallas twenty-three years ago. No one had even stayed in touch with him. Why would they help Robert, especially after so long?

"Okay, well, I guess I can let this other issue go another month."

Dallas felt the tension inside him uncoil ever so slightly. "That would be great. I'm sorry to leave you hanging, but if you could just give me a few more weeks, I'll have an answer for you."

He sighed audibly. "You got it. For the record, you'd be crazy not to do it. I'm not making the offer just because I respect your ability and everyone around here likes you."

That statement confused Dallas. "Then why are you doing it?"

"You have to ask?"

"I've often wondered why you mess with me. It can't be convenient that I'm gone half the year."

"I do it because I care about you, you knucklehead," he said.

Brian had been good to him. It was Brian's friendship and employment over the years that had helped him remain centered—as much as he *had* remained centered. "I really appreciate everything you've done."

"Stop. I'm not saying this to make you feel indebted. I just... with your father out of prison, maybe you need to hear me say... Well, I want you to know that you don't need anything he might have to offer, and what he did had nothing to do with you— wasn't any kind of rejection, even though it has to feel that way. *I* would've been proud to have you as my son. I love you like a son," he added, his voice suddenly gruff, and disconnected.

Dallas pulled to the side of the road. He knew he and Brian were closer than most employers and employees, but he'd never expected Brian to feel quite this strongly.

He chuckled as he recalled how quickly Brian had gotten off the phone. But the desire to laugh faded when he realized that Brian probably hadn't hung up to save *himself* the awkwardness and embarrassment of saying something so uncharacteristically sentimental. He'd done it to save Dallas from feeling the need to respond.

He'd just wanted Dallas to know that he had the love of a father, even if it wasn't a biological one.

CHAPTER TWENTY

Seriously? You think you've got the grounds to sue me?

Here it was: Ethan's reaction. It had come by way of a bitter and angry text. But that was better than a bitter and angry phone call. At least this way she didn't have to hear his voice.

"What took you so long to react?" Emery muttered as she debated whether to respond. She'd just arrived home from work, changed her clothes and gone down to the kitchen. Liam and Bentley were in their rooms, doing homework, Aiyana was still at her office and Dallas was on his way back from Santa Barbara. She planned to make dinner for the family so that she could feel as though she was contributing, and she wanted to get started on that right away.

But Ethan's text proved too provocative to ignore. She wrote back:

I have grounds. You're finally going to be held accountable for what you've done.

I haven't done anything, and there's no way the station is going to let you get away with this. You'll never be able to work in television again.

She was afraid that was already true. And it wasn't because of the lawsuit; it was because of him.

I'm not trying to get away with anything. I'm determined to see justice done—that's all. You humiliated me and purposely ruined my reputation and career. Did you honestly believe there'd be no consequences?

You lost your job because you suck at it. Don't blame me.

You're delusional! I'm a better newscaster than you ever were.

You're full of shit. I don't know what I saw in you.

Believe me, the feeling is mutual. And I was the one who dumped you, remember?

She knew she shouldn't add that last part. It was childish, petty. But she was so tired of taking his blows.

I don't care. You're the one who's missing out. It's truly over between us. And I'm telling you right now—you'd better drop the suit.

No way. I'm in it to win it, Ethan. After what you did, I won't give up until justice has been served.

You're going after the wrong man.

Is this where you tell me it was Tommy again?

She added a laughing emoji.

If you don't drop this damn lawsuit, you'll be sorry.

Because you'll try to take revenge? Like you did before, when you posted that video? I've talked to Tommy, Ethan. And Tommy has already spoken to my lawyer. He's going to tell the truth.

Leave Tommy out of this.

You're the one who dragged him into it!

You fucking bitch! You're trying to ruin my life.

She leaned against the counter for support.

Have you ever heard of a boomerang? You started this mess, and now it's coming home.

I swear to God you're going to wish you'd never met me.

Emery could feel the hatred oozing through those words and hesitated before blasting back another knee-jerk response. She felt safe while she was in Aiyana's house, an hour and forty-five minutes away from LA. But she'd have to go back to the city after Christmas and stay until she could figure out what else to do. She was only a few months into an annual lease and, after helping her mother and grandmother, she didn't have the money to buy it out. Even if she could scrape the necessary funds together, she wouldn't also have enough to put down a first and last month's rent and security deposit somewhere else.

She needed to be careful or, with Ethan behaving as volatile as he was, she wouldn't feel safe in her own home. I already do, she wrote. Then she refused to engage again, even though he kept texting her, and what he said grew steadily worse until he was screaming obscenities at her in all caps.

"What's the matter?"

At the sound of Dallas's voice, Emery shoved her phone in her back pocket.

"What is it?" he said when she didn't answer.

She shook her head. "Nothing. I—I have a headache—that's all. I'll have to get in bed early tonight."

He walked over and lifted his hand to feel her forehead. But while she was distracted by that, he used his other hand to reach around and grab her phone.

"Dallas, don't," she said, but he wouldn't listen. His eyebrows came together as he read her exchange with Ethan. She'd changed the name attached to Ethan's contact record to Voldemort, but the context of the conversation made it easy enough to identify him.

"This bastard doesn't know when to quit," he muttered, sounding incredulous, and the next thing she knew, he hit Call.

"Dallas, no. I don't want to drag you into anything. You've got enough going on," she said, and tried to take her phone away, but he easily fended her off.

"Hello? Is this Ethan Grimes? My name is Dallas Turner. I'm a friend of Emery's, and I need you to understand something... If you ever lift a finger to hurt her again, you'll have to answer to me, not her. Do you understand? So stop with the nasty insults and the threats—stop contacting her at all—or you'll be the one who's sorry."

He hit the red button to disconnect the call and handed her back her phone. "Don't let that asshole upset you."

She gaped at him, wondering how Ethan was going to respond to *that*.

Her phone buzzed. Ethan.

Who just called me? Are you seeing someone else already? Tell that bastard I'm not afraid of him.

You should be, she wrote back.

"What's he saying now?" Dallas reached for her phone again, but she was afraid the two would wind up having a serious conflict if she allowed this to escalate.

"Nothing," she said and was relieved when Aiyana walked in.

"You're finally back?" she said to Dallas, distracting him.

"Just pulled in."

"Did everything go okay in Santa Barbara?"

"It did."

"Thanks for going." She put down her purse and crossed to the fridge. "What should we do for dinner?"

"It's my turn to cook," Emery announced. "I was going to make stuffed bell peppers—a recipe of my mother's—if you think the boys will eat it."

"The boys will eat anything," Aiyana said.

"Then you go rest—or do whatever you need to do to keep the wedding on track. I'll call everyone when the food's ready."

"Really?" she said gratefully.

Emery smiled in spite of her recent exchange with Ethan. "Really."

"Thank you," Aiyana said. "That's very nice."

"It's my pleasure."

Aiyana looked at her son. "I still don't have all of my Christmas decorations up. Maybe I'll take this opportunity to finish. Dallas, would you mind lifting a few things down for me in the garage?"

"Of course not." He walked out with his mother as Emery got the groceries she'd brought home out of the fridge. She made some good progress on the meal, but after about fifteen minutes, she couldn't help taking another peek at her phone.

Ethan hadn't typed another word.

★ ★ ★

Her mother needed more money. Already. The request came via text after dinner, when the boys were helping Aiyana finish decorating for Christmas in the living room and Emery was doing the dishes. Connie was probably humiliated that she had to ask yet again, and it was easier to type such an unwelcome entreaty than to ask over the phone. She did add that a better offer would be coming from Emery's father soon—that she'd been promised as much by her attorney—but after talking to Marvin, Emery wasn't convinced it would be significantly improved.

Sure, I'll Venmo you another couple hundred. It's no problem.

She added the last words so that her poor mother wouldn't have to worry about her dwindling reserves along with everything else. Emery had never been a spendthrift, but it was expensive to live in LA, her job hadn't paid all that much to begin with—she hadn't been there long enough to work her way up the pay scale—and she hadn't anticipated losing it. She hadn't been prepared for such an unexpected and serious setback.

Her phone rang. Apparently, she'd been so nice her mother now felt safe to call.

"Thank you, honey," Connie said as soon as Emery picked up.

"Of course. No worries at all."

"Grandma is only getting worse," her mother complained. "Each day, she slips a little further away. It's so difficult to watch the woman who raised me regress into someone so childlike and lost. I'm just...beside myself," she admitted.

It was hard to hear about her grandmother, but the hurt and bewilderment in her mother's voice was even more difficult. "That's terrible."

"And someone broke the window out of my car last night. There wasn't even anything in it to steal! I hate to accuse anyone, but I wouldn't put it past that tramp your father has taken up with. Deseret seems to think he shouldn't have to pay me anything—as if his money is her money, and she's the one who can call the shots. After more than thirty years of marriage, this is what I get. She's what's making everything so much more difficult than it has to be."

Emery recalled her father saying that he had more people to consider then just his original family and had to admit her mother could be right. Deseret wasn't helping. But would her father's new girlfriend really go so far as to vandalize Connie's car?

Maybe it wasn't Deseret. Maybe Marvin had done it. It could be that he was so frustrated that he couldn't please the new woman in his life—and so afraid he might lose her—he'd broken the window himself.

Where would it all end? Emery asked herself. "I'm sorry, Mom. You don't deserve what you're going through."

"How are you doing?" Connie asked, but that question came across as somewhat timid—as though she was afraid of what she was about to hear.

Emery thought of Ethan's vile texts only an hour earlier but put some energy into her voice to make her response believable when she said, "I'm doing better. Much better. I'm going to be fine. Don't worry about me."

"What's changed?" her mother asked in surprise.

Dallas. Emery now had someone she could lean on. He'd come into her life right when she needed him most—but she wasn't about to mention him to her mother. She was afraid Connie would read too much into it. "Staying with Aiyana has given me a chance to catch my breath and recoup."

"Any word from Ethan?"

"No," she lied.

"Are you still going to sue him and the station?"

"Yeah, but my attorney will take care of that. I don't have to do anything, except wait to see how it all turns out."

"That's a relief."

"It is. And you know I'm working again. So…see? Everything's looking up. You don't have to worry because you have me. Just let me know if you need more money."

Her mother started to cry, which made Emery cry, too. "I love you, Mom."

"I love you, too, honey."

"We'll both get through this."

"I hope so."

Emery had hung up and was just blowing her nose and wiping her eyes when Dallas ducked into the kitchen. "Would you like to join us in the living room for a glass of eggnog?" he asked as he got the carton out of the refrigerator.

She kept her face averted so that he wouldn't be able to tell she'd been crying. "No, I'm okay. I'm just going to finish up here and go to bed."

"You still have that headache? Can I get you a painkiller?"

She tried to staunch more tears as she rinsed the last of the suds down the sink. "No, I'll be fine. Go ahead and enjoy your family."

He came over and caught her chin, forcing her to look up at him. "What's going on? That asshole isn't bothering you again, is he?"

She shook her head. She was afraid her voice would crack if she tried to speak.

"You'd tell me?"

She nodded and he kissed the top of her head before pulling her into his arms. "Whatever it is, it'll be okay," he murmured. "You'll see."

She closed her eyes as she rested her cheek against his chest and tried to absorb the warmth of his body, to somehow use his strength to bolster hers.

"Should we make some hot apple cider, too?"

Emery broke away from Dallas as Aiyana entered the kitchen and quickly returned to her work. She was fairly certain Aiyana had seen the embrace, but Dallas's mother pretended she hadn't. "Can you join us?" she asked Emery.

"Not tonight," Emery said. "I'm going to turn in early."

"Is everything okay?"

She managed a smile. "It's great," she said, but the only thing that was great in her life right now was Dallas.

And she had a feeling even that wouldn't turn out to be a good thing in the end.

"You know I was hoping that you and Emery would make a connection," Aiyana said.

Dallas arched an eyebrow at his mother. Emery and his brothers were in bed. Bentley had school in the morning; Liam and Emery had work. He was sitting in the living room with his mother in front of the Christmas tree, its lights sparkling in an almost hypnotic fashion. It was past the time she usually went to bed, since she had work in the morning, too, so he'd guessed she had a reason for staying up late. Apparently, this was it—a word in private. "You're always trying to play matchmaker."

"Because I want what's best for you," she pointed out.

"And that's Emery?"

"That's having the love of a good woman and, eventually, a family. Only..."

He rolled his eyes. "Here we go."

"I admit that what I saw in the kitchen earlier makes me a little nervous."

"You don't have anything to worry about, Mom."

"Emery's in a difficult situation, Dallas. I don't want her to get hurt—*again*."

"We're just friends. I'm not going to hurt her."

"I know you would never *intend* to..."

"But I might not be able to resist?" he said sarcastically.

"I'm not saying that. I'm merely pointing out that she might not understand how much you struggle with commitment."

"I don't struggle with commitment."

It was her turn to lift an eyebrow.

"I struggle in general," he said. "So I would never put myself forward as someone who would be good for Emery. She needs a different kind of man, someone who's willing to settle down and work a regular job. Someone who isn't as restless as I am."

"You don't have to be perfect to be perfect for someone. Lord knows I'm not perfect. And neither is Cal. But we're better together."

"Not everyone is going to find what you two have."

"No, but you don't have to sabotage your own happiness."

"I'm not. I'm coping the best way I can, and I'm being honest—with you and everyone else. I'm not going to give up climbing."

"You don't have to give it up. Can't you just…do a little less of it?"

"A little less? That wouldn't be enough to make anyone I'm with happy, and you know it."

"You can figure out how to get what it gives you while being there for someone else. You're here for me right now, aren't you?"

"It's winter. Besides, you don't require nearly as much as a spouse would require, and you know it."

She said nothing.

"Not everyone has to walk the same path," he said.

She frowned. "Then I hope you'll stay away from Emery."

He knew as long as they were living in the same house he probably wouldn't be able to do that, so he didn't make any promises. "Did you know my father is out of prison?" he asked. He'd been going to wait until after the wedding to mention this development but couldn't resist. She was the one person who would truly understand what this would mean to him.

She looked as though she didn't want to answer, but he could tell by her face that she wasn't surprised.

"You *did* know."

"Yes."

Robert must've included the fact that his parole had been granted in her letter, too. "And you weren't going to tell me?"

"Not until after Christmas."

"Because..."

"I didn't see any reason to ruin the holidays."

He supposed he couldn't blame her. She had her wedding coming up, too.

Dallas stared at the blinking lights on the tree, remembering another Christmas tree—the one his father had pulled down in a drunken rage, breaking most of the ornaments, only two months before he killed most of his family. And that memory, like falling dominoes, took Dallas's mind back to the terrible day when he was hiding under his sister's bed. Shaking. Terrified. Trying not to breathe for fear his father would hear him. He could still remember the cupboards slamming as his father searched for him. If their neighbor hadn't reported the gunshots and then come over to see what was going on, his father would've found him eventually. And then... "I can't believe a man can kill his wife and young daughter, and try to kill his son, and *ever* be allowed to go on with his life."

"It doesn't make a lot of sense," she agreed. "But the penal system is rife with inconsistencies. Someone can be put away on a drug charge and spend as long as your father did behind bars. Others can rape and murder and get less than ten years. I suppose we should be glad he served as much time as he did."

"It's not enough. I never expected to have to deal with this—not for another decade, at least."

She scooted to the edge of the couch, where she studied him as though she wished she could read his mind. "You wouldn't ever want to see him, would you?"

"Absolutely not," he said immediately, unequivocally.

"Because it would bring it all back?"

"Because I'd be afraid of what I'd do."

"He isn't worth going to prison for yourself, Dallas."

"Some days, I'm not so sure about that. I feel like I owe it to Jenny."

"That terrifies me," she admitted.

He stood. "To be honest, it does me, too."

CHAPTER TWENTY-ONE

Thursday, December 17

Over the next few days, Emery put her name into Google's search engine morning and night to make sure Ethan hadn't posted anything new and to send takedown notices to any website that still offered a link to the original video. When Ethan first posted it, she'd been absolutely dedicated to getting it removed. Her initial reaction was to do anything she could to get it down as fast as possible, which was why she'd quickly filed a copyright. According to the information she'd found as far as how to combat what'd happened to her—from support groups formed of people who had gone through something similar—that was the first step. But as the scandal grew, and she couldn't get ahead of it, she began to feel as though her actions were futile. As soon as one website took it down, another put it up.

Then she lost her job, and depression and despair washed over her like a tidal wave. That was when she gave up and did the exact opposite—stayed away from the internet so that she wouldn't have to be confronted with the reality of what she'd find there. Had she kept her social media pages, she had no doubt she would have found some supportive voices—fans who argued with her detractors that it was her life and her choice whom she slept with, that she and Ethan were dating at the time, that it didn't hurt others and, therefore, wasn't anyone else's business except her own. Those advocates had been there from the start. But from what she'd seen, any attempt to defend her only inflamed her critics. She still couldn't bear the thought of looking at Instagram, Facebook or Twitter and reading what people were saying about her.

Now that she was working again, however, even though it was only at a cookie store, she was feeling better. And as she regained her equilibrium, she felt fresh determination to fight the people behind the websites that kept the video circulating.

"How many tonight?" Dallas asked.

She set her laptop aside. They were naked in his bed, which was no longer unusual. They made love every opportunity they had. They knew their time together was short. She figured that must be what increased her desire for him, because she couldn't remember ever wanting anyone else quite so much. Providing she was in a relationship, sex had been a part of her life—since she'd become an adult, anyway—to a greater or lesser degree. And it had always been an enjoyable aspect. But sex with Dallas was somehow different, more fulfilling, more all-consuming.

Was it that there were no expectations or promises between them? It could be that, as much as knowing they didn't have long to explore their attraction...

She had no idea what made the difference, but this was the first time she'd ever felt as though she couldn't get enough of someone. She could make love with Dallas and want him again immediately afterward.

"Only two." It was getting late, but she didn't have to work until noon the next day, since Susan wanted her to stay until close, so she hadn't yet crept up to her own room. Wanting to spend as much time with Dallas as possible, she'd lingered afterward to do her computer work while he read various articles on his phone. "But there's no guarantee they'll respond favorably," she added. "I've been fighting with the owner of one of the sites I found on Tuesday. The link is still up, even though he told me he'd take it down."

"Let me write him a message."

She laughed. "No. That's okay. I'm not sure threatening him would improve anything. Besides, I don't want you to get yourself in trouble."

"So nothing new has gone up? Ethan hasn't posted anything else?"

"Not yet." She frowned. "His silence is a little ominous, isn't it? I haven't heard from Tommy, either, even though I've texted him several times. What a coward. I'm afraid Ethan has convinced him to back away from this."

"Isn't it too late? Your lawyer already talked to him, didn't he?"

"Just once. Over the phone. He'd like to speak to him again, only now Tommy won't respond."

"Hopefully he's just busy. It is the holidays."

"I doubt that's it. He doesn't want to cross Ethan. Tommy feels too much loyalty, even though Ethan would sell him out in a heartbeat if their roles were reversed."

She closed her laptop. "It's getting late. I'd better go." She started to get up, but he caught her wrist.

"Don't leave."

When she looked at him in surprise, his lips curved into a devilish grin. "Stay the rest of the night."

"And risk having your mother catch us in bed? No way."

"She wouldn't just walk in—she'd knock. So we'd have some warning."

"And what would I do if she did come down? Hide under the bed like we're still in high school? After what I've been through, I'm definitely not down for that."

He scowled at her answer but didn't argue. "My mother warned me away from you the night she saw us together in the kitchen," he said, sobering and changing tone.

"I thought she saw us and wondered if she might say something."

"Not much gets past her."

"Did it upset her?"

"Upset her? No. Why would it upset her?"

"I don't know. She was kind enough to take me in, and now I'm sleeping with her son. Isn't that sort of…predatory?"

"Predatory?" he barked while cracking up.

"Don't laugh at me."

"I'm a big boy, Emery. I know what I want. She was worried about *you*, not me."

Bless Aiyana. She'd been so kind, which was partly why Emery felt guilty. She didn't want to take advantage of that kindness. "So what'd you say when she warned you away?"

"That I wasn't going to hurt you. That you understand this is only temporary." He searched her face. "That's true, isn't it? Because I care about you, Emery. I would never want to hurt you."

"Yes, I understand that this isn't…*serious*." What she didn't get was why it felt so vital to be with him—and why it was hard to leave his bed for hers even now, when she was tired and just wanted to sleep.

"Then you'll be okay when it ends? You aren't getting in over your head?"

"You're pretty damn irresistible, but I'll manage," she snapped as she got up.

"Emery."

She grabbed her clothes off the floor. "What?"

"I was being sincere, not arrogant. If sleeping together is going to cause you some sort of pain, we should stop."

She hated that such a sharp edge had entered her voice—and

for no apparent reason. She believed he was being sincere. What was wrong with her?

He'd hit too close to home, she realized. She *was* getting in over her head—and yet she was reluctant to give him up while they were both in Silver Springs. It had to end too soon as it was. "Sorry," she said. "I didn't mean anything by it."

"You're okay?"

After how she'd behaved, she couldn't blame him for being uncertain. But what could she say? *No, this is more different for me than I ever imagined it would be? I think I'm falling in love with you?*

That was the last thing he'd want to hear. "I'm fine," she insisted, but once she was dressed, she hesitated at the door. "Actually..."

He narrowed his eyes, his handsome face showing concern.

"Maybe this *is* getting to be a little too much for me," she admitted. "It's been...pretty hot and heavy, and...after recent events... I don't know, maybe we *should* stop."

He frowned. "Is that what you feel would be best for you?"

How could she know for sure? She didn't have any way of foretelling the future, but she *did* know that she was relying too heavily on him. They texted each other all day, while she was at work, and spent the nights together. Even when they weren't in bed together, they were acting far more like lovers than friends. "Probably. I'm in no position to make a sound decision right now, so I guess there's no reason to take the risk." If she had to give him up, she might as well do it right away, before she got in too deep. The wedding was on Saturday and Christmas only a week after that. Her stay in Silver Springs—and their time together—would soon be coming to a close, regardless.

"Right. Okay," he said slowly. "I'll...honor that, of course."

He seemed disappointed. But she doubted he was as disappointed as she was, and that also indicated there was a problem. Better to chart a safer course as soon as possible. "I appreciate everything you've done for me. I really do. I honestly don't think

I would've been able to get back on my feet without you—at least not so soon. And the sex? Honestly, I've never had better. You've provided a glimmer of fun and happiness, and a sense of fulfillment, in a very dark time. So...thank you." She walked over and pecked his lips before hurrying from the room.

She was afraid if she didn't get out of there right away she'd change her mind.

What had just happened? Dallas had only meant to reassure himself that Emery was okay. He'd never dreamed that what he'd said could change the nature of their relationship, especially so quickly.

He sat propped up against the headboard and stared into the darkness long after she'd returned to her own room, feeling oddly bereft. But he knew he wasn't the best man for her. That meant their last few minutes together had gone the way they should have. At least they were able to remain friends. She'd kissed him before she left, and thanked him, which suggested she didn't have any hard feelings. That was the goal, wasn't it? To end on a positive note—one where no one got hurt?

Scooting down, he tried to force sleep, but it was impossible. He was too restless.

After fifteen minutes of tossing and turning and adjusting his position, he got up, pulled on some sweats and went upstairs to get a drink of water. He made more noise than necessary, even hung out at the kitchen table for a while, hoping Emery might hear him and come down. He thought he might feel better if they could just talk things over, or if she reassured him that she wasn't angry or too disappointed.

But she didn't come down. He listened carefully to be able to determine if she was up—and heard nothing.

When he finally left the kitchen, he paused at the foot of the stairs. He would've gone up to her room, except his mother's and brothers' bedrooms were close to hers, and he didn't see waking them as any kind of an improvement in the situation.

"Damn it," he muttered, shaking his head. Maybe he shouldn't have said anything. He could've waited. Things had gone so far now it was going to be difficult to establish a strictly platonic relationship. He'd become conditioned—like Pavlov's dogs. Just seeing her created an automatic hormonal influx. He'd become used to the way she felt beneath him, the sound of her breathing as he was driving into her, the feel of her curves beneath his hands. He knew how and where she liked to be touched and could tell just by the subtle tensing of her body when she was close to climax. She was sexy and gorgeous and fun, and...

He felt a profound sense of loss as he remembered how intense their lovemaking had been only an hour ago. That kind of passion wouldn't be easy to forgo or forget—not when they were still staying in the same house. The next week or two until one of them left would be a struggle.

In an attempt to distract himself, he sat in the living room and texted a climbing buddy he'd been with in Joshua Tree National Park for most of November. With temperatures in the sixties, Joshua Tree was the perfect place to climb through the winter. Damian Perego had stayed to ascend Illusion Dweller—a popular and difficult 5.10b climb Dallas had mastered just before he left. But Joshua Tree had over five thousand routes and more than a thousand bouldering problems. Damian had plenty of options even if he'd chickened out and hadn't yet tackled Illusion Dweller.

Hey, man. Did you get it done?

Damian would immediately understand what he meant. Dallas had coached Damian on that particular climb, told him how best to navigate it.

But he received no response. It was late. Damian was probably asleep—just like he should be.

With a sigh, Dallas sent a final glance toward the stairs, stood up and forced his feet to carry him back to his room, where he tried to stay in bed but got up only a few minutes later to tear off the sheets. He wouldn't be able to get Emery out of his head if all he could smell was her perfume.

Friday, December 18

Aiyana had been planning to get to the school as early as possible, but when she went down to pack up the treats she'd made for the Christmas party, she found Dallas in the kitchen. "What are you doing up?" she asked in surprise.

He'd made coffee and was sitting at the table with a cup. "I thought you might need some help at the school today, since it's the last day before Christmas break."

The fatigue in his face made it clear that he hadn't slept well. Had the same kind of nightmares he'd experienced as a child kept him up? Had news of his father brought them back? Or was it something else? Had Robert tried to contact him despite accepting money to leave town?

She watched her son closely as she said, "I could certainly use you. Both halves of New Horizons—the girls' section and the boys' section—are having a party together. I made a lot of Rice Krispies Treats I have to carry over. And Santa is coming at noon. If you could be on hand to make sure each student gets a gift and has a good time—that no one feels left out—that would be wonderful."

"*Santa* is coming?" he echoed. "Since when did you institute Santa? Aren't the kids who attend New Horizons a little old for that sort of thing?"

She was tempted to reach out and smooth down his hair. "They might pretend to be but, as you know, we have a lot of students who haven't had what you'd call an ideal childhood. I'm trying to give them a little bit of what they missed before they become full-fledged adults."

He took a sip of his coffee. "Where do you get your Santa? LA?"

"Oh no. He's not a professional," she said with a laugh. "For the past few years, it's been Sam Butcher, a farmer friend of Cal's who lives right here in Silver Springs. He's a little overweight and has a long white beard, so when you put him in that red suit, he fits the part well. And he's the most jovial man I've ever known. He does a great job."

Dallas had lifted his cup again, but he put it right back down. "Don't tell me the kids sit on his lap…"

"They do, but usually only with some of their friends for pictures. They might *claim* they're too old for that sort of thing, or that it's silly, but deep down they really want to do it, and I make it easy for them to save face," she added with a wink.

"How do you do that?" he asked.

She started cutting the Rice Krispies Treats into squares. "Everyone who turns in a picture with Santa for the school bulletin board in the cafeteria is entered into a drawing for an afternoon shopping trip with me to get a new pair of sneakers. Our boys will do almost anything for that prize."

"And Santa gives every kid a gift?"

"Every single one."

"How much does that cost you?"

"Fortunately, Sam doesn't charge me. I did originally buy the suit, but that was a while ago. These days I only have to pay for the gifts." She'd gone way over budget on those this year, but Cal had contributed a significant sum. He'd wanted to buy her a big diamond for her wedding ring—until she'd told him how short she was on Christmas for the students of New Horizons. When she'd asked if she could get a gold band and spend the diamond money on them, he'd agreed. To her, making them happy was worth infinitely more than having a big rock on her finger. "Some years, I don't have to spend much. Others can be expensive," she said. "It all depends on the donations we receive. But it's one of the more important things we do. I'd give up a lot before I'd cancel Santa."

He came over to cover the treats with plastic wrap for her. "What kind of gifts does he bring?"

"Mostly gift cards to places that sell a wide variety of items. We can't afford more than fifteen to twenty-five dollars per student, but a gift card allows them to pick out *something*, and then I can rest assured that they each received at least one gift."

"I see you provide the treats, too."

"Not entirely. Each of the teachers brings in a couple dozen cookies. I just provide the hot chocolate, the candy canes and half the Rice Krispies Treats. Gavin and Savanna, and Eli and Cora, provide the rest. The kids get a gift and a cookie or treat or two, and they play some games and make an art project. We always end with carols. It's quite a party. They look forward to it all year."

He slid the trays he'd finished onto the table, out of the way. "Sounds like you do, too."

"I love the joy it brings." She stopped cutting the Rice Krispies Treats and looked up at him. She'd hoped she could cajole him out of his dark mood, or that he'd tell her what was wrong without her having to ask. But she wasn't making any headway. He only wanted to talk about her and the school. "So what's going on with you today?"

He kept his face averted when he answered. "What do you mean?"

She put down the knife and leaned against the counter, watching him as he carried over another tray. "Something's bugging you. Does it have to do with your father?"

She held her breath as she awaited his answer. She really didn't want what she'd done to blow up in her face and ruin her wedding and the holidays. They were so close to getting through them. Dallas was far more important to her than any ceremony or holiday, but she had Cal and the rest of her children to think of. Seth and the twins would be coming in tonight. If she could put off the detonation of the "Robert" bomb until January, it would be much easier for them all to survive the shrapnel. Especially because Dallas might be gone by the time Robert returned. And Robert didn't have Dallas's address in Vegas. It would be a lot harder to find him there than in Silver Springs. That might take care of the problem right there. Without the resources to launch an extended search, he might settle in wherever he could survive and forget about his misguided attempt to apologize to his son.

They just needed to get through the next ten days or so without incident. Dallas hadn't indicated exactly when he'd be leaving, but she doubted he'd stay very long after Christmas—likely only a day or two. He never did. He had to keep moving, to feel as though he was free to go at will, or he became claustrophobic.

"No, I haven't heard anything. I'm fine. Like I said, I just wanted to help you out with the school today, so I set my alarm."

He would've set an alarm so he could help her if she'd asked him to. But she hadn't.

That told her right there that something more was going on than he cared to admit.

Emery waited to come out of her room until everyone was gone and she had the house to herself. She guessed Dallas was at the school along with Aiyana and the others because she'd heard him calling up to Liam and Bentley to come help load Aiyana's car.

After quietly descending the stairs, she checked out the front window to be sure, and saw that his van was gone.

Relieved that she wouldn't have to worry about running into him, she went into the kitchen to have some breakfast. With any luck, she'd get out of the house before he returned. As much as she cared about him, she knew the less contact they had the easier it would be to go their separate ways come January.

Now that she'd put a stop to the physical side of their relationship, she was kind of shocked she'd ever let herself get sucked in so deeply, especially while she was in her current position.

Or was it her current position that had left her vulnerable?

She'd been so hurt, and he was so attractive and good at supporting and defending her.

She couldn't decide exactly how she'd fallen into his bed—and still wanted to return there—but at least she was back on track.

After breakfast, she hurried upstairs to shower, but while she was getting ready, she couldn't help checking her phone every few minutes. She told herself she was looking to see if there was any word from her attorney, the station, Ethan or Tommy. And she was. But in her heart she knew she was also hoping to find a text from Dallas.

Something that would make what happened last night go away.

Something that would enable them to continue on as they were, at least until one of them left.

But he hadn't texted her, and he probably wouldn't.

She frowned as she read over their exchange last night.

You coming down?

Soon.

How long do I have to wait?

At least until your mother goes to bed.

I'm dying for a taste of you. We'll just close the door.

No way.

She'd felt giddy, breathless, waiting for the house to settle. And then, only two or three minutes later, he'd written.

Now?

She'd sent a laughing emoji, but she'd been every bit as impatient.

And then, only a few hours later, it was over.

Just that quickly.

She was ready for work by eleven-thirty and drove to the cookie store right away. She refused to take the chance that Dallas might return before she could leave. She knew she wouldn't have the strength to resist him if they had the house all to themselves.

Once she arrived at the shop, she sat in her car, waiting until it was time for work. She didn't get off until ten tonight. She was going to be at the store long enough as it was and figured she might as well reserve this last twenty minutes for herself.

Still determined to avoid social media, she read some news articles on her phone. Then she checked her email again. Her attorney had written to say he couldn't get Tommy to respond to him. He wanted her to reach out to him again, but she didn't have a lot of hope it would make any difference.

Just in case, she sent Tommy a text.

Really? You won't respond? Come on, Tommy. I'd be there for you.

She switched back to her inbox to let her attorney know she'd tried and would notify him if she heard anything—and found an email from an address she didn't recognize. She was half-convinced it was spam disguised as personal correspondence, except the subject line read: Emery, I loved it, and I love you! Since it had her name, and a positive subject line, she opened it just to be sure it wasn't something from an old friend.

It contained the picture of a man, naked from the waist down. His face was blocked out but he was wearing a Santa hat and showing off an erection so large it didn't look as though it could be real.

"Ew!" She was so shocked she dropped her phone, then had

to twist and bend to scoop it up so that she could delete the picture. Her spam filter was usually better than this. Figuring it had to be some porn site that had found a work-around to the latest firewalls, she sent it to the garbage.

But as it disappeared, some of the words above the picture registered in her mind. There was something personal in the message, too.

How could that be?

She retrieved it from the trash and, her chest rising and falling as her breath came quicker, read it carefully.

How would you like to work in the porn industry? It's not the nightly news, but I'd be happy to give you a ride you'll never forget—and we could capture what a real climax looks and sounds like. With the proper lighting, maybe viewers will even be able to see that little heart-shaped freckle on your thigh when I spread your legs.

She looked around as though she expected someone to jump out from behind one of the dumpsters in the alley and start pointing a finger and laughing at her. What was going on? Who had done this? And how did whomever it was get her email address?

She studied the sender's address: majorhardon. This wasn't spam. Whoever had sent the email had *targeted* her. Not only did he know her email address, he knew her name, her past occupation and about that sex video. She wrote back:

Who is this?

The answer came right away.

If you really want to know, meet me at the Blue Suede Shoe at midnight tonight. Then you can see the size of the woody you give me in person.

There was a knock on her window.

Startled, she screamed, but it was only Susan. Quickly shoving her phone in her purse so that her boss wouldn't look a little closer and see that obscene picture, she opened her door a crack.

"Aren't you coming in?" Susan asked, perplexed. "It's ten after twelve, and you're just…sitting here."

"Oh. Sorry," she said, and scrambled from the car. "I was reading a good article and must've lost track of time."

"No problem. What was it about?"

"What was what about?" she asked as she slipped past Susan to go inside.

"The article."

"Oh. It was about…it was about how…some guy mugged one of those bell ringers for the Salvation Army and stole all the money in his bucket," she said, grasping at anything she could think of.

"You're kidding!" Susan sounded horrified. "I haven't heard about that."

"It wasn't around here," she said, and hoped her boss would let it go as she put down her purse and moved into the front.

Fortunately, they were busy from the moment she put on her apron. Susan didn't have the chance to ask any more questions about that nonexistent article or anything else.

Emery was grateful that she couldn't dwell on Tommy's lack of response, that strange and upsetting email or how things had ended with Dallas last night. She was tempted to contact him, to tell him about the email she'd received, but she couldn't allow herself to lean on him. That wasn't fair.

He'd gotten her back on her feet. She had to navigate from here.

But as she closed up that night, she had to ask herself—was she going to the Blue Suede Shoe?

CHAPTER TWENTY-TWO

Emery felt self-conscious entering the bar alone. Because it was always busy on the weekend, and she couldn't imagine she'd be unsafe with so many people around, she'd decided to go. She'd once reported on a story about a spurned lover who'd impersonated his ex-girlfriend online and provided her personal information to men hoping to connect with women seeking a rape fantasy experience. Strange men had come to her house at all hours of the night, thinking she'd *requested* a sexual attack. Fortunately, nothing truly terrible happened to her, but it was frightening and sometimes difficult to convince her would-be "attackers" that her refusal wasn't part of the game.

Emery had to wonder if Ethan had posted her email address in a similar forum, hoping the men there would begin to harass her. If so, and she could prove it, the police would *have* to get involved. Setting her up went well beyond loading a sex tape onto the internet. Something like that could potentially result in physical harm.

She hadn't gone home to shower and change after work—she'd sat in her car and read for over an hour to pass the time—so her hair and clothes smelled like fresh-baked cookies. But at least most people liked the scent of vanilla. She'd been reluctant to return to Aiyana's for fear she'd bump into Dallas. She knew he'd ask about Ethan and if she'd heard anything on the lawsuit—they'd talked about that almost every day—and she'd decided not to tell him the latest. Not only was she determined to do a better job of handling her own problems, his brothers were coming into town today—she'd been hearing about their arrival all week—and she didn't want to get in the way of the family reunion.

After slipping through the crowd to reach the bar, she ordered a Sprite with a wedge of lime before picking her way along the wall to the far corner. She was hoping to find a vantage point from which she could view most of the people, but there were too many alcoves. She'd have to move around, actively search for whoever had suggested they meet here, even though she preferred to keep a low profile. After what'd happened the last time she'd visited the Blue Suede Shoe, she'd become a hot topic in town for something other than the video—or in addition to it—and this time Dallas had been drawn into the conversation.

Were they a couple? Had Dallas reacted in a jealous rage? Was he still the angry youth he'd once been?

But Aiyana claims he's gotten over all that… Aiyana must be beside herself… How can someone like Emery Bliss be good for him when she doesn't have any moral fiber herself?

Most of those comments hadn't been said to her face, but Susan had mentioned a few things, and she'd overheard others. Everyone seemed to be interested and hoping to learn a bit more so they could contribute to local gossip.

Her ears burned as people stared at her. She stood and sipped her Sprite, longing for the moment when everyone would just go on about their business. If she was lucky, she'd be able to blend in at some point.

No one else appeared to be out of place or expecting someone. But it was early yet. She had half an hour to wait. She'd just got-

ten tired of hanging out in her car, hadn't been able to concentrate on her book with so many other things on her mind and
had wanted to be the first to arrive, so that she could get into
position and, hopefully, be able to figure out what was going on.

As the time passed, she turned away a few offers to dance and
watched as several groups of people played darts or pool and still
more danced or hung out, talking and laughing at the bar. But
even at midnight she didn't see anyone who might be alone and
hoping to meet her.

It was almost twelve-thirty when she began to wonder if that
email had been a prank. Maybe Ethan had downloaded that
picture from a porn site and sent it himself as a way to intimidate her—and to remind her that he could still hurt her and it
would be hard to stop him.

That made sense. How would some random guy who'd received her personal information on the internet—meaning he
could live anywhere in the world—reach Silver Springs the same
day they'd exchanged emails? And how would he be familiar
with the Blue Suede Shoe?

On the other hand, maybe that wasn't such a stretch. After all,
there was nothing to guarantee he'd only received her information today. That exchange could've happened a week ago. Or...
LA was only an hour and forty minutes from Silver Springs. Any
online forum large enough could easily have members in such a
huge metropolis, especially if Ethan had used some kind of filter
to reach only those who were close enough to scare or harm her.

As for being familiar enough with the area to know of the
Blue Suede Shoe? That would only take a Google search.

She spotted someone who looked like Cain and almost walked
out. He was the last person she wanted to see—except for Ethan,
of course. But before she could take one step toward the door,
the person turned. It wasn't Cain.

Thank God. Still, it was time to go. She'd done all she could
here. Whoever it was hadn't shown up. Perhaps he was having

a good laugh from across the country over the fact that he'd probably sent her on a wild-goose chase.

She'd just stepped away from the wall when a tall, blond man in tight jeans, cowboy boots and a cowboy hat approached.

"Howdy," he said, tipping his hat.

It always surprised her when she found a true cowboy in California. That didn't happen very often in LA, but other parts of the state were quite rural. Cal Buchanon, the man Aiyana was about to marry, was a case in point. There were a lot of farms and cattle ranches up and down the Highway 5 corridor, especially between LA and Sacramento. "Hello."

This couldn't be her man. Any identifying details on that picture had been fuzzy and dark—the face intentionally hidden—but he didn't resemble the body type. Besides, he was only about twenty-three and came across as too young and too polite. She assumed he'd walked over to ask her to dance and was already formulating her refusal when he said, "A man over there said he'd buy me this beer if I let you know he'd meet you around the building in back."

Emery's heart skipped a beat as she began scanning the people in the area indicated. "What man?"

He turned to look. "Hmm. I don't see him. Must've gone outside already."

"What'd he look like?"

"I don't know," he replied with a shrug.

"You didn't see him when he bought you that beer?"

He seemed at a loss. "I saw him, but… Let me think. He was about this tall—" he lifted his hand to signify a height a few inches shorter than his own "—and had dark hair and dark eyes, I think," he added uncertainly. "The lighting in here isn't the best, and I don't come for the guys, so I don't make it a habit of looking at them too closely."

He chuckled, but she was too focused on what he'd told her to even smile. *Dark hair, dark eyes, average height.* That could describe Ethan. But it could also describe millions of other men. "What nationality was he?"

"White, I guess."

"Can you give me an age?"

"Thirties? Forties? I can't really say. Why? This comes as a surprise? You aren't here to meet anyone?"

"Not outside," she said.

"I'm sorry. I assumed the dude was a friend of yours. But I've done my part, so… I'll leave you alone."

She stopped him from walking away. "Are you familiar with Ethan Grimes?"

"Ethan who?"

Apparently not. "He's a newscaster on KQLA in Los Angeles."

"Never heard of him."

She used her phone to pull up a picture of him. "This guy here."

He reached up to scratch his head under his hat. "I don't think so."

"Well…did the man seem friendly to you?"

"Friendly enough to buy me this beer," he said with another laugh.

She got the impression he was slightly drunk and felt a twinge of irritation. This was serious. But only for her. He was just out having a good time and trying to be accommodating.

Emery hitched her purse higher on her shoulder and checked her phone as she tried to decide what to do. She couldn't leave the safety of the crowd to meet some stranger who could be dangerous out behind the building. Anything could happen back there. People had been mugged, kidnapped—or worse— in parking lots that were far better lit than this one.

"Well, thanks for passing the word along," she said. "But I won't go out there alone."

He finished his beer and put the bottle on the closest table. "I'll walk out with you, if you want."

She hadn't been hinting, but after what she'd said she could see why he might offer. "No, that's okay. I don't want to put you to the trouble."

"It's no trouble."

She was so curious about who'd sent that photo and whether she'd be able to tie it to Ethan that she was tempted. But she'd never met this cowboy before. "Really, I'm fine."

"Okay. Well, if the guy who wanted to meet you is out of luck, maybe you'll dance with me," he said and held out his hand. "I'm Terrell, by the way."

She just wanted to go home. But if there was someone waiting for her out back, who might be dangerous, she decided now probably wouldn't be the best time to leave.

With a smile she hoped did not appear as reluctant as she felt, she gave him her name and agreed to dance, and they danced several more times over the next hour. Terrell seemed a little immature, but being with someone was better than hanging out at the bar alone, waiting until she felt it would be safe to leave.

Just after one, she finally told him she had to go home.

"Can I get your number?" he asked.

There was an awkward moment during which she felt as though she had to give it to him, that maybe she'd misled him by allowing the friendship. But she knew she'd never be willing to go out with him, so she decided to be honest. "I'm sorry. It's been fun getting to know you, but I'm not open to a relationship right now. My life is...crazy. I need to figure out a few things first. Besides, I'm too old for you," she joked.

"Age doesn't matter," he argued.

She smiled and touched his arm to soften her words. "It matters to me."

He scowled and pressed a hand to his chest as though she'd just wounded him but seemed to take it good-naturedly. "Fine. At least let me walk you out to your car, make sure you get there safely. You seemed pretty leery of the dude who sent me over to talk to you. It might be smart to have someone with you when you go outside."

What he said made sense. And since he was willing, why not? "You're sure it won't be an imposition?"

"Absolutely not. As a matter of fact, I've going to take off now, too."

She peered closer at his face. "Are you sober enough to drive?"

"I think so, but I'm going to call an Uber, just in case."

He focused on his phone for a few seconds before shoving it back in his pocket. Then he jerked his head toward the door. "You ready?"

Grateful for his company, she left some extra money on the table for the waitress and walked out with him.

"I'm going to see if that guy who approached me is still waiting," he said as soon as they were outside and started toward the back.

She didn't think whoever it was would stand an hour in the cold and dark. More likely, if he knew what she drove, he'd be lurking around her car. So she followed Terrell.

It was dark in back. Only one dim light bulb hung over the back door so that employees could see well enough to haul the trash to the receptacle. Emery could see nothing else—just a fence and, behind that, raw land.

"There's no one here," she said peering toward that door from the corner of the building. She wasn't about to walk down there even with Terrell. The email invite had to be some sort of game, she decided—but the next thing she knew, Terrell grabbed her arm and jerked her out of sight so quickly she didn't even have the chance to scream.

As soon as she realized that he'd tricked her, that the entire past hour had been a setup, she opened her mouth to cry out. But it was too late. By then he had his hands round her neck and was squeezing so tightly she couldn't breathe.

"Leave Ethan Grimes alone. Do you hear?" he gritted through

a clenched jaw, his eyes glittering in the darkness like the stars she could see over his shoulder. "Drop the suit and do *nothing* to threaten him or his job—or this won't be the last you see of me."

His hands still around her neck, he pulled her away from the building only to shove her into it again, this time lifting her a few inches off the ground as he did so and banging her head into the rough brick.

After the big Christmas party at school, Dallas had gone to the airport to pick up his three brothers, who'd flown into Burbank. They'd hurried back to Silver Springs to do a quick rehearsal for the wedding, after which they'd all had pulled pork, potato salad and barbecue beans at Cal's ranch. It had been a loud, boisterous night with the nieces and nephews running around, trying to take the ornaments off the tree they'd decorated not only for Christmas but for the wedding.

Dallas had talked and laughed and played with the younger kids, carrying them on his shoulders or pretending to drop them to make them scream and laugh. He'd also enjoyed seeing the twins, Ryan and Taylor, who were on holiday break from graduate school, and Seth, who lived in San Francisco, worked as a sculptor and didn't come around very often since losing his wife.

But the later it got, the more concerned he grew. He'd expected Emery to come through the door long before now and was beginning to worry that she hadn't. The cookie store closed at ten and it was after one.

Where was she?

Aiyana had gone to bed and his two youngest brothers were gaming in one of the bedrooms since he, Seth, Ryan and Taylor were using the TV in the living room. They'd flipped off the lights, stretched out on the couches and put on a movie— a good one. Dallas should've been completely engrossed, and he would've been, except he'd finally broken down and texted

Emery about twenty minutes ago to see where she was, and he still hadn't received a response.

Was she angry with him? He'd known things were going to be awkward between them as they tried to navigate their friendship without sex, but he'd thought they could still communicate—until even his second plea went unanswered.

He thought of Cain and the night she'd had dinner with him. Had she met up with someone else from high school? Maybe she was having drinks with an old girlfriend and wasn't checking her phone.

It had to be something like that, he told himself.

But she *was* in a lawsuit with her ex-boyfriend, and he'd heard the threats Ethan had screamed at her over the phone.

"What are you doing, man?" Seth asked, distracted by the light of Dallas's phone going on and off every few minutes.

"Nothing," he replied but when he stood, Ryan paused the movie.

"What's up? Where are you going?"

"Mom told you about Emery Bliss, right?" Dallas said.

It was Taylor who answered. "Of course. That's why I'm sleeping in the same room as Ryan."

"Well, she should've been home by now. I'm going to drive to town, see if I can spot her car."

Seth started to get up. "Should I go with you?"

"There's no need to miss the movie. I'm sure everything's fine. I'll be back soon."

It was one-thirty by the time Dallas spotted Emery's car in the parking lot at the Blue Suede Shoe. It hadn't taken long to find. Since that was one of the only places that would be open so late, it was the first place he'd looked.

He called himself a fool for being so worried and would've driven on past it and returned home, assuming she was inside enjoying herself—except he spotted a piece of paper shoved under her wiper that made him curious enough to stop and get out to see what it was.

A group of two men and three women came out of the bar. He could hear them laughing and talking as they made their way to their various vehicles, but the parking lot was quiet otherwise.

He pulled out that paper and turned it over.

I mean it, bitch.

Those four words, written in black marker, took him back. He stared at them for a second, almost unbelieving. Then he looked around to see if he could spot anyone who might've left it or seen the person who did.

The three women and two men who'd come out were in their cars, pulling into the street and driving off. It was late enough that most of those who crowded into the Blue Suede Shoe Friday and Saturday nights had gone home.

He shoved that paper in his van and decided to park so that he could go inside. But as he drove down the row of cars that remained, still looking to see if someone was lurking about, he spotted police lights flashing behind the building.

What was going on? A sick feeling came over him as he parked, got out and walked over. Two police officers—one male and one female—were talking to someone who was crouched on the ground and huddled against the back of the building.

As he got closer, he could tell it was Emery.

CHAPTER TWENTY-THREE

Someone had choked her. Not bad enough to kill her, but bad enough to give her a good scare—and make him mad as hell. Dallas couldn't believe Ethan would have the balls to send someone out here to do what he heard Emery describe to the police, and he was determined to make him answer for it and everything else.

"You should go to the hospital and get checked out," the female police officer—an Officer Valentino—told Emery after she and her partner had finished taking the report.

Dallas agreed, but Emery wasn't having any of it.

"No. I'm okay," she insisted. "I don't want to go to the hospital. I got a couple of bumps and bruises, that's all. This was just a warning."

Dallas had so much adrenaline pumping through him it was difficult to stop himself from dropping Emery off at home and driving to Ethan Grimes's house tonight. But with Aiyana's wedding in the morning, he couldn't leave. Even if he could make it back in time for the ceremony, which wasn't until midday, she'd freak out if she woke to find him gone. And he didn't want her big day to start out like that, not now that Emery was safe with him. He could take care of Ethan later—especially because there was no telling what might happen once he got there. The confrontation could easily turn into an altercation, and fighting risked winding up in jail.

The officers promised to get in touch once they had a chance to investigate. As they went inside to see if anyone at the Blue Suede Shoe could identify the man Emery had described to them, Dallas helped Emery over to his van. They'd have to leave her car in the lot and pick it up later; there was no way he was going to let her drive home.

"You okay?" He lifted her into the seat instead of expecting her to haul herself up. He could tell she didn't have her usual strength. She was so rattled he even had to help buckle her seat belt.

She nodded and attempted to smile, but she was blinking rapidly, obviously fighting tears.

"We're going to get that bastard. Don't worry." He wanted to unclick the seat belt he'd just buckled and pull her into his arms—hold her close until she could stop shaking. That felt like a much more natural reaction. But, at this point, he wasn't sure she'd welcome it.

She nodded again, and he took off his coat and draped it over her to give her an added layer of warmth before walking around to the driver's side.

"Wh-what made you come look for me?" she asked as he climbed in, her teeth chattering—more in reaction to what she'd been through than the cold, he guessed.

"I was worried about you," he admitted. "When you didn't come home, I couldn't imagine where you were."

"Th-thanks for going to the t-trouble of c-coming out."

He hated the formalness that'd sprung up between them, especially when he was rattled and upset himself. "Why didn't you call me? Tell me about that dick pic and have me come with you tonight?" he asked, but he already knew the answer.

"Your brothers just got into town," she said, looking out the window instead of at him. "And it's your mother's wedding tomorrow. I didn't want to impose."

"*Impose?*" he repeated, bringing the van to a stop right in the middle of backing up. "*Really?* We've been fucking each other almost since I got home, Emery. You didn't think I'd be willing to help you? If you'd called me, this wouldn't have happened!"

He regretted being so harsh when the tears she'd been battling welled up.

"I'm sorry," he said, speaking more calmly. He was only yelling at her because he couldn't hold her, which was stupid. "I just... I can't believe you tried to take care of it by yourself. You didn't call me even *after* it happened. What'd you think, that you'd report it to the police and then drive yourself home?"

She didn't answer. He got the impression she was struggling to hold herself together and didn't dare get into an argument with him for fear she'd fall apart.

"He's not getting away with this," he said a few minutes later—to himself as much as her. "He has to be held accountable."

"You should've seen the guy who did it," she said dully. "You never would've guessed he could be c-capable of that." Her hands went to her throat as though she was remembering it. "He seemed so nice."

"I hope the police find that asshole. But even if they don't, I know where Ethan lives." She'd given him the address when he'd driven her to LA. He probably still had it in his maps, but he didn't have Ethan's phone number. "Share Ethan's contact record with me, will you?"

She wouldn't accept his phone when he tried to hand it to her. "No. I... I don't want you getting involved. This thing is already bad enough."

"Ethan and his friends won't do anything to me. I'm going to put a stop to it."

"You don't know that." She pulled the coat he'd given her up until only her eyes showed. "Maybe I should just drop the suit," she mumbled, more to herself than to him.

He looked over at her. "Are you serious?"

"I don't know. When that guy had his hands around my throat, and I... I couldn't breathe, it didn't seem worth it. The damage is already done. Everyone I ever cared about has seen that video. And I can't get my old job back."

Dallas didn't say anything. He *hated* the idea of her dropping the suit. He wanted Ethan and the station to pay for what they'd done. But he couldn't blame Emery for being tempted, not after tonight.

"You don't think I should?" she guessed when he didn't comment.

"Only you can make that decision," he replied.

As soon as they reached the house, he told her to wait so he could come around and help her out. She allowed that, but once they reached the porch and could hear the movie playing inside, she pushed him away so she could proceed on her own.

"Sleep with me tonight," he whispered, catching her hand before she could go in. "I promise I won't try anything. I just want to keep an eye on you. You could have a concussion."

"I'll be fine," she insisted. "You need to get a good night's rest. Tomorrow's a big day for your family."

"Come on, Emery—this sucks." He was referring to the distance between them as much as anything else, but she didn't answer. All of her defenses had gone up; she wouldn't allow him to get close to her again.

He missed her more than he'd ever missed anyone else. But he didn't get the chance to tell her so. She didn't wait any longer before opening the door, and the moment she did that, his brothers looked up and Ryan, once again, paused the movie.

"Everything okay?"

"Fine," Dallas replied as he watched Emery cautiously navigate the living room, as though she was afraid her knees might give out on her.

"This must be Emery," Taylor said, obviously surprised that there hadn't been any introductions.

Emery stopped when she heard her name. "It's been a rough night for me, guys, but I'm looking forward to meeting you all in the morning," she said, and grabbed onto the railing to help her climb the stairs.

"What happened to her?" Seth asked after she was gone.

With a sigh, Dallas shoved a hand through his hair. "Her ex-boyfriend put the fear of God into her."

"What does that mean?" Ryan asked.

"It got physical—at the Blue Suede Shoe," he admitted.

Taylor sat up. "She okay?"

"She's a little freaked out. Anyone would be. But I think she'll be fine in the morning."

"It's a good thing you went over there," Seth said. "Who was it?"

"I don't know his name, but I sure as hell hope to find out."

When his brothers glanced at each other, Dallas could easily guess what they were thinking, but it was Taylor who put it into words. "Is something going on between you two?"

"No, nothing," he said, but that only caused them to glance at each other again.

Saturday, December 19

Emery's throat hurt. She'd been so agitated and upset last night she hadn't considered the physical ramifications of that frightening encounter with "Terrell." She'd gotten off easy, considering what he could've done. But eight hours later, she could scarcely swallow.

She got up to go to the bathroom and was dismayed to see the discoloration on her neck. She could almost see where he'd put his hands—the bastard. Just remembering caused her to feel the same helplessness she had in those few seconds. She'd never forget the look on his face, the callous sound of his voice. Her throat would probably take only a few days to heal, but the emotional effects would take much longer.

Where had Ethan found this guy?

She'd never met him when they were together... Was his name even Terrell? She doubted it.

She could hear Aiyana and the many Turner men—as well as Cora and Savanna—talking and moving around the house. They were calling out to remind each other not to forget this or that, to ask whose turn it was to use the iron or to see if someone could sew on a button. She felt she should go down and help—but climbed back into bed instead. Although she had the day off so she could attend the wedding, she wasn't sure she'd be able to go.

After warring with herself for another thirty minutes, she finally gathered the Herculean strength it required to sit up and reach for her phone. Part of her desperately wanted to call her mother—the child in her who was hurt and craved comfort. But she knew how selfish it would be to worry her mother when Connie was already going through so much herself. She couldn't do that. She merely planned to see if she'd heard from the police.

No. Nothing.

She had, however, missed a call from her father.

Groaning when she saw his number, she debated whether she had the emotional reserves to call him back. Then she noticed that he'd left her a voice mail and, after listening to it, decided she definitely wasn't prepared to talk to him. He was asking for her help in persuading her mother to accept his latest offer, but she had no idea if it was a fair offer, and she wouldn't allow him to use her as a weapon against Connie. Although she was trying to remain neutral in the divorce—relationships could be so complex that she knew it would be unfair to judge—it was hard not to blame her father. After all, he was the one who'd already taken up with someone else.

It didn't help that Deseret wasn't anyone she liked...

"You're on your own with this one, Dad," she muttered. Why should she rush to *his* defense? He'd left her to manage Ethan and the loss of her job all on her own. He was actually making her life *more* difficult because he was being so stingy with Connie.

A knock sounded at the door. Pulling the covers up to hide the bruising on her neck, she called, "Come in."

Aiyana poked her head inside. "You awake, dear?"

"I am."

She crossed over to the bed. She was dressed in a robe, but her hair and makeup were already done for the wedding. She looked beautiful with her olive skin, her kind brown eyes and long thick hair, which had been curled. "The boys told me what happened to you last night," she said. "I'm so sorry."

Emery swallowed hard, trying not to succumb to the self-pity Aiyana's sympathy evoked. She couldn't allow herself to get emotional again. She had to buck up, couldn't cry all the time. "I shouldn't have trusted him. But he played it so well. I honestly thought he was safe."

She sat on the edge of the bed and took Emery's hand. "Of course you did. You'd never expect something like that."

Behind her, Dallas appeared in the doorway. He didn't come in, but Emery could see him leaning up against the doorjamb, his arms folded across his broad chest, his face a dark glower.

"Are you going to be okay?" Aiyana asked. "Dallas mentioned that you might need to see a doctor."

She reached up to touch the back of her head. It was tender there, too. But there wasn't anything a doctor could do. Only time could cause her bumps and bruises to fade. "That would be a waste of money that I don't really have at the moment."

"Have you heard from the cops?"

"Nothing yet."

"Well, I hope they find Terrell, if that's even his name, and that he gets what's coming to him."

"Ethan's the one who put him up to it," she said. "Even if they arrest Terrell, something like this could happen again. That's what I'm struggling with."

Aiyana made a sound of disgust. "I'd like to have a talk with Ethan Grimes."

"So would I," Dallas piped up.

"Maybe Dallas *should* pay him a visit," Aiyana said with a frown. "Someone has to stop him."

"It isn't Dallas's problem," Emery pointed out. "And you shouldn't be thinking about this, anyway. Not now. Please, enjoy your wedding day. It will only make me feel worse if this disrupts it in any way. I'll see you there."

"You don't have to come," she argued. "After what you've been through, you should stay here and rest. You have the day off and the house to yourself. Sleep. Recover."

Emery wished she could let herself do that, but she was too grateful to Aiyana. She couldn't miss the wedding, not if she could feasibly make it. "Are you kidding? I've been looking forward to it all month. I'll be there." She wasn't sure how, but somehow she'd manage it.

"Okay, well, Dallas and Seth will go over to the Blue Suede Shoe and bring your car back, just in case. Even if you don't come, at least you won't have to worry about anything happening to it."

"Can I get your keys?" Dallas asked.

Emery gestured at the dresser. "They're right there. Thanks for doing that."

"No problem."

He scooped them up as Aiyana said, "Really, though, don't put yourself under too much pressure."

"I won't," she lied, and forced what she hoped was a reassuring smile.

Aiyana squeezed her hand as she got up.

"You look beautiful, by the way," Emery told her. "Your hair turned out great."

"Thanks. Cora came over first thing this morning and curled it. She did my makeup, too."

Cora and Aiyana seemed especially close. "She did a wonderful job."

Dallas lingered after his mother left. "Are you really going to try to come to the wedding?"

She nodded.

Their eyes met and held, and she felt the longing she'd been trying to avoid tugging on her once again. She couldn't seem to squelch it no matter what she did, which just went to prove she'd let things go too far even though she'd known she shouldn't.

"You don't have to," he said.

"I want to." She couldn't tell what he was thinking, but he didn't seem happy. "Is there something else?"

"Yes. Will you give me Ethan's phone number?"

"No."

"I'm just going to talk to him."

"No," she repeated, unequivocally.

"Dallas?" Aiyana called up. "Will you come lift this big punch bowl into the back of my car? It's ridiculously heavy and somehow it didn't make it over to the ranch yesterday."

He shoved away from the doorframe. "Coming," he called down. He cast Emery a final, miserable glance and left without another word.

She thought that was the end of it, but about twenty minutes later, she received a text from him: I miss you.

She stared at those words. That was what he'd wanted to say when he was in her room. He just didn't know how, and she understood why. He couldn't say anything to follow it up, not what she most wanted to hear, anyway. It was as simple as it sounded, and she'd be stupid to construe it as meaning more.

It'll pass, she wrote—and prayed what she was feeling would pass, too.

The entire town turned out for the wedding. Dallas had expected it to be a big event, but he was still surprised by the number of guests who flowed onto the ranch like an engorged river. It was a testament to the number of lives Aiyana and Cal had touched.

Dallas smiled as he watched his mother greet each guest as though he or she were the most important person to have arrived and chuckled at the thought that she probably did the same thing with her sons—made each one feel as though he were her favorite.

She had a way with people and loved being around them. He, on the other hand, preferred to be out on the rock face alone, the sun beating down on his back, the sweat dripping into his eyes. He tried to remember the fact that he would soon be back in his element, no longer under the obligation he felt, for Aiyana's sake, to be more social. Because he could never match her genuine enthusiasm. He didn't feel comfortable in large crowds; all he wanted to do was retreat.

He stepped into the shadows so he could have a cold beer without having to smile or chitchat. He was gathering his reserves for the actual ceremony and the reception afterward, which he already knew would seem interminable, when Seth walked up. "Hiding out?" he asked drily.

Dallas loosened his collar. He rarely wore a tie, let alone a tux. "Basically."

Seth grabbed a glass of champagne off the tray of a passing waiter. "Great. I'll hide out with you."

"I think almost every one of us would rather face a firing squad than host a wedding," Dallas mused.

Seth's eyes roved over the crowd as he responded. "Of course. Take a look at the kind of children she adopted."

He was referring to the fact that they were all broken in some way, and since it was true, Dallas couldn't argue. Leave it to Seth to turn such an unflinching eye on reality. Dallas preferred to avoid such harsh truths. But Seth was an artist. He couldn't seem to ignore the things that made life so difficult. On the contrary, he noticed every damn nuance. "She looks happy," Dallas commented, watching Aiyana on Cal's arm as they made their way through the crowd.

"She *is* happy. And no one deserves it more."

"What about you?" Dallas asked.

Seth had been about to take a drink but held his glass in midair as he cocked one eyebrow. "What about *you*?" he asked, turning the question on him without answering.

"Well, I haven't settled into conjugal bliss like Eli or Gavin, but I just signed on with Xtreme Climbing Apparel, so I'm finally making some real money from climbing. And I'm managing—day to day."

"Managing day to day," he repeated. "That sounds reasonable. I'll say the same."

Dallas straightened as soon as he saw Emery walk in. She'd made it. She'd come even though she had the perfect excuse to stay home. He couldn't help admiring her for it. She looked beautiful, too, in a satiny black dress that fell to her ankles paired with a white blazer. She also wore a scarf to cover the bruising on her neck.

Following his gaze, Seth nudged him. "What's going on between you and our mother's pretty guest?"

"Nothing," he replied. "Why do you ask?"

His brother started to laugh. "Apparently, 'nothing' doesn't mean the same thing to you that it does to me."

"I like her," Dallas admitted.

"So do Liam and Bentley, but they can manage to look away."

"I explained it last night. Her ex-boyfriend is giving her a hard time," he said, his nose in his glass, since he was about to take a drink. "And I feel a little protective of her, that's all."

"You were beside yourself when she didn't come home last night, and you were even worse once you knew she'd been hurt," he pointed out.

"I was worried. And it turned out I had reason to be." He hated the defensive note that'd crept into his voice. It gave away the fact that he was a little more invested than he was willing to admit. But he couldn't help it.

"Have you slept with her?" Seth asked, point-blank.

Dallas shot him a withering look. "That's none of your business."

He laughed. "I'll take that as a yes."

There wasn't any point in trying to deny it. Seth missed nothing.

"Is it about sex, then? Is that all that's going on between you?"

Dallas opened his mouth to reply but couldn't find the right answer. It *was* all about sex—and yet sex had almost nothing to do with it.

When he hesitated, Seth said, "I'll take that as a no," and put his empty glass on the nearest table. "So here's my best advice. If this woman is different from all the rest—if she's the one who can fill the empty spaces inside you—don't let her go. Because I'm here to tell you that kind of woman doesn't come around very often," he added softly, and Dallas knew he was speaking of his late wife when he walked off.

CHAPTER TWENTY-FOUR

Emery heard several women in the audience sniff during the ceremony. Aiyana wasn't a young bride, but that made it even more meaningful. After spending most of her life as an unmarried woman, working hard and making it all on her own, she was finally getting the happy-ever-after so many people dream about.

To Emery's surprise, she began to relax and was quickly caught up in the magic of it. She was glad she'd come instead of curling up in bed and feeling sorry for herself. It was Christmastime—a time she normally loved—but she'd been so consumed with her problems she hadn't paid much attention to the beauty of the season. The wedding served as a reminder of all the little things she should still be grateful for in spite of her recent painful setbacks. There was music. The laughter of young children. The hope of better times ahead. The memories of Christmases past. The enduring love of family and friends.

Those things were what made Christmas what it was, she reminded herself. The holidays weren't only for those who had it easy. They provided a chance to rejoice *amid* difficulty. Maybe Emery didn't have everything she'd had before, but she had a friend in Aiyana, who'd taken her in when she needed it most. And she had a friend in Dallas, who'd been trying hard to protect her. They didn't *owe* her anything; she was lucky to have them. And, yes, she and Dallas had let things go too far, but even that had been wonderful while it lasted.

She also had the hope of better times ahead and the love of her mother, if not her father. If she really couldn't handle her own problems, her mother would stand by her just like she was standing by Grandma. Not everyone could count on that kind of loyalty.

And her father might get his head straightened out, eventually.

Susan slipped in late, and yet she made several people stand up to let her through so she could sit by Emery, which made Emery feel accepted and welcome—as if she belonged. When she'd first arrived today, she'd worried that her presence would create too much of a stir. There was the sex video, then the bar fight, then the police asking everyone if they'd seen the man who attacked her. She didn't want to distract from Aiyana and the celebration.

But her concerns had proved to be unfounded. The wedding seemed to be a time-out from regular life. Everyone was so happy for the bride and groom it pulled them together as a group and kept them focused on what mattered most.

"It's gorgeous in here," Susan whispered. "Who knew you could do so much with a tent?"

Emery studied the lights that had been strung overhead, the stand of real Christmas trees—three in varying heights—in one corner, decorated with silver ribbon and big glass balls, and the six-tiered cake not far away, with pink poinsettias adorning the frosting. "They've done an amazing job," she agreed.

The decorations weren't the only remarkable aspect. Emery had never seen a wedding line quite as large or striking as Aiyana's. Aiyana's eight sons stood beside her—all of them in the prime of their lives and looking so handsome in their tuxedos.

Cora and Savanna were there, too, sharing the role of maid of honor. On his side, Cal had four friends he'd known for years, together with one man who worked for him, three kids he'd adopted from a previous marriage and his brother, who'd come from San Diego to serve as his best man.

Without the tension and worry that had held her in such a tight knot since the trauma she'd experienced last night, Emery found herself smiling dreamily as she listened to Aiyana and Cal exchange vows. She was happy—happy for them if not herself—and she refused to think beyond that.

Susan nudged her. "Don't look now but someone can't keep his eyes off you."

Emery looked over to see Dallas watching her with an inscrutable expression. Her pulse quickened when she saw him, and she knew in that moment the truth she'd been trying to avoid. It was too late to save herself where he was concerned. She'd have to get over him along with everything else she had to do in order to rebuild her life.

But she couldn't bring herself to regret having slept with him.

Instead of overriding her natural inclination to single him out, as she'd been doing since she'd last left his bed, she allowed herself to meet and hold his gaze as she remembered what it was like to touch him, to taste him.

What she was feeling must've shown on her face because his eyebrows came together, and his gaze drilled into hers as if he was trying to read her mind. But then the priest instructed Cal to kiss his bride and the moment was lost as the wedding ceremony came to an end.

While those in the wedding party gathered for pictures, everyone else settled in to celebrate. The reception immediately followed, but Emery told herself she wouldn't stay for much of it. Aiyana would understand if she didn't make it through the whole thing. Before she'd left home, Emery had taken some ibuprofen to help with the soreness of her neck and head, but it was beginning to wear off.

After spending twenty minutes chatting with Susan and some of Susan's friends who were sitting at their table, she stood and was just reaching for her purse, so that she could go, when Dallas intercepted her.

"Would you like to dance?" he asked.

The quartet providing the music was playing "Make You Feel My Love," and several couples were already on the dance floor.

Emery knew she could use the excuse of what'd happened last night to decline—that she wasn't capable of being on her feet—but when she hesitated, he held out his hand and said beseechingly, "Dance with me."

Being in Dallas's arms proved to be as intoxicating as Emery knew it would be. She never felt more alive than when she was close to him, and it had been that way since he'd first walked into his mother's kitchen and taken her by surprise. She was afraid everyone in the room could guess how she felt about him.

But so what? She and Dallas were going their separate ways soon. She might as well let herself enjoy this moment. *He* was what this Christmas had brought her, and even though what they'd had couldn't last, she'd always remember him fondly.

"Seeing you walk in today took my breath away," he murmured in her ear as she settled against him. "That's how beautiful you are."

The warmth of his hand at her back seemed to travel through her clothes and skin, seep into her bones and begin to circulate through her bloodstream. "I'm glad I came," she said. "It's been good for me to get out and to think of someone else, for a change."

She assumed they'd keep everything polite and superficial and leave it at that, so she was surprised when he grew serious. "I'm sorry for how things ended between us, Emery," he said.

"But you deserve more than I can offer. You know that, right? I'm just not capable of being like Cal and so many other guys who can settle down and be steady and content. I wouldn't be able to make you happy even if I tried."

"Because you'd always be wanting to leave."

"Probably," he admitted.

"I understand. You love to climb, you're great at it and you have been given a fabulous opportunity. I would never want to stand in the way of you achieving your goals." She was trying to let him go gracefully. She didn't want him acting out of guilt or obligation, for God's sake.

But instead of relieving him, as she'd intended, what she'd said seemed only to make him more agitated. "I wish things were different," he said with a troubled scowl.

Letting her hands slip up to catch his face, she tilted it so that he had to look at her. "Since I'm in love with you, so do I."

What she'd said surprised her as much as it did him. Those words had come out spontaneously, but they'd also come from her heart, and that felt good. Honest. Regardless of anything else, they were, at least, true.

"What did you say?"

She dropped her hands and looked away, but she couldn't take the words back. Somehow, she didn't even want to. "You heard me."

"But…you can't mean it."

She could see several people around the room watching them, but she merely smiled. "I do. But don't let it freak you out. You can only feel what you feel. You can't make yourself love someone in return. I understand that."

"If you love me—why the hell have you frozen me out?"

"Because I had to at least try to save myself."

"Emery—"

"Don't worry about it," she said. "I'm not trying to put you on the spot. I just… I needed to tell you how I feel. It's—I don't know—*satisfying* to let it out, to quit trying to kill it or hide from it or deny it. There's no shame in loving someone, even if they don't love you back."

He stopped moving. "Are you sure? We haven't known each other for very long."

"We've known each other since we were kids," she corrected, and insisted he start moving again.

"I should've said we haven't spent a lot of time together."

"I can't explain how or why it happened, especially so fast, but it is what it is, and I can't change it. It's terrible timing when I'm dealing with so many other things, so I'm not any happier about it than you are."

"I care about you. I really do. I—"

"Don't," she broke in again. "I don't want platitudes. While I appreciate that you're trying to be nice, what you feel is so much less than what I want you to feel that it can't be any solace, if that makes sense."

He opened his mouth and closed it again before he finally said, "Any guy would be lucky to have you."

"I know," she said with a teasing grin. "But it might take a while to get over you."

"Emery—"

"It's fine," she insisted. "It won't even be awkward anymore. I'm going to go spend Christmas with my mother. She and my grandmother need me, and I should be there for them."

He stopped dancing again. "When did you decide that?"

She was slightly gratified that he didn't seem pleased by the news. "During the ceremony. The wedding made me realize that what I'm going through isn't the end of the world. My mother has lost the love of her life after sharing thirty-one years with him. My grandmother can't even remember my name. What both of them are going through is worse. I'm young and resilient. I'll find my way through what Ethan has done." She'd been hesitant to spend money she would need later, but she'd figure that out somehow. How could she not go and support them?

"But Christmas is only a week away."

"Meaning..."

"You must be leaving soon."

"You've stopped dancing again, and people are staring at us as it is."

Once more, he started to sway to the music. "So when are you leaving?"

"I'm thinking Monday."

"That's only the day after tomorrow," he complained. "That leaves us with almost no time."

"Right. This dance is about all I have left of you, so you'd better shut up and let me enjoy it," she joked. Then she closed her eyes and rested her cheek against his chest.

It was hard for Dallas not to go after Emery when she left the reception. She reminded him of Aiyana, who always offered her love without expecting anything in return. That was what made it so therapeutic, so potent and liberating.

Was he making a mistake letting her go?

"What's wrong?"

Hearing his mother's voice, he turned to find her at his elbow. "Nothing."

"I saw you dancing with Emery," she said. "The whole room was abuzz with it."

"This town loves gossip."

"Any small town loves gossip. Did she leave?"

"Yeah."

"Why? Is she okay?"

"Seems to be. She was tired of being on her feet and needed to lie down."

"I'm surprised she lasted as long as she did, poor girl."

He scowled at the doorway through which he'd seen Emery go. "She'll only be in Silver Springs another day."

"Where's she going? Back to LA?"

"No. To spend Christmas with her mother and grandmother."

Aiyana nodded. "That's good. I bet her mother will be very glad to see her."

He glanced around to make sure he could speak without being overheard. The room was crowded, but with the music playing and the roar of voices talking over it, he knew he was safe. "She told me she loves me," he said.

Aiyana, who'd just taken a drink, started to cough.

"Are you okay?"

Her eyes were watering by the time she was able to say, "Sorry, that went down the wrong pipe."

"I surprised you."

"That you would tell me surprised me. I already knew she felt something for you. You can see it in her face whenever she looks at you."

"So what do I do?"

"That depends…"

"On…"

"Whether you love her back."

"What if I don't know?" He knew a lot of things—that he enjoyed being with her. That he'd never been so turned on by someone sexually. That she was a wonderful person. But he'd always considered himself incapable of the kind of love a life-long relationship would require. And she deserved a man who could offer her that.

Besides, he couldn't settle down without giving up his sponsorship. What woman would be happy to see him head to Europe for half the year or more?

"Then I hope you find out soon, because letting her go could be the biggest mistake of your life," his mother said.

The conversation ended there. Cal approached and drew Aiyana away, and she was once again caught up in the whirlwind that was her reception. She chatted and laughed with her guests, cut the cake, spoke about her love and gratitude for Cal in a toast—and he did the same for her—and they danced their first dance as a married couple before driving off on their honeymoon later that evening.

But even as Dallas and his brothers got busy cleaning up and piling all the rental stuff in one section so he could return it on Monday, Emery's hands on his face as she gazed up at him and said, "I'm in love with you" played like a video loop in his mind.

Maybe he was foolish not to jump at the chance to be with a woman like her. She was the girl he'd wanted even back in high school.

But how could he take the risk of loving as deeply as she deserved to be loved?

Maybe he put himself in physical danger—challenged himself to climb steeper and steeper mountains—because he was too much of a coward to walk out on an emotional ledge. After all, he'd experienced the worst kind of fall. There were plenty of days when he felt as though that part of him—the deepest core responsible for trust and bonding—was still splattered on the ground.

CHAPTER TWENTY-FIVE

Dallas couldn't sleep with Emery right upstairs, knowing she wouldn't be around much longer. Every minute that ticked away felt like another minute wasted. They should be taking better advantage of the time they had left, shouldn't they?

He repeatedly checked his phone, hoping she'd text him. He even went up and stood at her door two different times, but he couldn't bring himself to knock. He didn't want to bother her if staying away from him was her best way of coping.

"Shit," he muttered, when he returned, once again, to his own room. He'd just taken off his clothes and was about to put his phone on the charger when he received a text message.

He grabbed his phone. Sure enough, it was Emery.

Would you quit prowling around the house? You're not making this any easier.

She ended it with a laughing emoji, so he knew she wasn't seriously put out and was surprised by the relief he felt that he now had the chance to engage her. He'd been losing his mind.

I know I'm the asshole who can't commit in this situation. But it's not like I don't feel anything. We don't have to make love, but won't you come down and sleep with me, at least? I just want to feel you next to me.

You know what will happen if I come down.

I can't say I don't want that. But even if it happens—would that be so terrible?

When she didn't respond, he thought the answer was yes—it would be too terrible.

But about fifteen minutes later, when he was lying in bed, wondering what she was thinking or if she'd just drifted off to sleep, he heard his door open and then the soft poof of whatever she'd been wearing as it hit the floor.

Dallas attempted to do nothing more than welcome Emery into his bed and curl up with her in his arms. He was glad she'd come to his room—grateful just to be with her. He didn't need anything else. But when she started kissing his neck and her hand slid down his stomach, he knew if he didn't stop her right away he wouldn't be able to prove he hadn't asked her to come down for that reason.

"I meant it when I said we don't have to do this," he told her, catching her hand.

"And you had a point when you said it probably wouldn't matter if we did, not with me leaving on Monday."

He hated that she sounded so fatalistic about making love with him, that she saw it as their last hurrah before she was gone and this Christmas became nothing but a memory. He didn't want to let her go; he just couldn't see another way.

"Dallas?" she whispered when he didn't release her hand.

Already rock-hard, he was too aroused to refuse what she was offering. He was always ready to make love to her.

"Okay," he whispered, and his heart began to pound as her fingers curled around him. If this might possibly be their last time together, he wanted to take it slow, to make love for hours. But all his good intentions came to nothing when she pulled him on top of her. Then he couldn't get inside her fast enough, and he didn't even care that the bed kept hitting the wall.

"We can stay in touch, can't we? Maybe after a few years, everything will be different," he gasped in the middle of it all. "A little time could change everything."

"But the opposite is also true," she said arching into him as though trying to join them even deeper. "We could hang on—and never go anywhere."

Despite the reality of her words, he couldn't think of anything beyond the taste and smell of her, and the warm friction created by the movement of their bodies.

"Damn it," he said when he came almost right away. "I couldn't stop."

"I didn't want you to stop." She kissed him and started to get up, but he pulled her back down. "No you don't. This isn't over yet. Give me a few minutes."

"But I can't stay. I'm afraid we'll fall asleep, and I'll forget to go back to my own bed."

"I'll set an alarm. Where's your phone?"

She gave him the code as she handed it to him, and he set an alarm for five-thirty. There was no way any of his brothers would be getting up before then, and Aiyana was gone. "Now we have most of the night," he told her.

She set her phone on the nightstand and spooned him as they fell asleep, and they made love again an hour later. This time Dallas managed to take it as slow as he wanted, and was gratified when she cried out, and he had to cover her mouth with his own so that she wouldn't wake Seth in the next room.

"God, that was good," she whispered as she fell back on the pillows, completely spent.

Dallas smoothed her hair off her face. "I owed you one."

They remained entwined until they'd both recovered, at which point he curled around her but didn't drift off. He stared into the darkness, waiting until her breathing evened out. Then he reached over to get her phone, put in her password and sent Ethan Grimes's contact information to his own phone.

Sunday, December 20

Emery had gone back to bed in her own room after her alarm went off, so she was alone when she called her mother the next morning.

"Hi, honey. How are you?"

She propped the second pillow behind her head. Although she'd listened before getting on the phone, she couldn't hear anyone moving around downstairs or anywhere else. Apparently the boys were sleeping in even later than she had. "Better."

"You are?"

Emery thought about the attack by that cowboy at the Blue Suede Shoe but decided not to mention it to her mother. There wasn't anything Connie could do about it, anyway. "I am. Definitely. And I've decided to come visit you for Christmas. Would you be able to pick me up at the airport tomorrow?"

"You're coming *here*?" her mother said, and immediately broke into tears. "I... I didn't want to ask you to come, but... I'm so glad you are."

A lump rose in Emery's own throat—along with a measure of guilt for making this decision so late and letting her mother believe they wouldn't be together for Christmas. But she'd been coping with her own difficulties and doing the best she could. "I considered surprising you, but the flight's going to be expensive. I decided to save the price of an Uber, if I could."

"Of course. I'll load your grandmother up, and we'll both be there. She'll be so excited."

If Adele could even remember who she was. Emery knew this probably wouldn't be the best Christmas she'd ever spent. She'd avoided going to Boston for a reason. But at least her mother wouldn't be left to continue to deal with Adele's memory loss on her own.

"What time?" Connie asked.

Emery hadn't even arranged her flight. Christmas was only six days away; she hoped they wouldn't be booked. "I'll text you as soon as I get my ticket."

They talked about the cold front that had set in back East, how much more it was going to cost to heat Grandma's house and what they should make for Christmas dinner. Emery was just about to hang up when her mother asked, "Have you heard from your father?"

Emery had never called him back. "He left me a message on Friday, saying he'd made you another offer. Is it one you can accept?"

"It's not much better than the other one, but I don't think Deseret will ever be fair. And there's something to be said for avoiding the upset and just...being done with the whole thing. What do you think?"

"I feel the same about Ethan and KQLA."

"Does that mean you're dropping the lawsuit?"

This was the question she'd been wrestling with since Friday night. She desperately wanted to walk away and leave it all behind her. But that would mean Ethan and Heidi and that "Terrell," or whoever he really was, would get away with what they'd done. "No. I can't. I owe it to myself to hold them accountable."

"That's true," her mother agreed. "And I owe it to myself to make your father treat me fairly. I'm going to reject his offer. We'll hang tough together."

Emery smiled at the sudden strength that had entered Connie's voice. Marvin had wanted Emery's help, and she'd done the opposite. But at least she felt good about it.

After she hung up, she went online and purchased a plane ticket that would put her in Boston at 9:30 p.m. It cost way more than she wanted to spend, but she tried not to worry about that. She'd get on her feet again.

She hated leaving Susan in the lurch at the cookie store, but she found solace in the fact that Susan wouldn't be any worse off than she'd found her. She'd actually given Susan some support when she'd needed it most, so she hoped that had helped enough. Because she couldn't stay any longer. She had to be there for her mother despite the expense. She couldn't believe she hadn't realized it sooner.

Planning to tell Susan when she went in that today would be her last day, she took a quick shower and went downstairs to make bacon and egg sandwiches for Aiyana's sons—the ones who were staying in Aiyana's house, anyway. She figured the least she could do was cook a final meal before taking off. Aiyana had done so much for her.

Dallas was the first one to enter the kitchen. He grinned the second he saw her, but then his gaze lowered to her neck and his expression hardened. She could tell he'd spotted the terrible bruises he hadn't been able to see at the wedding, because of that scarf, or last night, thanks to the darkness.

Grabbing her hand to get her to hold still, he ran a finger gently along the outline of them. "The man who did this had better hope I never find him. Ethan had better watch out for me, too."

She slipped away to put some bread in the toaster. "Enough terrible things have happened. The last thing I need is to worry about you."

"You won't have to worry about me. By the time I'm done with Ethan, you won't have to worry about him or his friends, either."

She lifted her chin defiantly. "I'm glad I didn't give you his number. With my luck, you'd wind up in jail."

Dallas didn't seem concerned. "I know where he lives. That should be enough."

"Don't go to his house. I'm not dropping the suit. When he realizes that he's not off the hook, there's no telling what he might do. If he could hire someone to hurt me, he could certainly do the same to you."

"I'm not scared of him."

She couldn't bear the thought of dragging Dallas any further into her mess, especially now that they were going their separate ways. *"Please?"*

"Sorry. I won't leave you at risk," he said simply and, using his body, pressed her up against the cabinets as he kissed her.

Emery's hands went up almost of their own volition and grabbed fistfuls of his shirt.

The sound of someone clearing his throat caused Dallas to step away.

"Good morning," Seth said cheerfully, and headed over to the coffeemaker to pour himself a cup. "You two didn't get enough of that last night?"

Emery's face went instantly hot, but Dallas tried to play it off. "Enough of what?"

Seth sent him a sardonic glance. "You forget—my room is right next to yours."

"God, don't you ever sleep?" Dallas grumbled with a scowl.

"Unfortunately, not very often. And thanks to the two of you, last night was worse than usual."

"I'm so sorry," Emery mumbled, but Dallas merely laughed.

"He's teasing," he said. "My brother has the driest sense of humor you'll ever find."

"I don't hold it against you." Seth lifted his cup in her direction. "Obviously, he's irresistible. It's him I blame."

"So? Take a nap this afternoon," Dallas said, and caught Emery's chin so he could kiss her right in front of him.

Seth watched dispassionately. Then he said—and even Emery could tell he was serious—"I hope you're not going to be a fool where she's concerned."

His words caused Dallas's demeanor to darken. But Emery had no idea how to interpret Seth's comment, because she didn't know what constituted a fool in his eyes.

"Stay out of it," Dallas warned, serious now, too.

Once Emery left for work, Dallas walked outside to call Ethan. Emery was gone, but he didn't want any of his brothers to overhear his conversation. Although he was tempted to drive to LA and teach Ethan the kind of immediate and painful lesson the douchebag deserved, he knew that might only get him arrested.

He couldn't be that stupid. Instead, he'd decided on what he hoped would be a better plan. He could always resort to a physical confrontation if this other idea didn't work.

After blocking his number, he called Ethan.

"I saw you on TV," he said as soon as Ethan answered, covering the speaker on his phone to disguise his voice.

"Who is this?" Ethan asked.

"You can't guess?" Dallas replied.

"I have no clue. How would I know?"

"I'm the one who threatened Emery Bliss for you. And now the cops are looking for my ass."

A heartbeat of silence preceded a befuddled "What are you talking about?"

Dallas tried to get even deeper into character. "Don't play stupid with me, asshole. After what I did, she's bound to drop the lawsuit. You should've seen her face when I had my hands around her neck. I did what you told me to. Now I need *your* help. I can't stick around here. I need some money to leave."

There was a long pause, then, "Is this some kind of joke?"

"Do you think it's funny?"

"Not at all. I just… I have no clue what's going on. Or how you got my number. I didn't ask *anyone* to threaten Emery. You didn't hurt her, did you?"

"Stop playing games, or I'm going to contact all the local news stations—including the one you work for—and tell them what you had me do."

"I didn't have you do anything!"

Dallas was beginning to believe him. He couldn't imagine why anyone else would be behind what'd happened, but Ethan sounded sincere.

"What'd you do to Emery?" Ethan asked. "You said you had your hands around her neck? You didn't *choke* her, did you? Is she okay?"

"She'll be fine. I just threatened her, like you said. And now it's time for you to make sure I don't get in trouble for it. Bring five hundred dollars and meet me at the Santa Monica Pier tomorrow at a quarter after midnight—right at the Ferris wheel—or the entire world is going to know that you sent me to Silver Springs to make her drop the lawsuit. Then the police will be coming for you, too."

"This is bullshit," he cried. "There's nothing the police can do. I'm not responsible for whatever you did to her."

"Stop fucking around! We both know that isn't true, so you'd better show up with the money—or else," Dallas said, and disconnected.

"What's going on?"

Startled, Dallas whirled around to find Seth standing in the shadow of the porch. "You followed me?"

Seth didn't answer the question. "Who was that?" he asked, pushing away from the wall.

"His name is Ethan Grimes. I told you what happened with Emery losing her job and all that."

"You did."

"That it was her coanchor who must've been behind the attack on Friday night."

"Let me guess—he claims he didn't do it?"

"Yes. I expected him to deny it, but... I don't know. He sounded pretty convincing."

"He *has* to be responsible," Seth said. "It doesn't make sense that it could be anyone else."

"That's what I thought. But...what about Heidi?"

Seth pursed his lips. "The producer?"

"Yeah. No doubt she'd like to see Emery drop the lawsuit against the station as much as Ethan would like Emery to drop the lawsuit against him—and if Emery dropped one, she'd probably drop the other. Having it go away could possibly save Heidi's job."

"I'd be stunned if it was her. Doesn't feel like something a woman would do."

"That's a stereotype," Dallas pointed out.

He shrugged. "You're right. I suppose it's possible."

"Well, I'll see if Ethan shows up with the money and go from there."

Seth tilted his head, a skeptical expression on his face. "Can't you get into more trouble for blackmailing someone than fighting?"

"It wouldn't be a fight—it would be a beating. And that's called assault. So, no. Besides, this isn't blackmail. I'm not going to take his money. I just want to find out who's responsible so that I can shut him—or her—down."

"Because you're *not* in love with Emery..."

Seth's sarcasm irritated Dallas. "I never said I didn't care about her."

Seth seemed to consider his response. "Fine. We'll give it a try."

"*We?*"

"I'm going with you tomorrow night."

"Why? You don't need to get involved."

"I'm jumping in to make sure a cooler head prevails," he said, but Dallas knew Seth was coming along to watch his back. He just wasn't the type to ever admit to something that sentimental.

"Sure you are," he muttered.

CHAPTER TWENTY-SIX

It hadn't been easy to tell Susan that she was going to leave town early. But her employer took the news well. "That's fine," she said. "My granddaughter just got out of school for Christmas break and is eager to earn some money to buy presents. She can step in. She's helped me so much in the past, I won't even have to train her."

"And you'll have Tobias, right? The way he looks out for you makes me feel a little better."

An affectionate smile curved Susan's lips. "I don't want to be a burden on Tobias. But you're right—he makes it a point to check in and do what he can."

Emery almost left it at that, but she was so curious about Susan and Tobias's strange relationship that she couldn't stop herself from asking how it had come to pass. "Is there a particular reason he's so attentive? I realize this might be none of my business, and it's fine if you'd rather not tell me, of course, but you mentioned that he's taught you not to judge others and… I can't help wondering how."

Susan stopped lifting the oatmeal cookies she'd just baked into the display window. "You haven't heard?"

"Heard what?"

Setting the spatula aside, she leaned one hip against the counter. "You know my son's a paraplegic. He worked at New Horizons but moved to LA a couple of months ago when he was offered a fabulous job as part of an IT team for a big company. He'll be home for Christmas, but you'll be gone by then, so you'll have to meet him another time."

Emery spotted movement outside the front window and thought they were about to get a new customer, but was relieved when the small group passed by the store without coming in. "If he's anything like your daughter, I'm looking forward to it."

"You'll like him—everyone does," Susan said confidently. "Anyway, when he was only eleven and my daughter was seventeen, she took him to a party without my permission. She wanted to see Maddox, her husband now, who had Tobias with him. Tobias was on some type of drug—acid, I think—and while he was wandering around the house, he found a handgun in the nightstand of the master bedroom."

Emery covered her mouth. "Oh no…"

"Oh yes," Susan said ruefully. "Atticus was looking for a quiet place to watch TV, away from all of those partying teenagers, but when he walked into the master bedroom, he startled Tobias at the wrong moment."

Emery's heart dropped along with her hand. "Don't tell me he fired the gun."

Susan nodded sadly. "I thank God every day that he didn't kill him, but Atticus hasn't been able to walk since."

"Wow." Emery bit her lip. "Tobias didn't get in trouble for what he'd done?"

"He did. They tried him as an adult, and he spent many years in prison. As a matter of fact, he's only been out for eighteen months."

"And you've forgiven him?" Emery asked, as shocked as she was impressed.

"There were a lot of mitigating factors to what happened—factors I couldn't take into account at the time. The way he was raised. The lack of intention. The severity of his punishment. The remorse he felt. It's taken me years, but I've finally come to terms with it all, and with him."

"What about Atticus?"

"He was able to forgive before I could."

"Wow." Emery puffed out her cheeks before letting the air go. "I had no idea. I'm not sure I've ever heard of anything like that before."

"No doubt about it—it's a tragedy. Although I'm sure we're not, I hope we're the only ones something like that ever happens to," she said as she returned to filling the display windows.

Emery moved one of the empty trays out of her way. "No wonder he takes such good care of you."

"It's hard to believe, but I love him now," Susan said simply.

Someone walked in, so Emery took their order and rang them up, after which she said to Susan, "Are you really okay if I go to Boston?"

"I'll be fine," Susan reassured her.

Relieved that her employer, who'd become her friend, wasn't disappointed, Emery hugged her. "Thank you for hiring me. I know I haven't been here long, but this job has been really good for me. And I'm not only referring to the money. It forced me to get out and interact with people when all I wanted to do was hide, and that was such an important first step to facing the world after...after what Ethan did."

"What he did was *so* unfair. But you'll put it behind you eventually, just like we've put our tragedy behind us. You're a strong woman. You'll rise to the top again. And I hope he rots in hell," she added.

Emery was laughing at that comment when the bell sounded over the door. Because Susan was intent on finishing the baking, she walked into the back so that Emery could wait on what would be their second customer of the day. But it wasn't a customer; it was Officer Valentino.

"Good morning." The officer rested her hands on her gun belt. "I saw the Open sign and thought I'd stop in to let you know that we've done everything we can to locate the man who assaulted you Friday night. We've talked to everyone who was at the Blue Suede Shoe, but we haven't had any success. Several people saw him, but no one can tell us his name, where he's from, anything that would enable us to track him down. He must've come from out of town."

"No one saw what he was driving?" Emery had slid to the ground after he choked her, hadn't even considered following him. She'd been too weak and shaky to even stand as she gulped in the air she'd been denied.

Now she wished she'd managed to do more.

"Nothing that will help," Officer Valentino said. "One couple claims he left in a white SUV, but you know how many of those are on the road. Without a license plate or something else…"

"There's nothing more you can do."

"I'm afraid not."

Damn it. Ethan was going to get away with this, too. "Thank you for trying," she said with a sigh.

"We'll continue to keep our eyes open. It's possible he'll turn up."

Not if he was smart. Emery guessed he lived in LA and would have no reason to come back to Silver Springs—not if she was in Boston and no longer around to bully and threaten.

As soon as Officer Valentino left, she texted her attorney:

Any word from Tommy?

It was a Sunday—not what she would expect to be working hours for an attorney—so she was surprised when she received a response: Nothing.

Are we going to be able to win this case?

All we can do is try.

That didn't give her a lot of confidence.

She texted Tommy again even though he'd never responded to her the last time.

If you know something, please speak up. Ethan had someone threaten me with bodily harm on Friday night if I didn't drop the suit. I still have the bruises around my neck from where he choked me.

She stared at her phone, silently willing Tommy to have some compassion. But when he didn't reply, she gave up and shoved it in her pocket. The store was getting busy. She couldn't continue to deal with her personal problems at work.

It was three hours later, when she took lunch and pulled out her phone to text her mother with her flight information, that she found Tommy had actually sent a message in reply: I'd drop the suit.

Her mouth fell open.

And let him get away with what he's done?

It's better than getting hurt.

No way. I won't do that.

But he wouldn't engage again.

Because her car would be safer in Silver Springs, and Aiyana had texted Dallas to say that it was okay for her to leave it at the school, Dallas drove Emery to LA after she got off work. Her flight wasn't until midafternoon the following day, but traffic could be uncertain, especially coming from almost two hours away, so she wanted to be closer to the airport. She also wanted to repack her bags with warmer clothing and check on her apartment before flying off to Boston.

They didn't arrive until after seven, so he insisted on taking her out for a nice dinner before they went to her place. He hadn't mentioned staying over, so when he carried her luggage up to her apartment, she assumed she'd take an Uber to LAX tomorrow.

Her apartment wasn't in the best possible shape. Seeing it through Dallas's eyes made it even worse. Dirty dishes were stacked up on the counter and filled the sink. Laundry was piled on the washer and the floor. Her coffee table and end tables were thick with dust. And all the houseplants she'd abandoned were dead.

Embarrassed, she opened a window to air out the place, and started dumping any leftover food in the trash or down the garbage disposal.

"Nice place," he said as he walked around, looking at the art on the walls as though he didn't see—or care about—the mess.

"I could barely get out of bed when I left here," she explained. "I'm glad I came home early so that I can get this place cleaned up."

"It's not that bad." He nudged her out of the way so he could close the garbage sack she'd filled. "Where can I take this?"

"I've got it," she protested.

"Let me help."

"But you have a long drive to get back home, and it's already nine o'clock. You should get going."

He frowned. No doubt he could tell that she was already pushing him away—at least in an emotional sense. "I thought I'd stay over and take you to the airport tomorrow, if that's okay."

"No need to put yourself to the trouble. I can grab an Uber." She tried to take the sack from him, but he wouldn't let go.

"After what happened at the Blue Suede Shoe, I'd rather not leave you alone."

"I don't need you to protect me," she said. "I'll keep the door locked. I'm sure everything will be fine."

Straightening, he held her gaze. "I don't want to leave when we still have more time, Emery."

She hated the thought that they were coming to the end of whatever had started between them. What they'd had was so unexpected and so good for her—something that had nothing to do with rational thought or checking off a list of traits and preferences that signified he'd be a good match. It simply felt right—natural, comfortable, instinctual. But she preferred to say goodbye now—to get it over with so that she didn't have to dread it any longer.

Still, she didn't want to be rude, not after everything he'd done for her. "It's just that… I know you don't get to see your brothers very often, and Seth won't be staying in Silver Springs for long."

His scowl darkened. "Stop with the lame excuses."

"Fine. The garbage bin is on ground level around the build-ing to your right."

"Got it." He walked out of the kitchen, but as he carried the garbage through the living room, she heard an ominous crunch.

"What was that?" She hurried out to see that he'd stepped on the broken glass she hadn't bothered to sweep up when she'd thrown a framed photograph of her and Ethan against the wall.

Dallas was bending down to see what he'd stepped on. "Noth-ing. I got it."

"Are you okay? You didn't get cut…"

"I'm fine." After staring at the picture of her and Ethan—their arms draped around each other at a friend's wedding—he dumped the frame, the glass and the picture inside the garbage bag. "Do you have a vacuum so I can clean up the smaller shards?"

"I'll take care of it."

She was just opening her broom closet when he came up behind her. Resting his hands lightly on her shoulders, he said, "Why won't you relax and let me help you?"

She was tempted to close her eyes, to let herself feel the heat of his body, the fulfillment that came with just having him around, but she didn't want him to know that such a small thing could mean so much to her. She was determined to respect the fact that his feelings for her were not as strong as hers were for him, and she refused to make him uncomfortable by coming off as needy or grasping. She thought if he hadn't been through what he'd been through, things might be different. But if he wouldn't open up and let her in, there was nothing she could do. She'd tried to talk about his past several times since she'd learned of it, but he'd shut her down every time. "There's no need—that's all. I've got this."

"It'll be easier to clean up this place if we both do it. It'll be easier for you to get to the airport if I drop you off. After what happened at the Blue Suede Shoe, it might even be easier for you to sleep, knowing I'm here. Why are you so anxious to get rid of me?"

"Because it's going to be hard enough," she said. "We should just...get the goodbye over with."

He turned her to face him and lifted her chin so she'd have to meet his gaze, but he didn't get a chance to say whatever was on his mind. A determined knock at the door interrupted.

Somewhat relieved to avoid whatever had been coming next, she hurried to answer it.

With Dallas in the apartment, she felt perfectly safe, didn't bother to check the peephole. She threw the door open, expecting a neighbor carrying a box that had been delivered while she was gone or something.

Instead, it was Ethan who stood on her stoop. *"You!"* she said.

"It's about time you came back," he responded. "I would've driven to Silver Springs, but it felt too much like entering the lion's den. Whoever you've been with certainly doesn't like me much."

"For good reason," she stated. "But…how'd you know I was home?"

"I asked the neighbor to give me a call if she ever saw you."

"My *neighbor* contacted you?"

He gave her a taunting smile. "She happens to be a loyal fan."

"A loyal fan of *yours*, maybe. Anyone who was loyal to *me* would never do such a thing."

His smile faded. "Look, I'm sorry, okay?"

"For…" She was dying to hear him admit what he'd done, to take responsibility for it. But he didn't answer. He leaned closer, his eyes widening in shock.

"Are those *bruises* on your neck?"

"Yes," she snapped. "That's what happens when someone chokes you! After everything you've done to destroy my life, I can't believe you'd send some thug out to Silver Springs to intimidate and threaten me."

"That's just it," he said. "That's why I'm here. I didn't send anyone. Would I like you to drop the lawsuit? Hell, yeah! But I would never have anyone *hurt* you."

"*You* hurt me!" she cried. "You posted that video online and—"

"Look," he broke in. "You're suing me. I can't comment on that. I'm sorry if anything I've done has caused you pain, but I didn't do this." He gestured to her neck.

The door slipped out of Emery's hand as Dallas opened it wider. "We're going to find the cowboy who choked her and prove you were behind it all, so you might want to admit the truth now. I promise I'll be in a far more forgiving mood if you do."

Ethan stepped back. "I know you…"

"I'm going to get to the bottom of this if it's the last thing I do—even if I have to hire a private investigator," Dallas went on, ignoring his reaction. "And when I have the proof I need, I'm coming after you."

Ethan lifted one hand. "You were the guy who came to the house and asked for Tommy. You said…" He glanced between them. "Oh, I get it. That was a setup. You're also the one who threatened me."

"Like I said, we're going to get the information we need—one way or another," Dallas reiterated.

"I can understand why you wouldn't believe me. But I didn't have anyone choke Emery."

"Maybe that wasn't what you specifically requested, but if you sent someone out there, you're responsible for it," Dallas insisted.

Ethan pressed a hand to his chest. "You don't understand. I really didn't do it! Having someone *attack* her is serious. I'm not that kind of guy."

The neighbor came out and looked down at them. "Thanks for the call," Ethan said, wearing a forced smile as he waved at her. Then he lowered his voice, "Can I please come in so that we can work this out in private?"

Emery shot her neighbor a dirty look for taking Ethan's side, and the woman ducked back into her own apartment as Dallas opened the door even wider. "I'd *love* to have you come in," he said.

Ethan shot Emery a worried glance. "This guy's going to hear me out, isn't he?"

"To be honest, I don't know," she said but only because she took some small pleasure in the fact that he was nervous. For all everyone had to say about Dallas's temper, she knew she could trust him not to go too far.

"You'll be fine as long as you don't lie to me," Dallas said and waved him in.

Emery perched on the edge of the sofa. She saw Ethan's eyes flick to the table where their photograph had once been, but he didn't mention that it was missing. "Where did you meet the cowboy who assaulted me—this Terrell?" she asked as Dallas settled beside her and he sat on the chair across the coffee table from them. "He wasn't anyone I've seen you with before."

"I don't know a Terrell, or any cowboys, for that matter," he said. "What'd he look like?"

Emery described him.

"I honestly can't think of anyone in my circle of friends who fits that description."

"You had to have met him somewhere," she insisted, but before Ethan could respond, Dallas spoke up.

"Could it be Heidi who's behind what happened?"

"Our producer?" Ethan said.

"*Your* producer," Emery clarified.

He blanched at the reminder of her lost job but responded to Dallas. "I can't see her doing anything like that. She knows if she were to get caught, it would only make matters worse. And she doesn't have the kind of friends she could ask to handle something illegal. I don't think she has *any* friends. All the woman ever does is work."

"It has to be you or her," Emery insisted.

"I thought so, too," Dallas said. "Until I remembered the email that came with that obscene picture. Whoever wrote it mentions the freckle on your thigh."

"I changed at work all the time," Emery explained. "She could've seen it. It even shows below some of my shorts—my cutoffs, for sure."

Ethan stretched out his legs and his chest lifted as he drew a deep breath. "I hate to even suggest this, but…do you think it could be Tommy?"

"*Tommy?*" she echoed. "Why would Tommy do something like that?"

"He's weird when it comes to me. He has this…crush on me, I guess. He always acted jealous of you."

Tommy had admitted his feelings for Ethan, and he'd certainly been protective of him—to the point he wouldn't help her with the suit—but she couldn't imagine he'd go so far. "He has a partner. And I'm out of the picture. Why would he try to do anything to me?"

"He and his partner are on-again, off-again. Now that I'm available, it could be some misguided attempt to curry favor with me."

"If that were the case, wouldn't you know if he was up to something?" Dallas asked.

"Not necessarily. He could be hoping Emery will drop the suit before he takes credit for making her do it."

"No," Emery said. "If it's not you, it has to be Heidi."

Ethan shook his head. "I don't see it. I would be shocked if it was her."

"Let's see if we can find out," Dallas said.

Emery looked askance at him. "How?"

Dallas directed his response to Ethan. "You tell Heidi, Tommy, everyone you know that a man called you, claiming you put him up to assaulting Emery, and now he's demanding you meet him at the Santa Monica pier tomorrow night at twelve fifteen with five hundred dollars in hush money. Tell them you're afraid that even if you give the guy the money, he'll tell someone and you'll lose your job and go to jail. Or he'll just come back and demand more. Say you aren't going to meet him because you didn't do anything wrong, but you're terrified to imagine what he might do when you don't show."

"Someone *did* call me and say those things. He…" Ethan's words suddenly fell off. "It was *you*! *You* did that, too."

"Yes," Dallas confirmed.

Confused, Emery scooted even farther forward. "You did

what? You mean you talked to him again, after you took the phone from me in the kitchen? How'd you get his number?"

Dallas sent her a sheepish glance. "I'll tell you about it later, okay? For right now..." He turned his attention back to Ethan. "What do you say? Will you do it?"

"I'd like to find out who's behind this as much as you—to prove it wasn't me—so I'm down. But I don't see how what you're suggesting will make any difference."

"I think whoever has gone to such great lengths to protect you will feel responsible for this latest bit of trouble and will show up to try to stop what's going on."

"That makes sense," Emery admitted.

Ethan bit his lip as he considered what he'd heard. "So you're hoping Tommy or Heidi will show up to pay off the guy or try to reach a resolution."

"Yes. They'll be afraid he might expose them. Wouldn't you get involved if you'd done something like that and then heard the guy was blackmailing the person you were trying to protect?"

"I'd be tempted," he admitted.

"Let's hope it's a temptation whoever it is won't be able to resist," Dallas said.

"Okay." Ethan stood. "But I want to be there tomorrow night, too, so that I can see for myself if anyone shows up."

"That's fine," Dallas told him. "You can hide someplace where you can keep an eye on what's happening. And I'll wait at the end of the pier."

"Fair enough." Ethan took out his keys. "I'll call Tommy and Heidi right away, start the ball rolling."

"Try to sound as natural as possible," Dallas cautioned. "You have to sell it, or this whole thing will be for nothing."

"I understand." He moved to the door, where he put one hand on the knob before looking back. "So are you two...you know...together?"

"We're just friends," Emery piped up.

His attention shifted to the table where their picture had once been. "I planned to marry you," he said softly. "I couldn't stand to lose you."

"So you wanted to hurt me?"

"I'm sorry. I never intended for things to go this far. I was... hurt and angry myself. I know that's no excuse, but... I didn't expect you to lose your job or...or anything else."

She shook her head. "That's pretty naive."

"I know. Again, I'm sorry."

Emery massaged her temples as she tried to decide how to respond. "I can't say I forgive you. You've cost me too much. But...who knows?" She thought of Susan and all Susan had for-given—and how much better off she was because of it. "Maybe I'll be able to one day."

He seemed to accept that, probably knew it was the best he could expect.

"That's got to feel good," Dallas said after he was gone. "He admitted what he did. I mean, he didn't come right out and say, 'I put up that video,' but he might as well have."

"It couldn't have been anyone else."

Dallas shoved his hands in his pockets. "Do you think he's telling the truth about not being the one behind the attack at the Blue Suede Shoe?"

"He seems adamant. I doubt he'd show up here to plead his case if he was behind it, especially because he did sort of admit the part about the video."

"I guess we'll find out tomorrow night."

"Are you sure you should go?" Emery hated that she wouldn't be around to do it herself, that someone she cared about felt as though he had to do this for her, especially when he could be spending the Christmas holiday with his brothers. "What if Terrell shows up, and the situation gets out of control—he has a weapon or something? We should call the cops and have *them* be the ones who are waiting."

"I have to be there to finish what I've started, but I'll call them if I need them. Maybe they'll be able to make an arrest."

She pulled her hair up and wound it into a bun before letting it fall. "It's not right to ask you to take care of my problems."

"You didn't ask."

"That's true," she said. "How'd you set all of this up?"

"Do I have to tell you?"

She thought it over and decided she'd rather not know. What was done was done. "I guess not. But after everything that's happened, I bet you're sorry you ever met me."

"And *I* bet I'll be sorry I ever let you go."

CHAPTER TWENTY-SEVEN

Monday, December 21

Preparing to say goodbye to Dallas was every bit as difficult as Emery had expected it to be. As the hours slipped by until it was time to leave for the airport, she kept coming up with compromises in her head—options she could suggest that might make him change his mind. But she knew if he wasn't willing to look for common ground and offer some compromises of his own, they'd never make it.

Bottom line, he had to fight for what they could have together, just like she was willing to fight, or she would only prolong the inevitable—and possibly screw up her life in the process.

She had to do what was best. That was the only way to make her future better than her present.

Afraid she'd falter at the last second, that all the longing she felt would come pouring out, she held herself rigidly as he turned into the airport. LAX was always busy, but today, with Christmas coming up, it was totally congested.

"Are you sure you have everything you're going to need?" he asked.

She watched the Christmas decorations on the light poles—green wreaths with red bows—creep past as they inched forward. "If not, I'll have to buy it while I'm there. We don't have time to go back to the apartment. I'll miss my plane if we do."

"I'll be in Silver Springs until after Christmas. I could always come get whatever it is from your apartment and ship it to you."

He knew she'd left a key out, in case she had to ask someone to take care of something. But she wouldn't ask him. She wasn't going to continue to communicate with him, not once she learned about tonight and whether he was able to find out who was behind the attack. Calling and texting each other after that wouldn't lead to anywhere good. "It's okay. I'll be fine."

They hadn't made love last night. As much as Emery wanted to be with him in that way, she couldn't do it again, not while she was trying to leave with some dignity.

He'd seemed to understand, because he'd simply curled up beside her to sleep—hadn't attempted anything more.

"Well, just know that I'm willing if you need me," he said.

"Thanks." She knew he'd be surprised if she told him that she planned to block his number and cut off all contact. He wouldn't understand why she had to do that. But he wasn't in her position. She had to do whatever she could to get over him and move on. Otherwise, she feared she'd hang on forever.

"This is it," she said when they reached her airline.

He got out and retrieved her big suitcase from the back of his van while she grabbed her purse and carry-on.

"Have a safe trip," he said as he brought it to the curb. "Call me when you land in Boston so that I know you arrived safely."

"I'll arrive safely. Millions of people fly every day without incident."

The frown he'd been wearing so often the past two days reappeared. "What's one phone call, Emery?"

"It's nothing, but we can talk after you've been to the pier. I'll be dying to know about that."

He acted as though he was tempted to argue but ultimately sighed in resignation. "It's three hours later in Boston. Do you really want me to wake you at three-thirty in the morning?"

"Absolutely."

"Okay."

She took her suitcase and gave him a smile she hoped didn't look too wobbly. "Thank you for everything. I really appreciate it."

He leaned in to kiss her, but she turned her face at the last second and his lips brushed her cheek.

"Thanks again," she said, and gave him a brief but impersonal hug before she rolled her suitcase into the terminal.

She could feel his gaze boring holes into her back as she started toward the counter, but she didn't turn around to wave. She was only pretending to check in while waiting for him to leave. She didn't want to face airline employees or fellow passengers quite yet.

As soon as she felt safe that Dallas was gone, she found a seat, sat down and buried her face in her hands.

Dallas arrived at the pier alone. Seth had almost driven to LA so that he could come along—he'd tried to insist on it—but Dallas had talked him out of it. Since Dallas had come to town with Emery and then stayed over, he was already in Los Angeles. There was no need to make his brother drive almost two hours for what would probably amount to a five-minute encounter, especially when Dallas felt confident he could handle it on his own.

The wind whipped at his hair and clothes as the lights of the Pacific Wheel, the world's only solar-powered Ferris wheel, showed a giant festive snowman that waved—so large and bright it could be seen for miles. This section of the California coast was almost always busy, especially during the holidays, but the attractions they featured here, like photographs taken with fully costumed merpeople, were long over and most everyone was gone. Although the park would be closing any minute, the pier was open 24-7, but tonight it was too cold for many people to have lingered.

He'd talked to Ethan half an hour ago and knew he was already in place, hidden to one side of a closed tourist shop. Ethan said he hadn't seen Tommy or Heidi, but he was being careful not to go too close to the Ferris wheel, so it made sense that he wouldn't. Dallas hoped one of them would show up and end his search for whoever put that cowboy up to threatening Emery. Providing they could catch that person, they should be able to catch the cowboy, too. All they'd have to do was search phone records, contacts, that sort of thing, and he felt certain the police would be willing to do that, given that the cowboy had gotten so physical with Emery.

Pulling his coat closed, Dallas ducked his head as he picked up his pace. He hadn't been able to get Emery off his mind since he'd left her at the airport. The way she'd acted once they returned to Los Angeles had been so remote. He could tell she was preparing to move on without him, and he couldn't blame her. He had to respect her for being unwilling to settle for less than what she wanted, but he definitely felt the loss. On top of everything else, his mother and brother thought he was crazy for letting her go.

It didn't help that he trusted their judgment.

But he was actually doing her a favor. He couldn't give her what she needed. For him, love equaled fear. He couldn't trust enough to step out of his isolation.

As he got closer to the wheel, the operator shut everything down and the snowman disappeared as the lights snapped off. "We're closed," the man announced the minute he spotted Dallas loitering near him.

"No worries," Dallas said, and stepped out of the way so he could leave.

He gazed out to sea, listening to the waves crash up on the shore. Occasionally, he'd turn around to see if he could spot Ethan, but Ethan was doing a good job of remaining out of sight. Dallas hoped he'd followed through with the plan and told his friends and contacts what he was supposed to tell them. But Dallas couldn't be sure about that any more than he could be sure his plan would work even if Ethan *had* followed through.

It was twelve-thirty when he began to think this would be a wasted trip. No one was coming to meet him. The last few stragglers who'd been at the pier when he arrived were gone. He seemed to be all alone.

He decided to wait fifteen more minutes, just to be sure, but still no one approached. A woman wearing a thick coat with the hood pulled up against the cold was the only other person in the area. She'd walked past him a few minutes earlier, and although he couldn't see anything other than her face, he could tell she was too old to be Heidi.

He pulled out his phone to let Ethan know he was calling it off. First he was going to turn off the app Emery had told him to download that would record the audio part of whatever happened, but right in that moment the woman approached. He assumed she needed directions, some change for a bus ride or a light for a cigarette, but she surprised him by pulling a bag out of her coat and tossing it at his feet.

"Here's what you want," she muttered before pivoting abruptly and hurrying back up the pier.

Scooping up the bag, Dallas shoved his phone in his pocket and took off after her.

She could obviously hear his footfalls on the wooden planking, which frightened her. Crying out, she started to run in earnest, but he was younger and quicker and was able to head her off.

Holding his arms out in front of him in the classic stop posi-

tion, he got in front of her every time she tried to turn a different direction and yelled, "Come on out!" to Ethan.

"It's about damn time." Ethan appeared from behind a re-
tail booth about twenty feet away and hurried over. "I was just
about to give up."

With Ethan on one side, it was easier to keep the woman
from getting away. Her eyes were wide with fear but now she
stood perfectly still.

"Who is she?" Ethan asked.

"Hard to say. But she showed up and tossed a bag at my feet,
which I assume has the money in it."

She was keeping her hood up and her head down, but Ethan
ducked so he could see her face and shocked Dallas when he
cried, "Mom! What are you doing here?"

Dallas's jaw dropped as he looked from one to the other. "This
is your *mother*?"

"Yes, but... She'd never... I mean..." Ethan shook his head,
momentarily speechless, until he managed to say, "Mom, please
tell me you had nothing to do with that cowboy—Terrell Something—who choked Emery."

She glanced behind her as though she wished running was
still an option. But she'd already been identified; it was too late
for that. "He wasn't supposed to hurt her," she said, finally removing her hood as tears welled up. "I just... I wanted to make
her leave you alone. I couldn't let her cost you money you don't
have, humiliate you in front of your fans and...and threaten your
job. You were so relieved when you were able to get it back."

"Oh my God," Ethan whispered. "I set a trap for my own
mother. I told her about the lawsuit and Emery going to Silver
Springs and about when you called and demanded that I bring
five hundred dollars hush money to this pier. I was so freaked
out, knew I didn't have anything to do with it. But I never
dreamed that... Oh my God," he said again.

Dallas remembered Emery mentioning that Ethan and his

mother were unusually close, and that she was overprotective, but the fact that it could be her had never even crossed his mind. "You're in some serious trouble," he told her as he opened the sack he'd grabbed before giving chase and pulled out a stack of twenty-dollar bills. He didn't bother to count; it looked like about five hundred dollars to him.

Ethan frowned when he saw the money. "Please. Don't drag her into this."

"*Drag* her into this?" Dallas echoed, putting the money back in the sack. "She's the one who's responsible for what happened to Emery." He pulled out his phone, which had recorded the entire conversation, and flashed it at them. "And now I'll be able to prove it. Who was the cowboy you hired?"

"Don't answer," Ethan advised, but it was too late. She spoke at the same time. "The brother or brother-in-law of a friend of mine from work. I don't really know. I never even talked to him. She arranged it all."

"For how much?"

"Three hundred for her and three hundred for him."

"I'm calling the cops," Dallas said.

Ethan caught his arm. "No, please. She did it for me. She was wrong, but her intentions were good. *I'll* take the fall."

"Leave Ethan out of it," his mother cried. "It was me. I'm the one who did it."

Dallas shoved the bag under his arm so he wouldn't drop his phone. Even though Ethan's mom and the cowboy deserved to be prosecuted, Dallas knew they probably wouldn't do much jail time since Emery hadn't been seriously injured.

If Ethan confessed to the cyberattack, however, Emery would be able to get a sizable settlement—both from him and the station—and that would be punishment enough for his mother, too, since protecting him was all she cared about.

While Dallas hated letting "Terrell" off, after taking a mo-

ment to weigh his options, he thought gaining the confession
served the greater good.

"I'll tell you what," he said. "I'll make you a deal."

Tuesday, December 22

Emery was glad she'd come to Boston. Connie had broken
into tears the moment she walked out of the airport into the
freezing cold of a Boston winter, and when she got in the car
and greeted her grandmother, Adele had actually remembered
her. Connie said it was the first hint of clarity Adele had had all
day—that it must be a Christmas miracle.

After they arrived home, they'd visited for an hour or so, but
then her mother had helped her grandmother to bed and retired
herself. Emery wasn't remotely sleepy. She'd slept for two hours
on the long plane ride. Besides, she was on California time, and
she was too wound up about what might happen at the pier to
even think about nodding off.

She closed the door to her room before going online to search
for possible jobs in broadcasting, which, with her experience,
would be her best bet. She probably couldn't work as an anchor
after what Ethan had done—not for some time—but it might
be possible to get on as the producer at a small, obscure station.
Even if she was just hired as a receptionist, or a gofer for a producer, it would be a start. She wanted to find work as soon as
possible, since she was the only one between her, her mother
and her grandmother for whom that was a viable option—while
she waited to hear from Dallas.

She didn't find a lot of opportunities, which worried her.
But she was willing to do almost anything, even if it wasn't in
broadcasting, to keep them afloat and hoped there would be
more offerings after Christmas. Surely in January there would
be plenty of companies looking for someone who was articulate,
conscientious and comfortable with people. She was a good em-

ployee—if the person doing the hiring was willing to look past the sex video that had created such a scandal, she thought wryly.

She watched the clock as it grew later and later. She'd expected to hear from Dallas by now. Had he forgotten to call her? Maybe no one had shown up and he'd decided that it wouldn't be worth the risk of waking her just to tell her so.

As four o'clock came and went—one o'clock in California— she began to pace, eventually pausing to lift the blind and stare out at the snowy scene all around her. If something was going on, she didn't want to cause Dallas's phone to light up or distract him. But she also didn't want him to forget to inform her.

He *couldn't* forget, she told herself. She was the reason he'd gone to the Santa Monica Pier.

"Have some patience," she muttered, and waited another fifteen minutes. It was now a full hour after he was supposed to meet whoever had hired "Terrell" at the pier. No matter what'd happened, he had to be done, didn't he?

Letting the blind fall back in place, she risked texting Dallas.

Is everything okay? What happened?

Give me ten more minutes. Almost done.

Done with what? Something *must've* happened.

She gnawed nervously on her bottom lip as she tried to while away another five minutes and then ten. At last, her phone buzzed with his call.

Although she answered immediately, she waited until she'd shut herself into the bathroom so she wouldn't wake her mother or her grandmother before saying hello.

"You're never going to believe who did it," he said without preamble.

"Don't tell me it was Tommy." She couldn't help feeling slightly hurt that Ethan's old roommate would put her in dan-

ger, and be so unfeeling about it. He knew Ethan was the one
at fault in the first place.

"No. It was Karen."

Emery couldn't immediately place the name. If it was a
woman, she'd been sure he'd say Heidi. "Karen who?"

"His mother."

"No!"

"Yes. That was who showed up at the pier to meet me with
a bag full of money."

Emery sat down on the closed toilet. "Did you call the cops?
Has she been arrested? Ethan must be beside himself."

"I didn't call the cops."

"Why not?"

"Because I don't think we should turn her in. It's up to you, of
course, but I've worked out something that will be a lot better."

"And that is…"

"Ethan has promised to confess to the cyberattack if we leave
his mother out of everything."

Emery began to massage her forehead. *Really?*

"That's what he says."

"I'm surprised he'd agree to that."

"Even to protect his mother?"

"Yes. He's so narcissistic, so used to her being the one to take
care of him. He expects it by now."

"That may be true, but he knows we will probably wind
up getting them both if he doesn't cooperate. There's a good
chance of it, anyway. And if she does have to serve time in jail
for what she did, not only would she lose her job, she'd have a
record. If you won the lawsuit, Ethan would lose his job, too.
It just compounds everything."

"What about the cowboy—Terrell?"

"He'd get away with it, so I'll understand if you don't want to
go this way. I could still call the cops, and you could take your
chance at winning the lawsuit without Ethan's confession. I re-

corded some stuff that should help, but it won't be as easy as if you have his cooperation."

She rubbed her forehead, stalling while she tried to think. "I suppose you're right. I'd rather win the lawsuit than see someone punished just for the sake of punishment."

"I agree. They deserve it, but this benefits you much more."

"I can't believe it was her," she said, still trying to come to terms with what she'd learned. "Or, actually, when I think about it, I guess I can. After witnessing what their relationship was like, it shouldn't surprise me. I just never even considered her a possibility."

"Me, either."

"I probably should've thought of her. She's seen me in a swimsuit, so she could've seen the freckle on my thigh. And they talked on the phone almost every day. That caused a lot of friction between Ethan and I. He always became so…puerile whenever he dealt with her. She didn't know when she was crossing boundaries."

"She still doesn't. She's not happy that his ass is in a sling. She'd rather take the fall. But if she does that, they both might wind up in a worse situation than they are now."

"What I don't understand is…why would Ethan help us figure out who did it if it was his mother?" she asked. "I can't see him ever doing that."

"He didn't know it was her. She arranged it with a coworker, didn't even have any direct contact with the cowboy. He just happened to confide in her about the call I tried to entrap him with, so she showed up at the pier to handle it."

"But she didn't get away with it—because of you."

"I'm just glad I was able to get to the bottom of the whole thing. It would've been really hard for me to leave California, knowing that you might still be in trouble."

"I doubt anyone would try to hurt me here in Boston, but it's nice to know I can go back to LA and won't have to worry."

Now she wouldn't have to fear returning to her apartment, and she'd soon be vindicated when she won the lawsuit. "Thank you," she said. "I can't tell you how much I appreciate…everything."

There was a moment of silence during which she could sense he wanted to say something—something he didn't end up expressing. "No problem," he said instead. "How're your mother and grandmother?"

"They'll be okay. I'm going to make sure of it."

"You'll have the means, once you win the lawsuit."

She imagined the relief that would offer. She couldn't get that video to disappear or go back in time and make it so that no one ever saw it, but at least she wouldn't have to take the first menial job she could find. She'd have time to spend with her family, as it was now, and her mother would be able to hold out until her father was willing to split their assets in a more equitable fashion. "That's incredible," she admitted. "It feels *so* good to have the answers, and to know the person responsible is admitting what he did."

"God, I miss you," he said. "And don't tell me it'll pass."

"Don't look back," she told him. "Go, be free and fulfill your dreams. And whenever you think of me, know that what I wanted most was for you to be happy."

His voice grew slightly hoarse with emotion. "Emery…"

She squeezed her eyes closed. "Goodbye, Dallas."

CHAPTER TWENTY-EIGHT

Dallas was exhausted when he finally rolled into Silver Springs. He'd been up all night, but he didn't have to worry about not getting enough rest. Aiyana and Cal were honeymooning, and he and his brothers were on Christmas break. He planned to sleep as long as he wanted, and he hoped that when he woke up sometime later he'd feel better about his decision to let Emery go. She was special. He couldn't deny that. But every time he considered embracing what he felt for her and actually making a commitment, the past rose up to mock him, reminding him of his poor sister, who'd meant the world to him. He couldn't allow himself to be that happy, not when she'd lost everything.

He yawned as he got out of the van and started trudging toward the house. At least he could rest assured that Ethan couldn't hurt Emery anymore and that the world would know her former boyfriend was responsible for the cyberattack that ruined her career. They'd also know that the television station fired her because of what Ethan did, not anything *she* did. She had to be glad for that, and knowing she was in a better place made things easier for him, too.

If only he could've done something to help Jenny.

Damn it! He knew he had to stop punishing himself, but he couldn't.

Forget, he told himself, and hoped he'd be able to do that once he returned to climbing and was once again caught up in the enthusiasm he felt for the sport. He might not be happy choosing the road he'd chosen, but at least he'd appease his sense of justice.

As soon as he let himself into the house, he was surprised to find the television on and Seth sitting on the couch. His brother had dozed off with the remote in his hand, but he startled awake at the sound of the door. "How'd it go?" he asked, sitting up when he saw Dallas.

"Great. It's all handled. She's going to be fine."

"What happened?"

Dallas was so tired his eyes felt like sandpaper, but he sat in the recliner next to the couch while he explained.

"So it wasn't Ethan," Seth said when he was done.

"No, but if he hadn't loaded that video onto the internet, none of this would've happened. So I don't feel bad that he's the one paying the price."

Seth grimaced. "I hate that the cowboy is going to get away with what he did."

Dallas did, too, but they didn't live in a perfect world, and he felt damn lucky to have achieved *this* much justice for Emery. "There's always karma. It'll come around and smack him down one day. And if I ever find out who he is, I'll smack him myself. At least Emery will get a sizable settlement. It'll ease a lot of the pressure she's under and will enable her to help the people she loves."

"I'm happy to hear that."

"I'm happy it's over."

"Mom called last night," Seth announced. "Forgot to tell you."

"How's the honeymoon?"

"Sounds like it's going great. She said she's happier than she's ever been. But when I told her what you were up to, she started to worry. You should give her a call."

"It's too early—I'll text instead, in case she's asleep. Will she and Cal still be coming home Christmas Eve?" Dallas asked as he gathered what was left of his strength and stood.

"She wouldn't miss Christmas. Not with us here."

"True." He covered another yawn. "Well, I'm going to bed before you start in on Emery again."

"Start in?" Seth repeated with a shocked laugh. "I've hardly said anything!"

Dallas gave him a dubious look. "But I know how you feel. You've made that clear."

"I think it's how *you* feel that's got you worried," he said, and Dallas hated that he couldn't deny it.

Emery's lawyer was ecstatic when she called him around noon her time to tell him that Ethan had agreed to confess.

"This case will be a slam dunk," he said. "I bet they'll settle out of court as soon as possible."

"How much do you think we can get?"

"Wrongful firing settlements usually fall anywhere in the range of five thousand to eighty thousand dollars, but your reputation was ruined as well, which takes this to an entirely new level. I know of one client who was fired for testifying on behalf of another employee in a sexual harassment suit who received more than a million dollars."

"You're not saying I could wind up with that much!"

"You could," he said. "You never know. It's all a matter of negotiation now."

Emery felt as though a giant weight had been lifted off her shoulders. And she had Dallas to thank for it. "It's going to be a nice Christmas, after all."

"Oh, the money won't come *that* quickly. The holidays will

actually slow the process. You're still looking at a month or more."

"I can last a few months. I'm just saying that the pressure is off. Now I know I'll be able to take care of my mother and grandmother."

"You'll be able to do that and have plenty left over."

She thanked him and, just as she hung up, her mother knocked on her bedroom door. "You awake?"

Emery propped her pillows up and sat against the headboard. "Yeah. Come on in."

Connie slipped inside the room and perched on the edge of the bed. "I've been trying not to wake you. I know you're on California time, but I'm so excited you're here I could hardly wait to see you. Thank you for coming."

Emery reached for her mother's hand. "I'm glad I'm here, too. And I want you to know that you're not going to have to worry about anything, not as far as money is concerned."

"What do you mean?"

"I'm going to win the lawsuit. Ethan has confessed."

Her mother's lips curved into a smile, but she started to blink quickly—an obvious attempt to avoid tears. She was hurting so badly that any kindness made her cry. "Thank you, honey. I'm so glad I have you. I promise I'll pay you back as soon as I receive my divorce settlement."

"I'm not worried about that. This will buy you the time you need to make sure it's a fair one."

"Thank you," she said again.

Emery pulled her into an embrace. "We're both going to make it through this."

Thursday, December 24

Over the next few days, Dallas felt his mood grow steadily worse. He'd tried calling Emery a number of times, but his calls went straight to voice mail; there wasn't even any ringing. He'd left her several messages, but she never called him back. It was as if she'd disappeared off the planet, as if their time together had been blotted out.

What was going on? He wanted to know how she was doing, how her mother was doing, even how her grandmother was doing. And he wanted to bask in the relief Ethan's confession gave them both—her, because it made such a difference to her immediate future, and him, because he no longer had to worry about her being in a terrible situation. Once she received her settlement, she'd be able to support herself until she found another job that she actually liked. And if she couldn't find anything right away? She could survive until a better opportunity came along. That sex video wouldn't hold her back forever. It would become old news as soon as someone else—a movie star or other high-profile figure—made headlines with his or her own sex tape. Or divorce. Or affair. Or other scandal.

Emery would soon be in the clear and he would like to have been able to celebrate with her. But there was only this strange, ominous silence.

Had she cut him off? He suspected she had, that she was handling their separation with the same grit and determination he'd seen when they parted at the airport and she wouldn't even let him kiss her.

But he truly cared about her. Couldn't they have *some* kind of relationship? Despite all of his issues, he couldn't help hoping for that, at least. Having her out of his life completely made him miserable.

He tried to tell himself that he had to let her do what she needed to do. *He* was the one who'd decided they couldn't pursue a relationship. And his reasons for it were still true. She'd crashed into his life like a comet—made a huge impact—and now he had to fill the hole.

He tried to do that by taking his brothers bouldering, as he'd promised. They went ice-skating, too, with the students who were still at the school. And they went Christmas shopping. Dallas even wrapped the presents he'd bought—for the first time ever. They were crudely done, but at least he'd put forth the effort.

He was doing everything he could to get into the holiday spirit, but the moment Emery left, Christmas had lost its sparkle.

"It feels strange not to have Emery here," Liam said as they were making dinner on Christmas Eve. Aiyana and Cal were due to arrive home at any moment, and Dallas had recruited his two youngest brothers to help surprise them by making the family's traditional Christmas Eve dinner of salmon in parchment pouches with slivered vegetables. "I was sort of getting used to having her makeup in the bathroom."

"Yeah, toward the end that didn't bother me anymore, either," Bentley chimed in. "We've never had a sister. I mean we have sisters-in-law, but have never *lived* with a girl. I really liked her."

"And I bet she'd be a lot better at this than we are," Liam said as juice rolled out of the corner of one of the pouches onto his lap, and he had to drop it and jump up to get a rag. "Mom makes it look easy."

"Mom makes everything look easy," Bentley agreed.

"What's Emery up to?" Liam asked as he returned to his station and continued to tie string around the packets Dallas was filling with food. "Is she having a good Christmas in Boston?"

Dallas had ignored the mention of her name, but he couldn't ignore a direct question. "I'm sure she is," he muttered because he didn't want to admit that he didn't know, but he'd spoken too gruffly and he knew it when Bentley shot him a dirty look.

"Why are you in such a bad mood?"

"I'm not in a bad mood," Dallas lied. "I'm just concentrating on making this meal. I want it to turn out halfway decent, okay?"

Bentley finished another one of the packets. "You know Mom will be thrilled that we even tried."

"She'll be even happier if it's edible," he snapped, but when both brothers looked at him in surprise, he realized he'd spoken too harshly again.

"Jeez, Dal," Liam grumbled.

He bit his tongue so that he wouldn't make it worse and was relieved when the twins came in and the conversation veered toward getting a game of football together tomorrow and trying to decide what time would least interfere with Aiyana's plans for Christmas Day.

Once it was settled that they'd head to the field after lunch, and they were finished with the salmon packets, Dallas put them in the oven while his brothers hurried out to play video games.

Relieved to be alone, Dallas sat at the table and, even though he told himself he was just making things worse by constantly checking, looked for a text or missed call from Emery.

Nothing.

His thumb hovered over her name as he considered calling her again, but he knew she wouldn't answer. "Merry Christmas," he muttered, and shoved his phone back into his pocket.

Aiyana couldn't believe the boys had attempted to make her salmon packet dinner, a meal she typically made only on Christmas Eve. As they sat around the table together, Ryan and Taylor complained that it didn't taste quite as good as when she made it, but the thoughtfulness behind the effort made it pretty darn delicious to her. She was proud of her family, had never been happier in so many respects, and yet it didn't take long for her to realize that something was wrong with Dallas.

She wasn't the only one who noticed it, either. When he'd grumble at this or that, or simply remained silent when he normally would've spoken, Eli, Gavin, Seth or the two younger boys would glance at each other. And when she asked about Emery and how things were going with her mother in Boston, she could hardly get him to answer.

"What's going on with Dallas?" Cal whispered when Dallas went to the bathroom and he was helping to clear the table.

"I'm not sure," she whispered back. "I hope his father has honored our agreement. You don't think he came here while we were gone, do you? Could it be that Dallas knows Robert's not only out of prison but close by and eager to make contact?"

"Robert promised he wouldn't interrupt the holidays. But we are talking about a man who murdered his wife and daughter. I doubt he'd have any compunction about taking your money and then doing exactly as he pleases."

"It doesn't have to be Robert. It could be that things didn't end well with Emery," she speculated.

"He texted you while we were gone that Ethan was going to confess. Won't that make things better?"

"For her. But I'm pretty sure he's fallen in love with her, and I don't think that's an easy thing for him to face."

He brought her fingers to his lips. "I'm just glad you're so open to love," he teased.

"Hey, I just rinsed off some plates—my hands are wet!"

He chuckled as he kissed them in spite of that. "I don't care. I'll take you any way you come."

She couldn't believe she'd waited so long to marry him, but her own life had not been easy. She guessed Dallas was battling some of the same trust and fear issues she'd dealt with in the past. He'd learned how to cope on his own, had eked out a life he enjoyed with his climbing, and he felt safer hanging on to that than trusting love—which was sort of ironic, given the more obvious danger of his job.

She was hoping for a chance to speak to Dallas alone, but he surprised her by going to bed early. He knew the rest of them were planning to visit the students who were still at the school and leave stockings full of Christmas goodies by each door, which he usually enjoyed, but he didn't seem to have any enthusiasm for it tonight.

"What's up with Dallas?" Cora asked after Dallas disappeared down the stairs.

"We think it's Emery," Cal replied.

"Really? Eli told me he's the one who chose not to pursue the relationship."

"He was," Aiyana said. "But maybe he needs a second chance to decide."

Cal gave her a suspicious look and Cora's eyes widened. "What does that mean?" they said, almost in unison.

A trickle of excitement ran through Aiyana. "Let's get the others together and see what we can do."

"There isn't anything *we* can do," Cora said, perplexed.

"Who says?" Aiyana responded with a wink.

Emery knew she'd done the right thing coming to Boston. She shuddered to think she'd almost left her mother on her own. Connie was bewildered and hurt, being rejected after so many years of marriage, and yet she was doing everything she could to support her own mother. Emery couldn't help but be proud of her.

She was also determined to follow her mother's example and fulfill her duty to both women instead of feeling sorry for herself. After all, the only thing she had to worry about now was a broken heart. But it still wasn't easy. She'd blocked Dallas's number and refused to let herself cave in and unblock him—an impulse she had to override every few seconds.

"You're quiet," her mother said as they sat in the living room after they'd finished the ham and scalloped potatoes she'd prepared for dinner, cleaned up the dishes, and put her grandmother to bed.

Emery held a glass of wine loosely in one hand as she studied the sad little Charlie Brown Christmas tree on a table near the front window. Her mother used to do a lot of holiday decorating—always went big—but this was the only token of holiday cheer she'd bothered to put up this year. "It's a very different Christmas."

"My first year spending Christmas without your father since we met," her mother said distantly.

Emery took a sip of her wine. "It's his loss, Mom. I mean that."

"His *loss*?" she echoed sardonically. "Deseret is half my age and probably thirty pounds thinner. Don't kid yourself. He traded up."

"That's not true. She's also selfish and controlling and spoiled rotten. I bet he'll make himself miserable trying to keep her happy."

"Regardless, I have to accept my new reality and figure out a way to soldier on."

"You're doing that, and it's such an inspiration. Anybody can do the right thing when it's easy. But you're doing it even though it's hard."

A gentle smile tugged at Connie's lips as she reached over to pat Emery's arm. "You were the best thing to ever happen to me, and your father is partly responsible, so I guess I can't regret marrying him."

Emery covered her mother's hand with her own. "You're going to be fine."

A buzz broke the silence—Emery's phone. For a split second, she hoped it was Dallas—until she reminded herself that he couldn't call because she'd blocked him.

"Who is it?" her mother asked as Emery checked.

Emery wished she didn't have to say. "Dad. I texted him about Ethan and the confession. He's probably calling to talk about that." Thinking she'd get back to him later, she started to put her phone on the coffee table, but her mother stopped her.

"Emery, it's Christmas Eve. Talk to your father. I don't want you to miss the opportunity just because things aren't going well between the two of us," she said and, taking her wine, left the room.

Emery was tempted to go after her. It had to be difficult for Connie to feel like the outsider when they'd always been a family. But she wasn't sure her father would have the opportunity to talk if she missed this call. There was no telling what he might have to do—or not do—to avoid an argument with Deseret.

So she answered.

"Just wanted to wish you a merry Christmas," he said.

"Thank you. I hope you're having a nice Christmas, too."

"It would be better if your mother and I could come to some understanding and agreement, but…"

Emery felt herself stiffen. She was going to draw a boundary here, too—refuse to let him complain when her mother was trying to be so generous. "I don't want to talk about the divorce, Dad. Please don't put me in the middle."

He fell silent. Then he said, "You're right. I'm sorry," and they were able to discuss Ethan and his confession and finish the call without getting into an argument.

After she hung up, she went to check on her mother and found Connie in bed.

"How'd it go?" she asked.

"Fine," Emery replied but was grateful when her mother didn't press her for details. Instead, they talked about what they planned to cook the following day. Then Emery said good-night and went to her own room.

She'd gotten so little sleep the night before she thought she'd nod off immediately. But that didn't happen. She kept shifting around and adjusting the blankets, trying to get comfortable, feeling lonely and even a little frightened by all the changes in her life and what might lie ahead.

She wished she could at least *talk* to Dallas.

At one point, she took her phone off the charger and nearly called him—until she asked herself what it was she was hoping to say. He'd already made his choice. She needed to let him go, not continue to hope that he'd change his mind.

Still, she probably would've broken down, if not for the example of her mother. She missed him that badly. But if Connie could remain strong and do what was necessary to rebuild her life, so could she.

CHAPTER TWENTY-NINE

Christmas Day

It wasn't even light yet when his mother, Cal and his brothers banged on Dallas's door and then flooded his room. He'd gone to bed early, but he still wasn't happy to be awakened. He assumed they were excited to celebrate Christmas, to eat and open presents, but he couldn't gather much enthusiasm for any of that. Not this year. He just wanted to get back to the person he'd been before meeting Emery—happy to know, with his sponsorship, that he had the opportunity of a lifetime and could, if he decided to, tackle the most famous climbs in Europe in the next few months.

"Let me sleep," he grumbled. "I'll get up in a couple of hours."

"But our present won't wait that long," Liam said, his voice filled with excitement.

Dallas couldn't imagine what he was talking about. He figured his family would give him a sweater, a football or maybe some new climbing gear, as usual—all things he would like and be grateful for but also things that could easily wait until he was ready to get up. "*How* old are we now?"

"Don't be a Scrooge," Seth said, and then it occurred to Dallas how odd it was to have Seth in his room—not just Ryan, Taylor, Liam and Bentley. What the heck was *Seth* doing up this early, trying to drag him out of bed? Seth was more reserved and withdrawn than the others; this wasn't like him.

"What's going on?" he asked as he threw his legs over the side and sat up. "I know it's Christmas, and you're excited, but this is the first time you've all descended on my room at once." Normally, Aiyana would call down to tell him to come up. Or *one* of his younger brothers would fetch him—not all who were currently staying in the house.

"We got you something we think you're really going to like," Bentley announced. He and most of Dallas's other brothers were bare chested and wearing sweat bottoms. That, together with their hair standing up and going every which way, served as a testament to the fact that they'd just rolled out of their own beds. They must've set an alarm for this and gathered upstairs before coming down. But why?

"Or maybe you won't like it," Ryan said. "I told them that if you wanted to be with Emery you wouldn't have let her go. You know what you're doing. Who would give up the opportunity you've got? You're going to be rich and famous. But even Seth thought Mom was right."

Dallas felt his eyebrows come together as he looked from face to face. Climbing and being with Emery wasn't really as mutually exclusive as he'd made it sound, but he was glad he'd sold Ryan, at least. "What does this have to do with Emery?"

Aiyana stepped forward and handed him a sheet of paper. "Merry Christmas," she said. "From all of us."

There wasn't enough light streaming in from the hall to be able to read what was on it. "What is this?"

Taylor snapped on the light. "Take a look."

Dallas had to cover his eyes for a second, but once they adjusted he could see that he was holding a boarding pass—and when he read the fine print he understood it was for a flight to Boston that left Los Angeles today at noon. *"You bought me a plane ticket?"*

"We bought you a second chance to decide," Seth said.

Dallas wasn't sure how to feel about this, whether he was relieved because he now had the opportunity to take off and go after Emery, which was what he'd wanted to do since she left, or irritated that those he loved seemed to be undermining his attempt to resist something he wasn't capable of managing. "Because I made the wrong decision the first time?"

"If I had to answer that solely by the way you've behaved since she left, yes," Seth said.

"This just enables you to reconsider," Aiyana explained, softening his answer. "In case you regret your decision. Even if you don't, you could always go to Boston to see Emery—just for a visit."

Apparently his mother didn't understand a mere visit was out of the question. He couldn't go to Boston only to tell Emery that he hadn't changed his mind.

"I know climbing is important to you," Cal said. "But I don't know anything more fulfilling than finding someone to love, who loves you back and makes you happy."

"Even if I decide to try to have a relationship with her, we don't know that it will last," Dallas said, giving them the argument he'd used on himself so often.

"Do you really want to deny yourself the possibility?" Seth asked.

Some things were more important than climbing. He understood that. But what they didn't understand was that he didn't deserve to be that happy. Poor Jenny had lost her life protecting him. Somehow grabbing hold of what he felt for Emery seemed too greedy—almost like a betrayal.

"She'll be better off without me," he said, handing the boarding pass back to Aiyana.

"See?" Ryan piped up. "I told you. Good thing we got him some other stuff, too."

"Can we open our presents now?" Liam asked.

With a disgusted shake of his head, Seth started for the door. "How about we go back to bed and start this day over in a couple of hours?"

Aiyana was obviously disappointed, but she didn't say so. "Okay. We'll let you sleep."

They all left, but when they were gone and Dallas was free to roll over and go back to sleep, he felt like throwing up—like the terrified little boy he'd been hiding under his sister's bed. They didn't know how deeply that had affected him, that he still had nightmares about it and felt so guilty about Jenny there were times when he felt he could scarcely breathe.

With a curse, he got up and paced across the floor. He couldn't give in, couldn't go to Boston. He'd only mess it up. He wasn't capable of giving Emery what she needed, and he sure as hell didn't deserve her.

But as the clock ticked away, and he heard footsteps on the floor above him and exclamations from his brothers as they teased and joked and enjoyed the holiday, a small voice—Jenny's voice—seemed to say: *Do it, Dallas. Don't let what I did go to waste.*

Tears streamed down his face as he closed his eyes and tried to listen closer. "Is that you?" he whispered, "Looking out for me again?" and felt such a tremendous warmth go through him that he couldn't believe any other way.

He sank onto the bed, trying to hang on to what he felt. It left soon after, but he knew what he had to do—what he had to be brave enough to do. "Wait a second!" he called, coming to his feet and charging up the stairs. "Where's that boarding pass? I'm going."

They converged on him as soon as he reached the living room.

"Seriously?" Ryan said when Aiyana, her smile wide, handed Dallas the boarding pass.

Seth leaned against the doorframe wearing a self-satisfied grin. "That's what he should've done in the first place."

Dallas hoped Seth was right. As he headed back downstairs to get showered and packed, his heart was pounding harder than when he was executing a tricky and highly dangerous move high above the valley of Yosemite. They'd awakened him so early because it would take time to make the flight. He needed to hurry.

He was ready within an hour, so he was able to take the time to have breakfast and open presents with his family. Knowing he was going to see Emery changed everything about how he'd been feeling. He was happier than he'd ever been, which still somehow made him feel guilty.

Trying to suppress that reaction wasn't easy, but he shoved it away as much as he could. After fending off the teasing and many jokes he'd suffered for acting so tough and then caving in, he was laughing when he opened the door to carry out his suitcase. He was going to put it in Seth's car while his brother finished getting ready, since Seth was the one who was driving him to the airport.

But he didn't make it past the threshold. There was an older man coming up the walk wearing brand-new jeans and a plaid flannel shirt. With his hair shaved so close to his head and all the changes nearly a quarter of a century had wrought in his face and body, he looked different, but Dallas easily recognized him.

It was his father.

Aiyana had had such a wonderful week. Her wedding had been beautiful, her honeymoon romantic and relaxing, and, so far, Christmas had been spectacular. She was excited to think that Dallas might finally allow himself to fall in love and grow some roots, especially because she really liked Emery. Aiyana thought she might soon have another daughter-in-law and was singing along to "White Christmas" while helping the twins pick up all the discarded wrapping paper when she heard the angry shouting that brought all of her holiday cheer to an abrupt halt.

"Get out of here while you can still walk!" she heard Dallas shout. "I don't ever want to see you again. Do you understand?"

"Dallas, hear me out," came the reply. "I'm not the same man I was. I found God while I was in prison, and He's changed my life."

Aiyana's hand flew up to cover her mouth. "Oh no."

She knew Cal had heard the same thing, because he looked equally shocked. "He's here," he said. "That son of a bitch didn't honor the agreement."

Aiyana's heart jumped into her throat. She'd contacted the prison while she was on her honeymoon to inquire about Robert Ogilvie—what type of man the warden and the correction officers who dealt with him thought he was, and had been disappointed to hear what they had to say. They claimed that he was manipulative, unrepentant and one of the most selfish human beings they had ever known—and that was saying a lot, considering the men they dealt with on a daily basis.

"You're so full of shit," Dallas said. "I could kill you for what you did."

Aiyana nearly tripped over a chair in her hurry to get out of the house. Dallas had been so happy once he'd made the decision to fly to Boston. Had Robert shown up fifteen minutes later, he would've missed him. She couldn't believe that he would have to face this during the holidays, after all.

"What are you doing here?" she asked when she saw Robert standing—surprisingly defiant—halfway up the walk to her house.

Dallas's father lifted a hand. "I'm sorry. I waited as long as I could. I'm not here to cause any trouble. I stayed away, like you asked me to, so that I wouldn't bother you during your wedding."

Like she'd *asked* him to? He accepted a thousand dollars to stay away but had still interrupted their holiday. "As if this is any better?" she said. "It's Christmas morning!"

Dallas whirled around to face her. "You knew he was in town and you didn't tell me?"

"I'm sorry," she said. "He came here a couple of weeks ago, but he promised me he wouldn't try to contact you until after the holidays. I wanted to give you that much time to enjoy being home."

"I would've waited and come in January like you wanted," Robert explained. "But I was afraid Dallas would leave right after Christmas, and I wouldn't be able to find him. I've waited so long!"

"How can you even say that?" Seth said. He and her other sons came pouring out of the house and were gathered around her on the porch, their faces filled with shock, outrage and anger for Dallas's sake. "How can you feel *any* self-pity after what you've done?"

"I wasn't in my right mind when...when that happened."

"In your right mind?" Dallas echoed. "Your boss had just discovered that you'd been redirecting funds and embezzling from the company! You were going to be arrested and you wanted to run away, start over."

"No, I was drunk."

"You did a lot of terrible things when you were drinking. That part's true. But you weren't drunk that day. I remember it all very clearly."

"That's not true!" he argued. "And even if it was, I'm not the same man I was twenty-three years ago."

"Oh yeah? What's changed?" Dallas asked.

"I'm sorry for what I did."

"I don't believe that. And your lousy apology won't help Jenny or Mom, anyway. As far as I'm concerned, you're dead, too."

"Forget him, Dallas," Seth said. "Mom will get rid of him.

We have to leave now or you'll miss your flight. Don't let him ruin what you have planned today."

Dallas didn't respond, didn't act as though he'd even heard what Seth said.

"Can I just...get your number or something?" Robert asked. "In case you change your mind? I have no one else. I would... I would love to figure out how we can have *some* sort of a relationship."

Dallas's voice dropped to a menacing level. "You're not hearing me. I've had nightmares my whole life because of you. I will *never* allow you back, never be able to forgive you for what you did. You need to leave."

Aiyana tried to grab Dallas's arm as he finished going down the steps of the porch, but he pulled away from her.

Robert backed up, but he didn't leave. "Dallas, please."

"He's not worth it, Dallas," Aiyana said. "I'm so sorry that I was tempted to believe him. I *wanted* to believe him, want anyone who's sincerely sorry to get a second chance. But I was wrong this time. I know that now."

He didn't answer. He was too mesmerized by the sight of his father, so she stopped trying to reason with him. "Get off my property," she said to Robert, "before I call the police. And don't ever come back."

"I thought you were good Christian people!" he snapped. "How can you turn me away, treat me like trash?"

"After what you did, you have no business being here," Dallas said.

"You heard him. You need to leave." Ryan went down the steps and Taylor, Liam, Bentley and Seth fanned out behind him.

Seeing that they weren't going to relent, Robert cursed. "I should've killed you, too," he said under his breath to Dallas and that was all it took to ignite the powder keg of emotion that was rippling through the entire family. Aiyana managed to grab Dallas and hung on for dear life, stopping him only because he wouldn't risk hurting her, but the porch quickly emptied as the rest of her sons went after Robert.

"Call a taxi," she yelled to Cal and let go of Dallas long enough to get in between Robert and her other boys.

"No," she told them. "I won't have this. His life will be difficult enough. Why do you think he's here? He's looking for a place to land, people he can live off of, but he can just keep on moving."

Although it wasn't easy, she managed to get Seth to help her stop the others, and by the time she felt she had things under control, Robert was walking as fast as possible toward the road, where she hoped the taxi would find him and deliver him to the bus stop so he could get out of town.

"Good riddance," she said, and tried to herd her boys back into the house before someone decided to run after him. She was so glad things hadn't gone any worse. But the moment she saw Dallas's face, she stopped. He was staring after his father with such a bereft expression her heart broke for him.

"Dallas, we have to go," Seth said gently. "You're going to miss your flight."

Finally, Dallas pulled his gaze away. But he didn't get in Seth's car. "Who am I kidding?" he muttered. "It's not going to work."

Leaving his suitcase on the porch, he stalked to his van, revved the engine and drove off.

"Damn Robert Ogilvie." Aiyana wished she were the one who'd seen him coming so that she could've chased him off before Dallas encountered him.

"Should I go after him?" Seth asked, obviously concerned and eager to do so.

She briefly considered letting him, but decided against it. "He's an adult. There's nothing we can do," she told Seth and the others, who were offering to go, too. "Just give him some space. This is something he has to come to terms with on his own. At least he knows we love him," she added, and hung all her hope on that.

CHAPTER THIRTY

Dallas thought his lungs would burst. He'd never run so hard in his life, but he had to get away from the town, the valley and the people—especially his father. How dare Robert Ogilvie reappear in his life, especially on Christmas! What did the bastard expect would happen when he arrived? Could Robert really have imagined, after what he did, that Dallas could embrace him and move forward?

Never! Robert had killed that possibility when he pulled out a gun twenty-three years ago. Any normal person would know that.

Although he was quickly growing weaker, Dallas forced himself to keep going. Not only did he need to outdistance the town and the people, he had to outdistance the images in his head.

Except that was impossible. He'd never forget the casual way his father had approached the house, as if it was just another day and what he'd done was no big deal. As if Dallas could ever want to see him or associate with him again. As if Dallas would *ever* betray Jenny like that.

His heart pumped hard and fast as he gulped for air and jumped over a rock, pivoted around a tree and continued up the narrow trail that led to the summit. He was somewhere in the Topatopa Mountains, but he didn't know where. He hadn't paid any attention. He'd just abandoned his van somewhere it probably didn't belong and taken the shortest route he could find to higher ground.

It almost felt as though Robert were chasing him. He'd always imagined avenging his mother and Jenny, if given the opportunity. And yet he'd done nothing, other than shout for Robert to leave. He felt as though he'd let them both down. But if he *had* done something more, it would've hurt Aiyana, someone else he loved, who'd been there, too, pleading with him. The opposing sides—the anger from the past and the desire to heal and be normal—warred with each other until he thought he'd be torn in two.

Tears streamed down his face by the time he reached the top. Staggering to a halt, he bent over, struggling just to remain on his feet. "Jenny!" he yelled as though she could step out from behind a tree. "Jenny!"

He fell to his knees as his own voice echoed back to him and grabbed a handful of dirt, letting it slip through his fingers. He owed her so much that he could never repay, and the fact that he'd done nothing when Robert appeared turned his stomach to acid.

"I'm sorry," he muttered. "I'm so sorry." But he knew he was apologizing for more than what he hadn't done this morning. He was apologizing for being alive, for the fact that she'd felt it was necessary to protect him, for the fact that she might've been able to hide or escape herself if she hadn't been so worried about him.

"God, Jenny," he cried, his voice growing hoarse. "Every day, I wish it was me instead of you."

A cold wind whistled through the trees. He hadn't bothered with a coat, and he was wet, dripping with perspiration. But he couldn't feel it. In his mind, he kept seeing his father come up the walk, over and over, and wondered what he could've done differently to make it so that he would hate himself less.

That was when he remembered Brian saying something he'd tucked away like a gold coin or other precious keepsake: *I love you like a son.*

Rocking back on his heels, he pulled his phone out of his pocket.

"I was just about to call you," Brian said as soon as he answered. "But you beat me to it. I wanted to wish you a Merry Christmas."

Dallas couldn't answer. He was too choked up.

"Dallas? You okay? What's going on?"

"My dad…" He only got that far before his emotions sealed off his throat.

"What about your dad?" he asked. "That bastard had better not have done anything else!"

Dallas squeezed his eyes closed as he fought to be able to speak. "He just showed up, out of the blue," he managed to say. "I… I should've done something, but I didn't. I just yelled for him to leave."

"Done something?" Brian echoed. "Done what?"

Dallas swallowed hard. "I don't know. Something for my mom and Jenny—"

"And gone to prison yourself?" Brian snapped. "That's bullshit. Who would that help? Certainly not them. They're gone, Dallas. You have to let them go."

"I…can't," he said simply. "I see Jenny…all the time. I miss her. I wish… I wish it had been me he'd shot."

"That's crazy."

The last spate of psychologists Aiyana had taken him to had harped about vanquishing the guilt he carried, which was why he'd refused to go back. He couldn't let himself off the hook that easily. He was afraid he'd be no better than Robert if he did. "She should…still be here."

Brian's response was stern and immediate. "That's true. But it's not your fault she isn't."

"It is," he shouted into the phone. "If she hadn't been trying to protect me, she might've escaped." There. He'd said what he'd been holding back since it all happened. Those words had been torn from him, but the release was instantaneous. He blamed himself as much as his father for Jenny's death—*for good reason.*

"You don't know that, Dallas. And even if it's true, it wasn't a willful act on your part. You were six years old! She did what she did because she loved you. Don't waste her gift by making yourself miserable, especially on her account. Do you think she'd want that?"

Of course she wouldn't *want* that, but...

"I've watched you over the years," Brian went on. "You hold back, deny yourself the love other people want to give you. And for what? Is it helping Jenny? Or your mother? No. Quit punishing yourself for surviving when they didn't. Leave it in the past, and live large and happy because that's the way they'd want you to live. Do it for them, if not for yourself."

Dallas was hunched over, staring at the ground as he listened to Brian. He'd recovered enough from all the physical exertion that he was beginning to feel the cold, was starting to shiver. "It was all so unfair to her," he muttered.

"You're telling me she died for you, right? Isn't that what you're saying? That it was a willing sacrifice on her part?"

Fresh tears rolled down Dallas's cheeks, and the lump in his throat grew so big that he could scarcely squeak out a one-word response. "Yes."

"Then don't let it be for nothing. Let her go. Let the past go with her. And quit punishing yourself."

Dallas thought of Emery and how much he already missed her. He hadn't chosen climbing over her, as he'd pretended. He'd turned her love away because he couldn't allow himself to be that happy without feeling guilt.

But as he sat back in the dirt and stared up at the clear blue sky on a beautiful Christmas Day, he knew Brian was right. Although it might be something he'd have to remind himself of over and over—and would probably always be a struggle for him—he had to say a final goodbye to Jenny.

It had been a long day. Emery and her mother and grandmother had exchanged only small gifts, but Emery was happy that her mother had managed to smile here and there, and her grandmother had been able to reminisce about Christmases past, something no one had expected. Earlier memories seemed to be easier for Adele to recall than more recent ones, so she talked about the Christmases she'd known as a child, which Emery was glad to learn about. Adele had grown up in such an interesting time. She'd been born on a small farm, helped to raise her younger siblings when her mother died after being bucked off a horse, and married young. Over the span of her life, she'd seen the invention of the telephone, the television, the personal computer and the internet. Emery doubted there'd ever be a generation who experienced such rapid and radical change in the way people dealt with each other and the world.

Maybe this Christmas hadn't been the best they'd ever experienced, but they were together. That was what mattered. They were together, they loved and supported each other, and Emery no longer had to worry about the lawsuit with Ethan and the station. She was grateful for all of that—which was why she refused to focus on what she *didn't* have.

She did, however, unblock Dallas and send him a quick message:

Merry Christmas. I hope you had a great day. You are such an amazing person. You deserve the best.

She waited to see if she'd get a response. She was breaking

her own rule—*already*—which was pretty pathetic. But she told herself she'd allow this one more exchange. It was Christmas, after all. And hearing from him was what she wanted more than anything.

She saw the three little dots that indicated he was either reading what she'd sent or writing back. But she never got a response.

She couldn't help feeling a little misty eyed when she put her phone on its charger but ordered herself to quit obsessing over something that wasn't meant to be. What happened to being strong like her mother? And what about all those things she was so grateful for?

She was being a baby, she told herself. But she couldn't stop the tears that rolled onto her pillow.

A ding indicated someone had sent her a text.

She slid over to grab her phone and had to blink several times to be able to see through her tears.

I was going to surprise you. But if you're awake, maybe you'll come pick me up from the airport.

Had she gotten this message by mistake? She wiped her eyes and read it again. It was from Dallas, all right, but she couldn't imagine she'd been the intended recipient.

Was this meant for me?

Yes. I don't know anyone else in Boston. [[laughing emoji]]

She jumped off the bed and blew her nose before she called him.

"What are you doing in town?" she asked as soon as he answered.

"Coming to tell you that I can't live without you," he replied.

She felt her heart jump into her throat. "Are you serious?"

"I missed my first flight, had to leave my luggage behind and flew clear across the country without it. I'd say I'm pretty serious."

"But...how could you be coming to surprise me? You don't even know where I'm at!"

"Our mothers are friends, remember? She texted me the address."

"So you're really here."

"Yes. Merry Christmas."

For a moment, Emery was speechless, and her mind was going in a million different directions. "What about climbing?"

"You don't have a job, and now you won't have to get one right away, so..."

She began to grab some clothes out of her drawers. "So... what?"

"I'm hoping you might agree to come with me."

"To Europe?"

"Is that too much to ask? I guess we could do the long-distance thing, but life could be worse than spending a year or two near the Alps."

She felt her chest tighten with the threat of tears again—only this time they were happy tears. "Because of you, I'll have the money to be able to do that. So I'll go, and we can leave it open-ended, see how it works out for both of us."

"That sounds perfect to me, but I hope you won't be sorry you decided to do something so spontaneous."

"This could be a once-in-a-lifetime chance."

"I'm glad you feel that way. Now hurry—I'm freezing my ass off," he added with a laugh.

"Boston definitely isn't California."

"That's no joke. But it's okay. I'd follow you anywhere."

Emery felt as though she had to be dreaming. Who would've thought that when Ethan did what he did her life would change *for the better*? She'd cared about Ethan when she was with him, and she'd loved her job. But nothing could compare to what she felt for Dallas. Even the idea of leaving herself open to something new professionally suddenly sounded exciting.

She told him she had to go so that she could finish getting ready and find the keys to her mother's car, but just before she disconnected she said, "What made you change your mind?"

He hesitated for a second, but then he said, "I decided that I've been carrying around enough baggage all my life. I won't let it keep me from you."

EPILOGUE

Saturday, May 15

Sweat rolled down Dallas's bare back as he basked in the sun while waiting at the top of a fairly easy 5a climb in Belgium for Emery to join him. Rochers de Freyr was a popular crag offering a dozen or so sectors of varied, high-quality limestone, and it was one of his favorite places on Earth. Here, he could ascend with Emery, who'd become interested in the sport and was still learning and improving, or tackle one of its harder climbs on his own. He'd recently been added to the short list of climbers who'd topped Le Clou, an 8c climb in the Al'Legne sector, and now, when he wasn't climbing with Emery, he was focusing on topping Slip a Clou or Big Bang. He planned to compete in the IFSC World Cup in the fall and hoped to place. He was starting the season off strong, felt he had a chance.

Emery's foot appeared first. She was wearing the latest climbing shoe his sponsor had developed. Then her head popped up and she pulled herself over the edge. "That was *so* hard," she said, dropping down next to him.

He chuckled at her dramatic exclamation. "You didn't think

you could do it, but you did. Way to go." He lifted his hand for a high five, and she mustered the energy to return it.

"How'd you get me into this sport?" she complained as she gasped for breath. "After today I'm thinking it was a mistake to tell Brian we were going to Europe instead of taking over the gym."

He smiled because he knew she was joking. "I talked to him last night."

"You did?"

"Yep. He's waiting a couple of years before he retires, to see what happens with me. And if I'm not done climbing when he wants to sell? I hope I've made enough of a name in this sport that we can open our own gym." Doing a push-up over her body, he kissed her when he was close enough to be able to touch her lips. "It's a risk, but I'm up for it. Because even if it doesn't work, and we're dirt-poor for the rest of our lives, I'll be happy as long as I have you."

She grinned as she sat up, leaned back on her hands and gazed out at the view. "Look at this. It's unreal, too gorgeous for words. Hard to believe that only a few months ago I was someone who spent almost all of her time working, or trying to build her career by chasing stories even when she wasn't working. Ethan did me a huge favor when he posted that video online."

He slid over so he could hold her hand as they looked out together. He enjoyed nothing more than feeling connected to her, which was partly why he was glad she'd started climbing: they were literally tied together quite often. "If he hadn't posted that video, you would never have come to Silver Springs, and we would very likely never have met again."

She slanted him a glance. "So you don't regret flying to Boston on Christmas?"

He tried to imagine his life without her and couldn't. That he'd almost let his father ruin the happiness he had now was terrifying. Sometimes, late at night, he thought about that pivotal moment after he'd seen his father for the first time in al-most twenty-five years. He still felt guilt whenever he thought of Jenny, but then he'd remember Brian's words: *Don't let her sacrifice be for nothing.*

He was determined it wouldn't be. That was why he'd spent a fortune on another plane ticket and boarded a Boeing 747 to Boston last Christmas without so much as a carry-on. And it was the best move he'd ever made.

Letting go of Emery's hand, he put his arm around her and pulled her close. She was such a part of him now. "How could I ever regret loving you?"

★ ★ ★ ★ ★

*Don't miss Brenda Novak's next book about family
and the ties that bind and challenge us.*

The Bookstore on the Beach

Coming soon from MIRA Books.

Turn the page for a sneak peek!

The bell went off over the door while Autumn was on the phone. The bookstore had been fairly busy today, but for every person who made a purchase she had a handful of browsers, so she didn't even try to see who it was.

It wasn't until she heard a man clear his throat that she realized the person who'd come in had walked straight to the counter. She signed off on her call, hung up and turned to find... Quinn.

"Hey," he said, treating her to that Hollywood smile of his.

She caught her breath. What was *he* doing here? "Hello."

He turned in a circle, making a point of taking in everything he saw. "It's been a while since I've been in. The place looks great."

"It should. My mother and aunt pour everything they have into this store. My mother loves it almost as much as she loves me."

He faced her again. "I doubt that. Your mother thinks you hung the moon. Have you been spending a lot of time here since you've been home?"

"Quite a bit," she admitted. "I help out most afternoons, once I've spent some time with my kids and have finished gardening."

He held a sack in one hand but leaned casually on the counter with the opposite elbow. "I didn't realize you were a gardener."

"I didn't plant it. My mother put it in. I just tend it. It gives me something to do while I'm here besides helping out at the store, and I like feeling the earth between my fingers, watching things grow and eating what I produce."

"You make gardening sound fun," he said wryly. "I wouldn't have believed anyone could do that—other than the eating part, of course."

She laughed. "You don't like getting your hands dirty?"

"I don't mind that. I've just never had the burning desire to plant anything, I guess. What types of things are you growing?"

She was tempted to cut straight to the part where she asked him if he needed help finding a book, to save him the effort of making small talk. But if he was going to be polite, so was she. "Watermelon. Sweet potatoes. Zucchini. Tomatoes."

"I have to admit there's nothing better than a homegrown tomato. If I was tempted to grow anything, it would be that."

"I make my own spaghetti sauce every fall, so we raise a lot of them."

Now that he'd spent a reasonable amount of time chitchatting with her—a nod to the fact that they'd gone to school together—she assumed he'd tell her it was good to see her again and ask where he could find the cookbook he'd come to purchase. Or maybe he was looking for a book on how to better manage a restaurant or survive a divorce. She was already wondering if they'd have what he wanted when he said, "I sent you a friend request on Facebook, but I'm not on there very much, and now I'm guessing that you're not, either."

She was on every night, hoping for some word from her husband—or from someone who could tell her what'd happened to Nick. Each time she logged on, the little symbol that signified she had a friend request waiting drew her eye again and again. But she didn't own up to having seen it. "Not since I've been here," she lied.

"Well, you mentioned how much you like our carrot cake, so I brought you a slice." He lifted the sack he'd been holding and put it on the counter. "I hope you enjoy it."

Shocked, she glanced at the logo of the restaurant before meeting his gaze. "Thank you. That's...really nice."

"No problem," he said and, with a parting wink, started to leave.

He didn't need a book? He'd come just to deliver this cake—*to her*?

Fortunately, there wasn't anyone else in the store at the moment. That was the only reason she allowed herself to call out to him. "Quinn?"

He had his hand on the door when he turned.

"I'm really sorry about your mother's cancer diagnosis."

"Thank you. I appreciate that."

"And..."

He waited patiently as she drew a bolstering breath.

"And I'm also sorry for how I behaved when we were in high school."

The words tumbled out so fast she wouldn't have been surprised if he needed her to repeat them. Fortunately, he seemed to have heard and understood. "You didn't do anything wrong," he said magnanimously.

"I did."

"When?"

Clasping her hands tightly in front of her, she was tempted to say "Never mind," in case he had really forgotten. But she was the one who'd brought it up; she was going to have the courage to see it through. "You know...when I did what I did in the tree house that day."

"What *you* did? I'm pretty sure we both participated."

"But I was so forward even though you tried to tell me you weren't interested."

The glimmer in his eyes suggested he was tempted to laugh. Once she caught that, she suspected he'd known what she was referring to all along. "I don't remember those being the words I used."

"Whatever you said, you were right. I was out of line. I apologize."

His lips curved into a sexy grin. "Is *that* why you won't accept my friend request?"

Damn it. He'd guessed she'd seen it, and he was right, so she figured there was no use continuing to lie. "Partially."

"I promise you—that's the last thing you need to worry about," he said and the door swung shut as he walked out.

The Bookstore on the Beach—*coming soon!*